I066603.3

THE CUTLASS TRILOGY
FLINTLOCK

Praise for CUTLASS

"I love how as a reader, I thought I knew all the secrets until a new one popped up right in my face taking me by surprise. These little surprises kept me on my toes, and made me love Cutlass even more." – *Chandra Haun, Unabridged Bookshelf*

"CUTLASS didn't disappoint. It's a rollicking, adventurous tale, centered around young pirate extraordinaire Barren Reed and his kidnappee (aka daughter of an important lord, aka his brother's fiancée, aka his eventual love interest-of course!) Larkin Lee." – *Nicole Singer at Write Me a World*

"I thought the use of elves, magic in a story centered around a pirates was unique and clever, and the myth of the bloodstone was intriguing. And yes I admit it, I was totally in love with Barren by the end of the book." – *Lipsyy Lost & Found*

"This really was a true epic adventure. It had every element to keep you glued to such a novel, if you enjoy this sort of plot. From sword fights, to romance, and even a few quite comedic moments, it was difficult to put down, and even more difficult not to enjoy." – *Lily at Bookluvrs Haven*

"Cutlass is the sort of book where you can never tell who all the bad guys are and betrayal, politics, and revealed secrets are constantly shaking the plot and causing problems for our hero and heroine." – *Ryan at Book Marks the Spot*

"I thoroughly enjoyed this pirate and elf tale! With brilliant sword fighting, a few adventures that drew out the tension, betrayal on all sides, and a story that finally comes together showing what a tangled web was woven, this was a wonderful, thoroughly enjoyable read." – *Tiffany at A TiffyFit's Reading Corner*

"I could scream out the window to the neighbors, I also want to stop people on the street and tell them to read this book. I honestly think it was that good. – *Michelle at Because Reading is Better Than Real Life*

"I would highly recommend this book to everyone who's looking for a great YA fantasy read. I can't wait till the next book in this series gets released!" – *Elien from So Bookalicious!*

"I freaking loved it! I'll definitely be reading the next book in this series!" – *Kendall at BookCrazy*

The story had me flipping the pages and wondering what was going to happen next! – *Erin at I Think I'm Obsessed*

Praise for FLINTLOCK

"If you enjoy YA fantasy, you definitely need this series in your hands right now. Especially if you like YA fantasy with well-rounded characters, gorgeous writing, some of the best world-building I've read, and an exciting plot." – *Ashley, The AP Book Club*

"After reading CUTLASS, I couldn't wait to see where Ashley Nixon took the series. With the release of FLINTLOCK, the answer is: bigger, broader and even more fun! The book grows seamlessly into the full scope and vibrancy of Nixon's world. The stakes are higher, the stage is wider, and the friendships we came to love in CUTLASS are tested in new and devious ways. Nixon balances the allure of ships, sailing and pirate battles with a growing threat of magic and the politics of both the mortal and immortal worlds. I will definitely be back for Book 3!" – *Nicole Singer, Write Me A World*

Well done, Ashley, Well done! I can't recommend this series enough for Young Adults and Adults, if you want something different with a strong handsome male, kick ass female and an amazing fantasy story, this is totally the book for you. – *Michelle, Because Reading is Better Than Real Life*

I enjoyed Flintlock immensely. Everything Ashley wrote fitted perfectly together, the characters, the world... Everything was just perfect. To top it all of Ashley her writing style is really addictive and I found it impossible to put this book down. I would highly recommend this book and it's prequel to everyone. Especially if you are a fan of Young Adult fantasy than this is a series that you have to read. – *Elien, So Bookalicious!*

THE CUTLASS TRILOGY
FLINTLOCK

ASHLEY NIXON

PUBLISHER'S NOTE: This is a work of fiction. Names, characters, places and incidents are either the product of the author's imagination or are used fictitiously. Any resemblance to actual persons, living or dead, business establishments, events, or locales is entirely coincidental.

Summary: Barren Reed must stop the spread of dark magic before the Orient is destroyed.

ISBN: 978-0-9911323-3-1 (paperback)
978-0-9911323-4-8 (e-book)

Copyright © 2015 Ashley Nixon
Book Cover design by Stephanie White
Chapter Art designed by Ashley Nixon
Edited by Jena O'Connor

All right reserved. No part of this publication may be reproduced, stored in or introduced into a retrieval system, or transmitted, in any form, or by any means (electronic, mechanical, photocopying, recording, or otherwise) without the prior written permission of the author.

www.ashley-nixon.com

STARSEED PRESS

DEDICATION

To my Prince Charming, Armand
Without you a lot of things would be impossible.
I love you.

Mariana

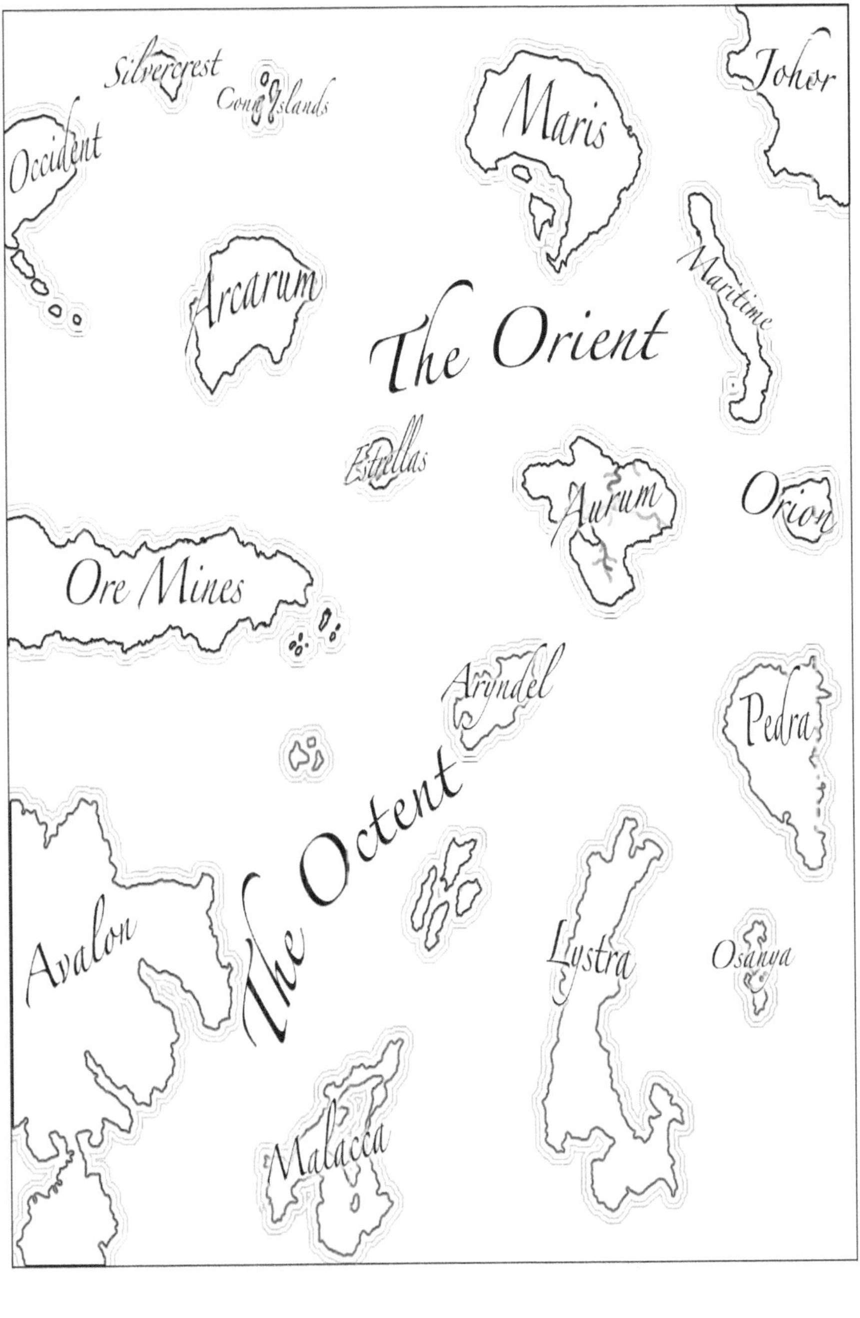

Silvercrest

Conch Islands

Johor

Occident

Maris

Arcarum

Maritime

The Orient

Estrellas

Aurum

Orion

Ore Mines

Arundel

Pedra

The Octent

Avalon

Lustra

Osanva

Malacca

Chapter One
ROUGH HOUSE

The note came to land discreetly upon the rough-grained table. Barren Reed stared at it for a moment before unfolding the message. Scrawled in his brethren Taisce's handwriting were two simple words. *They're here.*

He stared at the message for a long moment before mashing it between his hands and shoving it deep in his coat pocket. It was the report he had expected: privateers were using Occident, one of many islands nearest Silver Crest, as a launching pad for their campaign against pirates. Attacks had occurred all over the Orient, but the ones that bothered Barren the most were those that were closest to Silver Crest. King Tetherion and his sons, Datherious and Natherious, knew the location of Silver Crest, and their slow threat was teasing. Barren knew that one word from Tetherion and the entire island would be obliterated. He questioned only what Tetherion was waiting for.

In hindsight, delivering the princes and Lord Christopher Lee in chains to the king probably hadn't been his best idea, but it

1

was memorable and sent a message: he was ready for a fight. But Tetherion had been ready to fight, too, and sooner than Barren had bargained for.

Luckily, Alex and the captains of Silver Crest had begun to mobilize once word of Tetherion and the twins' betrayals reached them. Many women and children had been moved to Sanctuary, a fortified island that still remained a secret from Tetherion and the twins. After years of dormancy, the pirates would have to resort to what they knew best to protect Saoirse—piracy, in its most basic form.

People were losing their lives. The privateers who were meeting the pirates of Silver Crest were more skilled than previous privateers they'd encountered, and angrier. Barren had to wonder if they were out for revenge.

"Between the king's men and the sea-rats, we won't get no peace," the old man behind the bar spat. He rested a thick arm on the bar top. Barren could feel his disgusted stare.

The king's men were privateers whose aggressive campaign against pirates also affected the people of the Orient. They'd taken to occupying islands frequented by pirates, but they'd also been demanding and crass. Rumors abounded that the Privateers often ordered free shelter and food, citing their work against piracy as reason enough for special treatment. The inhabitants of these islands were poor and could not afford to accommodate so many; however, refusal resulted in death.

The privateers' actions were clearly far worse than any pirate's, but they acted under the king's law, and so their evil went unpunished. For now.

Boots tapped steadily on the wooden floor, and a man came to stand beside Barren's table. Some privateers preferred not to identify the island they were associated with to prevent possible backlash from pirates, but this man wore a red sash around his waist—a Maris Privateer. He was intimidating and tall, and his weapons were visible: guns in holsters over his chest, a sword at his side, a knife at his belt. He approached Barren in a way that suggested he grossly underestimated the so-called sea-rat.

"Sea-rats aren't welcome here," said the voice. "You best leave." The chatter in the pub quieted at the sound of his voice.

Barren did not bother to look at the man as he spoke. "I'm quite comfortable here, thank you." He took a swallow of ale.

There was a pause and the man leaned forward. "Perhaps you didn't hear me. *Leave.*"

Barren laughed quietly and then turned to meet the man's gaze. The privateer's eyes widened with recognition, but before he could speak, Barren moved. His head crashed into the privateer's, sending him backward. He fell like a board. There was silence. Barren pulled his hood back and then stood, draining the remainder of his ale. He slammed the tankard on the table and stared out at the crowd, waiting. The rest of the man's crew stumbled to their feet, drawing their blades.

Barren smirked and then extended his arms, welcoming their fight. A privateer charged forward brandishing knives. Barren drew his blade at the last second and shifted. The privateer stumbled forward, vulnerable, and Barren brought his sword

3

down upon the man's hands. He screamed, dropped his weapons, and then went silent as Barren's blade skewered his stomach.

Barren pulled his weapon free before the first man fell, ramming the hilt of the sword into another privateer's face. The man stumbled back, blood gushing from his nose, and Barren ran his blade across the privateer's chest. He continued taking down one privateer after the other, but the more men he fought, the more men joined in the fight.

Barren almost didn't notice the heavy rope coiling around his neck until the moment it began to tighten. He stumbled backward, hitting the ground hard, and his blade flew from his hand.

"Raise him high, boys!" One of the privateers yelled, and the room filled with a chorus of answering cheers. Barren stumbled as he was jerked to his feet once more, the noose still around his neck. The privateers tossed the other end of the rope around a rafter and pulled. The rope cut into Barren's neck until he could hardly draw air into his lungs. Beneath him the king's men hollered and bellowed in triumph.

He clawed furiously at the noose around his neck, trying to pull it away. Air escaped from his mouth in a haggard symphony. His heart pounded in his chest as panic left him. It was then that the door burst open, and Barren's crew filled the space. He wasn't surprised to see the former Lady Larkin Lee leading them. She was fierce, her skin touched by the sun, and a fire colored her cheeks. He found it strange that someone who avoided doling out death would crave a fight as much as she, yet she fought as well as any of them, maybe even better.

His quartermaster, Leaf, followed closely behind, wielding a blade. He fought with precision and a grace found only in the most skilled Elfin warriors. Behind him, Sam's large figure filled the doorway. Some of the privateers turned to run from him, but Sam was faster, and he took them down quickly. Seamus and Slay fought beside the others, Seamus with his chains and Slay with his cutlass.

With the privateers distracted, Barren suddenly found himself falling to the floor, the rope loosening its hold on his neck. He gasped for breath and coughed, tears filling his eyes. He rolled to his knees reaching for a stray blade and then stood. Larkin's eyes were ablaze as she attacked her opponent. Everything about her was fire.

"Down!" she commanded, and he obeyed, hitting the floor again. Larkin swung her sword, and it clashed with the sword of a privateer who had snuck up behind Barren. As the privateer stumbled back, Barren twisted and dealt the lethal blow.

"You were supposed to stay on the ship!" Barren said, his voice cracked and his throat hurt.

"And if I had, you'd be dead!" she replied.

"I had this situation under control!"

A bottle flew past his head and shattered against the wall behind him.

"Completely under control," she said and then she practically danced as she moved forward fearlessly into the fight.

There was the sound of more breaking glass, and then a fire

erupted, separating Barren from Larkin. On the other side of the flames she continued to fight.

"Larkin!" Barren growled. This was a perfect example of why she shouldn't be here. There were only two ways out of the pub—through the bartender's side entrance or the front door, both were unreachable from where Larkin was now annexed by the fire.

Some of the privateers fueled the fire by throwing full bottles of whiskey, rum and absinthe into the flames. The glass exploded and the blaze roared, the flames licking the ceiling. Barren could barely see Larkin through the inferno.

He searched the area for a way to reach her. Climbing onto a table close to the fire, he could feel the flames scorch his skin and sweat beaded off his face. He made a running start and then jumped over the rising flames. As he landed, he engaged a privateer who had been caught on the other side. With a swift swipe of his blade, he lay motionless.

"Barren!" Leaf called. "We have to get out of here!"

"Go! We'll meet you on the ship!" he called back.

The fire popped and hissed as if to challenge Barren's promise. Larkin cried out, and Barren's attention was again focused only on her. Momentarily distracted by the fire, she'd taken a blow to the arm. She was quick to recover, however, and her attacker soon found her blade in his own arm. Barren hurried forward, finishing him.

"Let's go!" he said and turned back toward the flames that separated them from the exit. He'd made it over them once; they could do it again.

Before they had a chance to move, there was a loud cracking sound and the ceiling caved in, sending sparks and smoke into the air. Barren pushed Larkin out of the way, his body covering hers as they fell hard to the floor. Quickly, he got to his feet and pulled her with him. "Come on!" He hurried to the back of the pub searching for an exit, but there was no way out.

He thought for a moment and then withdrew a flask from his coat. He tore a piece of his shirt free and stuffed it into the opening.

"This place is already burning to the ground...do you really think an explosion is the best idea?"

"If it gets us out of here, yes!"

He put the fabric to the fire and threw the flask. "Down!" Barren and Larkin hit the ground. He covered her head with his hands, pulling her close to his chest as the flask exploded. Pieces of the wall splintered, and the opening that remained was big enough for Barren to kick through. He rushed at it and burst through the wall. Larkin followed, stumbling out of the fire and smoke.

Outside, the night was cool but chaotic. Shouts and screams filled the air, people crying that pirates had attacked. In this pause, Barren turned to face Larkin, his eyes immediately focused on the blood running down her arm. She followed his gaze with her own and then turned so that the wound was hidden from him. Barren narrowed his eyes. He untied the sash from around his waist and reached for her arm, wrapping the cloth around the wound tightly. "Better that you don't bleed to death in the name of maintaining your pride," he said.

The sound of firing cannons caught his attention. He looked toward the port. His crew would be there now, attempting to set sail and make some distance from the shore. He exchanged a glance with Larkin and then the two broke into a run toward the shore. The dirt rose up beneath their feet as they hurried along. Around them cries of terror echoed, and now and then the word pirate tore the air like a curse. Barren wondered why no one decried the privateers for their thievery, but he didn't have time to worry about who the natives blamed for their misfortune. He and Larkin now stood at the edge of a thin cliff which loomed over the port like a dark cloud. The ships below them lined up almost perfectly beneath the cliff. From here they could look down and see men working furiously on board the privateers' ships as they sought to move away from the shore and pursue Barren's ship, which had not yet made enough distance from shore.

Barren felt Larkin's eyes on him, and when he met her gaze, he knew exactly what she was about to do. He reached for her, but she jumped. He watched her. She fell like a feather and landed lightly on one of the masts below. It was her lithe frame and her Elfin blood that made her so nimble. The commotion below meant that she remained undetected. Barren had no choice but to follow her lead.

He landed on one of the yardarms above her, and they exchanged a glance. Barren worked to remove a small powder flask. This one he'd filled with broken glass and pieces of sharp metal. He tore a part of his shirt, stuffed it into the hole, and lit the fabric. He threw it, aiming for a nearby privateer ship. The effect was immediate. The power flask exploded. There were terrifying screams as men found themselves filled with shrapnel. The sails of the ship caught fire and were consumed quickly. Those who were still alive retreated into the sea, but in the darkness, they did not resurface. Barren felt Larkin's disapproving eyes on him. She drew her blade, which flashed like the silver moon in the sky. Then she let herself fall to the deck below. It was like she was teasing him, seeing how far he'd go at her side. But he would go. He would follow her anywhere.

When she landed, she began her fight. Barren watched her for a moment, mesmerized by the way she moved. She'd been trained since her childhood to fight with a blade, something Barren had not known when he'd met her. He'd been too distracted by her beauty to notice the signs, the confidence. He knew many a man had fallen prey to her blade as a result of the same distraction. If he'd been in the thick of a fight when he first set eyes upon her, he'd have died instantly.

He shook his head, clearing the haze and followed her example, immersing himself in the fray. The clank of metal sounded, and it was two against many. They fought together, each building on the other's strengths and covering for weaknesses. Larkin was smaller but she moved faster. Barren was stronger but he hit harder.

Cannons rocked the ship, and Barren and Larkin swayed. His

ship had turned back; his crew had begun to attack. There were shouts from the privateers who scrambled below deck to defend their ship. Barren twisted as he fought to get a look at his ship. It wasn't far enough out to sea to avoid damage. His crew couldn't afford to become immobile so close to a nest of privateers.

He noticed the barrels of gunpowder that sat near the captain's quarters, an exposed weapon, a weakness. Barren whistled a command. He took off, hurrying for the barrels. His blade swept along, cutting down privateers as he went until he came face to face with a flintlock pistol. He stared straight into the barrel and watched as a slow, gritty smile spread over the face behind the gun.

As the privateer cocked the pistol to ignite the spark, Barren ducked, charging at the man with his blade and a small knife. He ran the man through, and as he fell, the blast from the pistol sounded, and smoke from the gun clouded Barren's vision. He stumbled over the fallen privateer toward the barrels, ramming his blood-covered blade through the wood over and over until a solid stream of gun powder poured from the barrel and spilled on the ground. Satisfied, he turned and hurried toward Larkin. He fought to reach her, and once he did he wrapped his hand tightly around her waist as they retreated, tumbling over the edge of the ship. Just as they fell overboard, a blazing arrow rushed past and landed in the gunpowder. The blast was loud, and debris rained down around them as they swam for the safety of their own ship.

"You're both thoughtless," Leaf said as they boarded. Behind them, the burning remains of the privateer ships groaned as the water consumed them. "And you're both arrogant!"

"Tell us how you really feel," Barren said, standing. He helped Larkin to her feet. Their clothes were soaked and water dripped off of them.

"Change before you develop a fever!" Leaf commanded. It was a well-known fact that Leaf did not like to treat colds.

Larkin moved to obey, but Barren reached for her. "Don't think you've escaped scrutiny," he said, eyeing the wound on her arm.

She rolled her eyes. "It wouldn't be a normal day without a lecture."

"He's just mad because you out fought 'im!" Slay called from the crow's nest.

Barren made his way to his cabin and slammed his door. This wasn't a competition, it was about staying safe. There were people who wanted to hurt Larkin, people who would hurt her simply to get back at him. She needed to be more careful. Instead, she ran headfirst into danger, and his crew seemed to have a good time encouraging it, even going so far as to follow her lead. He was going to have to talk to all of them.

He changed into dry clothes and left his cabin. He found Leaf finishing up a stitch on Larkin's arm. He cringed when he saw the blood, old and new, running down her arm.

Leaf cut the thread and sopped up the blood with a clean cloth. After smearing a salve on the wound, he wrapped and bandaged it.

"You'll be sore, but as long as you don't roughhouse, you'll be fine."

He glared at Barren, as if warning him. Barren moved to follow Larkin as she stood and walked away from him, probably trying to avoid the lecture she believed was coming. Before Barren could take a step in her direction, Leaf reached for Barren's neck, he winced. He'd been able to ignore the pain until now. A red wound circled his neck from where the rope had been.

"The noose was never a good look for you," Leaf said. "You're lucky Larkin was so incessant in her need to follow you." Barren guessed he couldn't really argue with that. Leaf continued, "She is very skilled. It should ease your mind." It didn't ease his mind. He'd seen the most skilled pirates go down in a fight. His father was the best example.

Barren shook his head, preparing to argue with his friend.

"You don't have to protect her, Barren," Leaf added quietly.

But he wanted to. Ironic considering he'd been so eager to show her the realities of this world, to prove to her that there were two sides to every story. Now he wanted to protect her from those truths.

"Didn't you feel the need to protect Fira?" Barren asked. He noticed Leaf's jaw tighten. Perhaps it was unfair of Barren to bring up Leaf's dead love, especially after all the Elf had suffered after her murder. Barren knew very little about Fira, but he knew no matter what, Leaf would have protected her.

"I did," the Elf replied, nodding and walking away.

Barren's chest felt tight with regret. He should not have

dredged up painful memories for Leaf. The Elf had been through enough. He let out a breath and turned to find Larkin.

She was leaning against the rail, looking down at the water toward the back of the ship. As he approached, she turned.

"You should be more careful, it's too dangerous, you could have died," she said. "See? I already know what you're going to say. Spare me the lecture."

"That's not what I was going to say," he said.

"You should have stayed on the ship," she said. "You never listen to me. Am I hitting the mark yet?"

"It's true that you never listen to me," he said.

"Leaf wanted me to listen to you this time." Larkin took a deep breath before going on. Barren lifted a brow, waiting. "He said maybe it'd teach you a lesson. To not go at things alone."

He chuckled, but as she spoke, he noticed her eyes focused on his chest. He didn't have to look to know what she was staring at—the myriad of scars that covered his skin. She'd traced those scars and asked questions he'd answered, no matter how difficult. Those questions hadn't come in a while, and he was glad for it. They weren't a part of the future he wanted with her.

After a moment, he reached forward, his fingers brushing her chin and forcing her eyes to his. "The fears you have for me are the same fears I have for you," he said quietly. He dropped his hand to her upper arm, squeezing gently

"The cut's minor," she said. "I'll be more careful next time."

"Next time? You plan to do this again?"

"Yes." She smirked at him.

He pulled her closer. "I don't know what to do with you," he admitted, and ran his lips along her jaw. She shivered beneath his touch but laughed.

"It doesn't seem that way," she replied.

He smiled against her skin and moved his lips closer to hers.

"I said no roughhousing!" Leaf called from behind them.

Barren groaned. He pulled away from Larkin but only fractionally. She laughed, but a blush touched her cheeks. Leaf took delight in embarrassing them, even knowing that Barren and Larkin had not made love. Barren had promised Larkin that things would progress slowly between them.

"Come," he said, taking her hands. "We'll go where there's privacy."

He pulled her with him and she followed, but Slay's voice reached them from the crow's nest.

"Before you go, you might wanna take a look north."

Barren sighed, rolling his eyes. "Slay, I'm not in the mood..."

But as he turned, he saw ghost-like sails on the horizon. He moved closer to the edge of the ship and Leaf joined him. The vessel moved with a familiar gait, cutting the waves with a precision Barren only found true of the pirates of Silver Crest.

"He's one of our own," said Leaf.

"Who?" Barren asked.

"Edward Merrik."

Chapter Two
SANCTUARY

Barren did not like Edward Merrik.

He watched Merrik's ship approach, apprehension making his body stiff. Edward was known by many pirates as the Elders' footman. It wasn't meant to be an insult to the Elders, as they were the most respected members of the Pirates of Silver Crest who lived; however, it was meant as a jab to Edward who performed any task as long as it resulted in certain perks for him. He and Barren had never gotten along, and Barren dreaded discovering the reason behind Edward's sudden appearance.

They dropped anchor and waited.

It wasn't long before Edward's ship was before them and his voice rang out. "It seems you've had your fair share of excitement, brother." Edward was small in stature but well muscled. He had blond hair and a plain face. His eyes focused on the fire and smoke in the distance. "May we board?"

Barren placed his hand over his heart, an important gesture of respect, especially when a courtesy was about to be denied. "May

I ask for what purpose this honor would be given?"

Edward smiled, but he was not amused. "Brother, let us speak in private."

"There are no secrets among brothers," Barren replied evenly.

A tight smirk crossed Edward's lips. "Very well," he said. "You have been summoned by the Elders. I have come to escort you."

Barren and Leaf exchanged a look. Part of him was not surprised. He'd suspected the Elders were disappointed in some of his choices, but the fact that it came on the heels of Tetherion's betrayal angered him.

"What does that mean?" Larkin asked. Barren looked at her, but not before he noticed Edward's gaze trained upon Larkin. Barren moved to block his view of her. He didn't like the look of disapproval on Merrik's face. Larkin seemed to understand what he was doing and stared back at Edward just as fiercely. "What does it mean?"

"It means he will go to trial," Edward replied.

"What are the charges against him?" Larkin demanded, stepping out of Barren's shadow.

Edward's gaze was not kind. "Do not demand information from me as if you are one of us."

"Thank you, Edward," Barren interrupted harshly. "I will do you a courtesy and follow you to Sanctuary."

"By the code, one of my men must board your ship," said Edward.

"You will take my vow that I will attend my summoning and

not offend my honor," Barren replied evenly. Edward hesitated in the silence but nodded in agreement.

They set sail. Barren's ship traversed easily beside Edward's. He refused to be watched from behind like a prisoner. There was tension on the sea, and Barren paced back and forth on the deck of his ship, a sign of his frustration.

"The insult of having Edward Merrik *fetch* me for trial," he sneered.

"I'd think you'd be angry about *having been fetched* for trial at all," said Leaf.

Barren was more worried than insulted. He'd been to trials before. His brethren would be there. The Elders would present the charges, allow Barren to defend himself against them, and make their decision. There were any number of punishments possible, but what Barren feared the most was the divide he'd witnessed among the pirates of Silver Crest. He'd seen pirates lose their closest friends and families at trial.

"Did you expect to be summoned?" Larkin asked. She stood nearby, her arms folded over her chest, and every now and then her eyes slid to the ship beside them.

"While a trial is not underserved, I'm not sure I expected it," said Barren. "And the fact that they waited until after Tetherion's treason is unnerving."

"But would you have answered before now? Without having your revenge?"

Larkin never really understood the weight of her questions. "I would have had no choice." Barren admitted.

"So do you believe you deserve their punishment?"

"I've never denied that I deserve their punishment," he replied. And he hadn't, but he couldn't imagine his brethren, people he'd known his whole life, deciding that his future did not lie with them.

Leaf cleared his throat. "Well, there's nothing you can do about it now except attend the trial," he said. "But I'll warn you that they'll try to make you angry. They want to demonstrate the behavior they seek to punish: they want to give your brethren a reason to mistrust you."

***

Larkin lay against Barren, her head on his chest. She couldn't sleep, though her eyes were heavy. It was so quiet in his cabin. She was used to sleeping in the hatch in a hammock in the back, where the groan of the ship was loudest. Then there was the heat of Barren's skin. She'd come to know his warmth, yet she'd also come to know the absence of that warmth. Right now, there was energy between them that had gone unacknowledged since they'd closed the door. Strangely, it made her restless.

She also had questions about this trial. What did it mean that one of Barren's brethren had come to escort him to Sanctuary? What did it even mean to have a trial among pirates? By the way Edward looked at her, she suspected she might have something to do with this.

"Will they take you from me?" she asked quietly, sleepily.

Barren was very still. She watched his chest rise and fall with the breaths he took. After a moment, she felt his fingers tangle in her hair. "Is that what you fear?" he asked.

"It is one thing I fear," she said. She feared being taken from him. She feared being sent back to Maris.

"In truth, I do not know what the Elders have planned for me," he said.

"Do they want to hurt you?"

"They will not kill me," said Barren. "I am not a traitor."

"But what you've done, it is punishable by the Elders?"

She knew by the silence that Barren did not know how to answer that question.

"By the code, I've done nothing wrong."

The code was a set of rules created by the Elders of Silver Crest. Larkin had once mocked the idea of pirates abiding by any type of law, but she'd come to learn that all Pirates of Silver Crest, even those touted as the most ruthless, were loyal to the code. It ensured that the pirates protect Saoirse, freedom.

"Why call you to trial then?"

"Because I've done something they do not approve of."

Larkin pushed herself up and stared at Barren in the darkness. His features were passive. It seemed so uncharacteristic. This should make him angry, because to her, it sounded unfair.

"So in truth this is against the code," said Larkin.

Barren chuckled and sat up. "The Elders advise and protect the code, Larkin. To say they do anything against it is blasphemy."

She regarded him for a moment. Barren's loyalty to the code of Silver Crest was strong, which meant his loyalty to the Elders would be matched.

"I was under the impression the pirates of Silver Crest lived a life dedicated to Saoirse," she said. It was one of the first things she'd learned about Barren, how important Saoirse—*freedom*—was to him. "If that is so, why do these men seem to have power over you?"

"The Elders are men and women," Barren said. "They are the eldest among us, those with the most experience, and they have no power over us, only wisdom."

"So they call you to trial to impart wisdom?" This wasn't making sense. A trial meant that Barren had been charged. It meant there were consequences for actions. He knew this just as well as she did.

"Larkin," he said and he ran his fingers over her cheek, tangling them into her hair, and secured his hand at the base of her neck. "I don't want to talk about this right now. It's in the future, but we're in the present."

He pulled her to him, and their lips crashed together, sending heat through her body, diffusing the tension that had built between them in the silence. His mouth moved from hers and trailed her jaw and throat. When he wrapped his hands around her thighs and pulled her to him, she forgot her frustrations—all she wanted to know was how she could be closer to him. The heat from his skin was addictive. It filled her senses, made her desperate.

He twisted, and she yelped as she found herself on her back with her legs still around his waist. He loomed over her and paused to stare, seeming completely focused, yet lost at the same time. She liked him like this. She often had power, but here she was in control. He would do anything she asked, bend to her will. So she reached for him, willing this distance between them to close, and he obliged, meeting her lips with a carnal growl.

***

Sanctuary was within sight. There was nothing special about the island from an outside view. It was barren, and a mountain covered most of the terrain. There were no trees and no life. Many avoided the area, believing that the island was merely a sleeping volcano, but the mountain itself was not a mountain at all. It was a fortified shelter, a fortress of sorts. Inside, there were rooms, an arsenal, and even a port. It had been built shortly after the Barbary Wars—a war that had split the pirates of Silver Crest—as a refuge in case Silver Crest was ever compromised.

The coordinates of Sanctuary were only given to pirates who had served the code for three or more years. Even then, it was said that those only most faithful to Saoirse could locate the island. Barren wasn't sure if he completely believed the second part, mostly because Edward Merrik never had any trouble, but he was glad for the first as it had kept the twins and Tetherion from discovering the whereabouts of the location.

"Pretty impressive, eh?" Leaf came to stand next to Larkin, arms crossed, a look of pride on his face.

"I hope that's your sarcasm," she replied, glancing at him.

"You haven't seen anything yet."

"You're right. I haven't."

"You will be impressed," Barren smiled, his eyes focused on Sanctuary. "You should know not to underestimate us. Slack the sails," Barren called. "Let's come to port."

Barren's ship moved forward fast, cutting off Edward's. As they made a sharp turn, a part of the mountain seemed to give way, creating an entrance large enough for several ships to sail through. As they passed through the opening, even Barren had a hard time taking his eyes off the magnificence of the port at Sanctuary. The ceilings were tall and the walls were made of strong steel, shaped to form simple archways. Lanterns had been strung on a moving line high above. The waterway was congested, and as Barren's ship made an appearance, he noticed how several of his brethren stopped to stare at him. They were here to attend his trial, and by their gazes, some had already made up their minds about him. His heart fell.

He exchanged a glance with Leaf who seemed just as uneasy. Unconsciously, Barren's hand rested on his blade. He caught Larkin's gaze and knew she hadn't missed the movement as her eyes burned.

They'd barely dropped anchor when a group of men came forward.

"Brothers," Barren greeted with a nod.

"Barren," A man he knew as Knightly nodded back. "We've come to escort you to the Chambers."

"I'm very much aware of how to get there," Barren replied.

"You do not have an option," Knightly responded. They stared in silence at one another for a moment. Barren watched the men, taking in their gazes, trying to guess their thoughts. Knightly seemed a little remorseful, but the others, men he knew, appeared harsher, and that frightened him.

"Has Alex McCloud arrived yet?" He needed to know that he had strong supporters here other than his crew. Alex had been like a father to Barren since the day his own had been murdered.

"No," was Knightly's only response.

Barren exchanged a glance with Leaf before moving down the gangway. The men he called brethren immediately surrounded him. Being lead from port in this fashion was an insult to the oath he'd sworn to the code. It insinuated he was not loyal.

The halls of Sanctuary were crowded with pirates—men and women alike, and their children—waiting for the trial. As Barren passed, the conversation quieted to a murmur, and people whispered, casting glances at him but never making eye-contact. What had changed since he'd been in Silver Crest only three months ago? This had not been his welcome then.

They came to a set of metal doors. Barren knew these doors led to the Chambers where all trials for pirates of Silver Crest were held. Designs had been worked into the surface, and the raised edges revealed a gold sheen. Barren might have considered the doors beautiful if he didn't think they were glaring at him, just like the people assembled here.

Two of his brethren moved forward and pulled the doors open. They stepped aside and allowed Barren to enter.

The room was dim like the rest of Sanctuary, except for a circle of light that poured like a waterfall from the ceiling at the center of the room. He knew people hid in the shadows around him and even more were filing into the open doors behind him. The air became heavier and hotter.

He stepped into the light, and as it spilled over him, he shuddered. At the very brink of the light sat the Elders in their carved wooden chairs. It was said the chairs were custom made for each Elder and depicted their triumphs throughout their lifetime. Barren knew those triumphs, and he knew the Elders by name. Sully, Ranger, Tristan, Sal, Eva, and Tobias. Light streamed down upon them, illuminating their harsh, unsmiling faces. Together, they'd worked to provide not just a haven but a home for a people placed in exile by the world at large.

And Barren had threatened that.

He waited, feeling like a pariah among the only family he'd ever known. He was eager to learn the charges against him, and he was eager to fight those charges. It might not be for the best, because arguing with the Elders was looked down upon, but Barren figured being summoned to Sanctuary meant things couldn't get much worse. He hadn't been eager to express that reality to Larkin. She would find out soon enough.

When the doors closed behind him, he turned. His crew was the last to enter the room. None of them were happy. Leaf kept his arms at his sides, within reach of his weapons, as did Sam. His large frame was intimidating and it was no surprise that people seemed to naturally gravitate away from him. Seamus and Slay kept their arms crossed, casting unfavorable glances around the room.

Then his eyes landed on Larkin, and he drew in a breath. He was still getting used to certain things. The first was having a girl on his ship. The second was having to tell her things about himself. The third was having to answer to her.

He'd noticed something unfortunate about himself in the last few weeks: his resolve weakened when it went up against hers. Even now, the stern mask he'd crafted in preparation for this moment faltered when he beheld her. He'd always thought she was beautiful, but the sea had done nothing but accentuate that beauty. Her skin was slowly darkening. The sunburn upon her high cheekbones made her emerald eyes even brighter. Her long hair was windblown and framed her face wildly. While he wasn't so sure she could be frightening, he was certain she could command. Her very presence demanded attention. He'd known that from the moment he'd met her, but he was much more aware of it now.

"Barren Hawthorne Reed." Tobias's voice rumbled deep in his throat. Barren turned around to face the Elder, knowing he'd already made a bad impression. "You are charged with kidnapping." *Of course he'd begin with that one.* "Recklessly endangering your brethren." Barren rolled his eyes. No one, not even these Elders suspected Tetherion's treason. "And culpable and reckless conduct." *That has to be the same as recklessly endangering your brethren.* Barren knew if they wanted to, they could find more charges, so he kept his mouth shut.

"You are here because you are careless," Eva's voice was sharp like glass. She had shrewd eyes and a thin nose. She stared down at Barren, and he got the sense that her dislike of him did not come from his most recent exploits. "Your trust in Tetherion and his sons has compromised the location of Silver Crest, and as a result, you have threatened Saoirse."

Barren was shocked. These were heavy accusations— threatening Saoirse *was* breaching the code. These were accusations that could get him stripped of his captainship, or worse, exiled.

"We fear the manner in which you will take your revenge against Tetherion will destroy us," Tobias continued.

"*What?*"

"We can't be any clearer than that," Sully said. "You stalked the coast of Maris to get revenge for your father, went as far as kidnappin' a young lady from her home. It scared people. It made people focus on all of us. When one of us does somethin', we're all considered guilty of it."

"So I'm here because you're afraid I'm going to kill more people in the name of revenge?" Barren's voice was flat, but he knew he'd done this to himself. He'd taught these people to expect this from him.

"We're treading a thin line here. We're one step away from full war at sea. There have been more battles at sea in the last two weeks than in the last two years. We do not have the numbers to withstand such a thing. Do you want to see our children at the noose? Piracy does not discriminate in the eyes of those people."

"I have no plans to kill anyone," Barren said through his teeth. "I just plan to keep an eye on Tetherion's actions."

"For what purpose?"

"To do what my father did."

The Elders exchanged looks, and Tobias's gaze told Barren he did not approve.

"And what was that?" asked Tobias.

Barren was surprised by their reaction; he didn't have time to hide it. Didn't they know already?

"If Tetherion attempts to extend his rule, I want to stop him."

The silence that followed told him none of them liked the sound of that.

"Pirates should not meddle in politics," said Eva.

"If we do not meddle in politics, how do you expect to protect Saoirse?"

"If you need proof, only recall the fate of your father," she replied harshly.

Barren glared.

"Your father might have sworn an oath to the Code, but he was always a prince to his people. It seems not even his son can escape that royal blood." She spat the words as if she despised everything about him.

Barren could hear Leaf's voice in his head. *They'll try to make you angry. They want to demonstrate the behavior they seek to punish. They want to give your brethren a reason to mistrust you.*

"My father believed in Saoirse," Barren argued. "His meddling had nothing to do with his blood."

"And I suppose you'd say the same thing?" Sal asked, and then he laughed, and Barren felt the sting of his insult. "At least your father knew what Saoirse meant before he started his campaign."

His father, the infamous Jess Reed, had known what it was to fight for Saoirse. So had all the Elders who sat before him. Around the time of the Ore Wars, the pirates had their own problems. A split had occurred between the pirates of Silver Crest, those who believed the Elders had too much power and those who felt they were upholding the code by defending the Elders. They referred to it as the Barbary Wars. The war had ended with those who had begun the war being exiled to a place called Avalon in the Octent. Their leader, a man named Dominique Esqueviel, started his own order of piracy, and they called themselves Corsairs. By the way the Elders were talking right now, Barren thought he might agree with them.

"Perhaps you feel your cause is noble, but you must understand our worry. Not only do we fear your future actions, but your choice in alliances is also concerning." Barren was confused for a moment. Was Tobias referring to his crew? "Emmalyn Levianth and Devon Kennings have been wanted by this court for years. I'm very interested to know why, of all the people they sought to help, they found you."

Em and Devon had never mentioned that they were wanted by the court. Come to think of it, Alex hadn't, either.

"And what did they do to deserve your punishment?" he asked, almost mockingly.

"The whole lot deserved punishment," said Sully, and Barren suspected that included his father.

"This involvement in magic," Eva cut in. "It must stop at

once!"

There were so many voices. Shrill judgment sounded all around. He wanted to cover his ears and beg for it to stop. "We weren't...*involved* with magic! We destroyed the bloodstone. We kept Tetherion from becoming invincible. Shouldn't you be praising us?"

"It is just like the son of Jess Reed to expect praise for irresponsible actions," Eva spat. "But we don't know what you are...what you are capable of, either of you."

Barren was confused, but he followed Eva's gaze and saw it fell on Larkin, whose green eyes flickered like flames in the dim light.

"You are of mixed blood. How do we know you don't wield magic?"

Barren couldn't believe it. They were suggesting that because his mother was Lyric, an Elf born with magic in her blood, that he might have magic, too.

Barren spat laughter. "What are you talking about? Of course I can't wield magic. I'm *mortal*." But the words fell weakly from his tongue. When it came right down to it, he *was* half-Lyric, and while he wasn't so sure half-Lyrics could wield magic, that didn't matter. Fear ignited their prejudice.

"You're half-Lyric. Half of the most powerful Lyric to ever exist. And she," Eva nodded toward the girl. "She is a danger as well. She's half-Lyric! How do we know she is free of magic?"

"Trust me, I'd would know if she had magic!" Barren said. He felt angry and desperate. This was unfair. They were making assumptions, and they'd offer their verdict based on these assumptions. This trial was no longer about the code.

"You may not even know if you have the ability to wield magic yet." Barren could not argue with that, but if there was a chance that they could, it wasn't Barren or Larkin they should be concerned with—it was Datherious and Natherious, who were also sons of a Lyric mother.

"What are you so afraid of?" Barren asked, careful to keep his voice level.

Eva hesitated for a moment, and then her eyes became more severe. "Magic does not belong in this world. Your father dragged the pirates of Silver Crest into the middle of a war they couldn't win. If it is magic against mortal flesh, there is no advantage. There is only death."

"Yet you're still alive," said Barren. "And my father is not."

Eva lifted her head. Her lips barely moved as she spoke. "You've already shown you cannot be controlled. We've presented the list of charges to you as proof."

Her words were drowned by voices rising to object Eva's words.

She looked at Tobias, and Barren suddenly understood that they had already made a decision. There would be no deliberation. His defense would not be heard.

"While destroying the bloodstone was a courageous feat," Tobias looked at Barren and his crew. "We feel you are a danger to all of us and it is best to send you into exile."

The clamor of voices rose, but Barren heard Eva's voice loud and clear.

"And the girl, she will be returned to her father. She has no place here."

The room erupted, and weapons were unsheathed. Barren turned to see his crew arming themselves. He raised his hand, directing them to put their weapons away, but the voices were still rising, some in protest, others in favor, as they argued among themselves about Barren's fate. The Elders shouted, requesting calm, but the root of the problem wasn't their decision, it was the way they'd come to their conclusion. The rules of the Code specified that Barren would have a defense, and that his defense would be considered.

It was then that the doors burst open, and for a moment, Barren thought a riot had begun, but the room hushed. Barren turned to see who had entered the chamber. A figure cloaked in black came forward. There was a familiarity about the way he moved. Behind the figure, Alex McCloud lingered. He did not enter but stood near the open doors, leaning heavily on his cane. He hadn't changed much in the time they'd been away from each other, but his features were clouded with anger.

The man in black paused before Barren. "It seems you're in a bit of trouble," he said. Barren could hear the smile in his voice.

Barren grinned, suddenly comforted by the new arrival. "Trouble would be an understatement, Albatross."

Albatross had helped Barren reach the bloodstone before returning to Arcarum where he was better known as Ambassador Cove Rowell. If anyone could get Barren out of this mess, it would be Cove. Albatross had leverage with the Elders. It was only today that Barren had discovered his own powerlessness.

"What is this?" Tobias demanded.

Albatross moved around Barren. Throwing his hood back, he bowed his head. "Elders," he said. "I have news."

"You didn't have to sail all the way here to tell us. That's what the Network is for," said Tobias.

It was clear the Elders didn't want him here. They were aware of Barren and Cove's friendship and knew the ambassador wouldn't approve of their ruling, much less the trial itself.

"I needed to deliver this message personally," he said. He looked about at all the bodies in the shadows. "You should all come into the light. What I have to say affects you all."

Slowly, people moved into the light at the center of the room.

"If you will look around, you will notice some of your brethren are not here. While many of you were sailing here last night, one of your brethren's ships went down, and three of our own were captured and hanged in Maris this morning."

There was that silence again, except this time it was heavy with shock. A pirate of Silver Crest had not been hanged in Maris in years, not since Cathmor's reign.

"Who?" voices demanded from all around."

"Gregory Mills, James Alaster, and Fredrick O'Neil," Cove said. "It is no secret to any of you that Tetherion has flooded our sea with privateers since his return to Maris."

"And what of the rest of Gregory's crew?" Tobias asked.

"As of now, not recovered," Cove's words were like a weight, and it fell heavily upon everyone in the room.

"This is your fault!" Eva exploded at Barren. "*You* drew their attention to us!"

The zing of Cove's blade sounded as he drew it and pointed it at Eva. The air was thick with tension. No one drew a blade against the Elders. By the code, that was a challenge.

"It is foolish to challenge us, boy," Tobias said carefully, raising his chin.

"So you're upholding the code now that it comes to your own well-being?" asked Cove. "I never thought it would be necessary to demonstrate to the Elders the meaning of Saoirse, but exiling a man who's done nothing but protect you from a tyrant king is not Saoirse, even if you fear his actions."

"This is about…"

"Your inability to control Barren?" asked Cove. "Because that isn't Saoirse, either. If you are placing him on trial, you must place me on trial, as I accompanied him to D'Avana to destroy the bloodstone. Tetherion is not ignorant of the place I hold in this world or the other. I am a danger to my crew and to Silver Crest."

"Come now, Cove," Tobias began. "This is ridiculous—"

"Your fear of Barren will work against you. If you push him away, you lose all advantage. He knows Tetherion best, and if it is magic you fear, you must know that the bloodstone could only be destroyed by Barren and Larkin, because they are of Lyric blood. What if you were to encounter something like that again? You'd have pushed away the only people who could save you."

"The decision has already been made," said Eva. "It cannot be undone."

"It can't? Did you bind the decision with magic?" Cove mocked. "You fear Tetherion will attack you. Well, he already has. It began with our brothers who were hanged this morning. You, as Elders, should realize that this was only the beginning."

"Beginning of what?" snapped Eva.

"War," Cove said simply.

"This is ridiculous to insinuate we would fail without Barren Reed," Edward's voice rose to mock them.

There was silence. The truth of it was that no one knew much about magic, but all feared it. The trial had taught the pirates of Silver Crest that the Elders were terrified of something they weren't sure how to fight, but Barren did and he had done so successfully.

"If Barren leaves here today with his crew and the girl, someone must watch him. See that his decisions don't lead to more trouble," said Tobias, staring pointedly at Cove. "Because if they do, just once, he will be exiled, and you will not be able to save him."

"I say let Ambassador Rowell be his guardian," said Sal. "He can take the fall for Barren's conduct as well. It does little harm to him if he is exiled from our world. He has another to turn to." There was bitterness in Sal's voice. "If Barren does fail to control his impulses, you will be exiled with him, Ambassador."

"If that is your wish," Cove said calmly. "But let it be known that anything I have given to further your cause will come with me. That includes the Network."

The Network was vital to how the pirates of Silver Crest operated, and Barren had a feeling, if war really was coming to them, it would become even more integral in the coming months.

"You cannot take what is not yours! Those who run the Network are pirates of Silver Crest and are free to do as they choose," Eva said angrily.

"Exactly," said Cove. "Shall we bet on whose side they will take?"

Eva narrowed her eyes. "You are full of conceit," she spat. "You came here with devastating news and used it as leverage to free your friend!"

"And you expected more from a pirate?" Cove asked. "Now if you will excuse me, we have somewhere we must be."

Cove looked at Barren, and the two turned to find Edward barring their way. The pirate drew his sword against Barren, a challenge. "You must be joking!" Edward's voice rose. "He has put us all in danger and you would let him roam free? So that he may do it again?"

Barren glared at Edward but said nothing. Those who were in agreement with Edward spoke up or nodded. Then there were others who couldn't seem to decide how they should feel.

Tobias spoke, his voice tired. "Barren has been given his terms. If he breaches the agreement, he will be exiled."

Edward's frustration colored his face red. He turned and reached for Larkin. Before anyone could stop him, he had her by the arm, his blade pressed to her neck. "And what of her? Do we fear Barren Reed and his mud-dog friend so much that we will allow the daughter of Christopher Lee into our midst?"

"Let her go,' Barren commanded, his voice even but deadly. He kept his hand on his blade but did not draw. He recognized the look in Larkin's eyes. If he waited long enough, she'd take care of this herself.

"Why?" Edward questioned. "This gypsy-witch has got you under a spell. She's here to spy for her father."

Larkin's head reared back, and with a snap, slammed into Edward's nose. She jabbed her elbow into his stomach and twisted, knocking him to the ground, but not before obtaining his sword. He fell with a moan, and laughter ensued.

Edward got to his feet, eyes ablaze, and reached for Larkin again. Cove stepped in this time, grabbing Edward's outstretched hand. The gross snap of bone cracked in the silence. Edward's desperate scream filled the air.

"By the code, I command you to stop!" Tobias's voice rose. "If any of you wish to spill blood, it must be at sea."

Barren shuddered. It wasn't a command to cease altogether, it was a command to delay. Larkin threw Edward's blade at his feet, and then filled the space beside Barren. They moved toward the door.

"Just remember," Eva's voice stopped them, and her eyes narrowed in a way that made Barren think she could see right through him. "Barren is tied to dark magic, and dark magic always leads its prey to death."

Barren felt his heart fall a little. He wondered just how much

Eva knew. Because Barren was tied to dark magic, but not through his mother. He'd destroyed the bloodstone, and as Lord Alder, the king of the Elves, had said, the bloodstone had kept Barren alive, but that only meant it wanted something from him, and Barren had yet to figure out exactly what that was.

Chapter Three
BRETHREN IN ARMS

It was storming outside by the time they managed to leave the chamber, which meant Barren and his crew would be staying put until it passed. He hated how uncomfortable he felt here at Sanctuary now, and it was even worse as he and his crew made their way back to the port. Barren kept his eyes forward, ignoring the way some chose to brush past him, striking his shoulder. He'd keep their names. They would not be allies.

Cove walked on one side of Barren and Alex on the other. His crew filed in behind them like a protective barrier.

"Did they tell you they had summoned me?" Barren asked Alex.

"I found out last night and sent word to Cove as quickly as I could. I knew it would not be good," the old man replied and paused. "This feels all-too-familiar."

"What do you mean *familiar*?" Barren asked.

"The Elders summoned yer father, too, after they learned of his dealings with the Elves. They didn't like 'em then, and they don't like 'em now."

Barren set his jaw tightly. "I can't help my blood," he said.

"Well, I know that, lad," said Alex. "And I'm not blamin' ya or yer father fer anythin'. The Elders believe anythin' that wields magic is bad. They've their own reasons fer those beliefs, but I don't share 'em."

"But the other pirates, they share the Elders' beliefs," said Barren. "And who could blame them? What I know of magic is bad, too."

"When things get hard, people take sides," said Alex. "No matter what, ya must remember, they're only tryin' to decide what is most right. They've families to protect."

Barren felt his heart sink a little. Yes, they had families to protect, and while he would always consider his crew to be his family, he couldn't help but think that he had no real family of his own.

"You speak as if you know this will get worse."

"It's already worse than you think," said Cove. They came to the port again. Here the thunder was louder and the waves restlessly rocked the ships. "Barren, a word before you return to your ship," Cove requested. He nodded. Alex remained with them while Barren's crew continued back to his ship.

Cove directed Barren and Alex to his ship, a small two-mast galleon he'd clearly chosen because he had intended for this trip to be quick. The hull was composed of glossy dark wood and the cabin sat above deck. As he boarded the ship Barren noticed a few familiar faces, men from Arcarum who had joined him on his journey to destroy the bloodstone. They took on many roles when at home, such as apprentices, lawyers, and senators, all men who lived double lives.

"Follow me," Cove said and led the pirates to the hatch of the ship. "We've got more trouble than just our men dying at sea," Cove disappeared into the darkness and Barren and Alex stumbled after him.

"What could be worse than that?" asked Barren.

"The way they're dying," said Alex.

Barren swallowed. He'd watched men hang before, heard the sickening snap of bone, and watched botched executions where the men merely hung by their neck, struggling until death smothered them. While the fugitive island of Estrellas had always been a popular form of punishment, hanging was still probably one of the most favored options for killing pirates. It allowed for humiliation both before death and after.

"Are they still there?" Barren asked. "Did they put them in gibbets?"

"Yes," said Cove.

Gibbeting was the practice of displaying the remains of criminals. It was meant to deter others from continuing acts of thievery or violence, but it just made Barren angry.

Cove moved forward along the creaking hull of the ship until he came to an area in the back, hidden by a ragged curtain. Albatross grabbed it and pulled it back. Barren hesitated to follow Cove and looked back at Alex, who had stopped moving forward. Barren guessed he already knew what lay in front of them.

"Cove," Barren said slowly. "What are you about to show me?"

He didn't really need him to answer. He could pretty much guess. There were irregular shapes beneath gauzy white sheets. Suddenly, he felt as if death were behind him, pressing the blade of his scythe to Barren's throat.

He watched as Cove strode forward as if numb to it. Of course Albatross was already numb. He'd had time to get used to *them*. He'd sailed with *them* from wherever they'd been fished from the water. Cove kneeled beside one of the mounds, one hand on his knee, the other lifting the white cloth as if it might break.

It wasn't until Barren saw the ghostly face that he realized he'd been holding his breath, and for some reason, even after he noticed it, he couldn't bring himself to take in air. There were things about this life that never got easier, and one was seeing his brethren die, especially the young.

Barren stepped forward and kneeled, mimicking Cove's position.

James. He was sixteen years old. Barren's stomach twisted as he stared down at the disfigured corpse that no longer looked like the James he remembered. His friend was now bloated and purple, and as Cove drew the white clothe back farther, Barren had to step away from the body. He wanted to vomit. He turned his back on what he'd seen, covering his mouth, tears stinging his eyes.

"What happened to them?" Barren managed to say, but he couldn't turn around. Even if he looked upon James again, he didn't think he could comprehend what he'd seen. A body riddled with...*disease*...but was it a disease? It was certainly nothing he'd seen before. James's chest was red, as if a rash was covering it, but there were dark blackish veins protruding from his skin, and it was all coming from a wound at his heart where the mark they'd sworn by was no longer visible.

Cove was careful to cover James again, and Barren heard the thud of Cove's boots as he came closer.

"I don't know," Cove admitted. "We know Tetherion has hired a new string of privateers, and we believe this is the result. I've never seen anything like it."

"Everyone died the same way?"

The ambassador paused before he whispered, "Yes."

Barren looked at Cove, and then at Alex, whose face was pale.

"Do you think it is poison?"

"We'd need to ask Leaf," said Alex. "But I doubt he's seen anythin' like this, either. Even yer hemlock wound does not compare."

In Estrellas, Barren had been stabbed with a hemlock needle. The weapon was laced with dark magic. It had nearly killed him, but thanks to the healing powers of Lord Alder, he'd survived, only to experience random bouts of paralysis. "Do you think magic is responsible?"

"We cannot rule out the possibility until the wounds are inspected," said Cove. "I'm taking them to Dr. Newell in

Arcarum. I'm hoping he can tell me precisely how they died," said Cove.

Barren shivered. That was something Leaf could not do, but if this was magic, Barren had to wonder what a mortal doctor could really do.

"Why did you lie to the Elders?"

"If we 'ad brought the rest of Gregory's crew before the Elders, there would 'ave been no argument for your release, and if this is magic, we're gonna to need you," said Alex.

Barren had to laugh at that. "I'm no expert on the subject."

"It doesn't matter. It's part of yer blood."

Barren couldn't quite place the feeling he got when he heard those words, but he knew he didn't like them.

"So you will take them to this Dr. Newell in Arcarum?" Barren asked Cove. "And after that? What are your plans?"

"I suppose most of that depends on what we discover, but these bodies, they must be returned to their loved ones in Silver Crest," said Cove. Barren looked between Alex and Cove. He assumed that's why Alex was here, but their expectant gazes told him otherwise.

"You want me to do it?"

"Alex must return to Silver Crest, organize the captains, and hopefully prevent further damage to your reputation," said Cove. "Besides, I'd think you might want to be there for the examinations anyway."

"There?" he asked. "You mean in Arcarum?"

"It wouldn't take long," said Cove. "Three days, perhaps.

You'd be well protected in my home."

"But what about that," he demanded, pointing to the five men on the floor behind him. "Do I let more of our men die like that?"

"Ya know just as well as we do that we can't do anythin' about it until we figure out what it is," said Alex.

That was true. And if Barren encountered the weapon or *thing* responsible for killing these men at sea, he wouldn't know how to fight it.

"Three days in Arcarum? Are you sure no one will find those bodies?"

"Dr. Newell works for me," said Cove. "He knows what I am involved in and he has for years."

Barren wanted to argue that Cove hadn't answered his question, but he knew the ambassador couldn't promise anything other than to keep them as safe as he could.

"Are you about to start elections? We would be a distraction."

"These dead men behind us are enough of a distraction," Cove paused. "Besides, I'm afraid I won't have much time to give you. The Autumn Ball is tomorrow night. I'll be busy preparing for it. My hope is that Tetherion reveals the identity of the privateers who killed our men."

"Would he be so bold around you?"

"Yes. We would be stupid to think he wouldn't boast. Besides, he needs some sort of triumph in the face of his unpopularity."

"What will you do if you discover the privateers' identities?" Barren asked, curious. He could think of a few things.

Cove shrugged. "That depends on many things, but the best we can hope for now is to learn how these killings were done. Until then, we are at a disadvantage at sea."

Barren shuddered. He knew without a doubt that was true. The sooner they discovered what this horror was, the better.

"You realize you both may be exiled along with me since you have chosen to hide this?" Barren asked.

"The code without Barren Reed isn't a code at all," said Alex.

"Many great things come to an end," said Cove. "It's our responsibility to be prepared for it."

Cove might feel prepared, but Barren didn't. What would he do without the only world he'd ever known? His identity as a pirate of Silver Crest was as much a part of him as his blood. To lose that meant he'd lose himself. But there were worse things at stake here. The proof was right behind him, and if he had to choose between exile and saving the people he cared most about, well, there really was no decision to be made. He knew what he would choose.

"If we do discover the identity of the privateers who did this, I call rights."

"Granted," said Cove with a laugh. "But you know you can't kill them until we have answers."

"I'll try to restrain myself," Barren said, and though he smiled, he turned again to look back at the space where his brethren lay. Those bodies could easily be the bodies of his crew. He would stop whatever this threat was, and fast.

Chapter Four
TUNNEL

The heat from the sun baked her skin. Her tongue was swollen and her lips chapped. She stared out at a huge crowd. Their skin glistened and dirt stuck to their faces. They squinted up at her against the bright blue sky. They were a subdued crowd, nothing at all like the normally boisterous mob that frequented these hangings, especially for pirates.

Though she was seconds from dying, all she could think of was her dry throat and the growing ache in her head. She just wanted it gone. Then she looked beside her and saw bodies hanging in a row, already dead but poised for another hanging. She knew them all: Barren was beside her, and Leaf beside him, then Cove, then Sam, Slay, Em, and Devon. They'd all met their end, and she would meet hers too. She screamed, and it tore at her throat and at her heart, ripping through her chest like a hot blade. Then the door beneath her gave way.

Larkin's eyes flew open and she sat up, heart hammering her in chest. Her hand closed around her neck where the phantom pain of the noose lingered, only to find soft, unscathed skin. She sat in the darkness for a moment catching her breath before swinging her legs over the edge of her hammock and jumping out. She pulled her cloak over her shoulders and headed for deck. She needed fresh air.

They'd set sail soon after the storm had ended. None of them had any desire to linger for very long at Sanctuary, though not everyone was excited to travel to Arcarum either. Larkin couldn't say she was particularly ecstatic, especially when she'd learned the Autumn Ball was tomorrow night. She'd attended many of those balls with her father as Lady Lee, and she knew how crowded Cove's home could get. The ambassador might promise he could hide them well within the large house, but those in attendance often explored the house and grounds.

And after what had occurred with the bloodstone only months ago, she couldn't imagine Cove, Tetherion, and her father in the same house together.

As she set foot on deck, she was awash in light. The stars were clear and crisp, and the moon was full. The air was cooler, as autumn was nearing. It would never really get cold at sea, and only the islands far west experienced ice, but after triple degree heat, these fall nights seemed colder.

She walked to the rail of the ship and looked down. This had become a habit, like looking out the window in the morning. She was never sure what she expected to see except water, but that didn't stop her from doing it.

She looked around, searching for Barren. She found him

sitting on one of the barrels at the back of the ship and approached him.

"It's not close to morning," Barren said. "Why are you up?"

She looked at him, and seeing that he had his canteen around his body, she reached for it. "I was thirsty," she said, drinking deeply. The thirst from her nightmare still clung to her throat.

Barren raised a brow. "Bad dream?"

"How did you guess?"

He looked at her with a smile in his eyes, and she felt her heart squeeze a bit. "Well, it's just a guess, but I'd suspect anyone might have nightmares after seeing what's in Cove's hatch."

She wanted to ask him how he knew, but he answered as if guessing her thoughts.

"I saw you sneak in," he said, shaking his head. "Always curious."

While there was a slight smile on his face, she couldn't help but feel he was disappointed.

"Oh," she said quietly, drawing her brows tighter.

She was stubborn, a fact she had never denied. She hated to be told what to do, especially when Barren tried to command her. After Barren had told them about the killings, she'd wanted to see the wounds, thinking maybe it would give her a better idea of what they were dealing with. It hadn't. Instead, the images rolled around in her head like a living nightmare.

"I guess you weren't able to sleep at all, then, either?" she asked.

"No, though even if I wanted to move from this spot, I could not at the moment," he indicated his left leg. She knew that meant he was suffering from another round of paralysis, a lasting reminder of the hemlock that had raced through his veins, made more potent by magic.

She knew he would prefer to forget his link to magic, but it was in his blood, *their blood*, as they had been reminded again today. Their mothers were Elves born with Lyric blood. It made them half-Elf, but also half-Lyric. Because of this, their lives were at the mercy of others' expectations. They were expected to retaliate, to betray. She supposed they both had a habit of meeting expectations in all the wrong ways.

Even stranger was that the Elders seemed more concerned with Barren and Larkin than any other threat that existed in Mariana, and after what she had seen today, she knew there were far worse things.

"Are you worried that the privateers who did this will attack Silver Crest soon?"

"I am worried," said Barren, but he did not elaborate.

"The Elders are wasting time having trials when they could be fighting."

"There was a time when they would have jumped at the chance," said Barren grimly. "I'm not sure why they think that avoiding the fight will make the privateers go away."

"Maybe they are looking to get out," Larkin said absently.

Barren looked at her, perplexed.

"What?" Larkin continued, "You cannot deny that this is a hard life, and it has clearly been hard on the Elders. They're working to protect a population that has grown to include women and children. You're more than pirates, you know— you're people, too."

"There was a time when you didn't believe that," Barren said, a brow raised.

"There was," she agreed. "But I know differently now."

"What you are suggesting, it doesn't make sense. It goes against everything the code stands for," he said.

"It does go against the code," she agreed. "But it didn't seem to me that they were overly eager to abide by it in the first place."

Barren said nothing. He had yet to openly express any disappointment or disagreement with the Elders, and he seemed to be uncomfortable whenever she did. Larkin watched as he looked out at the water, as if it might listen and report back to the Elders or perhaps retaliate immediately. To see Barren at the mercy of a group of old, bitter men and women was both frustrating and strange. Why was he giving them so much power?

"And to let the fight with Edward get so out of hand," she said. "Were they hoping someone would shed blood?"

Barren let out an irritated sigh, and raked his hands through his hair. "It was wrong of them to let that happen. It was wrong of Edward to challenge *me* in such a way."

"What do you mean?"

"Edward's attack on you was a challenge to me," he said. "The challenge went unmet. The next time we meet at sea, I may choose to engage in that challenge."

"I think Edward challenged me," she said. "Would you

deprive me of my first challenge? I'm sure I could easily break his other hand."

"I would not let you rise up to meet him," said Barren. "You are not trusted among the pirates of Silver Crest, and truly, you are not one of us. If you were to kill or even wound Edward, things would only become worse for you."

Why was it that suddenly everyone wanted to remind her that she didn't belong?

"You think you are any more trusted than I am at this point?"

"Yes," he said. "I'm not the daughter of Christopher Lee."

She set her jaw and glared at him. Why couldn't anyone separate who she was from who her father was? "Then let me swear to the code," she said.

"No."

"Why not?"

"Because you don't swear to the code just to prove something," Barren said, struggling to his feet, his leg still stiff. "You swear to the code because you believe in it!"

Larkin opened her mouth to argue that she did believe in the code, but there was a part of her that hesitated, and that was the part that didn't completely believe that the code was best. Perhaps it was Barren's trial or the Elders' conduct that was holding her back.

"I'm not my father," Larkin said quietly.

"I know that," he said and sighed. "They know that, too, but they also know there's a chance you'll decide this life isn't right for you. Then what? You take our secrets with you."

"Is that what you believe?" she demanded. Even if he didn't believe that, she was surprised these words came out of his mouth.

"No, but they do," he said. "It's not necessary to convince *me*, Larkin. You have to convince *them*."

"I didn't realize I needed anyone else's approval to be here."

Barren sort of laughed, but he was not entertained. "I asked you to join me," he said. "But we should have realized that our circumstances are more complicated than that. We're the children of Lyrics and our fathers were enemies."

"So maybe the circumstances aren't the best," she said. "Does that mean you are unwilling to fight for me?"

He stared at her and then pulled her forward. Her hands landed on his chest, and she stared up into his eyes and shivered. When he looked like this, he seemed so serious, as if he were prepared to swear an oath—and perhaps he was. He leaned forward, pressing his forehead to hers. She took in a shaking breath.

"I'll always fight for you," his voice was low, and as his lips covered hers, a fire ignited within her, filling her soul. She knew he told the truth. They had been raised as rivals, but this feeling told her that they had been bred for something more.

***

The moon was full and the stars were swollen with light, so when Arcarum came into view, its beauty was apparent, even in the full of night. The coast was like a grand mountain with houses stacked into its façade, rising like a terrace. Firelight burned outside several houses, welcoming beacons to all but pirates.

"Wonder if Cove will parade us through the streets," said Sam, as he turned the wheel ever so slightly to follow Cove's ship.

"You know he won't," Barren said. "You are being a cynic."

The helmsman smiled, showing his teeth. "Wouldn't be the first time."

Cove approached. He and a few other crewmen had decided to sail on Barren's ship so when the time came, they could crew the vessel to port.

"Since Arcarum is in view, I think it would be a good idea for everyone to hide," said Cove. "The port captains do not always patrol my port, but we should take precaution."

"What excuse have you for bringing this ship to port?" Barren asked curiously.

"It isn't uncommon to claim a ship one has conquered," Cove said with a smile. "I didn't get where I am today by being unprepared. Trust that I have a fitting story to tell."

His crew dispersed and Barren entered his cabin, shutting the door behind him. He walked to his desk and unlocked the top drawer, pulling out a leather-bound book. There were certain things Barren always took with him if he went inland, and one was his sketchbook. King Tetherion and the twins had taken great pride in relaying the humor of a pirate who drew. That had both embarrassed and angered him. It would also prove to be an incriminating detail if found on his ship. The second thing he always brought with him—indeed, he hardly took it off—was the compass he'd pulled from his mother's corpse.

It was broken, the needle tending to spin in rapid circles, which Barren found strange. Scorch-like marks marred the place where the stone had once rested in the back of the compass. The compass itself was a memory of his childhood, perhaps the only memory he had other than that of his father's death. When Barren had it on, he felt protected. Like there was a barrier between him and the rest of the world.

He also knew there was magic still attached to it. He could feel it, though it wasn't strong. That was another thing that had changed after he began the journey to find the bloodstone. It was also something that frightened him. If he could feel magic, did that mean he could somehow wield it? What if there was some truth to the Elders' fears?

He had to push those thoughts away. If he could wield magic, surely it would have surfaced by now.

He walked to the window as the ship came to port. Maris might be the biggest island in the Orient, but one thing was for certain, Arcarum was the most beautiful. It had every type of terrain: sandy beaches, tall mountains, and even a thick fringe of forest managed to snake its way through the island. It was a place he might visit more often if he wasn't a wanted fugitive.

He moved away from the window when he heard voices outside. They were low and cautious, and Barren suddenly wished Leaf was here to tell him what was being said. Several minutes passed before there was a rap on Barren's door.

"It's me," Cove called and poked his head inside.

"All is clear, but you must move fast. Hollow will take you to the tunnel," said Cove. Hollow had also accompanied Barren to D'Avana. He was Cove's best friend and a Senator in Arcarum. "I will take the bodies to Dr. Newell. It is late enough that no one will see me deliver them."

"I could accompany you to Dr. Newell's," said Barren. "If that is the case."

He didn't like the idea of Cove delivering five bodies in the middle of the night alone. Besides, he wanted to meet this Dr. Newell. He wanted to know what was so special about this doctor. Why had he been the first person Cove thought of when he'd found the bodies?

"It is not for the best. I have yet to inform him that you are visiting."

"Do you fear his reaction?"

"No, but Barren Reed should come with at least a little bit of warning, don't you think?"

Barren didn't say anything. Hollow approached. "The others are ready," he said.

Barren left his cabin, locking it tight behind him, and moved to join Hollow and his crew. Unconsciously he pulled his hat down farther and checked that all his weapons were near. It suddenly occurred to him that the decision to kill here was much harder than the one he had to make at sea. Here, a death meant a body, and letting someone go meant the possibility of a snitch. He pushed the thought away quickly. Hopefully it was something he wasn't going to have to deal with during his stay.

They followed Hollow through the bright night, traveling on the very edge of Arcarum where civilization had yet to invade. He led them up grassy hills overlooking Cove's private port. Hollow had referred to them as the Sea Cliffs because if you walked far enough south, the grassy ground became stone and plunged down into a cradle of waves and jagged rocks.

After some time, Hollow stopped and crouched to the ground. He pulled back a grass square to expose a set of wooden doors. Hollow knocked once, and from the other side Barren heard something like a rusted latch shift. After a moment, Hollow pulled the doors open. An aged man stood at their feet with a lantern in hand.

"Get in," Hollow commanded.

"G-get in?" Barren looked at the dark hole at his feet.

"Yes, this is a tunnel. Nob will take you straight to Cove's home," said Hollow. He peered around as if he were suspicious, which made Barren all the more paranoid.

"Nob?"

"How'd ya do?" The old man smiled without showing teeth, but it was a warm smile.

Hollow's voice suddenly became more urgent. "We don't have time for you to question loyalties, Barren Reed. Get in."

The pirate jumped into the tunnel and the others followed. Hollow did not. He shut the doors behind Sam, who was the last one in. The old man Hollow had called Nob reached up and latched the door.

"Let's get to walkin'. Gets cold down here fast."

The old man hobbled forward with the lantern and the pirates followed rather dumbly. At least this answered their question as to how they would get to Cove's home without being spotted. A tunnel. A tunnel straight to his home. Barren wondered when and why this had been created, but he had a feeling he already knew that this was an escape route just in case Cove ever needed it. Just in case he was caught.

"Where did Hollow go?" Barren asked.

"To check the ports," the old man replied.

"But he just came from there," said Barren.

"Mmm-hmm," Nob agreed and Barren heard Leaf chuckle behind him—he wasn't going to get any answers out of this man. Nob had been taught to keep his mouth shut. This was a characteristic Barren usually admired, until it kept him from getting what he wanted.

"You should take note of your surroundings and how you got here, for if there is a reason to flee, you'll be seeing this tunnel again."

"What does he mean, take a look at these tunnels? It's dark as night in here!" Leaf grumbled.

"Why're you complaining? You're a bloody Elf. It's not like you have trouble seeing," Slay countered irritably.

Barren shook his head and continued forward, following the old man as he made his way down the dark tunnel. It smelled of dirt, and the air was moist. His boots, caked with mud, became heavier as he moved along, and at one point he ran into an unlit lantern hanging from one of the wooden beams built into the side of the tunnel. Some good they did.

Though the tunnel was cold, Barren drew warmth from Larkin, who walked beside him.

"Were you aware of this?"

She looked at him surprised. "I wasn't aware that he was a pirate, how could I have known about this tunnel?"

"True," Barren conceded.

There was silence. "Do you think Cove is happy?" Larkin asked, which caught Barren off guard. What a strange question, he thought.

"Why wouldn't he be?"

"He smiles, but…it doesn't touch his eyes."

And then she moved ahead, down the dark tunnel. There were a lot of reasons Cove might be unhappy. Their brethren dying at sea might be one reason; the Elders' behavior at Sanctuary could be another, but the way Larkin had spoken made Barren think he was missing something.

Sometimes Barren forgot that Larkin and Cove had a relationship before he knew either of them. They'd known each other in this life, the one where Cove was ambassador and Larkin a Lady. They'd gone to balls, interacted socially, shared friends and drinks. It was sort of silly, but sometimes Barren felt a little jealous.

At last they came to the end of the tunnel. Nob stepped upon a short ladder and pushed another door open. He climbed out of the tunnel and the pirates followed him.

They found themselves in a dim basement. It seemed this was where all the extra decorations and chairs went when Cove wasn't having lavish parties, because there were boxes of fine garlands and stacks of well-cushioned chairs all about. Nob covered the hole they'd climbed from. The door fit in seamlessly, and for added protection, the old man moved a set of chairs over it.

"I will show you to the ambassador's study," he said and turned as a butler would to lead them upstairs. Nob opened the door after he mounted the stairs and they instantly felt a gust of warm air surround them. Barren welcomed it, as the chill from the tunnel pricked his arms. The smell of coffee and cinnamon filled his senses and he inhaled deeply, finding it odd that something as simple as a smell could make one feel safe.

Nob waited as Barren's crew filed into the hallway. They shuffled along, their boots sliding against the fine grain wooden floor. There was an air of awkwardness about them all. They were dirty, none of them had taken a real bath in weeks, yet here they stood in the pristine home of Ambassador Cove Rowell, and oddly enough, no one seemed to care that they were all a little wretched.

Around them, the very walls were lined with gold and cream. Iron sconces inlaid with shimmery gold and white gems added a warm halo around their shadows. Vivid landscapes surrounded with thick, intricate frames lined the hallway. This was the first time Barren had been in Cove's home. His other visits had been spent in the pub, Onyx Hall.

"Oh, it is good you have arrived!" came a voice from behind

them. Barren practically jumped out of his skin as he turned to face an old woman with rosy cheeks and a plump figure. She reminded him of Mary McCloud, Alex's wife, and he found himself feeling guilty that he even dared place his hand on his sword. By the slight tilt of her head, Barren guessed she hadn't missed it either. "I bet you are all famished. We'll have a nice little snack and some tea for you in a moment. Follow me."

She whipped around and led them through a door across from the staircase.

This room was just as nice as the hallway they'd entered. A fireplace lay directly before them, and upon the mantel sat a portrait of a man Barren could only assume was Cove's father, the late Canice Rowell. They had similar features—dark eyes, thin lips, high cheekbones. The only difference was this man had silver-streaked hair. On the day of his death, he had planned to betray the Arcarum pirates, which included brethren, friends, and his own son.

Windows stretched along the left wall, covered by heavy folds of fabric. The walls were white but accented by dark molding. The ceiling was an intricate crisscross of wooden beams, and at the center of the room a wrought-iron chandelier hung, tiered with candles. On the right side of the room, a dark wood desk rested, covered in parchment and rolled scrolls. It was evident Cove wasn't the most organized, which was a strange characteristic for Barren to observe in his friend considering he appeared so put together.

"I'll return shortly with some tea," the old woman said. "Oh!

And before I forget, my name is Camille, if you need anything."

Barren kept expecting the woman to react to them differently or to show her disfavor, but she seemed cheery, and if she didn't like them, she hid it well. He wondered how she felt about being placed in this situation. If Cove was ever exposed as having an alliance with pirates, she would be guilty by association.

A knock sounded at the front door of the mansion, and Barren's anxiety heightened. It was possible that every sound would cause him panic until they left.

"Better get that!" Camille said and hurried off, closing the door behind her.

After a moment Leaf said. "It's Hollow," he paused. "Huh, seems they've had some trouble with vandalism at Cove's port." As much as the Elf complained about his excellent hearing, it was a useful tool.

What kind of vandalism, Barren wondered. He went over their practices before leaving the ship. He'd made sure to bring his journal, and everything had been placed under lock and key.

The handle of the door moved and Hollow entered the study. He didn't appear any different now than he had when he shoved them all down the tunnel.

"Why'd you have to take the long way around?" asked Leaf. "Too good for the tunnel of dirt?"

Hollow was not amused. "We must at least attempt to live the lies we craft," he said simply. "Besides, you needed to be familiar with the tunnel. It is your only hope for escape if anything goes awry while you're here."

"You and Cove seem more nervous than usual," said Leaf, narrowing his eyes.

"Our situation is different now, in case the five dead men on Cove's ship didn't give that away," said Hollow evenly. "And while you are all here, let me be perfectly clear. While Cove finds you incredibly helpful, I do not. I cannot imagine why he brought you here unless it is to cause more grief for himself."

"Don't hold back your true feelings," Leaf muttered.

It had never occurred to Barren that Hollow didn't actually want him and his crew here. This was where Cove's duel life became difficult: What did he do when both sides weighed him down with pressures? Which did he choose? And who suffered without his help?

Before Barren could respond, Hollow held his hand up to silence him.

"Spare me the defense," he said. "I know why you are here, but we are not dealing with the same situation as before."

"So what has changed?" Barren prompted.

Hollow narrowed his eyes a bit. "There is a new power rising with a wish to overthrow the king. They are called the Commonwealth. Not surprisingly, they are also opposed to piracy. We believe one of the leaders of the group is a man named Ben Willow, a lawyer here in Arcarum."

"Ben Willow?" Larkin's voice rose to scoff at that name. "How has he gained popularity in such a small amount of time? Last I heard, he was just an apprentice."

"He's recently become a lawyer," said Hollow. "He works with

Frank Rosamund and is now engaged to his daughter."

Larkin appeared surprised. It seemed that bit of information had been unexpected.

"And why is he such a threat to you?" asked Barren.

Hollow stiffened and Barren could tell he hadn't expected that question.

"He is a threat to all of us, including you," said Hollow. "Specifically because he is running against me for the position I have held the last six years and because he has been able to pinpoint every last member of Cove's crew."

"Well, how odd can that really be?" asked Leaf. "You're all friends."

"Friends, yes. But Cove's crew is vast and our association with each other is private. Only those closest to us know who we spend our time with. Most of our crew and network do not openly interact with Cove or me. They man their own ships as instructed by Cove."

"Do you think someone has betrayed you?"

"Consider instead the possibility that Ben Willow is getting information from sources closer to the king."

That could be anyone but most likely the princes, Datherious and Natherious.

"If Ben were to win my position, he would use it to make the Commonwealth stronger. While he is not a fan of the king, his greatest motivation is to see Cove destroyed."

It was strange to hear Hollow say so much, but Barren knew what he was doing. Cove and Hollow had been friends a long time and Hollow, whether he'd say it or not, feared for Cove.

"Why?"

"Perhaps he is jealous." The way Hollow suggested it made Barren feel like there was more behind their rivalry.

"If Ben is Cove's enemy, why would he go after your position? Why not go after Cove's?" said Barren.

"Cove is too popular with the people of Arcarum to be attacked directly. Ben's job is to find something to shock people with. If he were able to take my position as Senator of Kentworth, he would not only oversee the province in which the ambassador lives but also be forced to work very closely with him. Ben will take full advantage of that if given the chance." The senator walked over to a cabinet and withdrew a decanter and a glass. He poured the golden liquid into the glass and swallowed it in one gulp.

"I'm not telling you this so you'll get involved. I'm telling you this so you'll stay out of it. I will deal with Ben Willow and the Commonwealth on my own. Understand?"

The warning in the man's voice was clear and to drive the point home, he glared at each of them with his coal-black eyes.

Shortly after Hollow's threat, Camille returned with food and tea, and Hollow excused himself. The pirates were thankful for something to diffuse the tension, though now the silence was filled with the clank of silverware and the sounds of chewing. Barren ate, though the food was not enough of a distraction to keep him from realizing Cove had yet to return from Dr. Newell's office. He began to worry that the ambassador had run into trouble, which made the food less appetizing.

Camille maintained her cheeriness as she led the pirates up four flights of stairs to their rooms. She instructed them to keep their doors locked and their window coverings drawn while offering up a silver key to each. Of course she was well-aware of who they were and it sounded as if she wasn't a stranger to these sorts of things.

Before she left Barren and Larkin at their door, she turned to Larkin. "I've often said that if God above has any humor, he'd have given Christopher Lee a son destined for the sea...boy did he ever pull one over on me."

Chapter Five
BURDEN

Datherious came here because he had to. The place was known as Wine Hall. Though the name implied a greater sense of sophistication, this pub had none. He moved through the crowded space, his hood drawn over his head. The farther he could retreat into the darkness, the less chance he had of being recognized. No good would come of his presence here.

He moved between the people crowded around the tables and the bar, guzzling their drinks and eating their fill of stew. Smoke created clouds that hung low from the ceiling. Most of the barflies smelled of sweat and salt and had probably retreated to this place after a day spent at port. Suddenly, Datherious was reminded of his times at sea with Barren Reed. He and his brother had spent two months with the pirate, learning Barren's weaknesses, his plans, his connections. It had all been a carefully crafted ruse, a service to his ungrateful father.

He'd experienced failure so publically then, when Barren Reed had returned him, his brother, and Christopher Lee to Maris in chains. Now, Tetherion only looked upon him with disdain, and his blood boiled at the thought.

Datherious moved to the stairwell and up to the loft, which overlooked the floor below. Though he knew he was alone, he could not help looking behind him. It was strange not to have his shadow, Natherious, the silent twin, but even he must remain ignorant of this. There was no other way. In good time, he would come to know. In good time, everyone would.

He sat in the farthest corner and waited. He had come early to Wine Hall, but he did not sit long before the silhouette of a man rose from the stairwell. He paused at the entrance, startled by Datherious's presence. Clearly he had thought to come early, too. The man moved forward.

"Prince," he said. "You seem ever-eager to meet."

"If I am early, it is only because I wish to get this over with," he said.

"I wouldn't expect anything more."

The man sat down, but he did not remove his hood. "So you are him?" Datherious kept his hands on the table, spinning a gold piece around and letting it fall with a clank. "The leader of the Commonwealth? My father has lost hair searching for you."

The man said nothing and Datherious laughed. "Are you afraid I will have you dragged away to the noose?"

"No," the man replied evenly, and truly there was no hint of fear in his voice, which set Datherious on edge. He didn't like when people weren't afraid of him. The spinning coin fell flat.

"Odd, perhaps you should be."

"I sit before a restless prince eager for his father's throne. I am in no danger."

"We are always in danger," said Datherious. "To think otherwise *is* unwise."

He picked the coin up again.

"It is unwise for you to linger here. For what purpose have you called me?"

"You are quite bold," he spun the coin. "I haven't decided if I like you yet."

"You called forth your enemy," the man replied. "You've little time to decide if you like me."

Datherious laughed. Slamming his hand down on the coin, he pushed it forward with his palm. "I am giving you a task. Find me an assassin."

The man reached for the coin, taking it into his hand.

"An assassin? For who?" There was no surprise in the man's voice, but his eyes seemed to gleam from inside the hood.

"That is my secret for now," replied the prince.

"It is not common for me to do this type of work."

"Oh, I think it is. You've a past, one you likely do not wish to be known."

It seemed he'd hit on something with that statement, and the man wrapped his fingers around the coin and stood.

"When do you want her?" he asked.

"*Her?*"

"Yes, I am assuming you want the best assassin I know, and she is a woman. When do you need her?"

Datherious narrowed his eyes and the man stood. "As soon as possible. Before the Autumn Ball."

"That does not leave me much time."

"Then you'd better hurry," Datherious replied.

The man nodded and turned, but as he was about to leave, he paused.

"You are correct, prince, it is a dangerous world. Do not be fooled by a pretty face or you'll find yourself in an early grave."

"Is that a threat?"

Datherious could not see the man's face, but he knew he smiled. "No, think of it as friendly advice...from a partner."

***

Cove stood behind his desk in his study. He'd gotten a late start to the day. He hated how unorganized he felt. Discovering three of his brethren had been hanged and finding five others in the Orient had thrown everything he'd been planning off course. He'd been preparing for the Autumn Ball, which would take place tonight. He needed this night to go smoothly. It would keep Ben Willow from gaining support and the Commonwealth from gaining momentum.

Cove was sure the two were connected, but he didn't have proof, mainly because he couldn't find any information on Ben Willow. He had gathered only enough information to know Willow's past had been contrived. He'd been in Arcarum for five years. He'd worked as Frank Rosamund's apprentice until recently, when he'd become a practicing lawyer himself. Now he was interested in politics, and not just any position would do. He wanted Hollow's province.

In reality, it was only a matter of time before someone challenged Hollow's position, but Cove didn't trust Ben Willow. Since he'd announced his nomination, Cove couldn't go anywhere without seeing him. Willow was always there, watching, waiting, expectant.

Their encounter this morning was just one such example. He had been visiting the courthouse when Ben approached.

"Ambassador Rowell," Ben said, *looking him up and down. "Feeling well?"*

"Perfectly," he'd replied.

"Really? I'd have thought you'd have to feel ill to visit Dr. Newell so late in the night."

He'd smiled. "That's the magic of a great doctor, Mr. Willow."

Ben had left then without another word.

After the encounter Cove sent Jonas to notify Dr. Newell, though he wasn't sure how much good it would do. He could only hope the doctor had hid the bodies he'd brought from sea well enough, and if they were discovered, he hoped Dr. Newell was a good liar. He knew it wasn't the best idea to bring the pirates here, but this was something he had to do.

A knock interrupted his thoughts and he uncurled the fingers he hadn't realized he'd been clenching. He waited, expecting Camille to answer or enter the study any minute to tell him someone was here to see him. Though he didn't have any appointments that he was aware of, it wasn't unlikely for someone to drop by for a few moments.

The knock sounded again. Camille and Nob must be busy, he thought. He strode into the foyer and opened the door.

"Cove!"

"Sara," Cove took a step back, trying to stifle the surprise in his voice as he took in the woman at his door. She was Sara Rosamund—a friend, and the daughter of Frank Rosamund. Her sapphire blue eyes were painfully innocent and so kind, and set within the prettiest face, heart-shaped and fair-skinned. Her blond hair was pinned up in a bun, but she could never quite catch all the strands, as loose curls always managed to make their way free. Her lithe frame was draped in blue, a coat with black clasps kept her gown hidden, and white gloves covered her fragile hands. They'd grown up together, both having fathers in politics, and had spent many nights walking the gardens behind his house during balls and their fathers' social calls.

"What a surprise," he gestured to his foyer. "Come in."

He closed the door behind her and as he turned to face her, Camille appeared from the hallway. "Apologies, Master Rowell," she said, and then her eyes moved to Sara. "Ah! Miss Rosamund, it is good to see you!"

She swept forward and took her hand. A warm smile spread across Sara's face as she folded her hand over Camille's. "You look as lovely as a flower!"

"Camille," Cove interrupted. They both turned to look at him, and he felt bad for halting their reunion. "Will you bring Miss Rosamund tea?"

"Why yes, of course!" she said and patted Sara's hand before running off toward the kitchen. An awkwardness fell between them in Camille's absence.

"Shall we sit?" Cove asked, indicating the open doors of his study. He permitted Sara to walk before him, feeling a little self-conscious at the clutter he'd allowed to overtake the space. She didn't seem to mind and went straight for the chair she'd always claimed as hers, the one closest to the windows. His heart felt heavy as he recalled the many nights she'd sat there, staring out the unblocked windows, admiring the starry sky.

"Does the daylight bother your work?" she asked, looking at the heavy curtains that now covered the windows. He hadn't bothered to open them since returning from his adventure with Barren. Perhaps this space offered too many memories.

"No, not usually," he said. When she did not seem to like his response he added, "Though it does get warm in here with the windows unblocked."

She seemed to comprehend, mouthing 'Oh' in understanding, but silence fell between them again, and tension built. Why was this difficult? Things with Sara had never been difficult before.

Camille brought tea. Any other time, her excited chatter would not bother Cove, but today he was feeling impatient. He had a long list of things to do to prepare for the ball, and there were pirates in his house. Not to mention Camille's love for Sara was just a reminder of what once was.

Camille left when the doorbell rang, and Cove was glad for it until silence filled the room again. For a while the clank of Sara's cup and saucer sounded as she sipped tea. After a moment, she set the china aside.

"I'm sorry if you are busy," Sara said. She played with the hem of her sleeve, pulling it down over her hand. Cove watched the motion closely. It was a strange thing to think, but he'd never noticed that habit before. Was she nervous? "I know the ball is tonight, and I could have waited to speak with you then, but I wasn't certain I could catch you alone. I tried to call earlier in the week, but Camille said you were away," she paused and finally met his gaze. Her sapphire eyes were so sincere. "You're gone so often now."

"It is the nature of my job," he said. "As you well know."

"Yes," she said with a hesitant smile. "I suppose, yet it was not so in the beginning."

"Times are changing. The sea is...unpredictable."

"Are you speaking of piracy?"

He stared back at her, taking a sip of tea. "Yes, among other things," he replied.

"Oh, it is awful," she said. "There were three men hanged in Maris just yesterday. I don't understand why we must make a spectacle of a human's life, no matter their transgressions."

"Many would argue pirates are not human."

"You don't believe that, do you?" She stared at him, almost demanding.

"I suppose it's never mattered what I believed," he said. He cleared his throat and stood. "But the news at sea won't affect your plans, will it?"

"Mine?" she was confused.

"The wedding," said Cove. "Ben's campaign centers on piracy. I can't imagine how he will balance the two—a new wife and his obsession."

She seemed surprised. "It's not like you to be so cynical."

They stared at one another, and then Cove laughed. "You'll forgive me, I did not intend to insult your beloved."

"Don't," she shuddered and took a breath. "Don't apologize."

Cove had a feeling that's not what the shudder was for.

"We digress," he took the moment to turn the conversation in a different direction and smiled politely at her. "What had you hoped to discuss in secrecy?"

She cleared her throat and stood, smoothing out the folds of her dress and pulling down on the sleeves of her coat again.

"I...," she began, taking a breath, but she hesitated, twisting her fingers together. It was strange to see her like this, so changed. Had her engagement made her a different person? Or had Ben?

"Sara," Cove watched her as she spoke, and her eyes seemed to grow wider. "You can tell me anything."

She opened her mouth to speak, but looked away. "I just...I just wanted to say that I'm glad you're back."

Cove raised a brow and stared. "Oh," and there was silence.

She curtsied. "I must go," she said, and turned quickly to leave the study. Cove followed closely behind her.

She reached the door when he called out, "Sara!" She turned around to face him, and suddenly he wasn't sure what he had wanted to say. There was nothing he could say that would bring her back to him and nothing that could undo the decision she'd already made.

"You will invite me to the wedding?"

"Cove," her voice was a whisper, and her eyes glazed with fresh tears. It might have disarmed him, but he had worked for a very long time to maintain the composure he had now. He reached behind her and opened the front door.

"Have a good day, Sara." His words were just above a whisper, and they urged her out the door. She turned and hurried to her waiting carriage. Cove watched it rattle off until he could see it no longer. When he closed the door and turned, he found Barren watching him from atop the stairs.

***

"So, that girl you said you could stand to be friends with?" he asked. "Is that her? 'Cause I think you lied."

Cove opened his mouth to speak, but instead left the foyer, returning to his study. Barren hurried down the stairs to follow quickly behind him.

"You should be more careful," Cove chided. "What if Sara saw you?"

"She didn't. I'm pretty sure she couldn't take her eyes off you."

Barren had to admit he was enjoying this more than he should. For the last couple of months, he'd been the end of these types of jokes. Dealing them was far more fun than receiving them, but sensing Cove's mood, Barren's humor faltered and he cleared his throat.

"What I really came down here to ask you was, have you heard anything from Dr. Newell?"

"Not as of this morning," said Cove.

His answer was short, and Barren watched him as he moved behind his desk, picking up random pieces of paper and moving them about absentmindedly; his mind was scattered.

"Did he seem to know what had caused the injuries?" Barren prodded.

"He didn't give any indication," the ambassador replied.

"And you haven't followed up?"

"Not in the last six hours, no, I haven't," Cove snapped, then seeming to realize what he'd done, he quickly composed himself, running his hand over his smoothed hair. He sighed. "I apologize, Barren. These last few weeks have not been easy. Dr. Newell wasn't as forthcoming with information as I would have liked, and he wasn't as eager to begin an autopsy as I'd hoped."

"Why did you think to bring the bodies to him in the first place? He's a mortal doctor. It isn't likely he's seen anything like this anyway."

"It's not a question of whether he's seen it before," said Cove. "I'd advise you to get comfortable. It isn't likely we'll have an answer before the ball tonight."

There was silence and Barren finished Cove's unspoken words. "Which you already knew."

Cove did not respond.

"You'll need me to carry off the bodies when the doctor has finished his autopsy," said Barren. He was putting the pieces together. Cove had something else up his sleeve. "It was a sure way to get me here, now what? Why did you want me here?"

A strange, slow smile spread over Cove's face, but it wasn't one of humor or happiness.

"You aren't going to like me."

"I'm not so sure you care at this point."

He gave a look that confirmed he didn't. "There are reports that an attempt will be made on Tetherion's life at the ball tonight."

Barren just stared. "So you wanted me here to do what? Watch?"

"No," Cove said slowly, though his eyes remained steady and a little fierce.

"I don't owe him his life! He's responsible for the death of my mother and father! Not to mention he's a traitor."

"Believe it or not, keeping Tetherion alive is definitely not for his benefit," Cove said evenly. "It's for mine. If they kill him tonight in my house, do you know what will happen to me?"

Barren didn't say anything, but he could only imagine. Cove's life here in Arcarum was all about his reputation. A murder in his home would be scandalous.

"And you think this has been organized by who? The Commonwealth?"

Cove seemed surprised. "Who told you about them?"

"Three guesses," Barren said mildly.

"I see," Cove said grimly. "I had planned to tell you, but Hollow was not in agreement with my plan to have you at the ball. I understand his reasoning."

"But you disagree."

"Yes," he said. "Hollow and the others will be busy entertaining guests, gathering support. They'll be distracted. I need you and your crew to keep watch."

"Doesn't Tetherion have guards for this? If someone's going to attack him, let them save him."

"We don't know if his guards support him. What if they are members of the Commonwealth, too?"

Barren raised a brow. While he'd have liked to brush this off, he knew Cove was right.

"I can only trust you," Cove added, and Barren felt his heart pull. The ambassador really knew how to persuade him.

"I think you forget who I am," Barren said. "I won't blend in easily at a ball."

Cove smirked, and this time he was truly humored. "Luckily, the Autumn Ball is a masquerade."

"Has it always been a masquerade?" Barren asked, the pitch of his voice rising. He wasn't going to know what to think if Cove said no.

"Yes," he smiled. "Tradition."

"You don't think Ben Willow has organized this assassination, do you?" Barren asked. He watched the ambassador. He expected him to look surprised at the mention of the name, but his features were neutral.

"It is a possibility," he replied. "I believe that Ben Willow would do anything to discredit me. Tetherion's death in my home would kill two birds with one stone."

"What's his vendetta?"

"I am Albatross. I carry all the knowledge that makes you strong," he said, and Barren felt a shiver go down his spine. Taking Cove down was a strategic move, a smart move. He was powerful in a way Tetherion and his sons weren't. His strength was garnered by a bloodline, but also by his ability to be everywhere at once.

"That name wasn't given to you recklessly. The story goes that killing an albatross is a bad omen. Your enemies would do well to heed that warning."

Cove seemed amused and added quietly. "It is too bad my enemies do not know that I am Albatross, then."

Behind Cove's joke, there was real worry. There was also real sadness. Larkin had been right when she'd said his smile no longer touched his eyes. He was very much a different Cove. Perhaps the burden of Albatross was taking its toll.

***

Larkin spent most of the evening with Camille after Barren had informed them they would attend the Autumn Ball. She'd bathed, scrubbing her skin and scalp until it burned. Now she sat in front of the mirrored vanity. Her long hair spilled over one shoulder, and she brushed the strands absently. She thought of how strange it would be to stand among people she'd once called friends. How strange it would be to hear her name thrown around in conversation, how strange it would be to hear what people truly thought of her.

Stranger still that she would be in the same room as her

father, but not as his daughter. Each time she thought of it, her stomach twisted into knots. She thought of how she and her father had parted. They had not spoken, and she'd tied her crimson scarf around his mouth to keep him silent upon his return to Maris. Her feelings for her father were confusing. When she'd been kidnapped, she'd just wanted his approval. Now, part of her wanted him to understand the price of his inattention.

And then again, she wanted answers. She wanted to know more about her mother. She wanted to know why her father remained close to Tetherion—was he truly as malicious as he tried to appear? Or was he seeking revenge? She wanted to believe he was somehow noble, but admitting that aloud made her feel silly when there was little to suggest that anything her father did was honorable.

The door opened and she looked up to see Barren's reflection in the mirror. He wore a clean white shirt and pants. In his hands he carried a towel and his mother's compass. His damp hair stuck to his face, and with the grime stripped from his skin, his scars were more visible. Despite this, he had lordly features—a strong jaw, sharp eyes, arched brows—and there was a grace about him granted by his Elvish heritage. He smiled at her and she flushed, her skin warming. She turned to face him, still sitting at the vanity.

He approached her, running his fingers through his hair, and she held her breath.

"Have you any instruction to give for my manners when

interacting with nobles?" he asked.

"Only one," she said. "Don't spill your wine."

He laughed and kissed her on the cheek. He pulled away too soon, but his lips lingered close to her skin, as if he was considering kissing her again. Larkin's heart fell a little when he moved away, but she watched him for a moment as he slipped the compass around his neck and dried his hair with the towel. It was strange seeing him in this manner made him vulnerable, human. It reminded her that he wasn't invincible. She turned back to the vanity.

"I'm surprised you agreed to this," she commented.

"I must help Cove in any way I can," he replied. "I'm indebted to him. Besides, though not ideal, this is the best way to learn more about the privateers who killed our brethren."

She did not respond immediately. She ran her brush through her hair, staring into the mirror without really seeing.

"You know my father will be at the Autumn Ball," she said.

"Yes," and though Barren did not say it immediately, she could hear the irritation in his voice. "He will look for you."

"Why? He will not know I am there."

"He's your father," he said. "He will always look for you, no matter where he is. I would look for you."

The only way Barren would ever stop looking for her is if he believed she did not want to be found. Her father had no such concern and took her choice to stay with Barren as a challenge.

"Which is why you must be mindful of your interactions tonight," Barren continued.

"Do you believe I will be careless?" she asked, looking at him through the mirror. She tried to keep her irritation at bay, but she knew she hadn't succeeded. Her tone was too sharp. It was the second time he had suggested she would betray him.

He met her gaze.

"I'm only advising you to be cautious. People who are familiar with you will recognize you with or without a mask," he continued. "It would be in your best interest to avoid contact with your father or anyone you were familiar with from your past. It should be easy. You aren't there to socialize."

"How do you expect to learn anything if you do not speak to anyone?" In her experience, gossip was probably the best way to gather information.

"By listening," said Barren. "And you can't very well do that while you're talking or dancing."

She stood and turned on him. "You obviously have little understanding of how a ball works."

"I know very well how this works for *us*, Larkin," Barren said evenly. He paused, and took a breath. "I know you want answers from your father, but tonight is not the night to demand them."

She was surprised by his assumptions, and even more surprised that he thought she would compromise their lives so easily. Did he think she was naïve?

"As hard as it might be for you, you must think of your father as the enemy. Once you start searching for his virtue, he has the advantage."

"Not everything is a battle, Barren."

He surprised her by smiling, and then he placed his hands on either side of her face. "But everything is a battle with you."

He leaned forward and kissed her. Heat rushed to her face and her stomach fluttered with feelings so contrary to the heaviness that suddenly filled her heart.

He pulled away, retrieving his jacket from the bed and moving to the door.

"I'll see you tonight," he said, and left the room.

Chapter Six
BATTLEFRONT

After his discussion with Barren, the day progressed into a flurry of chaotic episodes, all centering around the ball, so when it finally arrived, Cove was ready for it all to be over.

He had attended these balls when he was younger, but he'd never had a care in the world for what they were actually meant to accomplish or how much trouble and time went into their arrangement. For him and so many others his age, balls were about the frivolity. It had been about the drinks, the glamour, the attention. Unlike others his age, however, he'd inherited responsibilities much sooner, and simple things like balls became crucial tools for maintaining and gathering alliances and smoothing over scandals.

Cove turned to the mirror and buttoned his black jacket, ensuring his hair was slick and smart, bound at the nape of his neck. Oddly enough, the man who looked back at him was becoming more and more unfamiliar.

"Are you ready for this?" Hollow asked from the door. Cove

turned and faced his friend, smiling brightly.

"If you mean am I ready to flaunt my grace and charm? Always."

Hollow rolled his eyes. He stepped away from the door as Cove exited and they headed downstairs. "Great. You know the only reason women ever pay attention to me is to figure out if *you're* single."

Cove laughed. "Are you saying you actually want attention, Hollow? That is very unlike you."

"No, I'm not saying that at all. I'm saying many feign interest in me to get to you."

"Well, you can just tell them I'm unavailable."

"They know that," Hollow said quietly. "I suppose they are hoping you'll settle."

Cove ground his teeth. The reminders were everywhere. Sara Rosamund would never be his, but it was best that way and he'd always known it. If he were being honest with himself, it was his fault. He'd pushed her away, reeled her back in, only to push her away again. He was a coward, fearful that his life and the person he'd become wasn't meant for the innocent Sara Rosamund.

"At this point, Hollow, I don't think any woman could tempt me to think twice of her," Cove said, and he pulled open his front door and stepped outside as the first of the carriages arrived. The air was mild, and a slight breeze carried the smell of roses. It was the perfect evening for a ball.

Men and women dressed in velvet, lace and glitter suddenly converged upon his yard. The costumes were extravagant—big dresses, big masks—and people arrived dressed as all sorts of things: cats, jokers, swans. There were masks with feathers, masks with leaves, moon masks and sun masks. It was apparent that few in Arcarum were subtle, especially the nobility.

Cove and Hollow stood opposite each other as they greeted everyone. Cove made sure to smile, shake hands as a respected servant of his people would, and of course flaunt all that grace and charm. Overly dressed, extravagant, and boisterous, these people were all quite oblivious. They lived their lives in finery. Cove was no exception and he knew it. He utilized his high status every day to gain an advantage, to manipulate, to gain power. Sometimes he believed he was no different than his father. Sometimes he feared he would make his father's mistakes.

"Cove, m'boy!" the voice boomed over the murmur of the crowd, rupturing the calm of the ambassador's thoughts. A round man with a round face and red cheeks pushed his way between people and presented himself to Cove. No one protested the jump in line, however, for this man was the Governor of Arcarum, Matthew Dulcemer. He was a jolly man with no concern for others' ears. *Oh, would Leaf dislike him*, Cove thought. Matthew embraced Cove, patting him on the back loudly.

"Good to see you! You look well!"

Cove smiled pleasantly. "Great to see you, Matthew, Denise," he nodded to the Governor's wife who stood at his side, dressed in a blue gown that made her look long and thin like an umbrella. She had pulled her mask up and it sat upon her head. A long black braid snaked over her shoulder.

"You've not been by to dinner in some time! We sure miss your company!" It was always impossible to speak with Matt for very long as everything he said seemed to be a declaration. He very much liked company, especially Cove's company, and demanded it nearly every week. Cove wasn't as obliging as Matthew would like, but now and then the ambassador had to do the governor a favor and sit down with him. After all, he had been good friends with Canice Rowell, Cove's father. After Canice Rowell's death, Matthew had offered to help Cove in any way he could. It was the quietest Cove had ever heard him.

"I'll make time for that, Matt, I promise," Cove replied. "It's been very busy recently, you understand." The ambassador gestured to the ridiculous line that had gathered behind him.

"Of course! Wouldn't expect anything less from our ambassador!" the governor began to shuffle past Cove, nodding to Hollow. "How'd y'do, Hollow?"

Hollow nodded as the governor and his wife passed into Cove's home. After giving Hollow an amused look, Cove's eyes fell upon an all-too-familiar carriage. It had been in the driveway earlier in the day. His chest filled with fire. There were two people in that carriage he didn't want to see. Cove could try to be civil, but the bubbling inside him at the moment told him he wasn't going to keep his composure. Since returning from sea, he'd never actually seen Sara and Ben together. They'd been a rumor. A nightmare, really.

Cove glanced at Hollow and the senator nodded, not needing an explanation for his sudden wish to depart. Cove turned from the entrance and was about to disappear into the crowd when he heard his name called.

"Cove!"

He hesitated. Damn him, he could have acted like he hadn't heard her and continued on, but she would know he was ignoring her. He paused, took in a breath, and turned to face her.

"Sara," he intended to smile, but he found it difficult to think at all. He stood there numbly, taking in the length of her stature. She was dressed in a loose white gown, and the only embellishment was the diamond collar of her dress that dripped off her shoulders elegantly. Her curls were soft and fell around her face. Her cheeks were brushed with soft pink, and she glowed full of health, of life...of love for another person. It was maddening for him to look into her sapphire eyes, so round and innocent, as if she had never hurt him. Despite that, his fingers ached to brush her curls behind her ear. He had once, long ago when they had been just friends.

In her hands she held her mask, a brittle thing of white and black lace that glittered subtly. Sara was never one for extravagance.

"You..." He let out a breath. "You look lovely." He could feel the glaring black eyes of Hollow Dallon on him, cursing him silently for turning around.

Sara smiled as if she were relieved he was even speaking to her. After their encounter earlier in the day, this was likely her attempt to assure herself nothing stood between the two.

"I'm so glad I caught you," she continued. "H-how are you?"

"Well," he said nodding, then he smiled awkwardly, wondering why she always asked him that. "And you?"

"Good," she smiled. "Save me a dance?"

"Of course," he agreed, and just as he thought to depart, he froze and set his jaw tight. He could only imagine how he looked; he felt like he might kill. Sara seemed to understand because she straightened and leaned away from Cove, clearing her throat.

"My dear, you ran off so quickly!" Ben Willow appeared behind Sara and wound his arm around her waist. He was a tall man with brown hair cut short. He had a thin nose, thin lips, and gray eyes, eyes that never seemed to ease their critical stare when leveled at Cove. He was dressed smartly in a tailored white suit with a single red carnation blooming in his front pocket. With bitterness, Cove recalled that carnations were Sara's favorite flower.

"Ambassador," he bowed. "How kind of you to agree to host the Autumn Ball. I do not believe I have ever seen your home," his eyes rolled around the room once. "It is quite impressive."

"You pay the highest compliment, Mr. Willow," Cove replied curtly. Then he smiled. "If you will excuse me." He bowed to the couple and turned, disappearing into the crowded hallway.

***

The room grew warmer as people wandered in through two sets of doors on the other side of the ballroom. Barren watched them. Some were not fazed by the beauty of Cove's home, while others paused in the door to gape at finely crafted columns and marble arches which supported the second-story balcony. They were detailed with depictions of angels and Barren imagined the intricacy had made the stonemason's hands bleed. Or they might be gazing up at the crystal-encrusted chandeliers, which hung two in a row along the ceiling. Perhaps it was the actual ceiling that caught their interest, as angels and clouds roamed overhead. Perhaps it was the splendor of the entire room, as it was grand, with tall windows extending from floor to ceiling, draped with equally luscious red fabric and gold tassels. The floor itself was marble and glossy, the pattern composed of black and white diamonds tinted with gold.

Those who moved through the windowed doors on the other end of the room marveled at the rose garden which Barren had heard was filled with over one-hundred species of plants. They had been imported from all over the Orient and the Octent.

But the splendor did not end there. There was a couple dressed completely in silver, their bodies draped in long folds of supple silk. Their heads were wrapped in the same silk, strung with pearls, and their faces were covered with silver masks. A woman had entered with a gold half-moon mask. Stars and moons embellished the arc, and her dress was composed of black velvet and gold silk. Another woman was dressed as a jester, her mask pale white with black eyes. A hat sat on her head with two long ears weighted down by gold bells. Her dress displayed colors of red, black, white, and gold. A man wore a blue and silver suit fringed with lace. His mask was white and gold, and feathers seemed to shoot into the air from his head. Barren shuddered at his eyes, which appeared to be black holes.

There were some who were not so lavishly dressed. Men dressed in simple velvet suits with lace ruffles and simple masks that only covered their eyes. There were women who wore traditional ball gowns and masks fashioned from wirework. Barren liked them best. He did not feel comfortable in a place where he couldn't rightly conclude who was among his company, which was why he found himself holding onto the hilt of his knife.

Momentarily he would be even less at ease. Tetherion would arrive with his sons and his guards. They would fill the room, their red coats and gold sashes mottling the floor below. Barren had walked every corridor of Cove's home earlier in the day seeking escape routes. He felt guilty, but there were just some things Cove could not control. Barren had to be prepared if they were found out and if they couldn't make it to the tunnel. Luckily, there were enough woods about the property to aid their escape. The problems would come when they got to port. It was likely they could not get the ship to sea before gunfire sounded. There would be a skirmish, and people would die.

And what would Cove do? Left behind to deal with the aftermath of his choice to bring Barren and his crew to Arcarum, would he be able to avoid persecution by simply denying that he knew of their presence here? Or would he succumb to judgment.

Neither of those things were likely, and he needed to turn his thoughts elsewhere. He went in search of Larkin. He had not yet seen her, nor did he know how she would dress. Guiltily, part of him hoped she would decide not to come to the ball. He'd hoped that the fact that her father would be in attendance would draw her away, but her belief that her father had a secret did the opposite. Barren's fear was that she might try to learn that secret tonight. He knew he should trust her more, but he couldn't trust her curiosity. And when Larkin wanted something, she went after it, no matter the outcome.

He was also becoming less and less patient as she defended her father's actions. Sometimes it was simply because her father had a hand in his father's death. Sometimes it was out of fear. What if this life wasn't sufficient for Larkin? What if she found she missed life as a Lady? Part of him felt he could not blame her for wanting simple things like a hot bath, clean clothes, and a soft bed. He liked those things, too, but for him they were luxuries, experienced only on certain occasions. For her, they had been constants. Larkin had gone from one extreme to another. No preparation. He feared—no resented—the idea of her return to status, because that would mean he wasn't good enough.

Finally she entered the ballroom, and his eyes were drawn to her like he was drawn to the sea. It was the same pull that guided him, and he knew, even in places as unfamiliar as this, he would always find her. She was dressed in a purple gown, fitted to every part of her. A cape trailed behind her. Half of her hair was pinned with silver and pearls to hide her pointed ears. The other half was curled, and fell over her shoulders. Her mask was a light purple, almost silver, and glittered as she moved. Half of the mask bore a lace-like butterfly wing set with pearls. Her lips were red and her eyes the brightest green. She was not the most extravagant, but her presence drew gazes. She would be criticized for her tanned skin, a mark of lesser breeding, but there was no denying she was beautiful.

He felt something hot against his chest and grasped the compass at his neck. The metal was warm to the touch. He looked down at the device; the needle was still spinning out of control. This was not the first time it had heated his skin, and he wondered if the compass was reacting to something.

"Standing still as a statue will draw more attention than mingling," Leaf commented as he passed. Barren drew away from the balcony to behold the Elf. He was dressed in a gold suit that shimmered beneath the light. The mask he wore was composed of plaster, and green and gold diamonds covered its face. A long nose plummeted off the front of the mask and pointed toward the floor. The Elf had taken to holding onto it as he walked, which drew many curious glances. At least he chose something that hid all hints that he might be of Elfish blood.

"I'm drawing attention?" Barren questioned, raising a brow.

Leaf shrugged. "At least I'm approachable."

"*I'm* approachable!" Barren argued.

"As a cactus," Leaf muttered and walked away.

Barren scowled and decided to move from the balcony. He headed for the staircase, which would lead him into the very thick of the crowd, a sea of lace, feathers, and glitter. He would make a turn around the perimeter, observe what he could of the men and women below, make note of those who might be killers, and return to higher ground. He had reason to believe that if it was an advantage in battle, it would be an advantage here.

As he came to the end of the stairs, his gaze met Larkin's. She smirked, probably amused by how he looked. He wanted to go to her, but he resisted. She was still drawing too much attention. He nodded his head toward her and then moved into the crowd. Music which had been playing subtly in the background, grew louder, trilling through the large ballroom. Costumes converged, and the attendants of the ball began to dance in hypnotic circles. Barren watched as a man approached Larkin. They bowed to each other as she agreed to dance with him, directly defying Barren's instructions.

Barren kept his eyes on her as they danced. He wanted to look away, needed to look away, but his eyes held tight. He was reminded of his first encounter with her, watching her dance with his brother, William. The whole thing had been awkward and distant, no sign of splendor on either of their faces. Now she danced with a smile on her face, as if she'd missed it.

Another couple caught his attention. The girl who had visited Cove earlier in the day danced with a man in a white suit. She seemed so lithe and small compared to her partner, who was broad and almost jerked her about. It was not completely his fault, however, as she seemed distracted. Barren imagined she was looking for Cove in the faces crowding them. He caught himself wondering how she'd dance with the ambassador. He'd come to discover there was a lot to be discerned from the simple act.

When that dance ended, another partner rose to the occasion and claimed Larkin's hand for a dance. Barren turned away then, unable to watch further. He moved among the observers, who stood with glasses of champagne and wine. Some watched the dancers, others spoke among themselves. He listened to their conversations, looked to see if they had weapons, observed their stance. Were they relaxed or tense?

"I'm surprised the King would come so far with pirates roaming the seas in droves," he heard a man comment.

"Perhaps he does not fear them because he is in league with them."

Barren laughed. If only they knew the truth. It was likely that any pirate of Silver Crest would attack Tetherion if they encountered him at sea. He was a danger to them. But Tetherion was well versed in fighting at sea and so were his sons. The best trick of any war was to know how your enemy fights, to understand their weaknesses.

"It would be no surprise. The Reed line is prone to stray," the man continued. *"Perhaps all of this pomp and circumstance is merely so Tetherion can meet with the ambassador. If they are both piracy sympathizers, it would be no surprise."*

It was a ridiculous accusation, but it showed how disconnected the people of the Orient were with what really went on between the nobles. Barren wasn't so sure he liked that. It meant they were unaware of where enemy lines lay, unaware even, of magic.

"I have heard rumors that Tetherion is renewing his relationship with the Elf-king," the other man stated. *"I wonder if it has*

anything to do with the disturbances in the west."

"What would the Elf-king have to do with the revolts in the west?"

"Magic of course. Everyone knows he hoards his power. He's probably planning to use it against us one day."

These were dangerous thoughts. They made Barren's stomach turn. He knew the Elf-king could not wield magic, but that did not mean that the rest of the world believed it. They were not aware of Lyrics, which were a part of Elvish history, buried deep until recently. What had escaped from that history, however, were stories of magic. It also didn't help that Elves kept to an isolated island and maintained their own rule, independent of Tetherion's.

"I think if Tetherion were a good king, he would take away the Elf-king's power, maybe eradicate the species altogether."

"And what of half-Elves? The abominations born of inbreeding?"

"Perhaps kill them, too—though he should spare the women. They are quite beautiful. It would be a pity to lose them."

It was like they knew he was here, listening to them. He gritted his teeth so hard his gums hurt, and his fingers began to ache from clutching the hilt of his dagger. He wondered if these men belonged to the Commonwealth. The way they spoke made him think so, and if that were true, he hoped whatever notice they had gained was fleeting.

The band hushed, and Barren was brought back to the present. The voices he had been focused on were quiet. The dancers had paused, looking around in confusion at the silence. It was then Barren's eyes focused on Hollow Dallon who had moved to the center of the steps. He was dressed all in black, and no mask hid his features. Against the black, his pale hair and pale face were more severe, or maybe his features were severe because he was about to introduce the king.

"May I present to you his majesty, King Tetherion, Prince Datherious, Prince Natherious, and the royal court."

Barren scrambled farther into the shadows against the wall. It was easy to do since the dancers moved to form a pathway for the court to progress into the ballroom.

Two servants pulled the doors open and in paraded Tetherion's procession. The king's guard marched at the head, dressed in their red coats and gold sashes, cradling black weapons. They fanned out into the crowd and took their places about the room. Then the common people bowed. Begrudgingly, Barren followed suit.

The king entered, his presence striking in his blood red suit. White ruffles hung out of his sleeves and at his chest. A long cape dragged the floor, creating distance between him and the rest of his court. Upon his salt-and-pepper head sat a massive gold crown. In his hand, he carried a gold scepter, crowned with rubies. At his neck hung a beautiful medallion, though it seemed to contrast starkly with his other jewels. The medallion was a dark blue gem, and it appeared to have thousands of gold and white diamonds embedded within its surface. Eyes Barren had once found caring, now roamed the crowd, dark and austere.

The traitorous twins followed their father. Datherious was

dressed in emerald green, a red sash and simple gold crown designating him as royalty, not that anyone needed the finery to figure it out. He had dark hair, dark eyes, and severe brows. His lips always seemed too red for his pale face, as if he'd just bitten into a ripe cherry.

Natherious, always in the shadow of his brother, trailed behind him, dressed in blue. The thing Barren mistrusted most about Natherious was his indifference. Some might argue that Datherious shared the trait with his brother, but that was not so. Datherious reacted to things with passion and anger, violence even. Natherious appeared to have no emotional attachment to anything, making the tasks he carried out all the more callous.

Christopher Lee was also in the group, attired in his common blue suit. He walked with his black cane, something, as far as Barren was concerned, he used to keep others from realizing his true strength. There was a change in his features. Underneath the coldness, he was tired. Darkness sagged beneath his eyes and the folds of his face seemed deeper. No doubt he would field questions about his daughter while here.

Then Barren's eyes settled on a new face, a woman he had never seen in Tetherion's company before. What caught his attention was her bronzed skin and her dark hair. He bet if she opened her mouth, she'd speak with that clipped accent unique to the Octent. She was dressed in an extravagant gown, clearly meant to be the gem of the ball, despite her heritage. The bust was satin and gold, and teal and emerald threading created the images of peacock feathers. The skirt was a mix of gold, teal and emerald tulle. Her mask was gold embellished with emerald and a spray of peacock feathers. She walked with her shoulders back, and when she came to a halt at the center of the room, she surveyed the crowd, but the way her eyes roamed the faces surrounding her told him she was looking for someone.

Tetherion's voice finally sounded in the quiet. "You may rise," he said. "Come, let us dance."

He smiled as he spoke, and the crowd broke into applause. The music began again and the center of the room filled with dancers. The king and his procession moved out of the way of the dancers, and Barren took his opportunity to move. He navigated the crowd as if it were a sea and he a ship, avoiding rough areas and anything that might prove dangerous, like the peacock's gaze. As he moved around a column, he halted to observe from his vantage point, searching for familiar faces—Larkin, Leaf, Slay, Sam, or Seamus, but his search was halted by the peacock's gaze. She'd watched him as he'd moved. He knew his mask still covered his visage as sweat beaded off his skin and slid down his face.

Then he felt the hot metal of the compass against his skin and realized it was exposed. He wrapped his hands around it and tucked it beneath his shirt, watching the girl while she smirked. Perhaps she'd just admired it for its beauty. It was striking, and among all this finery, it was an unassuming addition to any costume. Unless someone knew what it was, unless someone recognized it. But who was this girl to have recognized a compass belonging to his mother and father?

He glared at her for a moment longer before tearing his gaze from hers and heading for higher ground. He'd fight his battles with a little bit of leverage for the rest of the night.

Chapter Seven
LEVERAGE

Cove roamed about, watching as people watched him. He looked to see how the room divided—who nodded respectfully and smiled, who glared and snubbed him. As much as this ball signified the start of elections, it also gave him an indication of the sides, whose loyalty he had and whose loyalty the Commonwealth, particularly Ben, had.

He'd found that since Sara Rosamund's engagement to Ben Willow, the divide between his supporters and Ben's had grown stronger. Perhaps this was Ben's intention, for it had been assumed for as long as Cove and Sara had been friends that they were a smart match, a handsome match. In fact, the people of Arcarum had adored Cove and Sara together so much that many had delighted in fantasizing about their wedding, something that would now never take place because upon his return from sea with Barren, he'd learned of her engagement to Ben Willow.

He'd ignored her for as long as he could, but the distance hadn't done him any favors. The public had questions: *What had Cove done to drive the poor, sweet, innocent Sara away? Was he really involved in piracy?* Ben Willow had to be something special to land Sara's interest.

Cove wanted to learn what had happened, too, but he wasn't eager to learn Sara's version, only Ben's. He didn't believe that Ben loved Sara; she was a strategic choice in bride. He only wished that Sara had seen that.

As if on cue, he heard her laugh, clear and sweet, like a chime. He gravitated to it despite the company she kept. Ben, always at her side, kept his hand planted around her waist. He had found company with the king and a few other pompous nobles. As the ambassador passed, a plump woman wearing a mask of fruit, reached out to him. She moved her mask, which sat at the end of a stick, away and said, "Oh, Ambassador Rowell! You've thrown a wonderful ball! Absolutely splendid!"

"Thank you, Madam," Cove placed his hand over his heart in appreciation. He'd hoped to move away quickly but the man beside her spoke next.

"Yes, very well done. I don't believe your father could have topped this," the man said. He had a mustache that moved as he spoke.

Cove smiled very faintly, and he imagined these people would take it as a grievous smile. "Well, he wasn't one for parties."

"So, your majesty," said Ben, diverting the conversation. "I see the princes are safe and well after their...little excursion with Barren Reed."

Now Cove stood closer, completing the circle that seemed to enclose the king. He wanted to hear what Tetherion had to say.

"Oh, yes," Tetherion's tone was colored in darkness. "The boy hardly believed it when he discovered their betrayal. He actually thought them loyal mates!"

Everyone laughed haughtily, and Cove clenched his jaw tighter.

"It is tragic, though, the lovely Lady Larkin is still within his treacherous grasp!" said the plump lady.

"Tragic, indeed." It was harder for Tetherion to maintain his show, and Cove knew the king couldn't wait until Larkin was exposed.

"She must be so distraught, living with those dreadful pirates on that dirty ship, knowing he murdered her fiancé," the woman continued, her face turning redder by the minute.

"What's being done to rescue the poor girl?" asked the mustached man.

"Ah, well, her father hopes he can save her. Of course, that will be difficult considering Barren Reed is surprisingly hard to locate. All in good time, though. Our privateers are making progress."

"Ah yes. The three pirates who were hanged just yesterday. A feat for your reign, sire," said Ben. Cove didn't think he was imagining the jab Ben threw Tetherion's way, but the king either didn't notice or didn't acknowledge it. "To which of your crews do we owe our congratulations?"

"That would be Miss Moore," said Tetherion, and he looked around. Cove did, too, hoping to catch a glimpse of whom he was speaking; but he quickly returned his attention to the party before him. "She is engaged at present."

"Miss Moore?" the old lady questioned. "You have a woman crewing your ships?"

"Yes, madam," the king said. "Females can be far more malicious than men sometimes."

The old lady's expression turned sour, as if she'd never considered the thought of a female murderer.

"And what have you done, ambassador, to combat pirates at sea?" Ben questioned, his eyes menacing. It was clear he intended to show off, but Cove only smirked.

"Well, Mr. Willow, you already know the answer to that." Ben's eyes grew wide for a moment, then Cove finished. "We deploy privateers to combat the pirates. It's the only way, really."

"I say you find their nest, exterminate them," Ben said evenly. "You know they amass somewhere."

"I think it would be a terrible thing to kill them...pirates are just humans. They deserve fairness," said Sara. Cove watched her as she spoke. She'd said the same thing to him, earlier in the day.

"Humans who take what they want, lives or otherwise," Ben said bitterly.

The ambassador raised a brow. "You seem to take this far more personally than others."

Ben narrowed his eyes.

"I think Ben is right," said Tetherion, looking evenly at Cove. "We must exterminate them. We must begin with their *hive*."

Cove was having a hard time staying calm.

"It's unfortunate you think that way," he replied tightly.

"What if there are women and children there? As all hives are prone to have."

"It doesn't matter what they are. They're all pirates."

"Piracy is an act," Cove countered. "If you cannot prove they have committed piracy, you cannot kill them."

Steady silence followed between the group until the round woman with the fruit mask began to fan herself and said, "I say kill the wenches, but the children, they have a chance. Raise them to be servants. It's better than the life they would have otherwise."

"You mean freedom?"

"Excuse me?" the woman was stunned.

"What you said. You would take them from their life, a life of freedom, and make them slaves."

"A pirate's life isn't free."

"That's exactly what it is," said Cove.

"It sounds to me like you sympathize with them," said Ben.

"I'm merely pointing out the obvious. It seems to me that in times of great distress, those with the most power disregard what's right for what gets the job done," he swept his gaze around, studying the faces. Faces that understood what Cove was saying, faces that were guilty. Then his eyes landed upon the king. "Of course, his majesty is fair and just, and would *never* let anything like that happen under his reign."

The king swallowed hard, but his eyes were menacing. "Of course not," and then he smiled darkly. "We would do what is fair and just."

"Cove m'boy!" Governor Dulcemer said as he slapped one hand on the ambassador's shoulder. "Are we ready to announce the candidates?"

Cove looked at the king. "Would you be so kind as to announce the candidates, your majesty?"

"I'd be delighted."

The ambassador, Matthew, and the king made their way up the stairs. When they were in the middle, they turned and beheld the crowded ballroom. Some already gave their attention, others were still talking among themselves, oblivious to the sudden shift in the air.

"May I have your attention?" Cove called. Voices hushed and all eyes landed on him, and he wondered for a very brief moment how odd he must look among them, so simple in his black suit. "Tonight we are not only gathered to enjoy each other's invigorating company, but to honor senators past and present. On this night, we announce the candidates for the senators of the seven provinces of Arcarum. On this night, let us put aside the campaign and instead be grateful that so many great men and women love Arcarum."

Cove shuddered at the seeming sincerity in his own voice. While he didn't believe what he said completely, he knew that the people in the crowd hung on his words.

Matthew then handed King Tetherion a document listing the names of the candidates.

Tetherion broke the wax on the paper and began to call out the names of the individuals who would run against each other for the provinces. As he did, Cove watched the crowd. There were smiles, and after each name was called, people cheered or clapped. When Ben's name was announced beside Hollow's, there was great cheer for both candidates. Ben took Sara's hand and raised it in the air with his, and Cove had to look away. It was like Ben was using her as a trophy, a way to lure votes.

Once the names were read, everyone cheered again, including Cove whose smile concealed the worry he felt inside. It was only a feeling, but after the conversation he'd heard tonight, he believed the battle for this election would extend beyond the shores of Arcarum.

***

Barren watched from above, leaning on the balcony. He'd lost sight of the peacock in the crowd. She had yet to dance with anyone, though she'd had plenty of requests. Barren imagined she declined in favor of watching. Larkin, on the other hand, had not declined a single dance. Barren suspected she was attempting to prove a point.

"Do you dance?" A voice asked from behind Barren. It was unfamiliar, but the accent made him think it could only be one person. He turned to see the peacock behind him. Her eyes were like storm clouds and completely focused on him, but a smile played upon her lips.

"No," he said. "I don't."

The smile on her lips grew. "Then why attend a ball?"

"It really wasn't a choice."

She laughed a little, moving closer to him. Her peacock dress bustled around her, and Barren drew his attention to the dancers below, wishing her away, but she would not be so easily dismissed. "You? Forced? You'll forgive me if I don't believe that."

"You would make assumptions about someone you don't know?"

"Who says I don't know you?" she asked, and Barren felt his chest grow tight.

He glanced askance at her. "What are you anyway? The castle pet?"

She laughed, throwing back her head, and then she leveled her gaze again. "You are not one for manners," she reached for his hand and he drew back as if she were a snake. The smile on her lips held. "Dance with me. I might tell you my secrets."

He gazed at her a moment longer and watched as she turned from him. He glanced at the ballroom floor seeing Larkin bounding along, oblivious that her identity might easily be ascertained, and then he followed the woman down the staircase and into the crowd as a new cadence began.

He danced with her, and they moved in hypnotic circles striding along the floor. The air around them grew hotter, and the tempo of the music carried faster. Barren kept his eyes on her as they danced. They were drawing attention of course. She was the foreigner, and he the stranger no one could place.

"Have you guessed who I am?" she asked after a moment.

"I know you're a privateer," he said. She had scars on her arms which he imagined she'd got from battle. "Why else would a woman from the Octent be among Tetherion's court? You're not exactly our favorite people."

"Nor are you mine," she said. "But sometimes gaining an advantage means working with those you like least."

"You must have gained some advantage to achieve this privilege."

"Perceptive," she said, spinning away from him, and as Barren drew her back, harder than he should have, he spoke between his teeth.

"Did you kill my men?"

She laughed. "Oh, Barren Reed, I shouldn't be surprised that you're not one for fun and games."

"They might be your sport, but the deaths of my brethren are not fun and games," said Barren. "You're bold to make this declaration before me as if there will be no consequences."

"I have admitted to nothing, Mr. Reed," she said. "You've only just accused me. And as for boldness, well, you are among your greatest enemies. Your identity is known to me. I could expose you."

Barren could buy into this, but he knew better. She wanted something. "What do you want?" he asked.

"I need leverage," she said, and as the music stopped.

"What?"

She took a step away from him and raised the compass. It glinted in the light, and Barren suddenly felt cold. "Leverage."

Barren went to reach for it, but she dropped the compass and chain down her collar. She smiled as she curtsied deeply. "I'll see you soon."

Barren watched her turn and part the crowd as she retreated.

***

Larkin stood near the window. She'd taken several turns around the ballroom, dancing with different partners who approached. When they asked for her name, she'd smiled and said Charlotte. She'd hoped to prove to Barren that she could come away with the most beneficial information at the end of the night. At first she'd taken pleasure in speaking with several groups of people, but then they started to speak of matters that involved her and Barren Reed.

"Charlotte, what do you think of Barren Reed and Larkin Lee? Scandalous, isn't it!" a girl named Alise asked. She'd taken off her mask and was now fanning herself.

Larkin hesitated. "I'm afraid I do not know much about them."

"How can you not? Their love story is the talk of town!"

"Nonsense, Alise. Do not give praise where none is deserved," a man beside her chided. "Barren Reed is a scoundrel, and Larkin Lee a traitor. She will learn of her mistake when it is too late."

"Do not be harsh, Max," she said. "Larkin is young, and I imagine Barren is quite the Casanova. She cannot be blamed for her crimes, not when her good sense was *clearly* charmed away by Barren Reed."

"You're ignorant, Alise. Do you not know her father's history? He once sailed with Barren Reed's father, Jess Reed. It is no surprise she would run off with a pirate. It is in her blood."

Larkin was surprised by Max's firm opinions of her. Max looked at her as if sensing her thoughts, "If you will excuse me."

She was left with Alise who moved closer to her. "Do not let him make you feel ignorant. He will kill a fantasy dead if you let him."

She giggled, but Larkin wanted to be far from here. "Excuse me," she said. "I need a drink."

She moved from Alise, but as she did, she saw Barren coming down the stairs with the peacock woman and when they danced, anger blossomed in her chest. They moved well together, and fast, gliding about the ballroom in a fierce and passionate manner. What was he thinking? He was doing the very thing he told her not to and with the woman who had been in Tetherion's party.

It was in these moments that she started to think of her father and yearn for the mother she'd never known, when she wished she had a real home to return to. She had a ship, and that wasn't even hers. She knew part of her was being silly, but then...there were things about Barren she still didn't know. Like whether he had ever loved. Was it possible that she would bore him one day? Did she bore him now? These fears lingered beneath the surface and they scared her.

She moved to the door of the ballroom, searching the crowd for her father. He stood proudly. Severe eyes, pointed beard, deadly cane. Even as Larkin observed him, fear crept into her soul. She wondered if he would know her even with the mask. *He's your father*, Barren had said. What did that mean though?

Sometimes, Larkin wasn't sure she knew. She hadn't even known when she'd lived under the man's roof.

"My Lady," a voice said and she jumped. Larkin whirled around to find a servant behind her, dressed in white. "The Lord Christopher Lee advised me to give you this."

The servant held out his hand and a piece of red fabric rested in his palm. It stood out like fresh blood. Larkin knew it well. It was a piece of her scarf, the one she'd worn the night of her engagement party, the night she had been kidnapped by Barren Reed. It was also the one she'd left tied about her father's mouth to keep him silent under the black hood. It held so much meaning.

She reached for it. "Thank you."

She closed her hand around the piece of fabric, but it felt hot in her palm and her heart pounded in her chest. This meant her father knew she was here, and if she confronted him, Barren would be angry. But would he even know? And maybe this meant he wanted to speak to her.

It was then she saw her father turn and leave the room. She took a deep breath and moved to follow him, walking slowly. She paused as she exited the ballroom to watch and see where her father was going, but he'd already disappeared. She hesitated, knowing Barren would be angry, knowing that she would only live up to the expectations he'd put on her, but even if she did follow her father, it wasn't like she had to engage him, and she might learn some valuable information. Besides, Barren had broken his own rule tonight. He'd danced with the peacock. Just thinking about how close they'd been angered her.

Gathering her dress, she moved down the hallway. She hated how the satin gown rustled. Ahead of her, she heard a door open and close. She paused for a moment to see if it was someone exiting a room, but no one made their way toward her, so she moved forward.

Sconces lined the corridor, casting dim light on the wood walls and carpeted floor. She stopped at a door with a piece of red ribbon tied around the handle. Her fingers brushed the fabric. She felt for her dagger at her waist. It was gone. Had the servant who delivered the ribbon taken her blade? Perhaps this wasn't a message from her father. Her heart hammered in her chest. As she thought to turn away, voices came from the other end of the hallway.

She turned the handle and pushed the door open, stepping into the dark room. Her breathing seemed too loud in her ears. Once the door was shut behind her, heavy arms encircled her. They were too large to be her father's. Panic flooded her body.

"Gypsy-witch!" A voice she didn't recognize seethed in her ear.

She reared back and her head connected with his nose. The man released her and she turned to face him. He growled, cupping his nose, and then raced toward her. She stumbled backward and fell, holding up her hands to protect herself from the attack, but as the man came forward, warmth surged through her body, and she felt heat in her hands. Colors of green and blue pulsed through her fingers and outward, hitting her attacker in the chest. He fell instantly, collapsing to the floor in a heap.

It was over as fast as it had begun, and Larkin was left feeling dizzy and weak. For a moment she was rooted to the spot, staring at her hands as if they weren't her own. Slowly she made her way to the man on the floor. She kept her distance, staring at a face she didn't recognize. He'd called her gypsy-witch, a term used to describe women who used magic. Anxiety filled her chest.

Voices sounded outside the door, and she heard the handle turn. She hurried to hide behind a chair in the dark room.

As the door swung open, Larkin peered out from her hiding place. She saw two figures haloed by the hall light. One was dressed in white, and the other bent down beside the body on the floor. He seemed to be checking for a pulse.

"Is he still breathing?" the man in white asked.

Larkin held her breath in the cold silence, waiting for the reply.

"Yes."

She covered her mouth and closed her eyes tightly. She felt relieved but also terribly afraid. That man would know something unnatural had happened to him. Worse, had he known who he was attacking when he grabbed her?

"What do we do?"

"We'll take him to Dr. Newell's," said the man in white.

When the door snapped closed, Larkin took a few deep breaths and stood. She stifled a scream when she came face to face with a man in the dark. He held up a lantern, and reached forward quickly, pulling her mask from her face.

Instinctively, she reached for her blade but remembered she did not have it. The man drew a pistol.

"Lady Larkin," he said. "Well, this is a delight."

She glared at him. She'd heard this man's name a lot in the last couple of days. This was Ben Willow. She'd had few encounters with him before her time at sea. He had not been born into her circle and had worked his way up, which would have been a quality Larkin admired in someone less bitter.

"I'm going to need you to answer some questions for me."

"Why do I feel as if I have no choice in the matter?"

He chuckled. "So fierce. Is this what piracy has done to you?"

Larkin did not respond. Her face was hot and she had yet to fully grasp what had happened when the man had attacked her. She didn't have time to deal with Ben.

"What did you do to him?"

She looked to where the man had landed and shuddered as she recalled what had happened, the feeling that had awoken within her.

"He attacked me," she said.

Ben just stared at her, and she wasn't sure what to think of his expression. It was blank. "It is no secret you have Elfin blood. It wouldn't be a surprise if you could...draw upon Lyric."

Larkin was startled mostly by the simple fact that Ben knew anything about magic. "That's ridiculous," she said, but she knew her words were too quick. "I might be half-Elf, but that doesn't mean I can draw upon magic."

"Let's say you did," he said with a shake of his shoulders.

"And I could protect you. Would you let me?"

"I don't need protecting!" She spat the words.

Ben held up his hands, as if to apologize. "Of course," he said. "But the public doesn't take well to your kind. You don't realize the danger you would be in. Not to mention…how safe can you really be with Barren Reed? Will he even want you when he discovers your secret?"

Her kind. She detested his words.

"You have no proof." She took a deep breath. "You must excuse me."

She tried to move around Ben, but he moved in front of her. Of course it couldn't be easy.

"I have a proposition for you," he said.

"I don't want to hear your proposition," she said through her teeth.

He smiled. "You have no choice. You take it or I expose you. Truly I hate for it to come to this, but you leave me no choice."

"I cannot help you with Cove Rowell," she said. "If that's what you want."

"I have Cove Rowell right where I want him," said Ben. "No, it is not Cove I need. It is not even a person. It is a thing. Bring me Barren Reed's compass."

"What?"

"You heard me, the compass. Bring it to me and I'll keep your secret."

How did he know about the compass? Larkin wasn't sure of Ben Willow's background, but surely a mortal would know nothing about that compass, much less find it useful.

"Why would you want it? It doesn't even work."

"Then he should have no trouble letting it go," Ben said.

"It belonged to his parents. It's all he has left of them. He will notice if it is missing."

"I suppose that's something you'll have to deal with," he said.

She narrowed her gaze. "You must be quite happy with yourself. You've risen from the low ranks to which you were born. Tell me, has it all been through manipulation and blackmail?"

He laughed, seeming truly amused. "You know, you manage to make me sound like the scoundrel but all I have ever fought were pirates. You believed as I did at one time."

"That was before I opened my eyes."

"Before you met Barren," he qualified, taking in a breath and stepping forward. "You know what you are? To everyone? A silly girl who gave up her life for a man. That's all you'll ever be." He straightened, still smiling. "Bring me the compass, Larkin. Tomorrow night at Onyx Hall. If you do not show, I'll drag you and Barren from this house to the noose. Follow the red ribbon."

He took a step back and turned, heading for the door, but before he left, he paused. "Ask Barren about Éire. Just ask. Maybe then you'll understand the kind of man you gave your life up for."

Then he left. She stood there for a moment collecting her thoughts before shakily putting on her mask and leaving. She ran upstairs, all four flights, not stopping once until she was safely inside her own room. She shut the door behind her, leaning against it and sliding to the floor. She looked at her hands, touching the tips of her fingers together. It was like everything within her was alive, wired. And she knew it was *wrong*. Because what had come from her hands, these hands—what had hurt a man tonight—was *magic*.

Chapter Eight
PINNACLE

Cove stepped out onto the balcony. The night was cool, and he could smell salt in the air. He felt calm here. Such a stark contrast to what lay behind him. If he wasn't obligated to stay at the ball, he would escape to the shore. Tonight had been trying. Everyone had an opinion about the pirates of Silver Crest, about Barren and Larkin, about him, about the pirates who had hanged in Maris. He'd taken it all in, and now he needed a break.

He breathed in the cool air, and exhaled too fast when he heard the door open and shut softly behind him. He didn't turn to see who it was. He didn't need to. He recognized the air around her. It was warm and smelled sweet.

"I knew I would find you here," the smile in her voice made him shiver. Though outwardly he was doing his best to be happy for her, he didn't understand how she thought everything was still okay. He took in a breath and turned to look at her.

"Dearest Sara, I am sorry. Did you need me?"

She was still smiling, but her eyes dimmed as she studied his face, and confusion flitted in her eyes.

"I was worried about you," she said quietly. "I haven't seen much of you all night. You promised me a dance."

"I have been busy. It is not easy to host a ball."

"I imagine not, well...now that you're all by yourself."

Cove raised a brow and nodded but quickly took his gaze off her.

"You are gone a lot now," she continued, sensing his unease. "Don't you miss home?"

"What is there to miss?" he asked. "Unfavorable memories rest here, Sara."

"You don't have to stay here. There are other places in Arcarum."

The Ambassador smiled wistfully. He wished in some way that he possessed her almost child-like understanding of everything. It was a reflection of her sheltered upbringing, her aversion to the outside world. She knew nothing of Cove's troubles or the horror he had seen and he wouldn't want her to know. That's why things were better this way.

"I always come back when I leave."

"Yes, but...there are times when I fear you won't."

He chuckled hearing that. "What danger am I in at sea, Sara?"

"Well, there are pirates and that dreaded Barren Reed."

Cove's brows came together but all he did was shake his head. "I do not fear pirates, Sara."

"I don't understand you. You should hate them for what they did."

And this is where Cove felt worse. She was referring to his father's death and the fact that it was believed he had died at the hands of pirates. That was true, but his death had come at the hands of Cove's own crew. How could Sara ever understand that he was the one responsible for his father's death? She would never forgive him. He could hardly forgive himself.

"Cove," she said softly. He caught the tremor in her voice and looked at her. "Why do you look at me with such wistfulness?"

He gazed at her for a moment longer and then looked at his feet. "Allow me to leave you, dearest Sara, for I do not wish to look upon you in such a way."

He stepped forward and took her hand, placing his lips against her soft skin.

"I feel safe with you," she said as he was about to pull away. "I feel safer when you are here."

He stared at her. Was this part of what she'd wanted to tell him earlier in the day?

"Sara, are you in trouble?" he asked.

Her smile was shaky but her eyes brimmed with tears. "No," she shook her head.

He took a step toward her, closing the space between them. He still held her hand. "Because if you are in trouble, you know I will protect you."

She dropped her gaze and gave a small laugh. "You might," she whispered and looked up at Cove. "If you were here."

She turned from him and left the balcony. For a moment he hesitated to follow, but his questions had still gone unanswered.

She'd come to him twice today, in secrecy, on the verge of tears. What secret was she keeping? He left the balcony in search of her.

***

As Cove stepped inside, he peered over the balcony. Below, a dance continued. The king was indulging one of the many women waiting for a turn about the room and they spun in elegant circles. He looked around for Barren's crew and found Barren tensely glaring at the crowd below. Cove guessed he couldn't find Larkin, because the ambassador couldn't find her either.

Then his eyes focused on Leaf, whose gaze was troubled. It wasn't until the Elf started to move in the direction he was looking that Cove got nervous. He followed the Elf's gaze and then found what had caught his attention, an inconspicuous figure standing across from him on the other side of the balcony, annexed in the shadows near the curtains. He was dressed in a long coat with his face covered with a plain black mask, head hooded. In his hand he held a silver flintlock pistol. He had not realized anyone had noticed him yet.

Cove had no time to think. His only objective was to distract the assassin. He drew a dagger from his boot, aimed for the chandelier, and threw the knife. The impact caused the crystals to shake and knock into each other; pieces broke away and began falling to the ground. It was just enough. Cove saw the figure hesitate as the king and the crowd moved out of the way of the falling glass. Cove made his move. Rushing down the stairs, he kept his gaze on the assassin. Knowing he had been caught, the assassin steadied the gun again.

Cove pushed through the crowd toward the king and plowed into him. The gun sounded, people screamed and chaos ensued. Some ran from the room while others collapsed to the ground. Cove and the king hit the floor with a hard thud.

Cove stood immediately and watched as the king's guard hurried up the steps in search of the assassin.

"Back! Everyone back!"

Hollow's voice cut deeply, and the crowd moved against the walls as far from the king and Cove as they could.

"You...you saved my life," Tetherion managed to say as he got to his feet, shaken. He was more surprised than anything. Cove knew what he was thinking: you should have let me die. They were enemies, after all.

The doors that led into the garden flew open and Sara emerged from outside, her cheeks red from the chill of the night. She ran to the edge of the circle of people, staring at Cove in bewilderment.

"Cove, you're bleeding," she said.

Cove looked down at his side as crimson dropped upon the floor. Sara tried to go to him, but Ben's icy hand slipped around her arm and pulled her back.

"He can take care of himself," he said roughly.

Cove's dark eyes showed no hint of his pain. He turned toward the exit. "Get them out of here," he told Hollow and left without another word.

***

Barren noticed the crystals fall from the chandelier, and he was suddenly brought out of his angry search for Larkin. He watched Cove take off running down the stairs, and he knew the assassin had been spotted. He'd been too distracted to notice.

He leaned over the balcony to see where the assassin might be. He had gone for higher ground too.

Barren took off running, pushing past unassuming attendees. When the gunfire sounded, there were screams and everyone flattened, making it easier for him to wind through them. He came upon the part of the balcony that was left in shadow, only to catch a glimpse of the gunman as he fled down the hallway.

Barren followed close behind.

"Stop!" he yelled. "Stop!"

The assassin turned, brandishing the pistol and Barren halted in his steps. He fired, and Barren hit the floor, the bullet whizzing past him. The assassin turned and ran again. Barren pulled a dagger from his boot. Tossing the blade, it landed in the assassin's calf, and he stumbled, hitting the ground with a loud thud. Barren pulled a thin piece of rope from his pocket and moved to tie the man's wrists only to discover the hands belonged to a woman.

She twisted around onto her back and Barren's heart went cold. "Well, we meet again, Barren Reed."

It was the woman from earlier. The one who'd stolen his compass for leverage.

"But you..." his voice faltered. He gritted his teeth. He only had moments. He needed that compass, but he had run out of time.

"Hey!" someone yelled from behind Barren. Tetherion's guards were coming for the assassin, and Barren knew he wouldn't be able to linger here or he'd have to reveal his identity. Barren's heart felt cold and he backed away from the woman, hurrying down the hall as the assassin was taken into custody.

Something wasn't adding up here. Hadn't that woman just told him she worked for Tetherion? Or had she gotten close to the king only to kill him for the Commonwealth? But Barren's most pressing question was what did she want with *him*?

***

Cove went to his study and locked the doors. Shoving off his jacket and vest, he unbuttoned his white shirt, craning his neck to get a good look at his side. By the firelight, he dug his fingers into the wound, his breath escaping through his teeth as he attempted to fish the bullet out. He felt a sharp pang as his fingers brushed the bullet and he cried out, grinding his teeth. He hated the feel of the torn skin and blood beneath his fingers.

A knock sounded at the door and Cove growled. He'd suspected he wouldn't get any peace while all these guests were leaving.

Cove braced himself against the mantle, sweat beading on his forehead. "Who is it?" he called, his breath short.

"Perhaps a decision between life and death?"

Cove sighed. As he moved from the mantle, he regretted his decision to attempt to remove the bullet himself. Pain shuddered through him, worse than when the bullet actually made its impact. He opened the door and Leaf stepped through.

"I am fine, Leaf," Cove shut and locked the door again.

"I'll be the judge of that."

Cove removed his shirt completely and leaned against the arm of his chair as the Elf examined his wound. He was doing a good job of ignoring the pain until the Elf started touching it.

"What the *hell* are you doing? I was shot, don't you think it hurts?"

"Touchy," Leaf chided. "It might not hurt so badly if you had left it alone!"

Cove looked away, rolling his eyes.

"It's going to have to come out," said Leaf.

"I don't suppose you have the tools with you?"

"Not in this room," said Leaf. "You might want to get them yourself. At least if you're saying goodbye, people will know you're okay."

Cove sighed. He could hear the commotion outside now. He hated to face the crowd, though he knew it would probably be good for him to seem composed among all of them. This would be talked about for weeks, and though it hadn't gone quite like he had expected, it would still work in his favor.

"Where's your stuff?"

"Upstairs in the room you so graciously offered," said Leaf, crossing his arms. Cove snatched his shirt from the floor and pulled it on. As he was walking to the door, Leaf called out. "You'll find it inside the nightstand. A brown bag."

"Got it," as he opened the door, he stiffened, finding Sara on the other side. Her arm was raised to knock, but she quickly faltered when she saw the ambassador.

Cove inclined his head. "Yes?"

"A-are you alright?" she asked softly.

"I'll live," he replied stepping out of his study and shutting the door safely behind him.

"Have you called a doctor?"

"Everything will be taken care of, Sara," he said as softly as he could, though his impatience was growing. "I am sorry your night was ruined by such an unfortunate event. Please accept my apology."

Cove bowed his head and went to leave, but Sara caught his arm. "Cove," she whispered. "How could you apologize?"

He searched her eyes trying to determine what answer she was looking for.

"How could you think I would be so selfish? To be concerned only with this ball?"

Perhaps it was unfair to accuse her of something so shallow, but it made the pain easier and the more he lied to himself about her motives, the more he understood her engagement.

He could tell she was desperately searching for something, anything in his gaze.

"Sara!" an angry voice cut through the air. Cove snapped his head in the direction of Ben Willow. He stalked down the hallway toward her. Putting his hands on either side of her shoulders, Ben drew her away from Cove roughly. "I told you the ambassador could take care of himself!"

Cove set his jaw tightly, and his dark eyes went black. "Of course I can take care of myself. You must forgive her for being so kind."

Ben's gray eyes narrowed, and he looked Cove up and down in disgust. "For a man everyone claims to be a gentleman, you do not present yourself like one, ambassador."

"I believe that can be argued. Remind me, were you the one who was shot this evening?"

"I'd be willing to bet that was a ruse. Trying to get your enemies off your back?"

Cove chuckled darkly. "Something like that."

Then Cove's gaze dropped to Sara. "You will excuse me." He bowed and then disappeared upstairs.

Cove made his way down the hall to Leaf's room. As he entered the room, dizziness overwhelmed him and he stumbled for a moment. Closing his eyes, he took a deep breath and moved forward, heading toward the nightstand where Leaf said his tools would be.

As Cove bent to open the drawer, pain tore through his stomach and he fell to his knees breathing raggedly. The ambassador reached for the drawer, pulled it open, and managed to retrieve the brown bag, though his arms felt weak. He braced his arms against the bed and tried to pull himself up, but pain shot through him again and he crumpled to the ground.

Chapter Nine
BLOOD & BULLETS

Everyone was quiet. They crowded into Cove's study, exhausted and unable to sleep while Leaf worked upstairs. Even Camille and Nob sat with them, staring off into nothingness, waiting to hear news of Cove's condition. Hollow had found the ambassador unconscious in Leaf's room. He'd had to wait until the house was clear to get Leaf in to heal Cove. By then, the ambassador had contracted a fever and Leaf expressed concern that infection had set in so fast.

Hollow stood, rubbing his face.

"What is taking so long?" he growled.

"The wound had to be worse than we thought," said Barren. "Leaf is doing as much as he can."

"And what if that's not enough?"

Barren just stared at the senator. No one wanted to think about what would happen if it wasn't enough. Hollow turned from them, scowling.

"None of this would have happened if you had all been where

you were supposed to be!" Hollow raged. He pointed at Larkin. "You weren't even in the room," then he pointed at Barren. "And you were dancing with the enemy!"

Barren met Larkin's gaze, and he could tell she wasn't happy about what she'd seen, just like he wasn't happy to discover she'd left. The tension in the room heightened.

"If she was trying to kill Tetherion, she's a little less of an enemy," said Barren.

"She sided with him for some reason and you can bet it wasn't for your gain," said Hollow. "Did she recognize you?"

"No," said Barren smoothly, though he felt guilty for lying. There was danger in the answer he'd give, for the woman, the king killer, was under lock and key, guarded by the very people who would like to see everyone in this house hanged. She might try to bargain for her life. Their whereabouts in exchange for her freedom. That was leverage enough.

Hollow stared at him for a moment, as if he hoped to catch the lie in his eyes, but he soon looked away.

"The assassin's name is Aethea Moore," said Hollow. "She's also responsible for killing five of our brethren and sending the other three to the noose, so it is a surprise that she would try to kill Tetherion, don't you think?"

"Well you said the Commonwealth wants to kill pirates and overthrow the king. She obviously felt she could do both," said Barren. "And perhaps she acted out of line from her command. You don't know until you talk to her."

"Talk to her?" Hollow scoffed. "There's no way to talk to her now. She tried to assassinate the king. Her hanging will be swift.'

That couldn't happen, not before he got his compass back.

"Something else is at work here," said Hollow. "And if you don't believe that, you're not the pirate I thought you were."

Suddenly, the door clicked open and Leaf entered the room. Exhaustion pulled at his face and he smelled strongly of mint and smoke. To the surprise of everyone, Cove also entered the room behind him. He did not look well. His face was sallow and perspiration powdered his skin. His eyes were lackluster, and he still wore the bloodied shirt he'd been shot in. As he walked, he held his side.

"What are you doing up?" Hollow and Barren demanded in unison.

"I have to see Dr. Newell."

"What? Why?" asked Barren.

"Because your Elfin magic wasn't sufficient!" Hollow accused quickly.

"On the contrary," said Cove. "Leaf's 'Elfin magic', as you call it, probably saved my life. Show them."

The Elf extended his hand palm open, and Barren and the others leaned in to get a look at what sat at the center of his hand. It was a bullet, only it was red in color and veins of black crawled over the casing.

"What is it?" asked Hollow.

"I believe it is poisoned, though I cannot identify the type. I can tell you that the poison was strengthened with magic," said Leaf.

Barren's gaze met Leaf's, troubled. "Like the magic tied to the hemlock needle?"

Barren had been poisoned by magic before and to cure him, Leaf had ended up needing his father's assistance. Even then, the two Elves hadn't been able to prevent the side effects.

"Magic?" asked Hollow. "What does that mean for Cove?"

"We can't say," said Leaf.

"That's why I need to talk to Dr. Newell," said Cove.

"The mortal doctor? What's he going to know about magic?"

"I've a feeling our men were killed with these bullets," said Cove. "I just need proof."

"But...does that mean you'll end up like them?" Barren asked. The question left a strange taste in his mouth.

Cove's eyes met his. "I guess we'll find out."

A loud knock sounded at the door and tense silence followed. Cove nodded to Camille. "Tell them I'm occupied at the moment, whoever they are."

She nodded, smoothing down her apron. She left the study, closing the door behind her. They were quiet while she was gone. It was Leaf who reacted first, twisting and drawing his blade as the study doors opened. A boy with wide, round eyes stood at the doorway. His hair was a mess of curls, and he wore a black suit. Perhaps he had been at the ball, yet Barren didn't remember him. The boy didn't even seem to notice them. He only had eyes for Cove.

"Jonas," Cove said, moving forward.

"I know, I know," he said, holding up his hands. "But we have trouble. It's Dr. Newell. They're going to hang him."

***

"Tell me what happened," said Cove as he moved from the study, directing Jonas to turn around. The others followed him into the foyer.

"There's a mob in the courtyard. They have Dr. Newell and five bodies that were found in his office."

"Who is *they*?"

Jonas hesitated. "I'm not sure who all is involved, but Ben Willow is leading it. Seems one of his men fell ill at the ball, and when he took him to John, they discovered the bodies."

"Nob, get the carriage ready," said Cove. "Jonas, I need you to get as many of our men down there as possible."

"Cove, you can't go down there. You were just shot!" Hollow protested.

"I can't let them hang John for something I did," he said.

"Then they'll hang you! What sort of explanation can you give for bringing five dead men to Arcarum?"

"I'll think of something," he replied as he moved out the door. He didn't bother to take a coat. Hollow followed him out, but the pirates had to stay. They had no choice. The carriage rambled up the driveway and Cove and Hollow hurried toward it. It had barely stopped when they leapt inside and urged Nob toward the courtyard at the center of town.

Cove clutched at his side as the carriage rattled hard over the cobbles. The streets of Arcarum were narrow and moved in a slow spiral toward the center of town where the gallows were ever-present.

Cove felt heat rush over his skin as he thought of how stupid he'd been. He wasn't surprised this was happening. Ben was bold and he had reason to be confident. He'd watched as Cove was shot hours earlier and probably supposed him to be incapacitated. He'd also been watching him over the last several weeks. He'd seen Cove at Dr. Newell's office in the dead of night. When Ben had called him out at the courthouse the other day, he should have had the bodies moved. This was the price he'd pay for underestimating Ben Willow.

Cove saw the torchlight first, scattered across the landscape, then he heard the cries and clamor. Several people crowded into the courtyard, others looked down from their windows far above, but they all joined in to rise in discord and demand justice for the display before them. And a display it was. Five bodies hung by the neck upon the gallows that rose like a dark shadow at the very center of the yard. The bodies had been frightening when Cove first found them, but now, between their wounds and the decay, they were horrific. Before the bodies stood Ben Willow and at his feet was Dr. Newell, who rested on his knees, bent over at his waist as if he'd been hit. His thinning gray hair fell over his face, hiding it from view.

"Stop the carriage!" Cove ordered as they came upon the mob. Cove climbed out of the carriage followed by Hollow. They stood for a moment, only a few feet from the crowd. He could feel the hostility in the air and it sprouted from one thing, fear.

He scanned the crowd. It took a moment, but his eyes finally found the men and women he had been searching for. Jonas had succeeded; members of his crew and network stood at the brink of the throng, waiting. Ainsley, Ean, Maddox, Sayida, and Jeanna. They all nodded, and as Cove made the first break in the crowd, they followed.

There was resistance at first, and the wave of the crowd made him dizzy. There was nothing calm or nice about how Cove moved through the bodies, elbowing, thrashing, demanding entrance. And soon there was no struggle, for the men and women began to move aside, creating a path for him. He walked forward, drawing closer to the gallows. Silence descended, and now Cove could hear Ben's voice.

"If you refuse to speak of what befell these men, how are we to believe you aren't responsible for their deaths?"

He had not yet realized why the crowd had suddenly gone so quiet. Ben bent to grab a handful of Doctor Newell's hair, forcing his head back so that his neck was exposed. Cove saw that the old man's face was bruised and bloodied. A dagger flashed in Ben's hand, and panic overtook Cove. He broke through the front of the crowd.

"This is madness!" the ambassador seethed. "Stop! I demand you stop!"

Ben straightened, letting go of Dr. Newell, who sagged to the floor of the gallows with exhaustion.

"Ambassador Rowell," Ben drawled. He didn't seem surprised to see Cove here. "You would halt the punishment of a man who has killed five men?"

The crowd reacted, shouting and throwing garbage at the stage, intent on hitting Dr. Newell. Cove moved, holding his side. His skin felt clammy and he was dizzy, but he maintained his focus. "Has this man had a trial? Has he been convicted of murder?" the ambassador challenged.

"This is all the jury Dr. Newell needs, and they have declared his guilt!"

The crowd cheered and the fire of the torches in the crowd swayed with agreement.

"What is going on here?" the voice boomed, but not in its normally cheerful manner. It was Matthew Dulcemer, the governor of Arcarum. The crowd parted even further for his large form.

"Governor," said Ben stepping forward.

"Is this your crowd, Mr. Willow?"

The man hesitated. "They're here for answers, Governor. These men were found in Dr. Newell's office. You will see that their wounds are...rather unnatural."

The governor's eyes moved to the men for a moment, and he studied them. Then his eyes slid back to Ben. "What is to fear of a dead man?"

Ben set his jaw. "And what of you, ambassador? Can you argue with the men behind you? Surely even you must agree that such an evil must be stopped."

"I do agree," said Cove. "Which is why I brought the bodies to Dr. Newell in the first place."

Ben smiled, his eyes alight with pleasure. Gasps escaped from the crowd. The air around them was thick with the smell of rain, and lightning began to flash in the sky. Cove wanted it to pour and douse the sick flames that had begun this panic.

"Say that again," Ben demanded.

"He said," Matthew's voice boomed. "That Dr. Newell was only doing what he was instructed, and you, Mr. Willow, should also know that I was aware of this agreement."

Cove was careful not to look surprised, but he felt it. Matthew had not been aware of such a thing.

Ben narrowed his eyes. "Why keep this a secret? Did you not feel the people of Arcarum had a right to know about this?' Some voices rose in agreement.

"The men were not found in Arcarum. They were found at sea," said Cove. "Besides, we cannot infer anything from what we have here, and we should not spread fear needlessly."

"But this is to be feared!" Ben argued, pointing at the men. "This *is* fear!"

"The only thing I see to be feared here is your disregard for what is right," said Matthew. Ben didn't look at Matthew. His eyes were on Cove, menacing and dark. Cove stepped forward to help Dr. Newell to his feet. He took a knife from his boot and cut the bonds from the doctor's hands.

"Are you okay, John?"

"Yes," he wheezed, leaning into Cove. "Thank you."

"You're bleeding, ambassador," Ben said. Cove didn't look at his shirt. He still felt lightheaded from the wound.

Matthew's voice rose. "Go to your homes! You should all be

ashamed!"

The crowd broke away slowly, and Cove helped Dr. Newell down from the gallows. Those who had come with Cove wandered to him.

"Take the bodies to the church. Alaster will know what to do," he ordered. As they obeyed, Ben's voice rose, catching the attention of those who remained in the courtyard.

"These are the bodies of pirates, are they not, ambassador?"

Cove paused and turned with Dr. Newell. "If they swore by the mark, we will never know," he said. And they wouldn't. The wound over their hearts had erased any traces of the tattoo. "We cannot make assumptions about things we do not know...that's how people die."

And he meant that as a threat.

Then he turned, moving past what remained of the crowd. He felt Matthew following close behind, like a thought he didn't want to recall. Matthew was reminding Cove that he still wanted answers.

As Cove helped Dr. Newell onto the carriage, he turned to face Matthew. The governor didn't look severe, but he didn't look jolly either. No, the look in his eyes made Cove's chest tighten up. It was a mix of fear and sadness. This was what it was like to be on the brink of losing.

"I expect a visit," said Matthew. "And soon."

Cove nodded, and while he was indebted to Matthew for what he'd done, he knew there was a profound change between them. Tonight had ensured that a seed had been planted in

Matthew, in the people of Arcarum. Cove Rowell was not to be trusted.

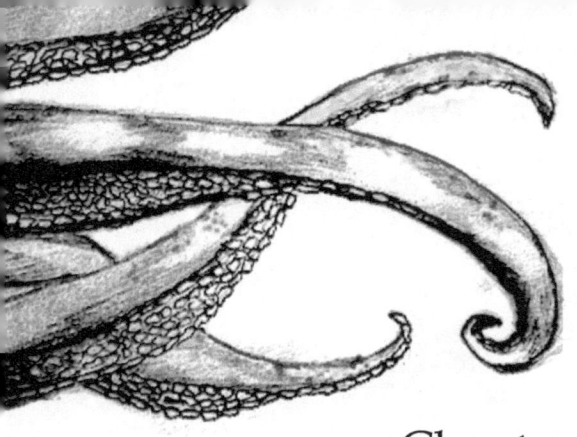

Chapter Ten
JOHN NEWELL

Barren studied the old man sitting in one of Cove's padded chairs, face bruised and bloodied. He'd heard his name a lot over the past few days—Dr. John Newell. He looked educated, with half-moon glasses perched upon the bridge of his large nose, a straight set to his shoulders, his head tilted slightly upward. But there was also something firm and rough about him. Maybe it was the way he had handled the beating he'd taken. Barren was more intrigued by the fact that the man hadn't once looked his way.

"I'm a doctor," the man was saying. "I can dress my own wounds."

"It's better that you rest," said Cove. "Besides, I'm sure Leaf has faster medicine for you."

"Just because his medicine is faster, doesn't mean it's better," he replied.

Leaf stood with his arms crossed, the look on his face passive. "You can have my help or not. It's your face."

140

"Scars and bruises are nothing to me," the man snapped. "Besides, I don't trust Elvish medicine."

Leaf exchanged a glance with Barren.

"Albatross, did I hear correctly that you were shot this evening?" he turned to Cove. Barren was surprised to hear the doctor call Cove by that name. Only pirates of Silver Crest used that name.

"You heard correctly, Dr. Newell," said Cove.

"Then may I be allowed to do my job and see that you are alright?"

"I am afraid the Elf has already beat you to it, though perhaps it is a good thing, as you have probably had little experience with these," he produced the bullet Leaf had extracted from his side and held it up for the doctor to see.

Barren expected the doctor to take the bullet and examine it, but Newell just stared and then swallowed, looking down at his feet.

"I know what you're doing, ambassador," the doctor said, and then he released his breath. "I have had time to consider why you have brought this upon me, but it must be that you suspect I've experienced something like this before."

Barren looked from one man to the other, confused. Cove hadn't been at all forthcoming about why he'd decided to show the bodies to John Newell of all people, but suddenly Barren understood.

"What's going on here, Cove?" Barren asked, but Cove didn't look at Barren. He kept his eyes on John expectantly.

141

"John Newell once served as the doctor of Jess Reed's crew," said Cove, not taking his eyes off the doctor. Barren was stunned. Perhaps Alex had given Cove this information.

"You knew my father?"

John didn't say anything for a long moment. "It is not a part of my life that I want to remember."

Barren flinched and felt his face grow red, though he couldn't tell if it was anger or embarrassment that colored his features.

"I quit because I was afraid to die, and because every chance he got, Jess would drag us into a new fight." He seemed older now and still afraid. His voice trembled. "You get tired of seeing your friends die. I got tired of failing to save them."

And no one could say much to that.

The old man hunched forward, his head down. He took a breath in, his whole body seeming to fold inward, and then he exhaled and reached into his pocket, extending his hand to the ambassador. "These were found in the wounds. There were several, and I'm not sure I got them all."

Barren moved toward Cove and looked at the bullets in his palm. They were all the same, coppery in color with strange black veins. Barren's brows knitted together and he felt the contents of his stomach turn to lead. These were the same as the bullet that pierced Cove. Panic filled him. What did this mean for Cove? Barren looked at the ambassador, but Cove didn't seem to share that concern.

"You were right," said the doctor. "I have seen this before, though I'd hoped I was wrong. No one wants to relive what we've seen these weapons do. No Elder, no pirate of Silver Crest, and not me."

"What are they? Where did they come from?" Cove demanded, obviously done waiting for answers.

"They are weapons powered by dark magic. *Vacair* is the Elvish term," Newell said without hesitation. "They were a problem before, back when Jess was alive and fighting in the Ore Wars. The stories you've heard about him intercepting ships to keep the war from progressing are true, but his greatest wish was to ensure that these weapons didn't spread. You've seen what they've done by themselves...well imagine what they would dc with a Lyric powering them."

"What?"

"You heard right. Cathmor had power over the Lyrics, a power that, thankfully, Tetherion has never come to know. During the Ore Wars, he used these weapons to level entire islands. It was a massacre and over in seconds. Lyrics...they don't even need weapons to use the bullets. They just use their minds."

"But why would they do such a thing?" What Barren was really asking was would his mother do such a thing, and had she?

"If I had my guess, it wasn't by choice," said Dr. Newell. "Though I never understood how Lyrics could be forced to do anything against their will."

"Why have these weapons resurfaced now?" asked Cove.

"Perhaps Cathmor had some sort of store and Tetherion has discovered it," said Dr. Newell. "Perhaps they linger in the dark markets...maybe it's a fluke."

143

"Your fluke found its way to Arcarum tonight and shot Cove," said Barren. "So what does that mean for him?"

Dr. Newell hesitated. "I...have never seen anyone survive a *vacair* wound," he took a breath.

Silence followed.

"How long does he have?" asked Hollow.

"It is dark magic," Dr. Newell replied. "He has as long as it wishes to give."

Barren found it strange that Cove hadn't asked any of these questions Even now, when hearing that he might die from the wound he sustained this night, he seemed unnaturally calm.

"What about the assassin?" asked Barren.

"What?" Larkin was incredulous that Aethea was being brought up again, but it was important they speak with her since she'd been the one to wound Cove with the same bullets used against their brethren. She knew where they came from.

"The assassin who was arrested tonight for trying to kill Tetherion. She had the bullets. We need to talk to her, find out where she got them. Cove, you can talk to her. Maybe she can lead us to someone who can help."

Cove shook his head. "It's much harder than that, Barren. She will be convicted of high treason, and Tetherion won't allow just anyone in to speak to her. We'd do better trying to figure out who she is and go from there. Besides, even if we were to talk to her, we don't know her agenda. She could be working for the Commonwealth or the Octent. If either, exposing ourselves to her would make everything worse."

"Do we have that kind of time?" Barren ignored the guilt pulling at his heart. She'd already recognized him, but maybe that's why Barren was pushing so hard to reach her, so he could silence her before she spoke up.

"We don't have a choice," said Cove.

"You can be sure of one thing," said Dr. Newell. "If these weapons have resurfaced, one thing you won't have on your side is time."

No, there was no time, because as Barren met Cove's gaze, he already knew the ambassador was dying.

***

Larkin couldn't sit still, so she paced the room. She still didn't feel like herself, and it had been hours since she'd discovered she had magic. What was she supposed to do now? If the Elders found out they would send her back to Maris, and she couldn't be sure what her father would do if he knew. Was she supposed to tell Barren? That would require admitting that she'd left the ball to find her father, admitting that she'd been attacked, and consequently discovered by Ben Willow, Cove's enemy. She should admit to those things. They were all things that put them in danger. But what held her back was others knowing what she was: a Lyric. Everything she knew about Lyrics was bad, from their magic to their tragic lives. If they weren't evil, they were enslaved and used as sources for mortals to gain power. She would not be a slave.

And yet that's exactly what Ben would make her. What did he want with Barren's compass anyway? If it was truly worthless, why would Ben want it? Most importantly, how did Ben know anything about it? If she wanted answers to these questions, she would have to tread carefully. Perhaps it was best to play into Ben's hands, but she needed an advantage. Something as damning to him as her magic was to her. The only person she knew who might have anything on him was Cove Rowell.

The door opened and she halted, facing Barren as he entered the room. She could tell by the look on his face that he was ready for a fight. He closed the door, sealing the tension in the room.

"Do you want to explain yourself?" he asked.

"Explain myself?"

"Why you left the ball?" he said.

She had no explanation she wanted to give and her hesitation cost her.

"Did you go in search of your father?" Barren demanded.

"I didn't meet my father," her voice rose to fight his abrasive tone. It was the truth, even if her intentions had been dishonest.

Barren stared at her, his gaze piercing, and she knew he didn't believe her.

"If you didn't leave to meet him, why did you leave at all?" he asked. "You had a job to do and you failed."

She glared at him. That was unfair. "How dare you! You left your station to dance with an enemy! And after you told me not to!"

"It didn't stop you," he hissed. "You stood up with every man who approached you."

"Oh, please," she seethed. "You sound jealous!"

146

"Jealous?" Barren laughed. "If you wish to return to Maris, I'll gladly take you myself. Just say the word."

"This isn't about going back to Maris!"

"Isn't it?" he said. "It is clear you miss your other life. The grand balls, the dancing, even your father. Why remain here, miserable in my company?"

She scoffed. "Is that what you think?"

"You're not like Cove," he said. "You can't live a duel life. You pick one or the other. You're either a member of my crew or you're not."

"I don't even have a place on your ship," she argued. "You pull me along like some doll on a string. I'm not something pretty for you to look at in your spare time! I deserve something more!"

"You can't even follow my orders! How am I supposed to give you a role on my ship?"

"Your orders never ensure that I am an equal!" she cried. "You have no problem sending Leaf out to fight, but when it comes to me, you hesitate. Why? I fight as well as any man on your crew."

She glared at him, and he stared back at her. There was a look on his face she couldn't quite understand, but she was certain he was hurt in some way.

"If you can't figure out why I don't want to send you into the thick of a fight, then I'm not sure what you're doing here at all."

She blanched. What was that supposed to mean? He turned to leave, but she wasn't done with him yet. There was one more thing she wanted to know.

"Who is Éire?"

There was a frightening pause, and Barren turned, taking a step toward her.

"Who told you about that?"

"Who is he?" She demanded again.

His stare was so severe, she felt she might break beneath it.

"Éire is a place, not a person," he said. "It's a small island where I made the greatest mistake of my life. I don't care to relive it, through memory or story."

"So you will not tell me?"

"Get your information from your source. It seems you believe they have everything figured out."

Barren turned and left, slamming the door behind him.

***

Barren hadn't realized he'd fallen asleep until he woke with a start as the door opened and closed. He sat up, his journal falling to the floor, and saw Cove. He'd come to Cove's study after leaving Larkin upstairs. For the longest time, he hadn't been able to sleep, and he occupied his mind by sketching in his journal.

"I didn't realize you would be in here," said the ambassador. His voice was tired and grim.

"Sorry," Barren grunted, bending to pick up his journal. He'd fallen asleep in one of the chairs near the fireplace and now he regretted it. His neck was stiff and his back hurt, though those pains paled in comparison to Cove's, he was sure. He met the ambassador's gaze. His face was drained of color, and his normally animated eyes were muted. His hair was loose around his face, but he was dressed in his black ambassador uniform. He moved toward his desk with a rigid walk. This was probably a normal reaction to having been shot last night, but Cove had been shot with a different type of bullet, and Barren couldn't help thinking that every hour that passed was an hour closer to the unknown.

"Shouldn't you be resting?"

"I am fine," he replied.

"Are you going somewhere?"

"I already have," he said. "I needed to speak with Matthew Dulcemer, and it gave me a chance to show people that I am okay."

Barren wasn't so sure.

"Have you learned anything about the assassin?"

Cove picked up a coin from his desk and moved it between his fingers as he spoke. "Nothing groundbreaking. I've had Maddox look into the matter. As far as he could tell, her life began the night she tried to kill the king."

"Well, she's an assassin. Find out where she was trained. If she's never had a job before this one, perhaps she's fresh out of training," said Barren.

"That will take time," said Cove. "Matthew tells me they're planning to send her to Maris tonight. They'll do it under the cover of darkness and hang her in the morning."

"So soon?" Barren was surprised. "We cannot let her die before we find out where she got the bullets! She is our only link."

Cove shrugged. "Christopher Lee is a link to those weapons.

He had a hemlock needle, remember? I don't doubt they are all connected in some way."

Barren scoffed. "Christopher Lee won't talk to us."

"Not to us," he said. "But he might talk to his daughter."

Barren set his jaw and stood immediately. He wasn't sure who Larkin had spoken to at the ball last night. Maybe it had been Christopher Lee and maybe it hadn't, but he wasn't going to encourage it.

"No, I won't allow it. I can't...I can't let Larkin near him."

"It would be her decision, Barren."

"No!" Barren ground out. "You will promise not to bring it up. You will not plant the idea in her head!"

Cove seemed troubled, but he nodded. "Very well," he agreed. "But then we are truly at a loss because Aethea Moore will die. Unless...she escapes."

"Escapes? Do you expect her to try?"

Cove shrugged. "It depends on the type of assassin she is, what she stands for. If she attempted to kill Tetherion out of loyalty to the Octent, then she will proudly die a martyr. If she took the highest bidder, say the Commonwealth, then she would not want to die for this cause."

"If she is working with Ben Willow, is it likely that he would want his king-killer to hang?" asked Barren.

"I wouldn't put anything past Ben Willow," said Cove. "I'm not sure what he's after but what I've learned of him over the years is that he is merciless. Perhaps we will make a visit to the Network tonight. Maybe they can tell us more about Aethea

Moore and if she's connected to Ben Willow in anyway."

"Finding out if she's connected to the Commonwealth will do us little good if she's dead," said Barren.

"Just trust me to figure things out," Cove said. "This is my territory, not yours. You don't get to make decisions, understand?"

Barren nodded stiffly and sent up a prayer that they'd be off land soon so he could make his own decisions.

Chapter Eleven
THE NETWORK

Cove sat in his study. The flame from his kerosene lamp flickered, causing shadows to dance on the walls, and he knew it was late. He had yet to sleep at all, and he would soon depart to the Network with Barren. He wasn't sleeping well, plagued by the wound on his side. He kept telling himself the pain would go away once the wound healed, if it healed at all. He'd been in a haze since last night when he'd learned the *vacair* wound might mean death. Everyone wanted a reaction from him, and he supposed he should be devastated, but he would get nothing done worrying about dying. He'd never lived his life like that and he wouldn't start now.

His clock chimed and a knock sounded on his study door. "Come in," he said.

He looked up when the door opened to see Larkin enter his study. Cove stood from his place at his desk.

"May I come in?" she asked from the door.

"Yes," he said.

She shut the door behind her and turned to face him. Her stance was elegant, the mark of the Lady she was bred to be. Her brows were knitted together in thought, and her jaw was set in a frustrated line, a result of fighting with Barren, no doubt.

"Are you troubled?" he asked her.

She seemed surprised and hesitated. "We've been friends for a long time, have we not?"

"We have," he agreed.

"Given the last few months, what I have to tell you might not be much of a surprise," she said. "But I need to know that you can keep a secret."

"Are you asking me if I can keep a secret from Barren?"

She stared at him and he took her silence to mean yes.

"Go on," he said.

"At the ball I was attacked by a man who called me a gypsy-witch. I bested him, but I was discovered by Ben Willow. He told me he wouldn't tell anyone I was there if I promised to give him Barren's compass."

Cove could only stare at her.

"I cannot give him Barren's compass, but Ben expects it to be in his possession tonight. I need something to hold over him, a way to gain an advantage, and keep him from exposing us."

He shouldn't have suggested he would keep this from Barren. But then again he needed this: someone who could get close to Ben Willow, learn his plans, become a true enemy to the Commonwealth. He turned from her and moved toward the fire, thinking.

"I am sorry if you are angry with me," she said. "If you wish for me to tell Barren, I will, but…"

"Ben Willow is my problem, not his," said Cove. "It was right that you came to me."

He started to pace and think aloud. "Why does Ben want Barren's compass?"

"How did he know Barren had it in the first place?" asked Larkin.

"The twins?" Cove suggested.

Larkin shook her head. "They never saw the compass," she said. "Even then, what worth would they find in it? It is broken."

"Yes, it is broken," said Cove. "So its use is not practical."

"Perhaps Ben feels he can trap Barren if he has it?" she suggested.

Cove shook his head. "No, he would have taken you," said Cove. "His priority isn't taking Barren down, it's exposing me for who I am."

"And how does the compass do that?"

"It's payment," Cove said at last. "Ben has struck a deal. He's getting something in exchange for the compass."

"What is he getting in return, and who did he strike the deal with?"

"That's exactly what I want to know," said Cove. "Tell Ben you know he is the leader of the Commonwealth, and if he's not ready to hang, he'll let you deliver the compass on your own terms."

"And that will work? He knows I don't have connections in

Maris anymore."

"Tetherion wants to find the leader of the Commonwealth. He'll take any report seriously. I'll have my men shadow you," he said.

"And what about Barren?" she asked.

"What about Barren?"

"If you tell him, he won't let me go."

Cove sensed she wasn't so much desperate to help him as she was desperate to hide something. She hadn't told him the full truth, and he supposed he shouldn't expect it. If she was keeping things from Barren, she was going to keep things from him.

"I'll keep your secret as long as it benefits me," he said. "That's all I can promise."

Her features hardened, but she nodded.

***

The air still felt heavy from the storm that had passed in the night. Thunder rumbled somewhere in the distance and lightning flashed in the sky above, illuminating the night. Barren took deep breaths now and then, reveling in the smell of salt. It almost burned his nose, which meant he'd been gone from the sea for far too long. An ache settled in his stomach.

The streets of Arcarum were cobble and the buildings clustered together. Lanterns illuminated the streets. Some were hung high on moveable wire so that they could be lit and extinguished easily. Others were placed in windows or outside on the streets. Barren would have preferred total darkness, but it did add to the island's charm. Because of all the light, Barren and

Cove kept close to the shadows, taking a maze-like path to wherever the Network was located. While Barren turned his head in all directions attempting to see if anyone followed, Cove remained perfectly focused on his target, eyes straight ahead. There were few who passed them at this late hour, but those who did kept to the shadows too, slinking about as if they belonged to the darkness.

Cove's easy stroll along the causeways made Barren impatient. He didn't like being out in the open even if he wore a hood and cloak to hide his identity. The ambassador had said he suspected people were watching his house, whether they be from the Commonwealth or just commoners curious about his condition. So they'd used the tunnel and come out on the side of the sea cliffs. Barren had questioned whether it was even necessary for him to tag along on this visit, but Cove insisted.

Sometimes Barren wasn't sure Cove knew what was good for him.

It was the smell of the sea and the cool breeze that made Barren feel refreshed again. He hadn't realized they were so close to shore, but Cove had lead him farther to the north where there were fewer trees. The road here was only dirt and it ran downhill. There were a few houses, but most of the block was taken up by a large stone church.

Barren halted when Cove moved in that direction. "Where are we going?" he asked.

"To the Network," said Cove.

"But this is a church," said Barren.

"Yes," Cove agreed and then nodded his head toward the door, moving forward. Barren followed dumbly. He supposed if the Network was going to be anywhere, it should be in the last place anyone expected.

It was then that Barren came to a realization. The Network, Cove's network, involved more than just the Pirates of Silver Crest. So the threat he had made to Eva was very real. It was possible, in fact, Barren was sure, that the majority of Cove's network didn't even include the pirates. If disciples of the church were members, then men of the government weren't excluded— men who were close to Tetherion. Cove had ensured that he would not suffer by someone else's hand.

Barren now understood that although the ambassador was prepared, the situation he constantly lived in was a balancing act—a precarious one. He supposed he'd always known that, but seeing this made it more real.

The doors of the church were large and wooden, held on with black hinges. The façade of the church was mostly flat, only interrupted by narrow stained glass windows. The largest part of the church was a bell tower which rose from the center of the building, and the rest of the church was hidden by a stone wall and willow trees.

It had been a long time since Barren had been in a church. Churches didn't give him a comfortable feeling, but Barren followed Cove as he stepped over the threshold. He found himself taking a breath once he was inside. Cove looked at him curiously.

"What?"

"I guess I was just waiting for you to burst into flame," Cove said and laughed. Barren rolled his eyes, but he'd been waiting for the same thing.

They looked ahead. The doors to the sanctuary were open, candles were lit at the head of the altar, and a heavy wooden cross was also erected there. Two sets of pews divided the room. There was a simplicity to the décor that Barren admired. The walls were white, trimmed with gold, and the pews were of dark wood. There were no large paintings or tapestries, no distractions. Barren imagined that with daylight streaming in through the windows, this place was probably uplifting, but with the darkness outside and few candles, the air felt heavy.

Cove moved forward and Barren followed in his shadow.

"Ambassador Rowell," a man in brown robes exited a door adjacent to the sanctuary. He sounded a bit surprised to see Cove in his church, though that might have been because the Ambassador had been shot the previous night. The man was older and small in stature. He was pale with a long face and he acted intimidated, though Barren couldn't tell if he really was or if that was just a part of his personality. "What can I do for you this fine evening?"

"Brother Gregory," Cove said, and Barren noticed he placed his hands behind his back, straightening. "I've come to visit Alaster. Is he available?"

"Yes, I'll see you to him," he said, but before he turned, the monk paused, his eyes settling on Barren, who he'd just noticed.

"You've no need to worry, Brother, he is in my company."

"Oh," the man gave a breathless laugh. "I see." But Barren could tell he was startled. Wasn't everyone in Cove's network aware of his connections to Barren? The way this man reacted told Barren that wasn't so true. "F-follow me," The monk said again and left the sanctuary through a side door.

They followed him, entering a narrow, dim hallway. The walls were stone, and it was cooler here. Barren wondered who this Alaster was. Cove hadn't referred to him as 'brother,' so it didn't seem that he was a man of the church, yet here he stayed.

"I have heard of the trouble in town," said Gregory. "Is Dr. Newell recovered?"

"Yes, I believe he is doing well," Cove replied.

"And…are you doing well, Ambassador?" the monk ventured. "You don't quite seem…like yourself."

"Yes, I am fine." Cove was less tolerant of questions in regard to his health. Barren wasn't sure if the ambassador was always like this or if he'd suddenly become defensive in light of the news that he might die.

The monk nodded and didn't ask how anyone else was feeling. At some point he turned and stopped them, putting out his hands as if moving forward one more step might cause the whole place to explode. "If you'll wait here a moment."

The monk entered a door to his right. Barren and Cove exchanged a glance. *This man was tedious.*

After a moment, Gregory reappeared. "Alaster will see you now," he said and stood aside while Cove and Barren entered the room. Barren tried not to make eye contact with the man, because even being in the monk's presence was uncomfortable.

They entered a small room and the door closed behind them. There was a table at the center, a bed to the far wall, and a washing cabinet.

A man sat at a round table. He was older and had a short white beard that covered the bottom half of his face. Glasses perched upon the end of his large nose. When he heard the door shut, he looked over at them.

The man's gaze met Barren's, and while he showed little surprise at his presence, Barren couldn't help feeling unnerved.

Shaking his newspaper closed, he cleared his throat.

"Albatross," he said, and when the old man spoke Cove's nickname, it was filled with the weight of its meaning, but also respect.

"Have the bodies been buried?" asked Cove. He was referring to the five men he'd found at sea, their brethren.

"Yes," he said. "Unmarked plots, but honorably laid to rest, all the same."

It was then Barren understood that Alaster was a gravedigger.

"What information have you gathered on Aethea Moore?"

"Little, but some. She has lived as Aethea Moore for the last five years. Most of that time was spent in Lystra, though her activities there are unknown. Her ship was purchased there."

"How did she come to work for Tetherion?"

"Datherious hired her, though where the recommendation came from, I do not know."

"Datherious hired a privateer for his father?" Barren questioned. The practice wasn't uncommon, but if Barren had to guess, Aethea was chosen deliberately.

"Or maybe Datherious hired an assassin for himself. Perhaps we are naïve. Maybe Datherious wants his father's crown," said Cove. "I'm sure he believes he can do a better job."

"Rumor has it the Commonwealth is pleased with Datherious," said Alaster. Barren shuddered. He couldn't imagine anyone being pleased with the twin. Something in Datherious's energy was malevolent. Barren had to admit, however, he was surprised Datherious would make a move for the crown so soon.

"I can't imagine why," said Barren. "He's done nothing to prove he will make a good king."

"No one is looking for a good king," said Alaster. No, Barren knew that. A change in reign would mean a change in the court, new positions, more power. "Besides, Datherious feeds into what the people want. War on piracy."

That was true. Ever since Datherious had returned, he'd condemned Barren and all who sailed under the code. It wasn't all that surprising. Datherious had to reestablish himself as a prince of his people, instead of a young and rebellious boy who'd run off with his cousin to sail the seas.

"For the time being, however, Tetherion is still king, and though an attempt was made on his life, it seems he's using it to his advantage," Alaster continued.

"What do you mean?" asked Cove.

Alaster pushed the paper he had been reading toward them. The title read in black, bold letters, "ASSASSIN FROM OCTENT ATTEMPS MURDER OF KING." The article touched on several aspects of the night: the success of the Autumn Ball up until the attack, Cove's injury and heroism, and Aethea Moore, the Octent assassin. But what disturbed Barren the most was the suggestion that this incident might reignite a war over the Ore Mines.

"Has this been printed yet?" asked Barren. Anything involving the Ore Mines wasn't going to be good. The Ore Wars had been waged over that territory and had ended in a stalemate. It was the war in which Jess Reed had become the most infamous enemy of his father, King Cathmor, by undermining the king's attempts to conquer the territory, and, as Barren had recently learned, to keep weapons from moving across Mariana.

"No," said Alaster. "But it will tomorrow."

"There are only two ways for the Octent to respond. They will either relinquish any claim to the land or they will go to war."

He said it so simply.

"I don't understand," said Barren. "Why is that place of such value?"

"An ore mine can be a valuable resource to a nation," said Cove. "It is a source of power and wealth. Two things we know Tetherion covets more than anything in this world."

"All this and the weapons, too," Barren muttered, thinking. "The attempted assassination could be a ploy. Just a power play so that Tetherion can come into possession of the Ore Mines."

"Yes," Cove agreed. "And the weapons work in two ways. They arm the privateers, Tetherion's army, and they deter war altogether because of their power."

"I suppose you'll have to ask the assassin herself if you really want to know," said Alaster. "But you don't have much time."

Barren looked at Cove expectantly, but the ambassador seemed to ignore Alaster's input on the subject and bowed his head. "Thank you, Alaster."

"Shall I see you out?" he asked.

"No, no. I know the way."

The ambassador turned then, and Barren followed.

Gregory didn't see them out, for which Barren was thankful. They stood outside in the night, cool air from the sea washing over them. It had been hot in Alaster's tiny room. Neither man spoke.

Barren ran through the information they'd learned. It was likely that Datherious had ties to the Commonwealth and had hired Aethea to assassinate Tetherion, though like Tetherion, he'd used the situation to his advantage. Now the Orient faced war with the Octent. With the tension over the Ore Mines and the weapons resurfacing, it seemed his father's past was coming back to haunt him.

Cove and Barren did not speak. They moved on, heading back to Cove's mansion in silence.

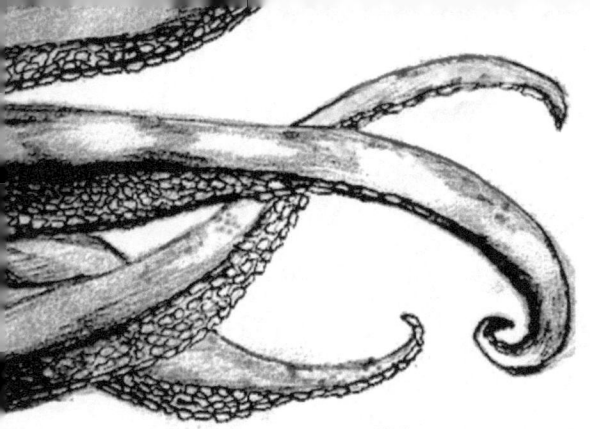

Chapter Twelve
TETE-A-TETE

They didn't take the same way back. Cove wanted to keep an eye on Dr. Newell's office. He didn't believe that Ben was finished with the doctor.

"We'll stop by John's and see how he's doing," said Cove.

Barren nodded.

Cove walked ahead, keeping his head down, not wanting to be stopped by anyone who desired his attention or help, especially with Barren Reed trailing a few feet behind him. They rounded a corner and Cove saw the back entrance of Dr. Newell's office. There were three rotten steps that lead to the door. He never used them, fearing they would collapse with his weight.

He approached the office just as the door swung open. A woman stepped down onto the first rickety step, and it caved beneath her weight. She yelped as she fell forward. Cove reacted, catching her before she hit the ground. He set her on her feet and stepped back.

"Are you alright?" he asked.

"I am so sorry," a woman's voice, a familiar one, said. She turned, fixing her hat in place. Even in this light, Cove could make out her sapphire eyes. "Sara, what are you doing out here so late at night?"

"I was...um," she looked back at the door.

"Is everything okay?"

"Yes," she was clearly uncomfortable.

Cove narrowed his eyes, but he didn't press her to explain herself. "I will escort you home." He glanced up at Barren, who seemed to understand and immediately melded with the darkness. He offered her his arm before she could decline. She seemed to hesitate for a moment, but took it, tightening her grip around him as if he'd be taken away. They began their walk toward her home.

"How are you feeling? I tried to check on you, but Hollow said you didn't want visitors."

"I'm fine, like nothing ever happened," he said, though he was most definitely lying because since he'd been hit, he hadn't felt the same. It was hard to put his finger on it. There was pain but something more. The look Sara gave him told him she didn't believe a word he said.

"When did you become a liar, Cove?"

"What do you mean?"

"How did you manage to get that bullet out?" she asked, pulling away from him. She crossed her arms. "You never visited Dr. Newell, did you?"

Cove rubbed his mouth, trying to stop the words that wanted

to spill out. They weren't truthful words, they were accusations. Why was she spying on him? Was it for Ben?

"Does Ben know you're out here checking up on me?" His voice was biting. Sara looked away, angry. "He doesn't have to know everything I do."

"You mean he doesn't have to know when it involves me, right?"

He watched her. She wasn't looking at him, and she kept her head tilted to the left. He saw her raise her hand up to brush her face and he knew she was crying.

"Hey," he stepped closer. Placing his fingers on her chin, he turned her head toward his. "Please don't cry. You know I hate seeing you sad."

Sara tried to wipe more tears away, but they fell quickly. She cried harder, placing her hand over her mouth to muffle the sounds.

"Shh," Cove pulled her to him. It had been so long since he'd felt her body against his. She was soft and warm. Perfection. He rested his cheek on her head and swayed slowly back and forth while she cried. "Sara," he whispered. "I'm not worth your tears."

She pulled away and stared up at him, her nose and eyes red.

"You're worth all my tears, Cove Rowell. I have cried for you day after day. What am I supposed to do? You're my best friend and you're always gone or...or getting shot in your own home! Then when I need to see you most, you refuse me!"

For some reason, Cove smiled. "First, Hollow refused you. Second, next time I'm shot, I will make sure you can see me."

Sara smiled, but pushed him for his sarcasm. "Cove, I'm serious!"

"So am I," the smile still lingered on his lips. "You know, I never gave you that dance."

He bowed suddenly and then held out his hand.

"Cove...it's late..."

"Better late than never," he said.

She laughed and took his hand. Their fingers threaded together, and Cove drew their bodies closer, placing his hand on her waist. Beneath the stars, they began to dance to their own rhythm, moving gracefully over the cobble road and never looking away from each other.

"You're such a good man, Cove," Sara said quietly.

Cove laughed. "Many would disagree with you. *I* disagree with you."

She frowned. "Why would you say that?"

"Well, for one, I'm alone with an engaged woman and to make the situation a little more compromising, I'm dancing with her."

She smiled, but it didn't touch her eyes. "I miss when this wasn't considered compromising. I miss how it used to be."

Cove grimaced. "This is what happens when we grow up, Sara."

"Does that mean I lose you?"

In reality, it did. He had lost her the day he returned from sea, and to a man that hated his very existence. There was no way Ben would allow her anywhere near him. And really, it wouldn't be appropriate. The public loved scandal. They had already gobbled up rumors involving the two, and when news of Sara and Ben's engagement broke, rumors circulated of betrayal. They would have to tread carefully with their friendship.

Given all that, he still said, "You won't lose me."

She interrupted their dance to hug him tightly, burying her face in his chest. She inhaled, as if she missed him. He returned the embrace, wrapping his arms around her, repressing his guilt and his sadness. Deep down he knew if Sara ever glimpsed him as he was outside of Arcarum, as Albatross, she would hate him.

And that thought was completely unbearable.

***

Larkin hurried through the night, feeling like an escaped prisoner. Her stomach was knotted with feelings of guilt and nervousness. She had debated about meeting Ben, told herself they would be leaving soon and whatever information Ben Willow had on her, it wouldn't matter at sea. But now she'd gotten Cove involved, and he seemed more than willing to let her continue this arrangement.

She wasn't all that familiar with Arcarum. She'd rarely been anywhere else but the courthouse and Cove's mansion. In the dark and with the weight of fear upon her, everything seemed a lot more confusing, but the shadows Cove had promised did follow her, and when she felt lost, she'd catch a glimpse of someone in her periphery.

Finally, she came to the building and the back entrance to a pub called Onyx Hall. She was familiar with the name only because the men she'd kept society with here frequented this place. Women of her level didn't. As she reached for the door, she found a red ribbon tied to the handle in a bow.

She swallowed and the knots in her stomach turned to knives. She pulled the ribbon from the handle. This felt like a horrible omen. When she tried the door, she found it was locked, so she knocked and waited in silence, pulling her hood farther over her head and praying no one recognized her, or worse, that this was a trap.

At last the door opened and a young man appeared in the doorway. He took one look at her and stepped aside. She wanted to ask him questions but decided it was best to keep silent. She didn't know who he thought she was, but she wasn't going to reveal her identity willingly.

"Stay," the young man said and left her in the dim light. She felt heat touch her cheeks. She was angry that he felt he could treat her in such a way and she wanted to say so, but again she kept quiet. She didn't like being vulnerable. Strange that with so much power coursing through her veins, she still felt helpless. But that's how this world had taught Lyrics to think of themselves, as sources of power, not powerful beings. The thought made her fingers clench, and she wondered for the first time if she might change that.

The young man returned. "Follow me."

Larkin was beginning to think his vocabulary wasn't very extensive. He led her up a dark set of stairs. At the top of the stairs, the young man just stood. She looked to him and he nodded in the direction of a door which stood ajar, light escaping from inside the room.

She moved forward and heard feet shuffle as the young man left. So she was by herself now with whoever or whatever lay beyond that door. She tried to slow her breathing. She'd hoped Ben was at least a little honorable and would stick to his word.

The door opened with a creak, and she found Ben sitting in a cushioned chair near the window. It likely overlooked the street she came down and she suspected he'd watched her approach.

He looked up from his paper as if he wasn't expecting her.

"Ah, Lady Lee," he said, folding the paper. She tightened her jaw upon hearing the title used in mockery. "What a pleasure. I presume you've brought what I have asked for. The compass," he held out his hand, and it irritated her that he felt she would be so obliging.

"No," she said, and Ben's face immediately fell. She began to think of ways she could fight him, where she'd placed all her weapons. "If I am to deliver you the compass, I will do it on my own terms."

"That was not the agreement," he said curtly, and a fire lit his eyes that instantly alarmed her.

"It will have to be," she said evenly. "I will have it no other way."

"Spoilt girl!" he spat and dared to move toward her. Part of her was surprised, which was why her knife found his face so quickly. He stumbled back, a large gash on his cheek. The blood that ran between his fingers made his eyes look like fire. She stood her ground. That was the only way she was going to take the upper hand here. Ben couldn't think she feared him, otherwise his power over her would be too great. "Wench! You don't have control here, you are nothing!"

"Do you want the world to know you are the leader of the Commonwealth?" she asked. "I can go back to Maris at any time. My father has made a place for me, and with my return, I will have your secret. I can bring you down swiftly. You may think you are safe but Tetherion wants your head."

"No one would trust you. Your reputation precedes you."

"For all they know I am playing the same role the princes once played. Pretending allegiance to a pirate to steal his secrets," she said.

Ben hesitated and she smiled. While the Commonwealth was growing and becoming more popular, a sign of their instability was the fact that they were unable to go public. If Ben was exposed now as the leader of the group, everything they'd work so hard for would be gone in an instant.

"Now we're one for one," said Larkin. "Let's see who can get two for two first."

"You think you're smart, but anyone who meddles with Barren Reed is ruined. Even if you were to go back and reclaim your spot beside your father, you would never be looked upon the same way."

"I'm not worried about falling into ruin."

"You think that now," he said. "You've no idea what it's like… to be rejected by society."

She raised a brow. "And you do?"

They glared at each other in silence.

"Two weeks," he said at last. "You have two weeks."

"Or what?"

Ben smiled, and her skin crawled. He was poison. "There's more to me than meets the eye, Lady. Bring me that compass in two weeks or I'll wage my own war against the pirates. I'll start with Silver Crest. I'll burn every building down. I'll kill every man, every woman, every child. Do you understand?"

She started at him. She wanted to believe this was an empty threat, but she knew it wasn't. It was part of the Commonwealth's goal to eradicate pirates.

"I said, do you understand?" he gritted out.

"Yes," she breathed, her gaze did not waiver.

"Good."

She turned to leave, but Ben stopped her. "Have you asked your lover about Éire?"

She did not respond.

"Make him tell you," he said. "It is important."

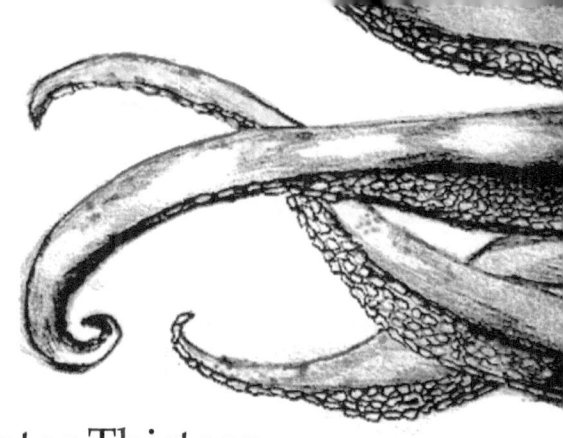

Chapter Thirteen
GRAPPLE

Barren had walked all the way to the courthouse, fighting with himself about hurrying back to Cove's mansion and locking himself in a room somewhere. He knew what he has about to do was a horrible idea, but the things he'd learned in the meeting with the Network were too troublesome. He couldn't let Aethea Moore get beyond his reach. He was going to have to free her. He couldn't bring himself to say rescue, because it was hardly that. It was more of a kidnapping. And as it turned out, he wasn't so good at those. But he needed her. She was the link to the bullets, to the magic. Cove was silly to think he could wait for the Network when it was obvious that Tetherion and Datherious were not idle.

Barren watched them from the shadows. A black carriage sat at the end of a wide staircase leading into the courthouse, an ominous building that rose into the night. Lanterns highlighted statues that looked like monsters, and Barren found it ironic that this would be their hall for justice. If there was anything he'd learned about politicians, it was that they were all about the show.

There were two guards standing at the door of the carriage and an additional man who would drive the carriage to the port. That meant he'd have to eliminate at least three people to get Aethea into his possession. Barren sighed. This couldn't be simple.

Barren watched as two men brought Aethea out of the courthouse. She wore the same clothes she'd changed into at the ball. Her hands were bound in front of her, a terrible mistake on the part of her captors considering she was an assassin. They probably felt her harmless because she was a woman. Barren knew their logic. She'd tried to use a gun to kill the king and couldn't even hit him. It would be their downfall.

The men shoved Aethea into the carriage and settled in after her. Damn. That made a total of five men he'd have to take down. He groaned inwardly. He had a decision to make. Did he kill them? Or did he leave them unconscious to wake and speak of what they'd seen? It wasn't like they had his best interest in mind. Then again, he shouldn't even be doing this. And when he was found out, he'd be in trouble with everyone, not just Larkin.

The carriage was off and Barren pulled his dagger from his boot, cursing as he hurried along. He kept telling himself he had to do this—for Cove, for his brethren.

The carriage bounced as it rolled down the road. He kept within the woods surrounding the courthouse at first, tripping over foliage and dodging limbs as he went. The two guards who had stood outside the doors hung onto the back of the carriage, riding along. They were the most vulnerable and would be the easiest to take out. He turned and looked back, taking care to see that no one was watching, but also that the courthouse was far enough away that no one noticed the carriage holding their prisoner had been attacked.

The carriage bumbled around on the wild roads leading to the port. Barren pulled his hood over his head and made his move as the carriage turned a wide corner and was finally out of view of the courthouse.

He jumped, latching onto the back of the carriage. The two guards on either side hadn't been prepared for someone to actually try to free their captor. With one hand clinging to the carriage, they tried to draw their weapons, but Barren moved fast. Kicking the one on the right, he sent the guard tumbling to the ground as the carriage kept moving forward. The other managed to draw his gun.

Damn.

Barren had to move fast. His fingers hurt from holding onto the carriage so tightly, but he was able to jump up and kick the man free of the carriage before he could fire his weapon. Barren swung for a moment, his boots dragging against the ground as he tried to regain his footing on the rungs. His next course of action would have to be quick because the men inside the carriage with the prisoner would know something was wrong, and the ones behind him would hurry to catch up.

Barren lifted himself up and sprung into the carriage driver's seat. He hit the driver on the head with the hilt of his blade, knocking him unconscious. Barren pushed him aside and took the reins, halting the horses. He was surprised, however, to hear nothing from inside the carriage. He hopped down from the driver's seat and approached the carriage door carefully, blade drawn, when suddenly, it was kicked open.

One of the soldiers who'd climbed in with the prisoner fell out onto the ground, dead. After him came Aethea Moore. Her hands were still cuffed before her.

"Did you strangle him?" Barren asked, meeting her gaze. Her eyes seemed alight with a vitality he didn't find inviting.

"They practically put the weapon in my hands," she said, smiling.

"And the other man?" Barren tried to peer behind her. "Two guards entered the carriage with you."

"I wouldn't look if I were you," she said. "His demise was much more…brutal."

Barren just stared at her.

"Oh, don't look so stunned, Barren Reed. I had a decision to make. I either kill them both, or let one keep me as a hostage."

"What makes you think I'm not taking you hostage?"

The woman smirked. "Better in your care than theirs."

Barren shuddered. He most certainly wasn't going to be taking care of her.

A gunshot rang out and Barren and Aethea turned to find that the soldiers Barren had thrown off the carriage were on their feet again, hurrying toward them.

"You didn't kill them?" she seethed.

"It's not as easy as you think!"

She glared at him and then turned toward the soldiers, putting up her hand in surrender. "Please don't hurt me," she whined, walking toward them. One soldier kept his gun pointed at Barren as the other went to take Aethea into custody. Barren wasn't sure what was happening here. Was Aethea walking right back into her captors' hands? Did she intend to have Barren captured? His hand tightened on his knife.

As the soldier reached for Aethea, she made her move. Using her shackles as weapons once again, she slammed them into the hands of the soldier who held the gun. He dropped his weapon, and Aethea turned to hit the other soldier across the face. They were both on the ground now and Barren hurried forward, knowing she would kill if given the chance. Enough damage had been done here in this moment without more murder. He had to get the assassin sheltered, and the only place he knew to do that was Cove's mansion. It was big and it was dark. He just hoped there were no eyes on it this evening.

He grabbed her arm, pulling her away from the fallen soldiers. "Into the woods!"

Surprisingly, she didn't protest and the two ran into the growth, allowing it to swallow them whole. They didn't stop running for what seemed like an eternity. It wasn't until Barren could no longer draw breath into his pained lungs that he halted.

Behind him, he heard the scrutinizing voice of his prisoner.

"You couldn't even kill those soldiers," she said. "What's so great about you?"

"Because I have killed, nothing is great about me," he said drawing in a breath.

She almost choked on laughter, taking in deep breaths as she moved about the small space where they stood. "And is it because of that girl that you suddenly changed your ways? Larkin Lee—is that her name? Has she reformed you?" She was mocking him and Barren glared at her. "So it is *her*!"

Silence followed and Barren started to look about, attempting to get his bearings straight so he could get to Cove's house quickly.

"So where are you taking me?"

"Somewhere we can hide," he said.

"Am I so important to you that you would risk your life for me?"

"I don't think you're important, but what you know might be."

"You realize I do not offer knowledge freely."

"You don't," Barren said. "But you will."

"Last I recall, I was the one with the advantage."

Barren turned to face her completely. "Yes, leverage, as you called it. Where is my compass? Give it to me!" He extended his hand as he stepped forward, but Aethea just laughed.

"You think I have anything I was arrested with? Your compass was confiscated. It's in Tetherion's hands now."

Barren's face fell, but his disappointment quickly turned to anger.

"There it is. That rage so unique to you," Aethea said, and her eyes gleamed with delight. She seemed to want to bring the worst out in him. He scowled.

"So much for your leverage," he spat, turning from her.

Aethea laughed, truly humored, and the sound echoed throughout the woods. "I got exactly what I intended."

Barren might have turned then to end her life, but a rustling sound caught his attention.

"Shh!" he commanded, and he heard the rustling again. He moved behind a tree, and peered out into the woods. The rustling was growing louder. Someone was running. He rushed out from behind the tree and tackled the cloaked figure, assuming it was one of the guards from the carriage.

What he got was much different.

He rolled with the body and found that it was soft and lithe. A woman. She was fiery and angry, and once she was on top, she reared her head back and hit Barren in the face. She rolled off him and stood, picking up his sword before his name spilled from her mouth.

"Barren?"

It was Larkin.

His head pounded from the blow to his face, and he felt blood gushing from his nose. He got to his feet.

"Larkin? What the hell are you doing here?"

"I should ask you the same!"

"Well, this is amusing," Aethea's voice joined the mix, and Barren knew Larkin was cutting Aethea up piece by piece with her eyes.

"Why is *she* here?" Larkin demanded.

"Yes, Barren, tell her why I'm here," Aethea joined in.

"I don't have time to explain!" he said. "Let's go."

Barren grabbed his sword from Larkin's hand before she could use it against him and moved toward Aethea. "Go," he commanded and she did, walking along steadily through the dead leaves. The whole way back to Cove's house, he felt Larkin's eyes burning into him. He looked back periodically to make sure she was still there. For some reason, he worried she might disappear. He knew he had to explain, but so did she. What was she doing in the woods in the middle of the night?

Barren finally managed to get Aethea into the stables, but once he was there, he wasn't sure what to do with her.

"Get down," he said.

"You expect me to wait here?" she asked.

"Yes," said Larkin, and without another word, she hit Aethea over the head with the hilt of her blade.

"Why did you do that?" Barren demanded in a hushed tone.

"You weren't going to do it!" she replied fiercely. "Besides, I might not have a chance to do it again."

They glared at each other for a long moment. "Stay with her. I'll go get Cove," he said and left.

None of this felt right, and his heart raced. He'd made enemies of all his friends tonight.

As soon as Barren entered the house, Cove and Hollow turned to face him. Barren wasn't sure how long the ambassador had been home, but when they looked at him, they were not happy.

"Where have you been?"

The pirate hesitated, preparing himself for what was next, but a harsh knock on the door interrupted him.

Cove set his jaw, and his eyes grew dark with accusation. "What did you do?" he asked evenly.

Barren didn't say anything and the knock sounded again. Hollow was already rushing upstairs to tell the others to hide.

Cove glared at Barren. It was the angriest he'd ever seen the ambassador, and when Cove spoke, the words slipped between his teeth.

"Hide. Immediately!"

And Barren did. He hurried down the stairwell and into the basement.

**

Cove stepped toward the entrance and stretched out his hand. He let air fill his lungs as he opened the door and found Ben on the other side, surrounded by soldiers. He released his breath.

"Ambassador," Ben stood silhouetted in his doorway. He appeared slightly disheveled and Cove wondered at the gash across his face. It appeared fresh. "What I have to tell you might require a seat, ambassador."

"I'm not faint of heart, Ben," Cove replied evenly. "And it doesn't take an army to offer me news."

Ben chuckled humorlessly. "These men are here to search your house. The assassin, Aethea Moore, has escaped our custody."

"Escaped?"

"Perhaps I should rephrase. They believe the assassin was helped. Three of the men who were knocked unconscious say someone attacked them. Two others are dead. Now, if you will be so kind as to let my men do their job," Ben said.

"Surely you do not think I would harbor an assassin," the words escaped Cove's mouth as a hiss.

"I would not accuse you of such treason, ambassador. But a scoundrel will hide anywhere he feels safe."

Cove raised his head and smirked, then he stepped away from his door and allowed the men entrance.

"Go ahead," he said. "Search."

"Check the basement," Ben ordered.

Cove stood aside, hands behind his back as the soldiers' boots thudded against his floor. Ben walked about the foyer, observing its finery. "I heard you inherited this house after your father died. Tragic that you would come into such wealth at the expense of his death."

Cove's jaw tightened.

"Tell me, ambassador. What do you make of this?"

Ben held up a thin piece of rope. It had once been white, but now it was frayed and dirty.

Cove laughed. "You cannot be serious. It's rope."

"Odd that when we found the assassin, she was already tied up, don't you think? To my knowledge there is one man who uses this rope to tie his victims."

Cove looked perplexed.

"Come now, ambassador, don't play dumb with me," Ben warned.

Cove's eyes narrowed. "I assure you, Mr. Willow, I would not do you dishonor."

"Barren Reed!" Ben said through his teeth. "It is a known fact that Barren Reed carries rope to bind his victims before the kill. Do you think it feasible that he was at the ball? And why would he tie up the assassin who was to kill his uncle, the man who tried to hang him?"

There was silence, and then Cove began to laugh. By this time, Ben's soldiers had returned from their search of the basement empty-handed. "You have wild theories, Mr. Willow, but it would have been impossible for Barren to infiltrate my ball."

"Unless you let him in," Ben accused.

"Oh yes. Unless I let him in," Cove said drily. "Lord Willow, let me advise you that the next time we have an escaped assassin on our hands, do not call upon me to suggest I'm in league with the enemy. There are far more important concerns at hand."

Cove opened his door. "Leave," he commanded.

Ben took a step toward Cove, and the ambassador felt his blood boil. "You keep your dirty secret for now. I'm on to you."

Ben stormed out of Cove's house, and the soldiers followed, sending apologetic looks Cove's way as they went. When they were safely outside, Cove slammed his door shut.

"Hollow!" he called.

The senator raced down the stairs. "See that Ben's men do not linger on my property, and send for Jonas and the others."

The senator nodded and left the house. Cove turned with deliberate steps toward the basement. The place was a mess. The soldiers had wasted no time searching behind things and throwing boxes about, but they'd never noticed the floor. Cove threw the debris aside and pulled open the latch on the tunnel door. He barely waited for Barren to climb out before he attacked.

"You helped her escape?" Cove's words were biting and he pushed the young pirate.

"Cove…" Barren tried to speak, but the Ambassador silenced him, placing a finger square in his face, grabbing his collar.

"Did you kill those men?"

"What do you think?" Barren glared at Cove and the Ambassador let go of him roughly. "They cuffed her hands in front of her."

"Where is she?"

"In the stables."

Cove ran his fingers through his hair and sighed angrily. "This was stupid, Barren!"

"I did what I had to do!"

"You did what you wanted to do!" Cove countered. "This is my realm, Barren. You don't get to make the decisions. I cannot undo what you've done."

Chapter Fourteen
CONSEQUENCES

Barren was silent. His throat worked. Words came back to him from the trial. Words that felt very heavy. *There are people who feel the repercussions of your choices.* He had known this, but when faced with the choice to allow their one lead to escape their grasp, to return to Maris and face the noose or to free her, he'd chosen the former, which meant Cove was left to deal with Barren's mess.

He felt invisible as he watched Cove. His eyes were dark, and a heat touched his skin that made Barren very aware of his anger. He gave orders and directed men to join the hunt for the escapee. They were still acting their part. Others were to find a way to get Aethea into the house. But it was the last order Cove gave that hit Barren hardest.

"And his ship. Burn it."

And as he said it, he looked directly at Barren.

"Burn my ship?" he wanted to be angry. Anger touched his words, but he knew he had no right, and Cove didn't really owe

Barren an explanation for his actions.

"It will be searched if it isn't destroyed," said Cove. Suddenly Barren understood what he'd heard the day he arrived in Arcarum. Leaf had overheard Hollow talking about vandalism at port. It had been a cover, an act. Something they could blame when the need for it arose.

When Cove's men had left to carry out his orders, the Ambassador came from around his desk. He ensured the doors to his study were closed, and he turned to Barren.

"What's done is done," he said, but Barren could hear the way Cove fought for control of his voice. "But I need you to know that I don't understand why you couldn't trust me."

"I..."

"*Don't* tell me you trust me," the ambassador interrupted him. His voice was a command. "Because if you had, you wouldn't have done this. I know your reasoning. You probably felt there was no other way. But there was. You had me. Of all the people who could have...manipulated this situation to our benefit!" He shook his head. "But you just refused to see it."

"But how long would it have taken you to 'manipulate this situation' as you say?" Barren asked. "After she's dead? She was to be hanged at dawn!"

"I had men prepared to ambush the ship and kidnap her. I asked you to trust me."

"Why couldn't you have told me?" Barren demanded. "Did you not trust me?"

"I do not broadcast my actions," Cove countered. "It's better that way, things don't go awry. But obviously I was wrong this time."

Barren opened his mouth to speak. He wanted to say he was sorry. But he also felt it was better that he didn't speak.

"I'm not sure you ever understand that you aren't alone," said Cove, and his voice quaked with anger. "But let me remind you that none of your problems are worth a life lost."

The ambassador turned from him at that moment. "They will take Aethea to the tunnel. We'll keep her underground, interrogate her, and proceed from there."

Barren nodded, and then looked directly at the ambassador. "Cove, I am...sorry for this."

"Perhaps you are," he said.

***

Barren, Cove, and Leaf made their way downstairs into the basement. Cove opened the door that led into the tunnel from the sea cliffs. His men were there waiting, and they helped lower Aethea into the tunnel. Her arms, feet, and mouth were bound. They carried her all the way from the end of the tunnel to the basement area. Once there, they placed her in a chair and bound her to it.

Leaf stepped forward and withdrew a knife at his belt. Aethea's eyes glinted. He cut the gag from her mouth, and she breathed heavily once she was free. Holders were attached to her thighs where guns and knives had been. Her hair was tangled around her face, and her eyes smeared with black. Barren found himself comparing her to Larkin in his head. They'd both been hostile, they'd both wanted to fight. While Larkin was fire, Aethea was ice.

"So what now?" she said. Her accent was thick, clipped. "You kill me?"

"We don't plan to kill you," said Cove.

"If I cooperate," she clarified.

"Well, that's only fair," said Barren.

She glared at him, and then at Cove. The way she looked at him, the way she talked—she was disgusted.

"Did Datherious hire you to kill the king?" Cove asked directly.

"Among other things," she said.

"And how did he find you?" asked Barren.

She smiled wickedly. "Through a partner."

Barren and Cove exchanged a glance.

"You are from the Octent. Why would you join a cause for the Commonwealth?" asked Cove.

"Because I have been a slave," she said between her teeth.

"But you are free now," said Barren. "And yet you chose to pledge to an organization that kills the freest people in Mariana?"

"You are free because you do not obey the law," she said. "But you have no idea what it is to be a slave, and you have nothing to fight for. That is why you steal and kill."

"I'm not really seeing any difference between you and me," said Barren. "Except that you have a weapon that I do not." She just stared. "Where did you get them? Where did the bullets come from?"

She had a smirk on her face, and then she laughed. "Men," she said. "You think I'll kneel before you? Spill all my secrets because you have a little muscle? Please. You'll have to try harder."

"I don't understand you," said Cove, narrowing his eyes. "You admitted to killing five of our men with those bullets. You turned the other three over to Tetherion. Perhaps to deceive him? And not three days later, you're the woman who tried to kill him with those same bullets. Why?"

"Tetherion is a madman," she said evenly. "You know he seeks dark magic to ensure his throne, and if he does get it, he'll destroy himself and everyone in the Orient."

Cove narrowed his eyes. "I'm not so certain that you don't want that."

"What sort of magic does Tetherion seek?" asked Barren. "The bloodstone has been destroyed, unless he seeks to use your weapons to gain power."

Aethea laughed. "Tetherion is not yet privy to my weapon of choice. But I thought you smarter, Barren Reed. If the bullets exist, it should be obvious to you that there is other magic for Tetherion to claim. Rumor has it he's in search of the King's Gold. It's said to be a channel through which mortals can wield magic. He already has one of the five pieces."

Barren thought of that jewel around Tetherion's neck. Had that been the King's Gold?

"And how did he come by that?"

Aethea shrugged one slender shoulder. "Shortly after Lord

Alder's visit, I am sure."

"My father? He would give nothing of power over to Tetherion," Leaf argued.

"Not willingly," she said. "But he must satisfy the Elfin treaty so that he may keep his throne. You destroyed the bloodstone. Alder had no choice but to replace it."

So Lord Alder had an alternate motive for keeping Barren from the bloodstone.

Why would he give something so powerful to Tetherion? His mother and father had hidden the bloodstone to keep Tetherion from coming into that sort of power. Perhaps Lord Alder was merely trying to bide his time. He had only given over one piece. There were four more, but where were they? And was Lord Alder planning to hand those over, too?

"Do you know where he's searching?"

She shrugged her shoulders. "There's only one place I know to get dark things," she said. "That's the Underground. And there's only one dealer in the Underground who will handle dark magic. No one else is brave enough."

The Underground made Barren uneasy. He and Leaf had a past in the market, one he'd prefer to keep secret. He met the Elf's gaze and knew Leaf felt the same way.

"Did he give you the weapons?" asked Cove.

"She gives nothing away," Aethea spat. "I bought them."

"She?"

"Yes, *she* goes by the name Sabine."

"And how does she come by these…weapons?"

Aethea shrugged. "How does anyone come by anything in the Underground? Things are stolen, things are traded."

"Can you take us to her?"

"A visit from the Ambassador of Arcarum won't win me any favors," she said.

"What about a visit from Barren Reed?"

"You're not asking the most important question," said Aethea, and the smirk on her face made Barren's stomach clench. "Don't you want to know where she is?"

The Underground was much like the Network. There were dealers spread all over Mariana. There was no limit to its geography, no limit to what it could provide. The only difference was the Underground dealt with illegal goods. "She is in Aryndel."

Barren knew his face drained of color. Aryndel was out of the question. Barren would never ask Leaf to relive that part of his life. Where Fira, his love, had died in his arms, stabbed to death by filthy men. After that, Leaf had let himself be taken to Estrellas where he was imprisoned. What horrors he faced there, Barren had never heard, but for some reason, he didn't imagine it was anywhere near the pain he'd felt losing Fira.

"No," said Barren. "We can't go there. We won't go there."

"You seem to perceive correctly that it is not safe," she said. "Take some comfort in knowing that you'll hardly stand out. You'll be among others who are sinners just like you."

"I will not take my crew there," said Barren. "Bring this Sabine here."

"Bring her here? To Arcarum? I highly doubt my supplier will accept an invitation to the ambassador's mansion."

"And I could not risk her here," said Cove. "You've all overstayed your welcome."

It didn't feel right. Going to Conn where his father had died had been hard for him. He couldn't imagine Leaf's grief. Or the thought of forcing him to relive Fira's death. The Elf was so quiet about his past. He bottled things up tight. Would a visit to Aryndel merely set him off? Barren didn't want to find out.

"If the supplier is selling the weapons or this *King's Gold*, she must be stopped," this time it was Leaf who spoke. "We will go to Aryndel."

Barren turned on the Elf. "No, Leaf"

He smiled at the pirate, and Barren could tell something had changed in the Elf's eyes. They burned with both grief and fury.

"We'll go," he said evenly.

And Barren didn't argue.

"Very well," said Cove. "I will make arrangements." He looked at Aethea pointedly. "Need I remind you, if you lead us astray, you will pay the price?"

"You threaten death as if you think I fear it."

"I'm not threatening a peaceful death," he said. "If you betray us, I'll ensure you die the same death my brethren did."

She glared at him, her lips thin. They turned their backs to her and left.

***

It was late, but there was light under Cove's study door, so she knocked. There was a pause and then he opened the door. He was still pale, but his eyes were lively.

"Larkin," he said and bid her to enter.

The room was empty and warm. She turned to face him and he closed the door.

"He wants the compass in two weeks," she said. "What can I do?"

"I've recently learned Barren is no longer in possession of the compass," said Cove. "Aethea Moore took it from him at the ball and it was confiscated. It is now in Tetherion's possession."

Now what would she do? Barren had not told her this, though there had not been time. She hadn't seen him since their encounter in the woods.

"What am I to do now?"

"The only thing you can do," said Cove. "Go to Maris."

Larkin's eyes widened. "But that would mean betraying Barren. And what would I do there? Take back the compass just to offer it to Ben?"

"Barren must think you've betrayed him in order for this to work," said Cove. "Go to Maris where you have stronger ties. Reestablish yourself as a noblewoman among your family, and discover why this compass is so important."

"Returning to Maris is not so simple," she said. Though she'd told Ben otherwise, he had been right. No one would believe her, least of all the twins and the king.

"It will be," said Cove. "Your father has left the door wide open for you. All you must do to gain Tetherion's trust is return with some secret that benefits him. Something that shows your loyalty to the crown."

"And what could I offer that would not destroy everything I have with Barren?" she asked.

"Nothing." Cove's honesty was brutal, and she felt the blow. "But you must consider that a position such as yours, within so close a range to the king, within range of your father, benefits us greatly. We would know the king's plans and perhaps your father has more information on these weapons."

"Do you mean it would benefit *you* greatly?"

"You can choose to see it any way you like," he said. "I'm not forcing you to choose this path."

"I thought you had men in Maris," she said.

"I do," he said. "But none of them can get as close to your father as you."

It was strange to find Cove so matter-of-fact. There were no emotions involved in his plans. He thought only of the practical need to make connections, to make decisions, to gain an advantage, and Larkin found it unsettling. She couldn't think in these terms because the only thing running through her mind was how wrong this was.

"Of all people, my father will know I've lied," she said.

"It won't keep him from sharing with you," said Cove. "He will want you to know their plans. It will be your punishment."

"You aren't making this easy, you know," Larkin said curtly.

Cove smiled slightly. "It's better to be realistic with you," he said. "At least you will not walk into it blindly."

She supposed that was true. "Barren has told you of the brutality of the world at sea, but let me assure you this is no different. Perhaps that's why I'm so good at it. These people will lie, cheat and steal to get what they want. They will kill you if the need arises. But the most important part of all of it is that we are no different."

Larkin set her jaw. "And when do you suppose I should leave?"

Cove shrugged. "You will know when it is time."

Would she? She couldn't imagine what might urge her return to Maris, but perhaps the division she'd felt between her and Barren over the last weeks was a sign that her time at sea was coming to an end.

The thought made her ill.

***

Barren opened the door to silence and darkness. He found Larkin standing before the balcony doors, arms crossed over her chest, hip leaning against one side. Part of him had hoped she wouldn't try to argue with him tonight, but he knew that was impossible. They both had things to answer for.

She didn't turn to face him. He walked to the middle of the room, the thud of his boots echoing in the dark.

"Well?" Barren asked, waiting for her attack, but it didn't come. She turned her head and looked at him.

"What?" she asked quietly, as if she were exhausted. Had she been crying?

"You're not going to yell at me?" he asked. "Tell me what a

big mistake I made?"

She stared at him for a moment and then turned back to the window. She was staring at nothing. The curtains were drawn.

"I don't know what to say," her voice was still quiet, strained.

Barren sighed, running his fingers through his hair.

"Look, I know I made a bad decision, but I couldn't let her hang in Maris when we have no answers," said Barren. "It was either that or Cove continues to live with this…thing…corrupting him!"

"I know," she said.

"What?" Why was there no resistance, no argument? This wasn't like Larkin. She would tell him how selfish he'd been, how stupid he'd been.

"You did what you believed you had to do," she said.

"Is that what you truly believe?" he asked her.

She didn't respond, and she didn't look at him. Was she resigned to let him suffer in the silence? Surely this was worse than arguing.

"Larkin," he said quietly. "Why were you in the woods?"

She looked at him, tears brimming in her eyes. "I did what I had to do."

Barren didn't know what that meant, but she leaned in and kissed him. She tasted of tears. He wanted to resist, to pull away and demand answers, but need ignited deep in his belly, and he wanted this, more than he wanted to fight.

Barren gripped her shoulders and pulled her to him, closing the space between them. She was warm. Her hands scorched his skin as they moved down his arms and under his shirt. He held her tighter, fingers twisting into her hair. He broke the kiss, breathing raggedly. Everything within him told him to kiss her again.

He watched her open her eyes, hooded with desire. "Please," she said, "I just want one last night together."

He couldn't figure out what she meant or even think at all. He scooped her into his arms and carried her to the bed. She kept her arms wrapped tightly around his neck, pressing herself against him, reminding him that she was there. He set her down and their eyes met. Larkin pulled him to her, and he kissed her eagerly, deeply, consumed by her essence. There was nothing else in this world he wanted more than her, but this was not happening now. He'd made a promise to himself and to Larkin. Things would be different, and under these circumstances, with the secrets he knew were between them, he couldn't go through with this.

He tore away from the kiss, and stood. "No!" He said. Larkin stared at him, stunned. "I won't make this mistake."

"Mistake?" Larkin's voice was a quiet whisper.

He left the room quickly. It was the only way he would stick to his promise.

Chapter Fifteen
STOWAWAY

They were up before dawn broke. Cove had to make sure Barren, his crew, and the assassin made it to the ship unseen. Once the sun rose, Cove and his crew began preparing the supplies. The scorched remains of Barren's ship still floated in the water from the fire the previous night. Cove's ships had not escaped the blaze. Two of them were charred from flames that had been farther reaching. Ships at the main port of Arcarum had been burned, too. There was a common belief that the ships had been vandalized to keep the assassin from escaping Arcarum shores. That worked well enough for Cove.

Surprisingly, the ambassador had been able to convince Matthew to let him leave. He'd had to tell him about the weapons, and he was given a time limit. Two weeks. Two weeks to figure out where the weapons were coming from before he had to be back in Arcarum. The sea didn't work well with timelines, but he couldn't argue with Matthew on this. He owed it to him.

There was another part of the agreement Hollow hadn't been

too fond of. Cove was the only one who could go. With Hollow and the others running for elections in Arcarum, they would need to stay to keep up appearances, and most importantly, watch Ben Willow.

"Cove!" he heard his name being called in the distance and froze. Turning, he saw Sara running toward him. Her dress flared wildly behind her, and her hat flew off her head, the ribbon pulled tight at her neck.

Cove dropped the crate he was carrying and moved toward her. He felt awkward—sweaty and shirtless. It was not appropriate for her to see him this way, but part of him didn't care. He was about to embark on a journey that was uncertain. He was going to lie to her again. He would leave her behind with her fiancé, and when he returned, she would be married.

"What are you doing?" she breathed harshly.

Cove sort of laughed. "I'm loading my ship."

"For what?"

He stared at her in silence.

"You're leaving again," she accused. There was a blush to her cheeks, and a strange anger to her eyes he wasn't used to seeing. "But you just got back!"

"This is my life, Sara," he gestured toward the ship that sat so gallantly at port, waiting. "I leave and I come back."

"No, no, this isn't your life! You're different. You've changed!"

"How? Because I won't tell you everywhere I go?" Anger sharpened his words. "I'm sorry, Sara, but I don't owe you that. I'm not your husband."

For a moment, he wasn't sure what she was going to do as hurt and anger flitted through her eyes. It manifested into a stinging slap against his cheek. He kept his head turned from her as he processed what had happened. Then she backed away slowly before turning and running.

"Sara!" he called, but she just kept going. He twisted his hair around his fingers and growled. "Dammit!"

Any other time he'd have run after her, but not now. There were witnesses, she was engaged. She'd made her choice and so had he. He was going to disappoint her.

Cove and his crew finished loading the ship, and when they set sail, he watched as Arcarum faded in the distance, knowing that upon his return, nothing would be the same.

***

Larkin sat on a bed in a small apartment below deck. The stillness was strange after she'd grown used to the sway and swing of a hammock slung from the rafters. On a normal day after having been inland for so long, she would be on deck, climbing the masts to get a better view of the ocean, but this was not a normal day. So much had changed since she'd arrived in Arcarum.

She hadn't spoken to Barren since last night. She'd barely looked at him. She was both embarrassed and angry. She had wanted one night before things were never the same again, but he'd called it a mistake.

A mistake.

He'd used that word before, when he'd made the decision to

kidnap her from her home to lure his brother to sea. She'd been more than he bargained for. She'd tested his limits and his boundaries. He'd failed every time, except last night. He'd had enough strength to turn away.

She was partly to blame for this. Barren knew she was keeping secrets, and he'd begun to build his wall the moment she'd inquired about Éire. She also knew that if she was going to follow through with the plans she'd made with Cove, she was going to have to start building her wall or leaving would prove to be impossible.

Something clattered to the ground outside her apartment. She looked in the direction of the noise and stood slowly, moving into the main part of the hold. It was not unusual for rats to be aboard the ship or for other crewmen to move about making racket, but it had been so quiet before.

She watched and heard nothing, but she caught movement to her right where a row of barrels lined the hull wall. She moved in that direction and almost jumped out of her skin. A familiar young girl recoiled from her.

"Shh!" Sara tried to hush her, rising to her feet, and then she halted. "Larkin?" she squinted her eyes as if she were seeing wrong, and Larkin sort of felt sorry for her. She's stowed away on Cove's ship only to find Larkin below deck. Things obviously weren't adding up in her head.

"What are you doing here?" Larkin asked.

"What are *you* doing here?" Sara challenged.

Larkin twisted, looking to see if anyone had noticed them yet.

She took Sara's arm. "Come with me."

Larkin guided Sara into the apartment and turned to close the curtain that served as a makeshift door, not surprised that Sara stood still, staring at her surroundings. She was probably shocked and disgusted all at the same time.

"You are going to want to sit down," Larkin said.

Sara turned to face her, but did not sit down. Her cheeks were flushed.

"Does he leave for you?" she asked in confusion. "Does he love you?"

Larkin had to laugh. If only she knew the truth. And she would soon. "No, Cove does not love me."

"Did he...rescue you? Are we on our way to Maris to return you to your father?"

Larkin just stared at her. How was she supposed to start? *I was kidnapped but I decided to stay. There's just a lot you wouldn't understand.*

There was still a lot Larkin didn't even understand.

"I just..." she paused. "Just wait here and do not make a sound, understand?"

"Wait!" she called as Larkin made it to the makeshift door. She turned and glared at the girl fiercely.

"What did I say about being quiet?"

"You won't tell him I am here, will you?"

"You can't expect me to keep you a secret," said Larkin. "That's hardly possible."

She bit her lip nervously. "Can ... can you just wait one more day? Until we're farther from Arcarum? Please?"

Larkin stared at her for a moment. "Yes. I will wait."

Then she left. She wasn't sure why she'd agreed to that request. There was a chance she couldn't keep the secret. Or that Sara would expose herself. But she had a feeling that the reason behind the request wasn't so much that the girl wanted to be here with Cove, but that she wanted to be far away from Arcarum, and Larkin could empathize.

She stepped out on deck, and the sun was bright. There was such a familiarity to the experience—the sound of the sea, the sway of the ship, the smell of salt water. She looked about as everyone settled into their roles once again with Sam at the helm, Slay lounging in the crow's nest, Seamus inspecting artillery, Barren and Cove discussing their plans. It was strange to realize that they all had a title, some sort of job they had to carry out to be a part of the crew, but she did not. It was like Barren couldn't quite figure out what to do with her or perhaps he viewed her differently. But she'd be damned if she remained some sort of figurehead. She'd asked to be a part of the crew, and that came with certain expectations. Like fighting in battle. The role Cove had given her, while difficult, at least gave her purpose.

She scanned the area again, and her eyes settled on the water canteens. She moved toward them. Maybe she could steal some bread from the kitchen. She would make sure Sara had what she needed until she could walk openly on deck.

For a brief moment, Barren's gaze met hers, and there was something there she'd seen often when he looked at her over the past few days. Distance and longing and anger. He wasn't good at controlling his features, not when it came to her, but maybe he wanted her to know exactly how he felt. She found herself wondering if it would hurt less if he hid it.

She reached the canteens when the scream escaped from below deck, and her heart fell into her stomach. *Well, that didn't take long.* She immediately turned to the hatch.

"What the hell was that?" Barren demanded.

Larkin hurried for the hatch. "Nothing...someone probably fell!" she called.

"That was a woman's voice," said Cove, following close behind.

"It was probably the assassin," Larkin said. "I will check."

She came down the steps and ran into Sara who was running toward them. So much for hiding her.

"I can't stay here! There are rats!" she squeaked.

Larkin let her breath escape between her teeth in irritation, but she didn't have long to be angry because Barren and Cove stopped behind her. She could just imagine what this looked like.

"What is she doing here?" Barren demanded. The anger in his voice made Larkin's ears ring. She knew what he was thinking: another secret she'd kept from him.

"I'd like to know the same thing," Cove said and Larkin and Barren flattened themselves against the wall as the ambassador passed.

Larkin could feel Barren's eyes on her, demanding an explanation, but she didn't meet his gaze.

"What are you doing here?" Sara demanded immediately. "You're on a ship with Barren Reed!"

"Do you realize what you've done?" Cove ignored her question. "Ben probably thinks you've been kidnapped, and everyone else will think you've run away with me. What were you thinking?"

"I wanted to know why you'd changed! I guess I have the answer."

Cove just stared at her. Then he shook his head and turned, moving up the steps and returning to deck.

"Turn around, Sam! Go back to Arcarum!" Cove commanded as he came on deck.

"No, Cove! You can't!"

"What? Will Ben ground you? What's a few days in your room to think about what you've done?"

Sara glared at him and then slapped him. "I am not a child! And if you were any sort of friend, you would not speak to me like that!"

"What you've done is childish, Sara! You have to go back."

"No," she crossed her arms. "Not until you tell me what you're doing here."

"Isn't it obvious?"

She spoke through her teeth. "I want you to say it. Tell me the rumors are true. You sail as a pirate. You've sworn an oath to the pirates of Silver Crest."

"Yes," he said, and moved the collar of his shirt to expose the 'X'. "I swore to them. I uphold their code. Now that you know, you can go back and tell your fiancé the truth he's been looking for."

"You think that's why I want to know?" she scoffed, shaking her head.

"Someone pull them apart. I'm tired! They're worse than Barren and Larkin on a *good* day!" Leaf cut in, covering his ears.

"If she goes back, there's a chance she will expose you," said Barren. "Can you trust her to keep your secret?"

Sara glared at both of them. "I will not promise anything."

"She wouldn't hurt me like that," he said. Cove did believe that Ben had gotten closer to Sara to gain more information on Cove, but he didn't believe Sara would actually talk.

"But Ben would," said Larkin. "He might hurt her to get answers. I believe that. Maybe Sara does, too."

Sara said nothing in agreement, and suddenly she was quiet again. The fierceness and the anger that fueled her words had dried up.

"Would you risk it, Cove?" Barren asked.

Larkin watched as Barren suddenly became the mediator of this argument. He never did this when he argued with her.

Cove looked at Barren. "You could be blamed for this," he said. "And you can't make another mistake or the Elders will exile you."

"That's not a real answer," said Barren. "Besides, my stunt with the assassin has probably ensured I have no place among the Silver Crest pirates now."

Cove sighed, pulling at his hair. "What if she's hurt out here?"

"I'll watch her," Larkin said.

Cove scowled and looked at Sara. "We're leaving for two weeks, but you go back with me," he said. "God knows what I'll return to with you missing."

"Help her get settled, Larkin," Barren said.

They exchanged looks, and she knew he wanted to ask how long she'd planned on keeping this from him. Larkin took Sara's arm and guided her back to the hatch, bringing the water canteen with her. They returned to her apartment below deck.

"You can sleep on the bed," she said, reaching under the bunk and pulling out blankets to tie to the rafters. She'd make herself a hammock. It was better than the hard floor.

"I thought you were at the ball," Sara said at last. "I remembered seeing your eyes and thinking they were familiar."

Larkin paused. "Strange that you remember them."

"Well, they aren't exactly normal," she responded, and then her eyes grew wide. "I'm sorry."

"It's perfectly fine," Larkin said and sighed. "It's never been a secret that I am half-Elf."

There was silence between them, a reminder that they were really just acquaintances and this was still strange.

"Is it not true that Barren killed your fiancé?" Sara asked at last. Larkin froze and turned to face the girl.

"I-I'm..." she was going to apologize again when Larkin cut her off.

"Barren did not kill William. I did," she said.

It was odd, admitting her sin aloud. It had been committed to save Barren and spoken of now to save him from more damnation. Sara seemed stunned.

"The sea is both beautiful and vicious," Larkin advised. "It will use you to its own gain, and it will change you."

Larkin felt the truth of those words more and more every day.

Chapter Sixteen
CHALLENGE

Sara did not sleep that night. Larkin only knew this because she didn't sleep either. Each time she would drift off, Sara would interrupt her slumber with another question.

"How long have you known that Cove sailed with Barren?"

"About three months."

"Only three months? How long has he known Barren?"

"I'm not sure. Maybe you should ask Cove."

Silence.

"Has he ever…hurt anyone?"

"That is not a question I will answer."

There was a lot of apprehension in her questions and Larkin couldn't blame her. There was no way to unlearn this. What she discovered about Cove was final, and it would shape the way she saw him from this point forward. She was sure Cove had feared the same thing. They would have to work through the same problems she and Barren were still dealing with.

She must have fallen asleep in the midst of Sara's questions because she woke with a start to a loud gunshot and fell out of her hammock to the hard floor. She rose to her feet quickly, reaching for her knife and running outside her apartment, only to find Sara holding a pistol.

"I'm sorry!" she said immediately.

"What are you doing?" Larkin demanded. She stormed toward her and wrenched the pistol from her. "You could kill someone!"

"What's goin' on down here?" Seamus appeared at the end of the steps followed by Cove and Barren. Larkin hid the pistol.

"Nothing," Larkin said, glaring at Sara. "We're fine."

"Sounded like a gunshot," said Seamus. Larkin glared at him too.

"It's nothing."

Barren and Cove exchanged a look.

"Sara, give Larkin and me a moment," said Barren. Sara looked between the two and then slowly stepped toward Cove. He allowed her to move up the stairs first, and then he and Seamus followed.

Barren reached behind Larkin's back for the pistol. "You said you would watch her. How'd she get the gun?"

"If she'd shut up for one second last night, this wouldn't have happened," Larkin snapped. "You try answering all her questions!"

He actually looked sympathetic for a moment. "Look, it's going to take all of us watching her. She's not like you."

"Teach her to fight," Larkin said.

"Teach Sara to fight?" Barren laughed at the idea. "Have you seen her?"

"She's small and she's probably never held a weapon until today, but you have to treat her like she's strong or she'll never be."

Barren looked at her for a moment. He ran his fingers over his mouth and then nodded. "Okay. We'll teach her."

They smiled at each other and suddenly it felt like things were right between them.

***

The crew stood in a circle around the deck. Most had wandered from their work to watch the training that was about to take place. Barren should have sent them back to work. It would be hard enough for Sara to train without so many eyes on her, but Cove had drawn their attention when he'd protested the idea of Sara's learning to fight. He'd finally conceded when Barren and Larkin had argued about how much better off she'd be if she could at least block an attack.

"Cove cannot be distracted trying to make sure you don't die," said Barren. "And we don't want everyone else distracted trying to protect you. You need to learn how to defend yourself, even if it's just the basics of swordplay."

"You want me to learn to use a sword?" she asked.

Barren shrugged. "Or a knife, or anything that will keep you safer than your tiny hands."

Sara looked down at her hands. They were pale, soft, and manicured. They rarely touched anything dangerous or unpleasant.

"Larkin," Barren called. "Let her use your sword."

Larkin stepped forward, pulling the blade from her sheath. The green gem glistened under the sunlight. It was the gift Barren had given her in Silver Crest, a symbol of trust.

As Sara took the hilt, the tip immediately dropped to the floor. She lifted the blade, her cheeks dusted with a fine blush.

Cove stepped forward. "Plant your feet," he said.

Sara tried to mimic him, but her dress got in the way. He showed her how to hold the sword and a couple of defensive moves, and then they tried them.

"Too slow," Cove commented. "Again."

It was evident Sara was surprised by Cove's shortness. They tried the moves again. Sara struggled with the blade, but she tried hard. For someone who had never held a sword, she moved instinctively to defend. Cove hit her blade too hard, and it clattered to the ground. He stepped back.

"Again," Cove said. She glared at him as she bent to pick up the blade. She held it tightly in both hands, her pale fingers turned pink.

Cove charged, and Sara swung her blade with all her strength. The shaft of the sword slid down Cove's blade fast and hit his fingers. The ambassador dropped his sword, and blood immediately dropped to the deck. Sara dropped the weapon as if it burned her and moved toward Cove, but he stepped away, hiding his injured fingers from her.

"You've done enough," he said.

She halted, snapping her mouth shut.

"Can I suggest a change in weapon?" Leaf asked.

Cove looked at the Elf as he grabbed his bow and an arrow. "Try this, Miss Rosamund," he handed her the bow. "It's simple, really. String the bow taunt, aim, release."

Sara took the arrow and bow. She fitted it easily and aimed with Leaf's guidance. "We'll aim for the center of that mast," he said.

She released the arrow with a pluck of the string and it lodged in the wood of the mast with a split. It wasn't centered, but it was a hit.

"Not bad!" Leaf proclaimed. "Looks like we found your weapon. You just have to practice." She tried to hand it back, but the Elf refused to take it. "Hold onto that. All these people are afraid your pretty little head will roll."

For a moment Sara looked bewildered, and then Leaf winked at her and she managed a smile. As the Elf moved back to his post, Cove stopped him.

"How did you know she'd be better with a bow?"

"Well, her hands are steady, but she's small and a sword is heavy," the Elf replied. "People are as strong as you let them be, Ambassador."

"Ship!" Slay called. "Eastward!"

Everyone paused and stared. It was closer than Barren expected which meant Slay had been watching the commotion on deck, not the horizon.

"They are holding a white flag," said Leaf, and he paused. "It is Edward."

"He's not wanting a truce," said Barren. "If anything, he wants to take me up on that challenge."

Barren turned and immediately found Larkin. He knew that look in her eyes meant she wanted to fight Edward. He moved toward her, and her gaze snapped to his, darkening. She knew exactly what he was about to do.

"You and Sara, in the hatch. Now."

She took a step back. "No," she said. "This is my challenge!"

Barren reached for her. "This isn't a game. Besides, you need to watch Sara. You said you would. She's never been in a battle. She needs to know when and where to hide. Can't you do that?"

Her response was to glare, but she could glare all she wanted as far as Barren was concerned. It would be too hard to ensure that both women were safe during this engagement. He held onto her arm as he made his way to the hatch. Sara followed close behind them. Barren cut through the hatch, searching for a reasonable place for them to stay.

"What about Aethea?" Larkin asked.

"I'll take care of her," he said, turning to Larkin. He clasped her shoulders. "Do this for me. If anything happens to her, Cove will never forgive us."

Sara sat down on the floor, and Barren guided Larkin to sit as well. He kept his eyes on her a moment longer, hoping that it was enough of a plea—and a warning—to make her stay. There was something about Larkin. It was like she was a magnet for danger. She couldn't stand it if she couldn't see it and immerse herself in the thick of it.

He left them then and hurried to the brig where Aethea was kept. The assassin stared at Barren as he approached.

"Having a little trouble?" she asked, tilting her head.

"I've not come to entertain you," he said. "We're about to engage in a fight, and as bad as I hate to, I need to keep you alive."

She smirked. "You're all charm, aren't you?"

He didn't say anything as he unlocked the door to the cell. He unlatched her arms from the wall. Just as he expected, she tried to reach for one of the blades at his hip, but his was already drawn and pressed to her neck. "Drop it."

She laughed a little, and then dropped the blade. "You're better than I thought."

"And you're not as smart as I thought."

He proceeded to chain her wrists together.

"If any cannon fire comes through these walls, lay on your stomach, and cover your head."

"You're going to leave me here, in this small box with nowhere to run?"

"You can run around in this box if you feel the need," he said. "But I'd advise you to stay as still as you can."

Then he left. Before he made his way to the deck, he watched Larkin and Sara from the shadows. They sat against the wall. Sara's legs were drawn up, and she stared forward, but it was as if she wasn't really seeing anything. Barren had a feeling that despite her innocent and sweet disposition, she dealt with fear in a quiet and brave way. Larkin, on the other hand, was tense. Her hand was on the knife she had drawn, her back straight. She had opened her senses to everything. She was ready to fight.

If there was ever a woman born in the wrong world, it was Larkin Lee.

***

Larkin hated the calm before the storm, especially now that she could only imagine what was going on above deck. When it began, it was sudden. The clash of blades rang out, and the ship groaned as if extra weight were coming upon it all at once. Beside her Sara sat staring forward, silent. Larkin was surprised by how calm the girl was.

"Will they kill us?" she asked. Larkin looked at her, but the girl was still staring forward, her wide-eyed gaze unseeing.

"They might kill me."

She blinked and then looked at Larkin. "Will they kill Cove?"

It was strange to watch these two. They'd been friends for a long time, and though there were secrets between them and anger divided them, their love for each other was unending. Larkin's heart hurt a little more.

"No," she said. "They won't kill Cove."

She said it because she truly believed it. Though their deaths were an everyday possibility, Larkin really couldn't imagine any of them dying. She didn't want to. It was better to think that the people she sailed with were invincible. Maybe that's why Barren pretended to be.

But Larkin had never witnessed pirates fighting pirates. She wasn't sure how skilled Edward was. What she did know was that Cove had broken his wrist easily, and it wouldn't yet be healed.

She heard commands and gunfire. She shuddered. How was she supposed to sit here while everyone else was fighting for their lives? She wanted to help, needed to help. After all, she was the one Edward was angry with. He'd threatened *her*.

"Stay here," Larkin told Sara, standing. "If shots are fired, lay flat and cover your head. I can't sit here and not know what's happening."

"But Barren told you to stay."

"Just because he tells me to stay doesn't mean I have to do it," she said. Larkin took a step away, and then turned around, offering her knife.

"If you have to use it, don't hesitate," she said. Sara reached forward and took the blade. It looked so strange in her small hands, and Larkin hoped giving it to her was a good idea.

She turned around, lifting her long sword in the other hand. She moved up the steps carefully but was surprised when the hatch flew open and a man rushed down the stairs. She did not recognize him, and he immediately engaged her, his blade dark. She blocked the blow with her sword.

"You're the one he's lookin' for," said the man. "The wench from Maris."

Larkin drew back, taking one step down. This was not the ideal place to fight. The man had the advantage, being taller and standing higher than she was.

"Better not fight too hard," he said, taking a step down. "This will already be bad for you. You don't want to make it worse."

"I'm not sure why men always think they can take me," she said. The man swung at her, and she ducked, moving her blade across his legs in a hard swing. He screamed, and fell from the steps. The fall would hardly kill him, but he wouldn't be able to walk. As she emerged from the hatch, she was immediately engaged by a pirate with a nasty gash across his forehead. And as she fought him, she realized she was not used to this. This pirate fought dirty. He used his body, hit and kicked. It was unfair, it was brutal, and she found herself tiring quickly.

She heard him before she saw him. Barren plowed toward her, cutting down the man who was fighting her. She was shocked by how easy he'd done it, and then she suddenly understood something about Barren. He had a switch—he could fight fairly, and he could fight brutally. He turned on her fast, pulling her toward him. She wanted to tear herself away, not because she was afraid of what he was going to say, but because he was angry. His eyes were ablaze, blood spattered his face, and sweat beaded off his skin.

"What did I say?" he snarled.

And then it happened. The ship rocked as cannon fire released from the opposing ship. Barren crashed into Larkin, sending her to the deck of the ship. She ignored the pain in her back and head and pushed against Barren to free herself. She crawled to the hatch. She imagined all the possible scenarios she would see once she was there. If anything happened to

Sara...well, no one would forgive her. She'd abandoned her post.

As she came down the steps and hurried to the back of the ship, she saw the damage. A gaping hole split the hull of the ship, debris was scattered everywhere, and one of the beams had fallen in exactly the place Sara had sat. She was nowhere to be found.

"Sara!" Larkin called. She dove into the debris, tossing aside pieces of wood and metal, thinking it would be a miracle to find her charge unscathed. She grabbed at pieces of splintered wood, feeling it cut her skin, but she didn't care. The faster she moved, the sooner Sara would be safe. As she pushed a barrel out of the way, she could see the end of Sara's dress.

"Sara!" she breathed, relieved, but as she went to reach for more debris, she found herself being ripped away from where she stood. She screamed and then landed on the hard ground, her blade out of reach. She faced Edward and other members of his crew she recognized from Sanctuary. They had entered the ship from the blast site. He stood over her, smiling, his arm hanging from a sling at his neck. She knew if she hit him there, she would beat him, but what about the others? They weren't injured and their weapons were ready.

"Too bad we don't have more time. I'd like to teach you more than one lesson."

He lifted his blade, took a step forward, only to find an arrow in his hand. He screamed and the blade clattered to the ground.

"You're really pushing it," said Barren. "One more mistake and you won't have hands at all."

Edward turned and glared, breathing heavily through his teeth. He was unsure of what to do with his injured hand. He couldn't pull the arrow out or even break it because his other hand was broken. "What are you going to do? Kill me? That's against the code."

"You challenged me," said Barren. "You were to fight only me, instead you chose to attack my crew. Now you are an enemy."

"And what have you become? Choosing her over your brothers?"

"I didn't have to choose her over anyone. She chose me. Now you can either return to your ship and leave or…"

"Or what?" He spat. "Will you kill all of us? Get rid of your problems just like that, huh?"

"Or I'll take your hand," said Barren. "If you choose the former, Leaf will remove the arrow from your hand and heal it. He might even help you set that nasty break to your wrist. I'm sure it has been causing you some pain."

Edward looked down at his hand and the expression on his face said everything. "Fall back," he ordered his men, snarling. His crew seemed confused, and it took them a moment to drop their weapons. From their perspective, their captain had turned coward.

"Leaf, do what you have to," said Barren. The Elf stood on the steps leading down into the hatch, his bow still in his hands. He nodded and stepped aside so Edward and his crew could move up the stairs.

Barren waited until they left. He hurried to the pile of debris and began shifting it aside. Cove was soon beside him and after a moment, they pulled Sara from beneath the rubble. She seemed frazzled, and there was no blood, but Larkin knew that they wouldn't know what damage had really been done until she was out of this mess.

"Are you okay?" Cove asked.

She nodded.

"You're not hurt?"

She shook her head, but her silence made Larkin think otherwise. Larkin stood from where she'd fallen and moved to pick up her blade. As she did, Barren turned to face her.

"I asked you to stay with her!" She thought he might keep his voice down, but he didn't.

"I thought she would be safe."

"You thought wrong. Does it never occur to you that sometimes I tell you to stay because I know what you're capable of? Because I knew you'd know what to do if this happened," he indicated the mess around him. Larkin felt dizzy. She wasn't sure why. She'd been fine throughout the whole attack even when she'd fallen. "You tell me I don't consider my life. Well, you don't consider yours!"

"I was afraid of what I couldn't see," she replied.

"You don't get to ignore my commands any more than the rest of my crew, Larkin!"

"You're supposed to remind me why I chose this life, not make me feel confined to *your* law!"

"If you can't remember why you are here, maybe you are better off with your father!"

Larkin glared at him and then tried to move past him, but as she took a step, she staggered. Barren caught her as she did.

"Larkin, are you alright?"

That's when she felt the large splinter of wood in her side. It must have happened when she fell. Her head spun, but she steadied herself. She wrapped her hand around the splinter, finding it was much bigger than she'd thought. She tried to pull on it.

"Don't," Barren moved her hand away, and she looked at him. His eyes were still on the splinter. His fingers moved around the wood and the pain seemed to increase, burning into her side and running to her head. Without warning, he lifted her into his arms and called to Leaf.

***

She woke in a cold sweat. There was a dull pain where the splinter had been removed. She sat up slowly. Barren was asleep in a chair near the bed. His arms were crossed over his chest, and his head fell back. She moved from the bed slowly and walked to the washbasin. Pouring water into the bowl, she blotted her face with a cool cloth, washing away the clamminess.

When she turned, Barren was watching her.

"You should lie down," she said.

"You should rest."

"I have."

He kept watching her. She set the cloth aside and moved back toward the bed. She sat down. "Are you going to scold me?"

"No. All the blood and the screaming took my words."

She cringed but teased, "You're not squeamish, are you?"

"When it is your blood that covers my hands, I am."

She was quiet. They hadn't been this close in proximity since he'd fled their room in Arcarum, and the space between them was strained.

It was their last encounter that made her ask her next question.

"Have you ever loved?"

"What?"

She regarded him for a moment before asking the question again. "Have you ever loved another woman?"

She couldn't quite describe the look on his face. He just stared at her, still as stone.

"No," he said. "I have never loved another woman."

It was strange to hear that word love spoken as if they'd said it to each other before. Larkin was well aware that they hadn't. She was also well aware that she wasn't so sure she knew what it meant.

"Why?" The way he asked, he was both intrigued and a little defensive. Larkin looked at him. This explanation should be obvious.

"Because you are a pirate."

Barren regarded her for a moment, raising a brow. "Now I don't think you're asking the same question."

"No love, but a lover, then?"

Barren laughed and let his hand fall into his lap. After a moment, he lifted his head again, running his fingers through his hair. "You want to discuss this?"

"Is there a better time?" her voice was barely more than a whisper.

Barren shook his head, looking away. "Then, yes," he said, shrugging.

"That's it?" she said. "That's all you'll say?"

"There's nothing else to say," he said.

"How many?" she asked.

He scoffed. "Larkin…"

"How many?" she demanded.

"I don't know. Four—five!"

"Well, which one is it?"

"Does it matter?"

She glared.

"I don't know," he said, sighing. "See? Isn't it best not to know?"

"I don't know," she admitted. Silence stretched between them, and they didn't look at each other. "You loved none of them?"

"You don't have to love them," he said.

Larkin cringed.

"You haven't?" he asked, now curious.

"What?

"I mean…it happens."

"No!"

"Well, that's a little bit of a relief," he said.

"What?" she demanded.

"I just…if you'd…with William…I—"

"Not in my world, Barren Reed," she cut him off curtly. "That's how reputations are ruined."

The dynamic was ridiculous. Why should her reputation be ruined? Why not a man's as well? Or better yet, neither. There was silence again.

Barren took a breath. "I never thought I would have you, Larkin," then he laughed and it was a true laugh. "And I'm sure you never thought you'd want me. But here we are, me with my sins and you with yours. I can't promise you'd be my first lover, but there are many others firsts yet to come."

She hugged her legs tightly to her chest. Barren stood and reached forward, wrapping his hand around her neck, he pressed his lips to her forehead.

"Sometimes I don't know what is going on between us," he said. "Sometimes I can't figure out how we will work, but I need you to know that I want you to be my forever."

His eyes were like fire. She wanted to say something in response, but she had no words. He moved away from her then, heading for the door.

"Rest," he said.

"Where are you going?"

"To breathe."

Then she was left alone.

Chapter Seventeen
ARYES

Cove sat at the back of the ship. He was bent over, his elbows on his knees. Leaf had bandaged his hands earlier and given him a warm drink to relieve his pain. It had left a bitter taste in his mouth, and while his fingers did not hurt, they seemed to pulse. The wound was his fault. He shouldn't have made Sara mad. She shouldn't even have had a weapon. This is not the life he wanted for her.

From the corner of his eye, he saw her approach.

"I'm sorry I hurt you," she said.

Cove sort of laughed. How strange those words were.

"I shouldn't have been so demanding," he said.

"And why not?" she asked. "You should treat me no differently than you would a member of your crew."

Cove looked at her then. She had no idea what she was asking for. "But you are not a member of my crew," he said. "Nor are you a pirate."

"I am not," she said. "But how am I to learn if everyone is

afraid to break me?"

Cove opened his mouth to speak, but he could not find any words. She did not want to be weak or appear vulnerable, especially among pirates. But there was nothing for her to learn here because she would not be staying.

"You will not be among us long enough to need the skills Barren so desires you to learn," said Cove.

"Why do you dismiss me so easily?" she asked. "Where others see potential, you only see weakness. Is that why you never told me the truth? Did you feel I could not withstand it?"

Cove laughed bitterly. "I never told you the truth because I am selfish and I am a coward. I couldn't stand the thought of you running from me, of you hating me. But this is where you face the fact that I am not a good man and that you were wrong."

"I am not wrong," she said, shaking her head.

"Do not forgive me so easily, Sara," he said. "I do not deserve it. Even now I should confess my sins to you, yet I am still too cowardly. If I really wanted you to run, I'd tell you everything. Remember that when you're angry that I have kept secrets."

***

Larkin was between wakefulness and sleep. Her body was alive. She could feel someone in the room with her. A dark presence. Part of her felt like she was dreaming, but her heart was racing and her fingers itched to reach for her blade.

The air changed and she opened her eyes. A shadow rose above her, arms raised, blade glimmering in hand. Larkin threw up her arms, and she felt the foreign rush of magic come to her fingertips. But the person who stood over her quashed the magic that had pooled into a ball. Their hands closed over hers harshly and pushed them down to her stomach. Now the weight of the shadow was upon her, and fear gripped her deeply.

A voice rose in the darkness. She was quiet, but her words were venom—she was like a spider, wrapping Larkin in silk, only for the kill.

It was Aethea.

"So," she whispered, and her eyes widened at her discovery. "You're Lyric."

Aethea rested there for a moment, her hands keeping Larkin's pinned against her chest. Finally, Aethea released her and stepped away. Larkin reached for her blade.

"And what are you going to do with that? Wound me?" she asked, and Larkin glared. "You'd have to explain why, and you don't want to do that, do you?"

"Why are you here? Who freed you?"

Aethea laughed. "No one *freed* me. I am already free," she said. "But you need not worry. After this, I'll wander back to my part of the ship and replace my bonds as if none of this happened."

The wicked smirk on Aethea's lips did not waver.

"I've been around pirates long enough to know there has to be a catch," said Larkin.

"I am not a pirate," Aethea said, as if she were offended.

"You aren't so different," said Larkin. "But you're welcome to prove me wrong."

She smile. "You're pretty," she said. "And smart, too. It is a pity you won't capitalize on your power."

"All I've ever seen Lyric do is spread evil. No good can come of it."

"So you would reject your magic completely? When it is a part of you just like your blood?"

Larkin glared.

"I suppose it is no surprise. You abandoned your father for a pirate."

"You know nothing of me," Larkin snapped and then narrowed her eyes. "How is it you know about Lyrics?"

"Everyone knows a little about magic," she said.

"Ben knew about magic, too."

"Are you trying to make a connection?"

Larkin shrugged. "You both happened to be interested in Barren's compass, you both have knowledge of Lyric, and you both work for the Commonwealth. That's a lot of commonalities."

Aethea raised a perfect brow. "That is *not* uncommon."

"Perhaps not so uncommon," Larkin agreed. "But when they happen within the span of a few days, one begins to wonder *if* they are connected. Do you want to know what I think?" A slow smile spread across Larkin's face. "I think you were asked to find the compass. My question is, why do you want it, and who has hired you?"

Aethea was not humored, but she smiled and took a step toward Larkin.

"You're perceptive, and those are good questions," she said as her gray eyes seemed to turn black. "I suppose they deserve an answer. But, then, if I gave an answer, I could not keep *your* secret."

It was Larkin's turn to laugh. "See, you're not so different from a pirate."

"You're careless in your comparison," she said. "For when you see what I am capable of, you will wish for the droll antics of a pirate."

"Are you threatening me?"

"No," she said. "I'm already watching you fail. For when your pirate-lover learns of your magic, his love for you will evaporate as if it were never really there. A pirate cannot truly love anything other than the sea. He yearns for it like a lover. He will sacrifice human touch for it. He will kill for it."

"You sound jaded."Aethea laughed. "You know I am right. Barren has changed. He no longer welcomes you with a smile. His disdain will grow, and if he must choose between you and the sea, he will most certainly choose the sea." She laughed and took a step back. "I hope I am here to see it."

She was gone then. She melded with the shadows like smoke. Larkin stood for a moment in the darkness. She wanted to run to the brig and check that Aethea was bound to her chair because what had just happened felt like a nightmare, but she didn't want to see Aethea. She didn't want to hear her voice.

How had Aethea known she was a Lyric? Had Ben told her? She had the forethought to test Larkin's powers, too, and to stop her magic. She wasn't denying knowledge of Lyric or claiming to be an expert, but didn't quashing magic take some skill? A mortal couldn't do such a thing, but that's what Aethea was.

And now Aethea knew Larkin was a Lyric. She wanted to see Larkin fail. If Barren discovered Larkin's powers through Aethea, Barren's trust *would* evaporate. When it came down to it, if Larkin did not tell Barren her secret, he *would* choose the sea over her.

***

Larkin moved across deck. It was morning and the sun was not yet on the horizon, but she had been unable to sleep since Aethea's visit. She'd struggled all night between the decision to tell Barren she was a Lyric or keep it a secret. Part of her just wanted to keep the secret a little longer, to hold onto the freedom she had as Larkin Lee.

She came to Barren's cabin door and knocked. She'd never knocked before, but what Aethea had said was true. Things were different between them. She set her teeth, angered by the woman's words, and threw open the door to his cabin. She found Barren at the door, a look of surprise on his face.

She took him in. He was half-dressed. His chest was exposed, bronzed from days in the sun. Under this light, his muscles seemed even more defined. He towered over her, his shoulders broad and toned. She knew his skin would be warm and rough. She wanted to reach out and touch him.

"Are you okay?" He asked her and she flinched. His question was sincere, but she also realized that she wasn't okay. Her chest felt tight. She moved to close the door and then turned to face him again.

"Don't look at me like that," he said. His voice was hushed.

"Like what?" She approached him, but he didn't move away. Suddenly, any thoughts of telling Barren she was a Lyric were pushed aside because she wanted something more. She wanted him, and she wasn't going to be refused again.

She stood on the tips of her toes and touched his face. She felt him shudder. Her heart picked up speed. She moved her hands to his blond-streaked hair. His hands latched onto her forearms, but he did not pull her away.

"What are you doing?" His voice was a gruff whisper.

She inhaled sharply. "I need you," she said.

His eyes burned into hers. "I'm here," he said.

He drew her against him and kissed her lips, slowly at first, but fiercely. His teeth grazed her lip, and their teeth clanked, but he kept kissing her, deeper and deeper until the air around them was too hot, and she knew he needed her too.

He lifted her against him, and she drew her legs around his waist. One of his hands clasped the skin of her thigh, and the other wrapped tightly around her waist. He kissed her jaw and her neck. His lips grazed the tender skin of her chest and then found her lips again.

He moved her so easily, as if she weighed nothing, and suddenly they were on the bed, bodies pressed together. She kept her legs wrapped around him, and he broke the kiss to stare at her, his eyes like embers.

"You won't leave me again," she said.

"No," he rasped, and she knew he regretted his decision to leave her before.

He drew her up, and she sat in his lap, arms wrapped tightly around his neck, their lips crashed together. She couldn't think, and her breaths came in gasps. Feelings clashed inside her. Guilt, need, fear. They mixed with the magic in her blood, and for a moment she feared her power would make itself known, but it regressed as soon as Barren's cabin door flew open and Barren tore away from her.

Leaf stood in the doorway. A lopsided smirk was on his face.

"Dammit, Leaf!" Barren seethed.

"S-sorry," he said quickly. Larkin hung her head in her hands and let out a sigh. There really was no privacy on a ship, even in private quarters. "But...we may have trouble. I thought you'd like to know."

Barren grumbled. "If you're making this up for fun, I will kill you," Barren said, and got to his feet, swiping a shirt from the bedpost and pulling it on. "I'm sorry," he turned to tell Larkin, and then he continued out to the deck.

Larkin stared at the closed door for a long moment. Had the sea just won?

***

"You embarrass me," Barren said as they exited his cabin.

The Elf was amused. "Next time I will knock."

"You should have done that in the first place!"

"I would not have disturbed you at all," he said. "But we're close to the Octent now and it appears we might be approaching a ship. Maybe a Runner or a Cutter. I thought we should be more careful."

Leaf was right. They needed to be more careful. This part of the sea was never safe. If they sailed to the west, they would come face to face with the Ore Mines, and if they sailed east, they would come to the island of Estrellas. Their course was set for the south, however, where the sea was far more violent.

Here, survival was a daily struggle. It could be argued that the Corsairs of Avalon were the main commanders of the sea, but there were others to worry about, too. Runners were the names given to sailors who delivered illegal goods for the Underground. They were a vicious sort and killed without mercy. It was said that many of them appeared rabid at sea, as if their minds had been lost to a drug. There were also Cutters, notorious for their hatred of the Orient, and their ships were designed with large metal blades protruding from the hull. One good ram from their ship and the enemy was sunk.

Barren was familiar with Runners. He had personal experience with them. Luckily, he had not encountered Cutters and he hoped he never did. What probably concerned him more was the fact that they did not know how far the weapons had spread. If Aethea had managed to purchase them from Sabine, others probably had too, and he wondered if the Runners were using them to defend their ships and supplies. It was definitely a technique that would leave them unopposed.

"Look to the horizon. The ship is there," said Leaf. He

pointed and Barren looked, but his vision was not as sharp. He saw nothing. Moments passed, and Barren held his breath. The sound of the ship cutting through the ocean was loud in his ears.

"It's an Elfin ship," said Leaf at last, and his tone suddenly changed. "It has been destroyed."

"Destroyed? But there is no smoke, and it has not yet sunk, so it cannot be very old."

Leaf did not respond. He just kept staring. A great unease spread across the ship. It wasn't uncommon for humans, pirates or otherwise, to sail Elfin ships, but it was uncommon for them to be so close to the boarder of the Octent.

Barren recalled Aethea's words. Tetherion and Lord Alder were working together. Lord Alder would need to provide something in order to satisfy the agreement in the Elfin Treaty. Perhaps it extended beyond offering up a piece of the King's Gold.

Barren kept his eyes on the horizon. It wasn't long before he could make out the outline of what was once a ship. The mast had toppled over and the sails ballooned above the water. The debris slowly floated away from the scene. Barren smelled the air, but there was still no sign of smoke or ash. If the ship hadn't been destroyed by cannon fire, why exactly was it in pieces?

They neared the ruins of the ship, and without warning, Leaf dove into the water and swam to the wreckage.

"Leaf!" Barren called after him, but the Elf had already made it to the thick of the flotsam. He pulled himself from the water onto the main part of the wreckage and crawled to an area where the sails of the ship still billowed from the water. It was then Barren saw the yellow hair of a person in the midst of the ruin.

"Get as close to the remains as possible and weigh anchor," Barren instructed before jumping into the water himself. He emerged surrounded by debris. Chunks of wood and pieces of rope from the sails floated around him. He pulled himself onto the wreckage to find Leaf bent over the body of an Elf.

Leaf patted the side of the Elf's face, trying to get him to respond. "Aryes! Aryes, I am going to need you to open your eyes."

The young Elf groaned but did not open his eyes.

Leaf put his ear to Aryes's chest. "He has a heartbeat, but it is faint."

Barren couldn't tell if Leaf was talking to him or not. Then Leaf turned, and Barren's eyes followed. The Elf's legs were pinned under the fallen mast. Leaf crawled toward the mast and tried frantically to push it off Aryes's legs.

"Albatross!" Barren called. "Help us!"

Barren hurried to Leaf's side to get a better look at the fallen mast. It was situated over broken and buckled pieces of the ship, making in nearly impossible to lift.

"Leaf, you have to stop. His legs are crushed."

Leaf looked directly at Barren, and his sea-green eyes were a storm of emotion. "You can't ask me to leave him."

No, he couldn't. He knew that. It was just that even if the boy survived, he would never walk again. There was no Elfin magic to cure crushed bones. The wreckage shifted as Cove joined them. Leaf positioned himself above Aryes's head, and lifted him up so that his hands were anchored underneath Aryes's arms. Barren and Cove lifted the wooden mast enough for Leaf to pull Aryes out. Cove was the first to drop the mast. It crashed into the remains, and caused the debris to shift beneath them. He gave out a cry, and his hands went quickly to where he'd been wounded at his side. He seemed to realize it would draw attention and straightened. Barren managed to keep his footing and lowered the mast carefully, but his eyes were on Cove, questioning.

"Are you alright, Albatross?"

"Yes," he said quickly, his breath sounded short and his body seemed to slump, his hands pressed to the area where he had been shot. Barren knew it was the *vacair* poison, but he was carrying the burden silently.

Leaf scooped the young Elf into his arms, cradling Aryes against his chest as if the boy were his child. Seamus and Sam laid a boarding plank out to connect the ship and the ruins, and Leaf moved carefully along it.

Barren and Cove were left to observe the remnants of the deck a moment longer.

"This couldn't have been destroyed with gunfire," said Cove.

"Then what do you suppose did this?" asked Barren.

The ambassador looked around. "It looks like...well, it looks like it was crushed."

There were no other Elves among the wreckage, and Barren wondered where they'd gone. The ship Aryes had been on was too large to be captained by one person.

Barren moved forward, kicking at some of the debris when he spotted shining bullets on part the deck not covered by water. He stopped to pick one up, noticing they were similar in color to the ones used to kill his brethren and the one pulled from Cove.

"Where did you come from?" he muttered. He turned and held the bullets up to Cove, whose eyes grew dark. Then Barren took off, scrambling toward their ship.

Aryes lay motionless on the deck, and Leaf scrambled beside him, trying to evoke some sign of life from the boy even as he worked to mix one of his Elvish concoctions. Barren fell to his knees with a loud thud beside the two.

"Aryes, I need you to tell me why this was on your ship." Barren demanded desperately. He patted the boy's face. "Who attacked you?"

Cove pulled the pirate away from the unconscious Elf. "You're not going to get an answer out of him, Barren. Not yet."

Barren twisted towards him. "That ship was carrying the same bullets that harmed you and killed our brothers!" He shoved the bullet into Cove's hand and turned to look at Leaf, as if he had the answer.

"We're not going to discuss this right now," Leaf said evenly. He looked at Cove. "Will you help me get him into Barren's cabin?"

Albatross gave Barren the bullet and did as Leaf had asked. Barren watched them as they entered his cabin. He hoped the Elf made it because the bullets spilled all over the deck of that ship needed an explanation. Not only that, where was Aryes heading? Had he come from the Elfin kingdom of Aurum? Why was he near the border of the Octent? Worse, who had attacked the ship, and did they know exactly what they had in their possession?

***

Barren didn't see Leaf until the sun set. Cove had come out of the cabin soon after they'd gone in, but Leaf couldn't bring himself to leave the boy's side. When he emerged hours later, Barren knew what he was going to say.

"He is dead," Leaf said. His voice was low and raw, and a sadness hung around him unlike anything Barren had seen before.

Sometimes it was easy to forget that Leaf was the prince of the Elves, but when things like this happened, Barren always remembered, and no matter how much Leaf despised his royal blood and dreaded the day he might take the crown, he cared for his people. He cared deeply.

Barren hesitated and then managed to say, "I'm sorry, Leaf."

Though he had nothing to do with the boy's death, he felt guilty for hesitating to free Aryes from the mast in the first place. He was sure whatever happened to the boy had been horrific.

Leaf sat down on one of the barrels and silence stretched between them. Barren wanted to ask questions. Needed to ask them, because even though the young Elf had died, there was something greater at work here. He needed to know if the Elf had awoken long enough to reveal his attackers.

"We have only two possibilities," Leaf said very quietly. "Either Aryes brought the weapons from Aurum or he picked them up somewhere. Perhaps the Underground. We are close to the border."

Barren was silent for a long moment.

"Perhaps that piece of King's Gold and a promise for more was not good enough," said Barren. "Perhaps your father has offered the weapons to meet the treaty and to ensure Tetherion wins the Ore Mines for good."

"We have no proof," said Leaf. "And my father does not condone the use of magic."

That was true. While they had been in Aurum months ago, Alder had refused the idea of using magic, citing how abusive dark magic was.

"Someone among your people does," said Barren. "Aryes died for it."

"You do not have to lecture me," said Leaf, bitterness coloring his words. "I will not jump to conclusions about my father. He's lost enough. I've lost enough!"

Barren sat quietly. What Leaf had said wasn't untrue. Lord Alder had lost. He'd lost his power, and, as he saw it, his dignity. Lord Alder had become bitter, and Barren believed that the Elfin king would do whatever he must to keep the power he still held, even if that meant using magic that might destroy the world. Leaf had spent a long time running from Lord Alder's bitterness. Exploring the world beyond the borders of Aurum had led him to dislike his father's policy of isolation and become more

240

accepting of mortals, whom he found no different from his own race. It had also led him to experience discrimination and hate in the bitterest way, through the murder of his love, Fira.

"My father..." Leaf paused, frustrated. Then he sighed. "All of my father's actions, they're all for one purpose. To protect his people."

Barren stood. Placing his hand on Leaf's shoulder he said, "He is what every king ought to be. Come, let us send Ayres to the Otherworld."

Leaf nodded in agreement and the two settled the broken body into a dinghy. Barren watched Leaf as he smoothed the young Elf's hair and arranged the boy's hands atop his stomach.

"He is only a child in our years. No more than fifty. His father serves in the Elfin Guard. Ayres would have been an apprentice at this point."

"It is not often your people sail," said Barren.

"It isn't," agreed Leaf, but he said nothing further.

The rest of the crew gathered about as they lowered the small boat into the ocean. Leaf withdrew an arrow from his quiver and picked up his bow. He watched as the waves carried Aryes away. Leaf lifted an arrow to his bow. Barren lit the arrow and Leaf pulled the string taut and released. It came to land in the boat, flames springing to life from within and they watched the beacon until it died on the horizon.

"Pirates send their dead to sea, believing that the sea will carry them to the Otherworld to rest," said Leaf. "The Elves believe our souls go to a place called Nonlos to heal, to recognize the

lessons they learned in this lifetime. After, they pass onto Elos."
He smiled a little, as if he'd touched on a memory of the place, and somehow Barren knew he was thinking of Fira. "There is no sadness there, no pain. Just understanding."

Barren had no words for Leaf, but he found himself hoping that his father had found a place like Elos in the Otherworld.

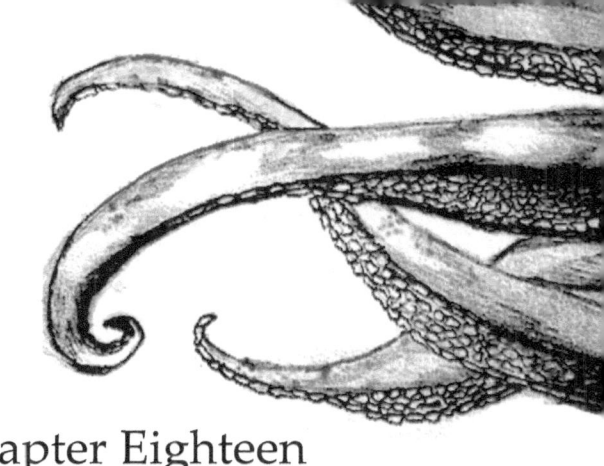

Chapter Eighteen
ISLE OF IONA

"We are close to Iona," said Cove. "We should stop there, gather news. It would be good for us to know the current state of the Orient before we are too far from her waters."

"It is out of our way," said Barren.

"Only by a few hours," Cove argued. "Kerry may be able to give us some information on Aryes's death. It is the only Network we'll have access to before we enter the Octent."

It would be beneficial to have an update on the status of the Orient before they entered the Octent. Barren was curious to know if there had been any more attacks on their brethren and if Aethea Moore was missed. Cove would need to know how Arcarum had reacted to Sara's absence so he could plan his return. He would have to leave them soon.

"Sam, set course for Iona," Barren called. The helmsman nodded and adjusted course.

"Iona?" Larkin questioned.

"It is an island of the Network," said Leaf.

"I have never heard of it."

"It is on no map you have seen," said Cove. "None of the Network islands are."

"So how do you get to them if you have no map?"

"Their coordinates are learned upon swearing to the code," said Cove.

"But most of the locations you've established yourself, is that not correct?"

"It is correct," said Cove. "And when I pledged to the code of Silver Crest, I also pledged the use of my Network."

"But at trial, you threatened to revoke use of the Network. How can you when all Silver Crest pirates know of their locations?"

"If it comes to that, I will have them destroyed."

Barren didn't like the conversation they were having. Destroying the Network locations at a time like this would likely mean doom for the Silver Crest pirates unless new ones were established quickly. Barren did not believe his exile was worth losing their best means of communication. On the other hand, if the locations were betrayed, they would have to be destroyed. He felt guilty, but part of him wondered if it was wise to even allow Larkin the privilege of seeing Iona. He had yet to determine who she'd spoken to in Arcarum. He had yet to broach the subject of Éire. And if he could get away with it, he never would.

***

There was a strange feeling about the ship. After Ayres's death, things had been quiet. Larkin imagined her feelings were much different than everyone else's. She felt unease. A sick feeling had begun to fill her stomach. She knew Cove's words were true. Her time with Barren, her time on this ship would soon be over.

The wind was heavy as they approached Iona. Like Sanctuary, there was nothing spectacular about the island. In fact, there was nothing to Iona but sand.

"You should not stand in this wind," said Leaf, coming to stand beside her. "You may fall ill."

She smiled at Leaf. "I do not wish to be below deck," she replied.

"You can take refuge in Barren's cabin," he suggested, raising a brow. She felt her cheeks color with embarrassment.

"I think not today," she said, and there was silence between them. "I'm sorry about Ayres, Leaf."

A ghost of a smile touched the Elf's lips. "Thank you."

The sound of the water rushing against the hull of the ship occupied the quiet. Larkin inhaled deeply, and for a moment the calm of the sea filled her. Then she heard the hatch door open and turned to see Barren lead Aethea from below. She was in chains and blindfolded, and though the assassin said nothing, the smirk on her face seemed to mock Larkin.

"Should she not stay on the ship?" Larkin asked, her voice harsher than she intended, and it also sounded alarmed.

"We have plans to make," said Barren, and he seemed surprised. "We need her input. Besides, she has to be somewhere she can be guarded."

Barren lead Aethea to sit, and Larkin ground her teeth, turning back to look at the approaching island.

"Jealousy is fickle, is it not?"

"I'm not jealous!" Larkin seethed, and Leaf lifted a pale brow. She sighed, feeling the weight of the last few days fall heavy upon her. "Things are not the same between us."

"Barren does stupid things all the time because he doesn't communicate. I need not give you examples, and, unfortunately, you're not immune to his actions. Barren always communicates by fighting physically. He picks up a sword."

"Are you telling me to fight him?"

Leaf shrugged a shoulder. "It would get his attention. And be amusing."

Larkin narrowed her gaze. "I never know if your advice is sincere."

Leaf tilted his head. "Just see how long you can deal with brooding Barren...you'll want to fight him by the end of it!"

***

Larkin and Sara moved through the water toward the shore. Larkin watched as Barren lifted Aethea and carried her through shallow water to the sandy beach. She was very conscious of the anger igniting her blood and heating her skin. Was her anger born from jealousy? Or the fact that Aethea gained so much pleasure from this act? The assassin kept her arms wrapped around Barren's neck tightly. Larkin had held onto him the same way only this morning.

When they reached shore, Barren let go of Aethea

immediately and let her fall to the ground. She caught herself before she hit, and it made Larkin wonder if she'd said something to make him angry. He kept one hand on the assassin's shoulder as they marched forward.

"Will they kill her?" Sara asked quietly. Larkin turned to look at her, surprised. She hadn't thought about that. Whether or not they'd kill her.

"I do not know," she said, pursing her lips. "But I do not think I would protest that execution."

Sara did not seem appalled, but she set her lips in a tight line.

They were both surprised when children ran to them from across the island. They called out the names of members of Barren's crew. Some ran for certain people. Barren took a small girl's hand, and Sam reached down and picked up a little boy. The pirates smiled at them, and the children asked questions.

"Children? There are children here?" Sara asked.

"Yes," Larkin said, though she was a little surprised they would live here on the isolated island of Iona, and a Network location at that. Wasn't it dangerous? Especially if Cove chose to dissolve the Network? He had said that would require destroying these locations. If anything, it was another reminder that the pirates of Silver Crest were more than just a rogue lot of men and women. They had become more like a whole other people, governed by their own rules and their own beliefs, and they fought to protect them.

They continued across the island, moving through the sand until they came to an entrance in the ground. There was a metal door and dark stairs. Barren took the lead this time and helped Aethea down the steps. The process was slow, and Larkin moved down a step at a time behind them, tempted to push them the rest of the way.

Finally they came to an underground shelter. Barren led Aethea down a hallway that branched off of the main room. Larkin stood in her spot at the end of the stair, staring at the room in wonder. She wasn't sure what she'd expected. There was simplicity to Silver Crest, a grandness to Sanctuary. And this, this was simply impressive. The shelter wasn't huge, but it was spacious. People moved around her, going about their business as if the visitors hadn't even arrived. Children played on the floor, some areas carpeted and others exposed, cold stone. The main area was filled with various things including beds, tables, and chairs. Sheets hung from different parts of the ceiling, creating privacy for sleeping areas. The walls were covered with old wooden planks, and built in shelves were full of books and other strange ornaments. There were two hallways that led off the larger room, but Larkin's attention was drawn to a long wall of darkness where water seemed to reflect on the surface. She moved toward it and pressed her hand against the wall. It was cold and glass.

"It's a window," said a voice she didn't recognize. Her gaze met the face of a young man in the reflection of the window, and she turned. He had olive skin, a head of thick, dark hair, and an inviting smirk.

"Why?" she asked.

He shrugged and approached her. "Why not? Don't you think it's charming?"

She smiled a little. "I don't think a pirate creates for charm. She creates for safety, for protection."

The man raised his brow. "You think us so single-minded? Some of us are romantics."

She laughed. "Single-minded? No. Practical, yes."

She heard someone clear his throat behind them, and she turned. Cove was standing there, eyes narrow. He'd been the one to clear his throat, but Larkin's gaze went straight for Barren, whose eyes burned into hers. It was that angry passion that ignited her senses, but it was jealousy, too.

"Xavier, don't you have chores to finish?"

The boy hesitated, looking between Larkin and the two men who'd joined them. It took him a moment to understand, but when he did, he hurried off. Larkin moved toward Cove and Barren.

"Did you build this?"

He laughed. "No, I didn't. This particular station is older than my Network. I'm not sure who built it, but I'm thankful for it all the same."

"You never worried that whoever made it would come back for it?"

Cove narrowed his eyes a bit. "It's been abandoned for quite some time. Whoever created it isn't come back."

That made Larkin shudder. Cove and Barren turned and walked down one of the hallways. Larkin followed. They turned into a room on their left. It was a small office, simple but enough for someone living underground. A man stood behind a desk. He had dark skin and eyes, and his head was covered with a scarf. He was reading a long letter. He looked up from it and took a breath before addressing Cove and Barren.

"Good to see you boys, unexpected as it is," he said.

"Kerry," Cove nodded to the man.

"I've heard about your encounter with Edward," he began.

"It doesn't surprise me that you have. He would be quick to profess his innocence."

"He is innocent, from the Elders' perspective," said Kerry.

Larkin watched as Barren grew tense, and she started to wonder if they really had friends here.

"It seems Edward came after you because the Elders placed a bounty on Larkin's head," then he looked at Barren. "They also want you to appear at Sanctuary for sentencing."

Barren went rigid, and Larkin felt her heart pick up speed. Barren moved to cover her.

"We're not going to have a problem here, are we Kerry?"

"Not from me," he said. "But it should be a warning to you that others might not be so dissatisfied with the Elders."

"What are the conditions on the bounty?" asked Cove. "Is she to be returned to the Elders or Maris?"

"Maris," said Kerry. He looked around on his desk for a moment then picked up a piece of paper, moving it before Barren and Cove. Larkin peered around Barren to look. A face stared back at her. It was her own. She compared it with the one Barren had drawn of her, finding that whosever hand had penned it felt she was much harsher and more wild than Barren had. There was a crudeness to her features, a sneer on her mouth. "They want her alive."

"That is bold of them," said Cove. "Larkin is not one of their own. They do not have a say in her life or death."

Larkin wondered why the Elders wanted her in Maris so badly. At the trial they'd wanted her gone. Had they discovered she had magic? Or did they believe she was a traitor?

"Regardless," said Kerry, looking at Barren. "Every Network has been advised to retain Larkin and turn you over for sentencing. It is only safe to harbor you one night. Any longer and you may be discovered. Further, a split has occurred among us. Your supporters remain in Silver Crest. The others have taken refuge at Sanctuary."

This was terrible and Larkin couldn't help but feel it was her fault in some way, but at least Silver Crest held out in support of Barren. He had not completely lost everything.

"Are there Elves frequenting these parts?" Cove asked. "Just before our arrival, we encountered an Elfin ship, destroyed. There was only one surviving member of the crew, and he later died. It seems strange they would be so close to the boarder of the Octent."

"There have been more in the past weeks," said Kerry. "Some come from the Octent, others come from the West. We believe they may be using the Ore Mines while the Orient and the Octent come to a compromise."

"You've not followed them to confirm this?" asked Barren.

"It is not easy to follow a ship of Elves," said Kerry. "They know we're coming miles away. Besides, their concerns have never been ours."

"It is our concern if they are using the Ore Mines. The Elves are as much a part of the Orient as the king," said Cove.

"They've never felt that way," said Kerry.

It was true that Lord Alder did not wish to associate himself with mortals or their world. The only reason he did was to protect his kingdom.

"Any news from Arcarum?" Cove asked. There was an edge to his voice, as if he dreaded this conversation.

"The last bit of news we received was this," he picked up a newspaper from one side of his desk and placed it before Cove. The front page announced Ambassador Rowell's departure to search for the escaped assassin, the belief that pirates had been involved, and the disappearance of Sara Rosamund. The article hinted at two possibilities, that Sara had been kidnapped by pirates or that she had sailed away with Cove to elope.

"You know what I'm going to say next," said Kerry. "There is no lack of rumors."

Cove grimaced. "Well, in this case, they are all half-right. Sara was a stowaway on our ship."

"You didn't think to return her?"

"It was not that simple," said Cove, and he left it at that. "Send word to Alaster. Request information, specifically on what Ben Willow's activities have been."

Kerry nodded. "I will see it done."

They left then. Larkin was shown to her sleeping quarters. She was surprised to find that it was an actual room with two bunk beds. It was small, but she wasn't going to complain. Sara was already there, sitting on the bottom bed. When Larkin walked in, Sara was sewing the hem of her skirt, though it was still wet from wading through the water earlier.

"While we are here, perhaps we can find you some clothes," said Larkin. Sara was smaller than Larkin, and none of her clothes would fit.

"I am fine," she said.

"Surely you would like to change," Larkin suggested. Sara's gown was stained, and the salt water on the hem would discolor the fabric.

"I said I am fine," she snapped.

Larkin regarded the girl for a moment. Tears fell and hit her hands as she worked to sew her dress. Larkin sat down beside the girl. "You can tell me," she said. "Are you homesick? Do you wish to go home?"

"No," she said, and she covered her mouth as her crying grew louder. "No, I do not wish to go home."

She took a deep breath and wiped her eyes with the back of her hands. "He will not speak to me," she said. "I don't know what I have done."

Larkin sighed and then moved to kneel before the girl. She took the needle and thread from Sara and then took her hands. "Do you not see why Cove is angry?"

Sara just stared.

"You are not oblivious," she said. "I think you realize the mistake you made, and now you cannot take it back. That's why you're here. What was between you and Cove, it means you can never be just friends. You were never destined for that."

"Just as it was not your decision to marry William, it was not mine to marry Ben. I warned Cove. If he left too often, my father would move on, and he did," she paused to swallow a sob. "But what I know of him now and this life… how can I accept this? It was better that I were ignorant of it all."

Larkin smiled a little. "But you weren't ignorant of any of it," she said. "Cove doesn't want this life for you. You're a lady. All you've ever known is finery."

"But you're a lady and have only known finery," she argued. "And you fight."

"I do," Larkin said. "You and I, we come from very different backgrounds. My father, whether he realizes it or not, prepared me for this world."

"My father prepared me for marriage," Sara said, almost bitterly, but then perked up quickly. "Will you teach me to fight?"

"Leaf is already teaching you with the bow. What more would you want to learn?"

"I want to fight with a blade," she said, her blue eyes hardened with determination. "It was the first weapon I was given. I want to master it."

Larkin studied her for a moment. "Are you doing this for

yourself, Sara?"

"Yes," she said. "Yes, more for myself than you realize."

"Okay," she said. "I will teach you."

Sara reached for Larkin's hands. "Thank you."

There was a knock on the door and it swung open. Barren appeared. Larkin rose to her feet.

"Come," he said. "We are meeting."

***

They crowded into a small room with a long table. The feel of this shelter was much like being on a ship. The ceilings were low, and the same creaks and moans ensured that it was never quiet.

When they'd arrived, Slay had been sleeping with his feet propped up on the table. Sam had slammed his fist on the table to wake him up, and the dwarf had drawn a knife to illustrate his anger. Cove glared at them, and Slay put the knife away.

With the door closed, the air became hot. Larkin wasn't sure how long she could stay in here. Her anger had already flared when Barren left them to retrieve Aethea from whatever hole she'd been placed in. When he walked in with her, her eyes were no longer blindfolded. He directed the assassin to a chair at the table, and she sat, back straight, arms tied behind her back. Larkin kept her eyes averted.

Barren sighed and ran his fingers through his hair, as if he were irritated. "We cannot all go into Aryndel," said Barren. It was the same tune he always sung before they did things like this. "If we leave our ship unwatched, it will likely be looted, and if we all entered Aryndel, there will be no one to help us get out in the event we are captured." Larkin glared at him, daring him to tell her to stay. He met her stare. He already knew what she was thinking. The last time he'd asked her to stay on the ship, she'd snuck into one of the worst prisons in Mariana. It hadn't gone well for either of them. "I would like to bring Leaf and Sam with me. Aethea will lead us to Sabine. Everyone else will remain on the ship. If we need aid, Cove can organize a rescue party."

"What am I to do?" Larkin asked.

"I don't want you there," said Barren.

"You don't want me there?" The pain she felt at his words just made her angry. "Yet you'd trust the assassin to lead you to Sabine? The assassin who used the *vacair* to kill your brethren? As if *she* doesn't have plans to kill you!"

It was dangerous for her to speak about the assassin in such a way, especially considering what Aethea knew, but Larkin was tired of being overshadowed.

"Aethea has nothing to do with this," Barren grated.

"You both keep talking like I'm not here," Aethea's voice made Larkin's skin crawl. "If it will ease your mind, Lady Larkin, I assure you I do not intend to kill your beloved."

"As if your word means anything," Larkin spat.

It was the first time Aethea didn't smirk at something said to her. The assassin pressed her lips together tightly, and her eyes seemed to burn into her. There was silence, and then Barren spoke.

"It's hard enough to go back to the Underground without Christopher Lee's daughter. You will be a target."

"Go back? What do you mean?" Larkin asked. She'd never heard of Barren going to the Underground in the first place. And if she was merely a target, then why hadn't he sent her back to Maris already? He was starting to sound like the Elders. He was turning her into a burden. "Are you going to explain this to me, or are you going to pretend like it never happened?"

He stared at her for a long moment, biting the inside of his lip. Everyone in the cabin looked away, and Larkin realized she was the only one left in the dark. "There is little to hide, I suppose. There was a time when the Underground benefited Silver Crest as much as it has the king. My crew and I worked for the Underground. It's how I met Leaf."

"So what happened?"

"Silver Crest broke from the Underground," Barren said with a shrug. "More than likely, it was to ease tension. The Underground works with the Avalon pirates, too."

"And what were you made to do?"

"We were Runners. We did what we were asked," said Barren. "I'll let you imagine what that means."

"I don't want to imagine!" she hissed.

"We moved inventory, destroyed rival shipments, killed lead dealers," said Leaf. Barren glared at him. "The Underground is as much a market as it is a race. We did what we did, and we don't anymore. That should be all that matters."

"Just like Éire doesn't matter?" She stared at Barren, waiting for him to speak, but harsh silence filled the room. "Leave us," Barren said, and his crew stood and left. Cove directed Aethea from the room. She was clearly amused. When the door shut, heat built in the air between them.

"While my crew and I were Runners for the Underground, I was betrayed by one of my own. Isaac Noble spoke of a traitor on the ship. He believed Ambrose, one of my closest advisors, would betray me to the Éire fleet. We were delivering a shipment from the Underground. I kept Ambrose close to me. I never voiced what I suspected. When we were attacked, I killed him quickly. There was a battle, and it wasn't until after that I learned Isaac was the true traitor."

There was silence, and Larkin just stared, shocked. That was not the story she expected him to tell.

"I want to know who told you about Ambrose," he said. His voice quavered as he spoke, full of pain and anger. "I deserve to know!"

She just glared, and he grew angry, hitting the table with his fist.

"Tell me, dammit!"

Her throat worked, and the words tumbled from her mouth.

"Ben Willow," she said.

"Ben Willow?" He was surprised. "How did you happen to speak with him?"

She averted her eyes, but they grew red and watery with tears. "At the ball."

"You spoke with him at the ball?"

"I was attacked," she said. "It was a trap."

"You were attacked and told no one?"

"I-I couldn't."

"You couldn't tell anyone? Why? Because you didn't want to admit you were looking for your father? Larkin, I already had that figured out."

His voice rose. It made her want to cover her ears.

"So what did Ben Willow hold over your head to bring you to his side?"

"I'm not on his side!" she argued.

"To hell you're not!" he countered. "You've lied to me. You're supposed to tell me everything!"

"Well, you don't make that easy!"

"It isn't always going to be easy!" he growled, and he shook his hands in the air. "Ben Willow gave us hell in Arcarum, and now you're telling me it's because he knew we were there. Don't you think this is dangerous for Cove? Don't you realize it could get him killed?"

She had realized that. That's why she'd told Cove the truth, or most of it anyway. As she stared back at Barren, taking in the pain and disbelief on his face, she knew she should tell him that Cove was aware of the situation, that they had a plan—that things would be okay. But she couldn't. If Barren knew, he would not let her complete her goal, and his relationship with Cove would be wounded. No, the burden would fall upon her.

"My choices were just as bad as your choices," Larkin argued. "I cannot justify them, but you brought soldiers right to Cove's door when you kidnapped Aethea. It is the same thing."

"Is that where you were that night?" he asked, ignoring her

accusation. "You went back to *him*?"

She did not speak, and Barren leaned forward, pressing his palms against the table. "If Ben Willow is the man I think he is, you had better think twice before you place your trust in him."

"Who said I trusted him?"

"Your actions speak volumes."

The door opened and Cove stood there. "Larkin, a word."

"Gladly," she said, and hurried from Barren, knowing her world was falling apart.

***

Cove moved down the hallway, and directed her into a room. Larkin turned to him, tears streaming down her cheeks as he closed the door behind them. "I cannot do this, hurt him like this!" she dragged her hands over her face, wiping the tears away. "He sees me as a traitor!"

"Larkin, it's hard now, but I promise it will get better. For now, we must keep our secret."

"Yes, with no consequences to you!"

"Oh, I will have consequences," said Cove. "My friendship with Barren will never be the same after this."

And yet he showed no pain, no regret.

"How do you do it?" Larkin asked. "Choose Mariana over your friends?"

The ambassador's gaze was unwavering, as if he didn't understand.

"Even as a pirate of Silver Crest, your concern is Mariana. You swore to the code, and yet you're the one willing to defy the

Elders and dissolve the Network. You would sacrifice your relationship with Barren. You've let the love of your life slip away. All for the greater good of a world that has been so unfair to you. In the end, what will you have? Power? Did your father not die for power? Did your father not die alone?"

"I think you've said enough," Cove replied, and then he turned and left. Larkin wouldn't have any friends after this either.

***

Cove stood by the ocean. He'd come out here to think. Since he'd found those five bodies in the ocean, nothing had been the same. He wasn't so naive as to believe otherwise, but things were going in a direction he wasn't sure he could return from. Larkin's words had hit their mark. Tonight he'd realized why she was so infuriating. She told the absolute truth, and while it was hard to hear, she was right.

He spent his days distancing himself from his emotions, making decisions that benefitted the cause rather than the people. It was the only way he could do his job. This was the burden of Albatross.

Since his injury the night of the ball, he had not felt the same. He'd kept quiet about the pain, he'd kept quiet about the lethargy, but each night it grew harder to sleep, and when he did, it was harder to wake up. The wound at his side had not yet begun to heal either. The skin had yet to turn red and pink, instead it looked bruised, black and blue, and black veins had begun to branch forth from it. Leaf had requested to look at it, and Cove had refused him. He knew he only had so much time before the Elf got his way. Dr. Newell said he had never known anyone who survived a *vacair* wound, but Cove wanted to keep that as far from his reality as possible.

He hoped he could return Sara to Arcarum before the *vacair* wound claimed his life, but as far as staying, he was not sure he could return to his life as ambassador. His father always said nothing was forever. Perhaps he had been anticipating his betrayal when he'd spoken those words, but Cove had come to find out they were true.

"Do you always wander off by yourself?"

He came out of his thoughts and turned to look at Sara. She seemed sad, which made him sad. At least so long as he kept his secret, he could make her smile.

"Not always," he said. "I just needed...the quiet."

"You have been quiet," she said. "At least...toward me."

He heard himself laugh a little. "What am I supposed to say to you?"

"If you cannot speak to me now, how am I to think you were ever sincere about anything you told me?"

He turned fully to look at her. "You don't honestly think that what you and I...that our friendship was a lie?"

She shrugged her lithe shoulders. Sometimes he forgot how small she was, how young she was. "I thought we could tell each other anything."

He laughed again, but there was no humor.

"I know you think I'm a child..." He started to interrupt her, but she continued, speaking louder when he tried to stop her.

"But I thought I understood our relationship. That no matter how bad things were, we would never lie. The reality is, you didn't trust me. Don't you think all of this would have been easier if you'd just told me the truth?"

"And put you in danger? Absolutely not. Sara, you don't understand!"

"You've never given me the chance!"

"People want to kill me, and you, by association. Don't you understand that? Anyone who stands up next to me is as good as dead."

"But I would risk my life to stand up with you," she said. "Does that make you afraid? Is that why you run away?"

"Because I love you!" When he realized what he'd said, he paused and took a deep breath. "You cannot forgive the things I have done, and I don't deserve your forgiveness."

She glared at him with those round eyes, and when she spoke, her voice trembled with anger. "How can you tell me you love me now? When it is too late?"

He hadn't meant to say it. It had just slipped out. "I should never have said that," he paused. "I did not mean it."

"You're a liar," she said.

He was a liar, but no matter where she was in this world, or who she was with, she was still engaged to Ben Willow.

"Why'd you say yes?" he asked. "I was coming back for you."

"My father didn't give me a choice. He waited for you just as I waited for you, and he grew impatient."

"You could have said no."

"And if I had you'd still be leaving and coming back for me," her smile was sad. "I suppose we do not realize what we've lost until it is gone."

She turned slowly then and walked back to the shelter. Cove kept his fists clenched tight. The pressure ensured that he did not move from this spot, though everything in his being wanted to run after her.

Chapter Nineteen
ARYNDEL

They departed Iona early the next morning. Several things fell heavy on Barren's heart, and he knew his crew felt the same way. There was a lethargic feel about the ship. Perhaps part of it was from being so close to the Octent, knowing that Aryndel would be within their sights soon.

Finding Aryes in the wreckage with the weapons and learning that the Elves were frequenting this part of the Orient made Barren think the Elves were involved with the *vacair*. He hadn't broached the subject with Leaf since Aryes death. Indeed, he was avoiding it. They were going to need more evidence.

Then there were the Elders, who would exile Barren if they ever got him back to Sanctuary to carry out the order. Until then those who did not support him would hunt him. Further, they'd had the audacity to place a bounty on Larkin's head. He suspected they wished to return her to Maris to gain favor, but he had no way of verifying this belief.

Then there was Larkin. He had no ability to really understand her actions. She'd been attacked at the ball and was consequently discovered by Ben Willow, though she had told no one. He also believed she'd visited Willow a second time. He wanted to believe that she would not enter into any sort of contract with Ben, but her silence on the subject made him think otherwise. In any case, they had not spoken since yesterday.

He'd decided to bring her along into Aryndel. He hadn't trusted her to stay on the ship anyway, but now he wasn't so sure he could trust her at all.

Since Cove had called her away yesterday, she'd hardly left his side. Even now, they stood in each other's confidence. He thought about interrupting them, calling Cove away for some menial task, but when Larkin's gaze turned to his, he pushed the thought away. Her features were raw. She was angry, frustrated, sad. She turned back to Cove, leaving Barren alone.

Leaf approached Barren.

"Can you hear what they're saying?" Barren asked Leaf.

"They are discussing Sara," said Leaf.

Barren did not question that.

"Larkin learned of Eire from Ben Willow," said Barren. "I can't imagine how he would know about something so close to me, unless he heard it from Isaac Noble himself."

"Why would Isaac chose to relay that story? It does him no justice," said Leaf.

"Isaac would not care what light it cast upon himself. It shows the kind of person I am," said Barren quietly. "It shows I am a monster."

"Larkin does not think you are a monster, Barren."

"You did not see the way she looked at me." She'd been shocked. Clearly she had not expected him to relay such a story. It just showed how much she didn't know about him and how she'd run if she did know.

"I see the way she looks at you every day," said Leaf. "She does not love you any less. But you must be forthright about your past. It's hard to hear, yes, but harder when you try to keep it a secret."

"She keeps her secrets," said Barren. "Why am I not allowed mine?"

"You must see what you've done," said Leaf. "Even now she takes confidence with Cove and not you. She's taking comfort in someone who does not lecture her as if all her decisions are wrong, someone who has shared, no matter how hard, the truths of his circumstances. She's afraid of your reaction. She's…"

"Afraid of me," Barren finished. "I get it."

Leaf stared at Barren, irritation in his eyes.

"If she was afraid of you, she wouldn't defy you. She's waiting for you to trust her."

Barren met the Elf's gaze. "There is no chance of that now."

"Was there a chance to begin with?" The Elf's sea-green eyes were harsh. "You've set her up for this. You've expected her to betray you. If anything, this is your doing." Leaf turned from him then.

Barren had always felt he trusted Larkin, but maybe Leaf was right. Maybe he had set her up for this. But of everyone she might listen to, why Ben Willow? He still didn't understand what had happened at the ball, but maybe there was more to the story than she was letting on. Maybe Ben had some sort of advantage. Leverage, as Aethea had called it. Perhaps this had been his fault. When his identity was found out at the ball, Aethea might have relayed that information to Ben, who could then identify Larkin. He'd kept sight of her all night. Anyone with eyes would have seen that.

So when Larkin had left the ballroom, Ben had followed like a hawk waiting for its prey.

Barren found himself moving below deck, and his feet carried him quickly to the brig. Aethea was already looking up, as if she knew he was coming.

"What a surprise," she said. "Has the pirate captain come to visit?"

Barren regarded her for a moment. Aethea had maintained her arrogance since she'd been captured. It made Barren think she had secrets, some sort of power over them they had not yet realized.

"You work for the Commonwealth, which means you know Ben Willow," he said. "So once you discovered I was at the ball, it was probably easy to ascertain who my crew was, you being an assassin."

Aethea did not speak.

"But I can't understand why Ben Willow, having the chance to take Cove down before everyone, would refuse in favor of attacking Larkin and holding her to his will. Further, I cannot quite grasp how Ben acquired information on a man I once sailed with. He was much like you, a liar and a good killer, and he hated me. His name was Isaac Noble."

He watched her to see her reaction, and while she still smiled, she had gone completely still. She knew Isaac Noble, and whatever connection he had to Aethea or Ben Willow would not be good. Barren wanted to know why, after years of hiding, he'd decided to come back.

Aethea inhaled and then spoke. Her eyes narrowed, and seemed coal-black under the dim light. "Do you really believe Ben is holding Larkin to his will? Really, what sort of power does he have? By now Larkin has experienced true magic and should realize mortals hold no true power."

Barren found that comment odd, but it was partly true. Larkin had experienced true magic in the form of the bloodstone. She'd seen mortals vie for its powers, but it wasn't like they had any of that magic, so they were all just mortals against mortals.

"Perhaps," Aethea continued. "She merely does not wish to be a part of this world anymore."

Barren set his teeth. She was preying on his fear.

"I don't believe that," he said.

"Maybe she was sent to betray you from the very beginning. Her father has ensured she was made for battle, and he's also maintained her position in Maris. You cannot deny these possibilities," she said.

If he wasn't aware of the secrets she'd kept and her correspondences with Ben Willow, he might not have let this bother him, but it did.

"Though, it will be a pity and awfully damaging for you to confront her, especially if you are wrong," said Aethea. "You would prove that you mistrust her, and your relationship cannot carry forward without trust, but that's what you get when you love a proud beauty."

Barren glared. "What do you know of this?"

Aethea laughed. "I know you," she said, and there was a gleam in her eyes. "Brooding, angry. You'll never find true peace because you have no wish to be happy. You're a disaster waiting to happen."

"And you think you're any better?" he said. "An assassin with a history wiped clean, bent on revenge? Someone was not good to you."

"You're right," she said, lifting her head a little. The light spilled over her features, making her cheekbones seem shallow. Someone was not good to me. My mother was slaughtered, and I was taken and enslaved."

"Was Tetherion responsible?"

"No, he was not."

"So why try to kill him?"

She smiled. "For practice."

Barren knew that wasn't completely true. She might have tried to kill Tetherion for practice, but he suspected the king played some role in her agenda. Something about her was completely off and Barren shuddered. He turned from her, disgusted.

"It is strange you know so little about your world and yet you are the one who tries so desperately to save it."

Barren didn't respond, he kept walking.

"I am curious. Why care at all? The nature of your occupation is to be content to let the world and all its trouble pass you by."

Barren turned back. "There will be a time when the troubles won't pass me by. When they hurt those I love. Besides, my father had something to do with all of this. I want to know what."

She kept that annoying smirk on her face. Barren wondered what it would take to make it go away. "You might do battle, Barren Reed, but it is still for selfish reasons."

He was done listening to her. He'd been told a number of times how selfish he was—by the Elders, by his friends. What would it take to prove them all wrong?

***

When lights blazed on the horizon in a haphazard manner, Barren brought Aethea above deck and removed her bonds.

"And what about a weapon? You would not leave me unarmed."

"I would and I will," said Barren.

Slay scoffed. "Listen to 'er! It was kindness to free you from those shackles, and now yer demandin' a weapon?"

Aethea glared, but Barren knew that if she wished it, she'd come by a weapon on her own. He only hoped he could stay one step ahead of her.

They all changed in anticipation of entering Aryndel. They

wore dark clothing and kept their weapons strapped tight. Barren kept an eye on Leaf as they approached the island.

"Leaf," Barren caught him before they departed the ship. He'd wanted to say something helpful, something sincere, but the Elf turned to him, and his sea-green eyes were hard and dark.

"Every life is hard, Barren," he said. "Stop acting like mine is an exception."

When they were close enough to their destination, Aethea, Barren, Larkin, and Leaf approached the island in a dinghy. They unloaded onto a slimy set of wooden steps that jutted out from the ocean and led to a wide cobbled walkway, which narrowed into a street. From there, Aryndel unfolded before them.

What was beautiful about Aryndel, about the whole of the Octent, was that these islands seemed to cling to the ancient world. Though it was nighttime, the lamplight fell like oil onto the slippery ground. The cobbled way wound through cluttered buildings composed of distinct stones or white plaster and dark beams. The streets themselves were crowded with tents and people selling goods, drinking ale, and living in filth. The smell of alcohol and urine was ever present. Barren had never actually entered the city of Aryndel before, but he'd sailed to one particular landmark, a large bridge that ran over a wide river. It was beyond this bridge that things got rough.

"Draw up close," said Leaf. There was an edge to his voice that made Barren's skin prickle. "Here they will claim you as property."

"Women are not property," Larkin said. "No human can be property."

"A human can be property," said Aethea. "Though that does not make it right, does it?"

With that, Aethea settled into the space beside Barren, giving him a grin. He looked back at Larkin who had taken the comfort of Leaf's arm but did not remove her fiery gaze from them.

With that, they began their journey down the cobbled road. Any other time, Barren would have been perfectly at ease walking among these people. They were people he knew, a lifestyle he'd seen countless times. There were certain times, however, when he felt more Elf than human. In these places, the only thing they would see was the Elfin blood.

Barren was jolted out of his thoughts. The crowd had become thicker, more rambunctious. Music roared to life, and men, women, and children danced in the streets.

"Move faster," said Aethea, and she broke free from Barren and hurried ahead.

"Hey!" Barren said angrily and he moved rapidly through the crowd. He didn't have time to look behind him to see if Larkin and Leaf were following because the assassin moved too fast. Her small frame made it easy to dodge people, but Barren was bigger, and his attempt to catch up with her was drawing attention.

He saw the end of her cloak as she rounded a corner. He almost slipped as he followed, charging after her down the causeway, but he suddenly found that she was nowhere in sight. He halted, and Larkin and Leaf did too.

"Imagine that, she's led us astray," said Larkin. "And quickly, too!"

"Yes," Leaf said grimly. "And what worries me is who she'll find now that she's free."

Barren kept his eyes on the crowd, searching for her silhouette. He caught sight of it. The back of her dark cloak, hood drawn up, probably hoping to blend in with the crowd and the night. He ran for her. When he reached her, he grabbed her arm and twisted her around, but the woman staring back at him wasn't Aethea. It was Em, Emmalyn Levianth, the assassin who had saved them in Estrellas, Devon's love, and a friend of his father's. He stood shocked.

"Em?" he asked breathlessly.

He was even more surprised when she tore away from him and ran. "Em!" he shouted. What was she doing here of all places? And why was she running from him? Was it coincidence that both Aethea and Em were here? Both were assassins. Perhaps they were working together?

He took off after her, but Em, true to her nature, was fast and agile, and by the way she ducked around corners and maneuvered the causeways, he guessed she knew these streets well. Their chase drew more and more eyes. While he tried to ignore the attention, he knew that they couldn't avoid the trouble coming their way for long.

And he was right.

"Barren!" the voice belonged to Larkin, and when he halted and turned, he saw that she and Leaf were surrounded by a set of grizzly men. Leaf had drawn his bow, the arrow rested against the string with stillness.

Barren drew his sword and approached, but the circle of men opened, and more men came out of the shadows to surround the three of them.

"You pickin' on that lass?" One asked, his teeth looked black, and he spit at Barren's feet. He had a feeling these men didn't really care, that they were just looking for a fight. Barren and Leaf instinctively moved closer to Larkin. They had a shared unspoken fear.

"Let's get one thing straight boys," said Barren. "I'm not looking for a fight, but if you want it, you'll rue the day you messed with us."

The men laughed. "Sure didn't look that way to us," said another.

Barren surveyed the men, locating weapons. A few had swords, others had small knives, but most—and he was sure by the scars on their knuckles—fought with their fists.

"I'm not so sure any of you are a good judge of character," Leaf replied.

There was sudden movement from behind him, and the Elf turned to release an arrow. It lodged straight in the heart of a man. He fell with only a final gasp. Barren gaped and watched as Leaf drew back his hood, exposing his heritage to everyone who surrounded them. The words he spoke next made Barren's skin crawl. "Challenge me," he said. "I will bathe in your blood."

And the men did challenge him because Leaf was something

they wished to destroy. Barren tightened his grip on the blade and swiveled quickly as one of the men tossed his dagger. The blade twirled fast, and he somehow managed to hit it with his sword, shifting its trajectory. It landed far away in the darkness, but the man charged at Barren, and he had no choice but to attack him head on.

His hood flew off his head and someone yelled, "He's half-elf!"

That seemed to stir even more commotion, and the fight became all that more violent. Barren was distracted. He heard the whiz of arrows and the clang of Larkin's blade. The harder they fought, the more men piled up around their feet, yet still more came out of the darkness.

And then suddenly, the ground shook violently. Barren found himself struggling to stay upright. The buildings around them seemed to moan, as if they, too, feared falling. Pieces of brick and mortar broke free from the buildings and tumbled to the ground. If the earth shook any harder, the whole of Aryndel would crumble. The tremors seemed to last for a lifetime, and when they were finally over, the men who had surrounded them, ready for blood, fled.

The pirates watched them flee, dazed.

"Well, I would say that was luck," a familiar voice sounded from the shadows. It was Em.

Barren turned to face her.

"You're here? You watched us struggle?"

"I wasn't going to let you die, if that is what you are

insinuating."

"And what are you doing here in Aryndel?" Barren demanded, ignoring her jibe. "And running? From me? Like I am some enemy?"

"You can never be sure of your enemies, Barren Reed. You of all people should know that."

Barren wasn't sure which he should be more upset about, the obvious jab at the twins' betrayal or her insinuation that she couldn't trust him. If he had to guess, this was about the Elders.

"I suppose we should move along. Those Earthquakes aren't so common."

She moved between them, and they watched her as she did. They exchanged glances and then followed her, drawing up their hoods.

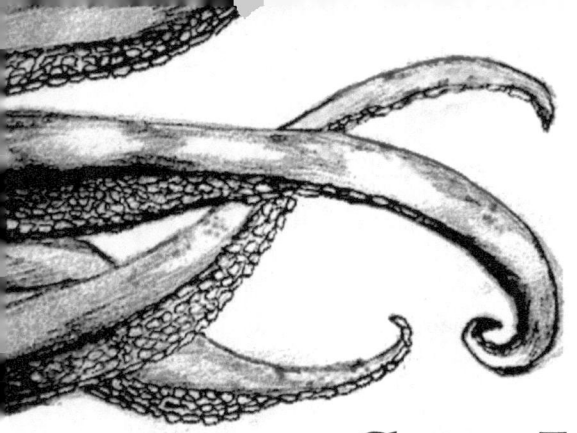

Chapter Twenty
ILLUSIONS

It started to rain as they headed farther into Aryndel, moving around corner after corner, spiraling into the heart of the island. Barren was nervous here, and even more so now that Aethea had escaped them. They needed to find her, but if she'd made it to the Underground already, they would have no advantage. No matter what sort of pull Aethea had in the market, Barren and Leaf's presence would be a problem for some. There were few ex-Runners in Mariana, and those who were didn't venture near the Underground.

Em kept them in the shadows. He hadn't thought to ask where she might be taking them, because, truly, there were things he wanted to know about Em. Was she staying here? The way she moved through the darkness, the way she cast her eyes about before moving between streets made him think she wasn't any more comfortable here than the rest of them.

At last, she slipped down a short set of steps into the basement of a building. She held the door open for them, and once they were inside, she shut it tight behind her, leaving them in darkness. Something scrapped against the floor, and then there was silence. Their air was stale and they were uncomfortable in their wet clothes. After a moment, a candle ignited in the room, and Barren saw that Em had pushed a small wooden dresser in front of the door.

"Are you afraid you were followed?"

"I don't believe we were followed," she said. "But you can trust few here."

There was a tension between them Barren couldn't quite place. None of them were strangers, and yet this felt strange. Barren exchanged a look with Leaf and Larkin.

"Does Devon know where you are?" Barren asked.

"No," she said nothing else on the subject. "I will make tea."

He'd seen Em kill, so it was unusual to watch her as she did something so normal like making tea. She placed a cast iron teapot over the dying embers of a small fireplace, and fumbled with the cups a bit. Perhaps she was nervous.

"We don't really have time to have tea," said Barren.

"Oh yes. The girl you were looking for when you found me." Em continued to make tea. "What is your hurry? If she knows these streets, she will find you."

"She will only find us to ensure we are dead," said Larkin, and she glared at Barren as she spoke.

Em paused, looking at them. "Either way, she will find you. Is she why you are here?"

"She is part of the reason," said Barren. He paused for a

moment and reached into his pocket. "She used these bullets to attempt to kill Tetherion. She missed and hit Albatross instead. A man named John Newell said these weapons are called the *vacair*, and that Cove will die."

Em stopped making tea, and her hands fell to her sides. "And this girl, she got these from the Underground here?"

Barren nodded. "She said her supplier was a woman named Sabine."

Em turned away and started to pace.

"Five of our brethren were also killed with these bullets," said Leaf.

"Do you know who killed them?" she asked.

"The same woman who shot Cove," said Barren. "Her name is Aethea Moore."

"Do you know of the dealer she spoke of?" Leaf asked. "Is that why you are here? Because you know about the *vacair*?"

"I did suspect the *vacair* were running through the Underground," she said, and hesitated. "The Corsairs have intercepted ships recently carrying Underground goods. Among them were these weapons. Their leader, Dominique, has told me that a woman named Sabine funnels the weapons through her channel, though we are not sure who her supplier is."

If the Corsairs were intercepting ships, it was possible they were responsible for destroying the ship Aryes was on. It was also possible Sabine's supplier had gone through other channels to funnel weapons.

"The Corsairs?" Barren couldn't believe what he was hearing.

280

"You're working for the Corsairs?"

"They have information," she said with a shrug. "And I'm wanted by the Elders. Do you think the mark I swore by counts for anything now?"

"Yes," Barren argued. "Yes it counts! You swore to uphold the code!"

"Sometimes you take chances to get the upper hand, Barren, and this is one of them! You don't want anymore of these weapons to move beyond these shores, trust me." She took a breath to calm down. "The *vacair*...they...they drain life forces. There is only one man who still lives with a *vacair* wound." There was quiet. Everyone knew Cove's fate, but somehow it still didn't seem real.

"There is no cure," Barren said quietly.

She shrugged. "Dark magic can cure dark magic, but for a price. You know that's how it works."

"We know how it works, what we don't understand is why it is so cruel," said Larkin.

"It's all about the intentions, what energy is placed into the magic," she said. "Ruthless intentions create ruthless magic, pure intentions create pure magic. It's simple."

But it didn't seem that simple, because everything they'd encountered from the bloodstone to the hemlock needle, and now the *vacair*, had been evil. The only commonality was that his enemies had a handle on it all.

"So are these weapons being made anew?" asked Leaf. "Or are these old?"

Barren lifted his hand and extended it toward Em, who seemed apprehensive. She took a few steps toward Barren but did not take the shells into her hand. She stared down at them, her face grim.

"These are new," she said. "Recently made."

"How can you tell?"

"Because the magic feels new."

Barren met her gaze. He could feel magic, but he didn't know the difference between old and new magic. And how did Em know? Could she feel magic, too?

"So what? That means the Lyrics are alive? Does that mean they are the suppliers?"

She smiled faintly, but it was not a happy smile. She reached for the bullets, but she drew back quickly and bent at the waist, holding her hand to her stomach as if she'd been struck by something. Barren reached for her, but as she uncurled from her position and straightened, there was a new Em before them. There were parts of her that were the same. Her long blond hair was still streaked with silver, she still had blue eyes, and there was a fierce air to her. But she was different. There was an ancient quality to her features, and her ears were slender and pointed, and there was a sharpness to her whole appearance. She was an Elf when minutes before she'd been human.

Barren stumbled back. "Who are you?" he whispered. He didn't think he really needed her to answer that. There was power here now, stronger than that which had radiated from his compass.

She looked down at her hands and he swore he saw colors of green and blue pulse from her fingertips.

"I am Emmalyn Levianth," she said.

"You're a Lyric," the tone of Leaf's voice made them all stare. He had never really come face-to-face with one. He'd seen Illiana, the twins' mother, briefly, but had not known what she was until after she'd died. Lord Alder had taken care to ensure no Elf remembered what a Lyric was, and his son was not immune to the brainwashing.

"So you knew the whole time? Where the bloodstone was? How to get to D'avana? You've always had your memory?"

She said nothing. Barren wasn't sure how to feel, but mostly he was angry and he felt betrayed.

"Does Devon know that you're...that you're a..."

"Lyric?" she asked, her features were cold. "He remembers that I am Lyric, but his memory of me as this," she gestured to herself. "Was taken with everything else."

Barren just stared without really comprehending anything.

"If you're a Lyric, how many others are there?" asked Leaf.

"Of those who lived on D'Avana, only me. But of the others who were born after us, I do not know."

"What do you mean, *born after* you?"

"Lyrics are born to Elvish parents," said Em. "It is an unpredictable gene that no one, not even the King of the Elves, can control," Em met the prince's gaze. "I know what you are thinking. You are thinking of your father's words. He told you Lyrics do not exist, and he made sure they did not exist in

Arcarum by taking them from their parents."

"And what did he do with them?"

"He has had to imprison them somewhere. Lord Alder is too frightened to destroy his only weapon," said Em. "A king can only sit by so long and watch his race waste away."

"You said you haven't had magic in the last five years," said Barren. "Since my father's death? Why? What changed?"

"The bloodstone was destroyed," she said. "Upon Sysara and Kenna's death, they agreed to place a cap on magic. If no one could access it, no one would be tempted to use it. When it was destroyed, the cap was removed."

She didn't need to say anything else.

"You knew this," he accused. "And you begged me to destroy it!"

"I did," she said, and her features were proud and severe. "We were all in agreement that the bloodstone was dangerous. I would prefer magic in my hands so that I might use it for good, rather than a bloodstone in the hands of your king."

"He is not my king!" Barren yelled, and his chest heaved. Heavy silence followed, and Barren didn't feel like he could be in this room anymore. He moved toward the door, but Leaf's next questions stopped him in his tracks.

"How is it possible to make a Lyric a slave?" Leaf asked, and when Em did not respond, he asked again. "You're saying my father imprisons Lyrics. How does an Elfin king with no power over Lyric keep them as slaves?"

"He took our power," she said. "He used an amulet as a

channel. It was called the King's Gold." There it was again. The King's Gold. Barren still could not understand why Lord Alder would relinquish such an important piece of magic to Tetherion, even if it was to secure his own kingdom. "It was made up of five Relics from the ancient Lyrics," she continued. "After the bloodstone was hidden, Jess took it from Alder and hid the pieces, only returning mine."

Em pulled on a glittering gold chain around her neck. At the end of the chain, hung something that favored a star, but Barren felt like each edge of the star resembled a blade, and each edge bore small rubies that sparkled under the faint light. It was likely the piece was as deadly as it was beautiful.

"Relics are all representations of our greatest strength. My strength...is war," she paused.

"So what are the other four, then?" asked Larkin.

"Kenna's was earth. Her Relic was a flower crafted of opal and diamond. Ara's was water. She had a gem called the heart of the ocean, it is a blue crystal. Illiana's was light, her Relic resembles a star-filled sky," said Em, looking at Larkin, and then her eyes turned to Barren. "You should already have Sysara's. You took it with you when you found her body in D'Avana. The compass, for she was strong in everything."

The compass. The ache of its absence felt heavy around his neck. Aethea had known it was important enough to be considered as leverage. When he'd captured her from the Maris guards, she'd said all her belongings had been confiscated and the compass was now in the hands of Tetherion. Had Aethea intended to hand over the Relic to Tetherion? And if so, why had she tried to assassinate Tetherion at the ball? Unless it was all a ruse?

"I do not have the compass," said Barren. "It was taken from me."

"Let me guess. This Aethea Moore has taken it?" asked Em.

Barren met her gaze.

"This woman you've spoken of, Aethea Moore, I've a feeling she is not who she appears to be," said Em. Suddenly Barren thought of how Em had kept up an illusion of being mortal. Could Aethea be a Lyric as well? "There are few who would know what value your compass had as a Relic of Sysara. Few of mortal blood, anyway. If Aethea is a Lyric, I suspect she wants to be in a position to obtain the King's Gold."

"For what purpose, if she can already wield magic?" asked Barren.

"Relics are powerful magic," said Em. "If she wanted to, she could raise your mother from the dead."

The thought was unsettling, and yet somehow hopeful.

"So why let it fall into Tetherion's hands so easily?" asked Leaf.

"Because he is a mortal man and no threat to her. The magic will corrupt him before he can wield any power."

"We have to find her," said Barren.

"You must let me find her," said Em. "If she is truly who I think she is, you can do nothing to stop her."

"You can't just throw up a flashing sign that says you're

magic," Barren argued.

"People are not aware of Lyrics. Why would you invite panic sooner by exposing yourself?" asked Leaf. "We can't risk that. Whatever you do will reflect on all Elves."

"And what if you are captured and used as a weapon?" asked Barren. "If Aethea and this woman, this Sabine, are in league together, don't you think she's prepared for something like you?"

"She will never be prepared for something like me," said Em. and Barren shuddered.

Barren was slowly beginning to understand the tangled web of his father's past. After the Ore Wars, his father, his mother, even Lord Alder had all done what they could to quash magic from existence to keep it from evil hands. They had succeeded for a time, as Barren had grown up in a world where magic was only a rumor and those who believed in it were thought of as superstitious. But it was back and for the first time in his life, he feared losing a fight, because a fight lost to dark magic meant the end of Mariana.

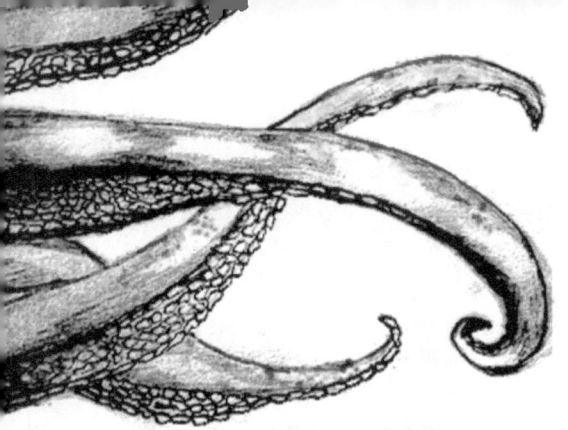

Chapter Twenty-One
THE UNDERGROUND

Em was a Lyric.

Larkin kept repeating the sentence in her head. She was both thrilled and frightened. Here was someone who could help her understand what she was, teach her about the power rising within her, maybe even help her accept what she now hated about herself. But the fear came when she looked at Barren and Leaf. She knew they were angry, and they had not yet developed a complete opinion about magic. In fact, they were probably more conflicted. Em was someone they knew and trusted, but the magic within her...well, they'd all learned to hate it.

Em had said that magic took on different forms depending on intention. That meant not all magic was bad, that meant that *she* didn't have to be evil, she didn't even have to *create* evil. Maybe she could *destroy* it.

Larkin dared a glance at Em. The gaze was familiar, set within a face she didn't really recognize. It was strange to see her as an Elf; she seemed harsher in some way. Perhaps it was from the burdens she carried.

Em's eyes narrowed, and Larkin averted her gaze. There was no denying Em's prying stare. She knew. But how? Did they share some strange connection because of their magic? She prayed Em could keep a secret.

But her magic was not her only concern. Barren's compass had turned out to be just as important as she thought. It was one of five Relics, and Lord Alder had used it to control the magic running through Lyric veins. Ben had to know this, and Aethea, too. She already suspected Ben's knowledge of the compass originated from Aethea, and if Aethea turned out to be a Lyric, she would be even more certain.

"Once we reach Aryndel Bridge, you will no longer have my aid," said Em.

"Why?" Barren asked. "Where will you be going?"

"Nowhere," she said. "But you'll deliver me to Sabine as a weapon."

"How is it to be believed that I have captured a Lyric?" asked Barren.

"There are ways. We are not above weakness," said Em. "If we were, our history would not be as tragic. Magic is as great a weakness as it is a strength."

"I will not put you in danger," the words were ever, unwavering. But Em wasn't having it and it sort of made Larkin smile, though she agreed with Barren.

"I'm putting myself in danger. Besides, how else do you propose getting to Sabine? You cannot approach her without goods. She will not see you."

"I suppose she can afford to be exclusive if she is in this business," said Leaf.

"You've kidnapped before," said Em, looking at Larkin. "So you can pretend you captured me. If she asks questions about where you found me, you can afford Leaf the credit. She'll believe him, he's the prince of the Elves."

Leaf didn't look happy, but he nodded.

"Where do we take you once we hit the bridge?" asked Barren. Larkin could tell by the way he spoke that he didn't like this. "I do not know Sabine."

"I don't know," Em admitted. "But in my experience in the Underground, if you wander around long enough, someone will ensure you get where you're supposed to."

That made Larkin shiver. She watched as Em stepped forward to place her hand on Barren's face. "You are like your father. But you are also Barren Reed and there is much to love about that."

But he doesn't believe that, Larkin thought. Barren had spent most of his life trying to be his father. She wondered if he'd ever live for anyone other than Jess Reed.

***

They replaced their cloaks and secured their weapons. Em added to their supply. She'd given everyone small round balls which she said would explode and ignite everything in their path. She instructed them to aim for anything that looked like it could store weapons.

"Let's head out," she said.

They slid into the night, moving soundlessly through the shadows. The streets were all slick with the passing rain, causing an odor to rise from the cracks between the cobbles. Larkin tried hard to focus on Em, who moved so effortlessly before her. She found herself wondering what Em's sacrifices had been. She already knew one. She'd had to make the decision to stay separated from Devon twice now, but it was clear that magic had not been her friend and had brought more burden than aid.

Why did it have to be like that? Something told her that Lyric didn't start out as a burden; it had been a gift, but mortals and immortals alike had corrupted its purpose.

Larkin, struggling to move slyly, caught up to Em. "What was the purpose of Lyric? Why are there Lyrics?"

Em glanced at Larkin and then said, "In the Elvish race, Lyrics were supposed to be guardians on earth, our magic comes from the earth's energy."

"So what happened?"

Em paused. Larkin had a feeling it was because she knew Leaf could hear, but shouldn't the Prince of Aurum already know this? Sometimes she wondered if Leaf had repressed everything he knew about the Elves to keep himself separate from them.

"Volos, Lord Alder's father, began to believe he needed to keep the Lyrics controlled, so he gave them their own island and they were to be admired for their abilities, but also restrained by strict rules. When Lord Alder came to power, he took it a step further after meeting resistance to his rule from humans. He felt the magic held by the Lyrics was his only advantage and if the Lyrics were to be guardians on Earth, then he had free use of their magic."

"So you became slaves to the will of the Elves," said Larkin.

"Part of me can reason that Volos and Alder only believed they were doing what was right for the Elves," Em said. "But their fear made them forget the purpose of the Lyrics. And instead of guardians, we became weapons. So what we would have done out of love was suddenly done from hate. Hence the birth of dark magic."

Larkin didn't ask any more questions, and she found that she suddenly moved slower, falling behind Em and even Leaf in the line heading for the bridge. She was half-Elf but she had not been raised among Elves. How was she supposed to begin to understand what it meant to be a Lyric?

She knew one thing: she had to protect people. She had this magic for a reason. Whether people believed it to be good or evil, well, that didn't matter. All that mattered was what she chose to do with it.

***

At last the space between the buildings grew farther apart, and the streets widened. They emerged from the thicket of stone to find the Aryndel Bridge. It rose like a tower with several houses stacked on either side, some three stories tall, others five. Lights illuminated windows, but most were dark, and even the starry sky above couldn't make this place any less foreboding. It was almost like its own town, suspended over the river that separated Aryndel, but Larkin realized it meant more than that. The Underground had infiltrated this place. It had set itself up so that it could control what moved, and if it had done that here, it had done that everywhere else it existed.

Larkin shivered. So many times over the months she'd spent with Barren, she'd had this feeling. It was the knowledge that if she'd stayed in Maris and never been kidnapped, she'd never know the truth of Mariana, the truth of the world.

"So it will begin," said Em. She turned and took out a black hood and a piece of rope. She turned to Barren. "Once we reach the bridge, I cannot help you and there is no turning back."

She eyed them all, as if she were waiting for them to bow out. She shoved the hood and rope into Barren's hands and Larkin watched him as he hesitated to follow Em's orders. Surprisingly, it was Leaf who retrieved the hood and rope. He placed the hood over Em's head and tied her wrists together before her. Then he grabbed her arm like she was a prisoner.

"If we cannot convince them, we will not make it out of here alive," said Leaf. "Let's go."

And they moved toward the bridge, dragging Em along as if she were a stranger whose life they did not value. Sadly, Larkin had a moment to think that Cove might be better suited to play captor than Leaf.

The bridge was wide and the houses that rose up on either side of them were encroaching. Ragged tents lined the streets, and there were few lanterns to illuminate the goods within, but light wasn't needed to buy what these people sold. Men and women moved about inside and outside the tents.

Barren kept his hand on the hilt of his sword, and though Leaf directed Em through the streets, he, too, kept his hand hovering over his blade.

A bent man ran up beside them holding a wooden box in his hands. "I got what you need...poisons, untraceable. All you gotta decide is how you want them to die."

Larkin shuddered.

"Away with you, scum," she almost didn't recognize Barren's voice.

"The lady might fancy priceless gems, rarest in the world," a woman ran beside Larkin.

"Or fine silk," said another.

Larkin ignored them and moved on. There were more, though. Sellers ran up beside them, walked backward in front of them, tempting them with various goods.

A man came up to Barren and showed him a set of knives. Larkin was surprised when he took one and examined it, but after a moment, she realized what was happening. Barren twisted the blade in his hand and pointed the tip at the man's neck.

"I'm looking for Sabine."

There was a strange light in the man's eyes and he pointed across the street to a tent. Barren pushed the man away and tossed the blade on the ground.

As they crossed the street, Larkin tried to keep her eyes forward, but she knew everyone they'd passed on the way here was watching them.

The tent the man had directed them to was much nicer than the others—blue with jeweled trim. Behind it, a three-story building was illuminated, spreading light into the tent. A man reclined in a chair, whittling away at a piece of wood. He didn't look up as they approached. On the table before them, there were crates of strawberries. The sweet smell made Larkin's stomach turn.

"I'm looking for Sabine," Barren repeated his statement to the man.

The man did not stop cutting at the wood and he didn't look up.

"Sabine does not accept meetings with pirates of Silver Crest," said the man, his accent was thick.

Did that mean Aethea had reached her already?

"I've brought her a gift," Barren said.

The man paused and looked up from his work. "A gift?"

"A powerful one. One that will make her a queen."

The man's features did not change. After a moment, he leaned forward, setting the trinket he'd made out wood on the table, then he stood, folding his knife. It disappeared somewhere in his robes.

"Follow me."

Larkin did not like this. She watched as Leaf and Em moved first, then Barren. She reached out for him, grabbing his arm. He twisted, expecting it to be someone else and she backed up a little. "Barren," she whispered. "What if this is a trap?"

She already knew he'd considered that, but this is what it was like to have no options.

"I will fight for you," he said.

And then he reached for her, and she felt his hand hook around her neck. He kissed her hard and heat race through her. How could he do this? Fight for her, kiss her, touch her when all she had done since Arcarum was lie?

He broke the kiss too soon, and her lips pulsed. He said nothing else and turned, entering the house. She followed.

The house was elegant, which was contrary to everything outside. The floors were wood, the walls white and lined with gold. There were wrought-iron chandeliers that hung from the ceiling, draped with crystals and alight with candles. Music even managed to resonate from somewhere in the house. But they weren't really going into the house. No, the man took them down a spiraled set of steps that lead deep into the abyss of the bridge.

The farther down they went, the less she was able to breath. She'd heard Barren say it before, and believed it was true now. Higher ground was always in their favor, and if they were to burn this place to the ground, wouldn't they trap themselves?

The man opened the door to what seemed like a large storeroom. There were crates lining the walls, and at the very end of the room, a large burlap curtain hung. The sound of the river was faint, but the rancid smell and the cold were strong.

"Wait here," said the man and he left, shutting the door behind him.

The four were silent for a long moment, and they looked around them.

"Why bring us exactly where we want to be?" asked Larkin.

"Because they think we will not win," said Barren.

A door opened, and they whirled around to find a tall woman dressed as if she'd just returned from a ball. Or made an important sell. Her gown was white, crafted with silk and lace, and she wore pearl and diamond jewelry. Her hair was dark and pulled away from her face, but not in a severe manner. No, the curls were soft. She had a lovely face, too, with dark eyes and blood-red lips.

When she saw them, her eyes lit up and those blood red lips curled into a smile. "My, it is a rare thing to see pirates of Silver Crest here in Aryndel, especially former Runners," she said, her voice calm and soothing. She could probably sell anything, and it was clear Barren and Leaf had made a name for themselves in the Underground.

"We've brought you stock," said Barren and he looked at Leaf, who pushed Em forward.

"Stock?" she asked, raising her brow. "That looks like a woman."

"If it is your wish to call her a woman, you can," said Barren. "We call her a Lyric."

This was the first time Larkin realized just how well Barren could play pretend. Minutes before he'd been concerned about Em's safety, on the brink of refusing anything she suggested, but now he'd dropped all of that and became cold and calculating. This was how he survived.

"And you brought her to me?" she asked. "In exchange for

what?"

Larkin looked to Barren who hesitated, but it was Leaf who saved them with a sarcastic laugh. "We have many reasons, but I'll give you the top two. Money and revenge."

Sabine seemed to consider this for a moment, but she held the elegant purse in her hands tighter. She moved toward Em and when she stood before her, she said, "Take off the hood."

Leaf obeyed.

Sabine studied Em for a long moment. She kept her eyes narrow, her lips parted. "Hmm, she is pretty," she said. "And powerful, you say? Well, I cannot very well purchase her if I have not seen her magic."

"And I cannot very well conduct magic with ropes around my wrists," she said.

"I cannot see that they would hinder your magic," said Sabine. "To my knowledge, only iron will do that."

The two had a moment, and it seemed that Sabine finally gave in. "Fine," her voice was sharp. "Cut the ropes."

Barren stepped forward to cut the ropes, but laughter interrupted him. Familiar laughter. They all drew their weapons as Aethea stepped from behind a set of crates. She was dressed in black velvet robes, and she drew back her hood. In her hand she held a sterling blade and tapped it against her palm.

"Dear, dear Sabine," Aethea said. "So beautiful, but so gullible."

Sabine's features became hard and she turned toward Aethea. "You know nothing of this market, Miss Moore. I suggest you let me handle this transaction."

Aethea arched her brows, but her amusement evaporated. As quick as a viper, she struck, her silver blade sliding into Sabine's stomach. Crimson spilled down her white dress. "But I know more of dark magic." Sabine's dark eyes went wide and she fell with a final breath to the floor.

The pirates were left to lift their weapons and Em drew back, trying to free her hands from the binds.

"So it is you," said Em. A sudden burst of energy exploded from Em's hands. Moving in colors of green and blue, it raced toward the woman they knew as Aethea. She raised her hands to block it, but as she straightened from the blow, they saw that the block hadn't protected her.

"You look just like your mother, *Halya*," Em said.

Aethea had changed as Em had changed. Once she'd been human, and now she was an Elf. Unlike Em, there was something dark about her presence. Larkin remembered feeling it upon meeting her, but now it was stronger, and she imagined it was because her illusion had been lifted.

"Ah," Aethea stretched her arms out wide. "It is so much better being in my true form."

"So you *are* a Lyric," said Barren. "Why did you let us capture you? Surely you could have escaped."

"I could have," she agreed. "And I did. Ask your lover." Larkin's heart beat fast in her chest. Barren looked at her, but there was not enough time for an explanation. "I let you lead me here so I could carry out my orders," she said. "A kiss of death was issued for Emmalyn Levianth per King Tetherion's orders."

"But... you tried to kill him!" Barren argued.

"No," she whispered and smiled. "I hit my target."

Then chaos ensued. Power radiated between Em and Aethea and men suddenly emerged from behind the crates inside the storeroom. They attacked fiercely, carrying all-too familiar swords. They were long, black and curved. Made so their victims would bleed out, that's what Leaf had said. They were Estrellas prisoners, the same men they had all encountered not four months ago, and they lusted for blood.

Larkin's sword hit hard against their blades, but this was a different kind of fight. It was harsher, it was something she hadn't yet learned how to adapt to, and she could feel the magic in her body welling up inside her. It wanted to protect her, but that couldn't happen now. She couldn't expose herself now, so she gritted her teeth and fought as hard as she could, hoping she could repress it long enough to get through this, but the more Em and Aethea fought with magic, the more her body wished to use it.

Em and Aethea were zoned in on each other. They circled one another as animals fighting for dominance.

"I'm surprised you'd choose to serve Tetherion," said Em. "When you could just kill him and take his crown."

Aethea laughed. "I like a challenge," she replied. "Besides, Tetherion is quite a malleable puppet. I think I'll keep him."

Em struck, but so did Aethea. There was a surge of energy and colors of red-orange and blue-green collided in the air and repelled each other. Some of the energy smashed into crates, and within seconds, they erupted into fire, and flames rose up and spread.

It would have been a beautiful scene if it wasn't so hostile, and when they were drained and could no longer use their powers, they drew weapons. Again, they circled each other, swords in hand.

"I've killed for a living this long, I'm not about to die now," said Aethea.

"You've forgotten that I've done the very same thing."

And when their blades met, it was with murderous passion. The anger that was between them ran deep, and it would end unresolved.

For a while they fought, evenly matched, and perhaps that's why there was so much hate. Em blocked a blow to her head, and then pushed Aethea back, breathing heavily. Aethea straightened and without any indication, she released a blast of energy from her hand.

After that, it was like everything happened in slow motion. Em fell to her knees, the air left her lungs. It was clear she was disoriented and her hand loosened from her sword. Barren's voice tore the air as he screamed her name, and Larkin turned to see the catastrophe.

Aethea pushed her blade through the middle of Em's stomach and released it. Em's eyes were wide, and she still hadn't managed to catch her breath. Even then, Aethea wasn't finished She came toward Em, the fire growing stronger behind her.

"This is the only test that ever mattered, Em," she said. She reached forward, snapping the chain that held her Relic about her neck, then she kicked Em into the fire.

And suddenly, time seemed to stop. Barren, Leaf, and Larkin all froze. Even the men of Estrellas hesitated to strike as Em's body writhed in the flames and soon went still. The smell of charred flesh made Larkin vomit. Aethea's harsh laughter filled the air, and she sprinted toward the exit. Leaf and Barren moved to stop her, but their hesitation cost them. Barren cried out as a blade moved through his chest.

It was Larkin's turn to scream, and then there was no stopping the magic within her. As she rose from her feet, it tore from her body and surged before everyone. The Estrellas men in its path were crushed, and the only thing that saved Barren and Leaf was that they had flattened themselves to the ground. It was Aethea who stopped it from going further with a simple wave of her hand. Larkin collapsed to her knees, out of breath but her gaze never left Aethea, whose eyes were alight. Larkin's secret was now known.

Then she retreated.

Larkin crawled to Barren as the fire raged about them. Her hands shook. "No, no, no," she whispered desperately. This could not be the end. This would not be the end...but she didn't believe even Leaf could heal this wound.

The blade was still in his chest, blood seeping from it fast as he struggled to breathe. She gripped it with her hands and pulled it out. His breath grew more uneven.

"Barren!" she cried desperately. His eyes were open, but they stared, unseeing. She touched his face with her hands, oblivious to the blood that seeped down his face from his lips. She was losing him. "Please don't leave me! Please, please, please."

She kept pleading, as if her words could reverse this terrible thing.

She fought the hands that pushed her aside until she realized it was Leaf, trying to get to Barren. Leaf lifted Barren to his feet, hurrying to the back of the store room where the burlap cloth hung. Larkin followed numbly. Leaf prepared to enter the water with Barren, but before he did, he swiveled toward Larkin, his eyes severe, and she flinched. She did not know this Leaf.

"You're a Lyric," he said.

"I couldn't tell you. I don't even understand what I am."

"After the choices you've made, it is impossible to trust you."

And then he entered the water, somehow managing to drag Barren along with him.

Her heart hurt for her secrets, for Barren's wounds, but more for what she had to do now. She couldn't be here anymore, not with Barren and not with these powers. She entered the water, and when she emerged on the other side of the river, her eyes met Leaf's.

He knew her decision.

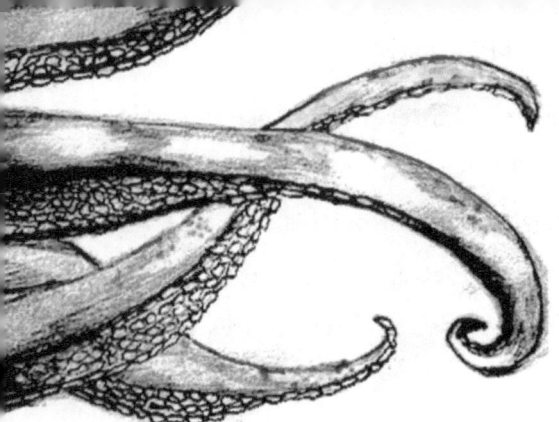

Chapter Twenty-Two
A PROUD BEAUTY

Her return to Maris had to be dramatic. It was the only way she would live. Her offenses were not unknown to Tetherion or his sons, and while her father had been able to maintain that she was still a captive of Barren Reed's, she knew the king and his sons would prefer to hang her.

The last few days had been a struggle. Physically, she was exhausted and dehydrated. Her muscles were knotted from keeping herself crammed into a tiny space in the hatch of Aethea's ship. It was the only one she knew for certain was headed for Maris. If she'd been captured, well, it would have been the end for her. Mentally, she wasn't even sure she could process what had happened to her in the last few weeks, or what had happened to Em. Barren had warned her that if she went with him, she would see things she never wished to see, things that might make her wish she had never agreed to stay. Surely he'd had no idea then how true his words would be. Surely even he hadn't been prepared for the way Em had died.

There was no going back now. The weight of her decision was heavy. She knew what she would have to do. She needed all the pieces of the King's Gold. There were at least three Relics in Maris. One was Sysara's compass, one had been given to Tetherion by Lord Alder, and the third Relic was on this very ship in the hands of Aethea Moore, who has taken it from Em before pushing her into the fire. Larkin would reclaim that piece if it meant an end to her life.

And where was her mother's Relic? Did her father know about it, and would he tell her if he knew?

When Maris was in view, Larkin slipped from the cannon window and swam to shore. She climbed onto the dock and walked through the markets at port. Her clothes dripped with water, her hair stuck to her face. She moved slowly, exhausted but also ensuring that she was seen. The markets were crowded and the throng parted almost immediately. People stared in shock. Behind her, the crowd converged and followed. She marched toward the castle, which loomed over the port mockingly.

As she neared the long set of stairs, two soldiers met her there on horses. She regarded them for a moment, unsure of what they had been ordered to do. One solider dismounted and helped her onto the horse.

Those who had followed her from port also followed her up the steep stairs until they passed beyond the walls of the castle and they could follow no more.

Everything was familiar as she passed down the halls of the

305

castle, except that it was darker, and the servants who wandered about stopped in their tracks to gawk at her. She had to get used to the stares. They would be a part of her world from this day on. No one would ever forget that she had spent months at sea with a pirate.

She was led to the throne room. The guards pulled the doors open, and she entered.

"So it is true," Tetherion's voice reached her as soon as she stepped into the room. This room was also dark. All the windows were covered, and Tetherion sat on his gilded throne at the head of the room.

When she was before him, she bowed and Tetherion laughed.

"Rise," he said, and she did. He regarded her for a long moment, and she studied him. He was the Tetherion she had encountered at sea. Untrusting, fierce. She took note of the chain about his neck, at the end of which a glimmering blue gem rimmed in gold hung. It was beautiful and drew the eye when the light hit its facets. So that was the King's Gold. She guessed this must be Illiana's piece, as it favored the night sky. How strange, Larkin thought, that Lord Alder would gift Tetherion his wife's Relic.

"Why have you returned?" he asked.

Larkin leveled her gaze with his. "I have come to deliver the information requested on behalf of my father, Lord Christopher Lee."

"What information?" Tetherion sat up in his chair. "Your father spoke of no such thing."

"She is a liar," Datherious said, and his voice rang out in the halls like a bell. "She would have us believe she is our ally, but she is a serpent. Hang her swiftly and be done with it!"

She smiled wider. Serpent, indeed.

"Silence!" Tetherion ordered, and his eyes returned to Larkin. "Let us have this information."

"Weapons of dark magic are moving through the Underground in the Octent," she said. "We believe the weapons are being used to arm the Commonwealth against you."

"You have no proof," Datherious hissed.

Larkin reached into her pocket and withdrew the spent shells that had been used to kill Barren's brethren and wound Cove. "If I may, your majesty," Larkin indicated the bullets in her hand. Tetherion nodded, stretching out his hand. She let the shells fall into his palm. The king stared at them as she spoke.

"Ambassador Rowell was shot at the Autumn Ball with one of these bullets meant for you. The effects will kill him. The assassin chosen for the job works for the Commonwealth. She is using her position to gain power until she can kill you."

"You liar," Datherious' face had grown red, and he strode forward.

"Enough!" Tetherion's voice had grown dark and frightening. He rose from his seat, pointing at his son. "You hired a traitor to serve me?"

The doors opened behind them, and Larkin turned to see Aethea Moore enter the room. She appeared triumphant, until her eyes landed on Larkin.

"Guards!" Tetherion's voice was like thunder. "Take her to the dungeons!"

"What?" Aethea demanded as she was seized.

"You would believe the words of a sea-witch?" Datherious growled.

"I believe my envious son would conspire to take my throne," Tetherion replied.

Datherious's gaze was dangerous, and he strode toward her. "You," he spat the word as if it were poison. "You really are putting on a show. I know you love him, and it will give me great pleasure to watch this break you."

Datherious swept past Larkin. She met Tetherion's gaze.

"Guards, see that Lady Larkin gets home safely."

***

It was raining when she arrived at her father's house. She stood outside, staring at the door for a long moment. She had not been dry since she'd swum from Aethea's ship to get to shore, and her body yearned for rest. Yet somehow, she couldn't bring herself to knock on the door before her.

Luckily, she did not have to. The guard who had accompanied her rapped on the door. There was a pause and it opened.

Ms. Jenkins, the housekeeper, answered with a smile on her face, but it faded instantly when she saw Larkin. She did not move to let her in. She just stood there, holding the door ajar, staring wide-eyed at the girl she used to know. Larkin felt disappointment.

308

"Who is it, Ms. Jenkins?" There was an edge to her father's voice that made her heart beat faster. He came around the corner and immediately pushed Ms. Jenkins aside.

"Lord Lee," the soldier said and bowed his head. "I was ordered to see Lady Larkin home safely."

"Thank you," the Lord said. He was not able to mask his shock. He ushered Larkin inside and closed the door behind him. Water dripped onto the wood floors and she imagined she was a pitiful sight. She hated to be pitied.

"What are you doing here?" He wasn't demanding the answer, and he didn't sound angry. This emotion she couldn't place.

"I…" she hesitated. "I came home."

He led her to his study, wet clothes and all, and shut the door tight behind them.

"Sit," he told her. She looked down at her clothes compared to the furniture. What a contrast. She sat anyway. There was silence for some time and she looked around her, unable to concentrate very well. This all felt unreal. She'd never imagined herself here again once she'd decided to sail with Barren. She felt a cold glass in her hands and looked down. Her father was giving her a glass of water. She took it and gulped greedily. He disappeared again while she downed the glass and reappeared with a blanket. It wouldn't do much good while she was still wet, but it was thoughtful, nonetheless.

"Why are you here?" his voice was low, as if he feared listeners. Larkin met his gaze. It was strange to look into his eyes and see nothing. No anger, no concern. She worked to string a sentence together.

"I told you...I came home."

"Is that all you're going to say?" he demanded, his voice suddenly harsher.

She looked up at him. His gaze was not kind, not fatherly at all. Perhaps she would have been better received if she had returned sobbing and begging for forgiveness. "What would you like me to say?"

"I would think you would wish to apologize," he said. "You humiliated me!"

"*I* humiliated *you*?" she sneered. "This has never been about you, father, but you've always made it about you. Mother's death was all about you, your revenge was all about *your* pain. You've never lived for anything but your past. You've never lived for me!"

And somewhere deep down, she realized she could say the same thing to Barren, and it would be true.

"Do not blame me for your behavior!"

"I am not blaming you, but I am not apologizing for my behavior," she said standing. "You were wrong to assume I returned in hopes that my reputation remained intact."

"If you had no hope of returning to this life, I wonder why you came at all."

She hesitated, and then raised her head, setting her teeth. "I am tired," she said, and moved to leave the room.

"Larkin," her father said her name deliberately. There was no anger, there was no frustration, only warning. "Tread carefully. The world out there at sea, it is vicious, but this, it is not any easier. I cannot protect you."

"I didn't ask for protection," she said.

She left him then, taking a candle from the candelabra and hurrying upstairs to what was once her room. The door creaked open and she entered. The lightning from the storm outside illuminated her room. It was the same as the day she'd left. Nothing out of place. Her bed was at the center of the room, red velvet covers and a canopy of the same fabric covering it. Her vanity was scattered with oils and her brushes.

She moved forward slowly, taking in the smell of the room, the groan of the floor. She placed the candle in its holder and then moved to the window seat. She sat there, drew her knees to her chest, and watched the storm as it illuminated the roiling sea. She could make out the remains of the Cliffs, their broken slabs a reminder of the night she had been kidnapped. She had come full-circle now. It was the first time she'd ever wondered if she'd survive this.

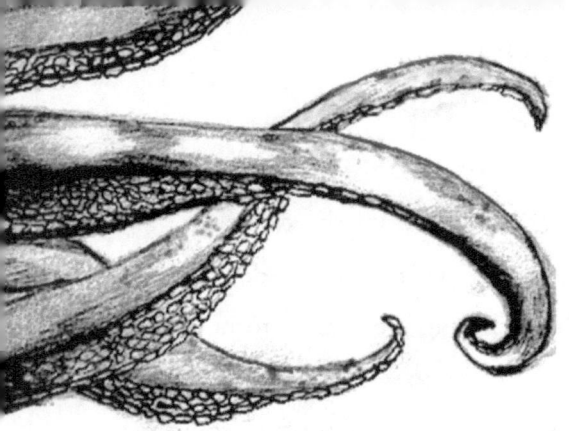

Chapter Twenty-Three
AFTERMATH

Barren came to consciousness, and while he felt feverish, he felt strong. There was something different about him, a feeling he couldn't quite place. It made him uneasy.

He opened his eyes and found Leaf sitting by his bed. He lay there a moment, trying to recall what had happened and was filled with profound sadness. Em was dead, stabbed and then burned alive by Aethea Moore. He had also been wounded. The only thing he could recall from that point on was the pain.

"You're awake," Leaf said, and his voice was rough and tired. Barren sat up and looked at the Elf. Leaf was pale, but it was not just his face, it was his eyes and lips, too. He looked sick.

"Are you well?" Barren asked. Leaf hesitated and when he did not speak, he looked around the room.

"Where is Larkin?"

He hesitated again and all Barren could think was that she had died. "Is she…is she alive?"

"She is alive," the Elf replied with some effort.

"Where is she?" he demanded a little more fiercely.

After a paused he said, "She is gone."

"What do you mean, she's gone?"

"She left," said Leaf. "She ran away."

He couldn't bring himself to believe that she wasn't on this ship. Frantically, he began looking around the room for any sign of her presence. She wasn't there. He threw the covers off and stood. He moved quickly, and Leaf had no time to stop him before he was out of his cabin and rushing on deck.

"Larkin!" he called. "Larkin!"

He turned in circles but was only met with the eyes of his crew. They shared Leaf's pale expression. It was pity because they knew she was gone, too.

Finally, Barren met Leaf's gaze again. "Barren, I am sorry."

All Barren could think to do was scream. Rage formed from deep in his belly and exploded in a growl so deep and guttural that his crew flinched away. Despite his wound, he punched the mast in front of him. Over and over again, he hit the hard wood, crying out as he did.

"Stop it, Barren!"

Finally, Leaf pulled him away, and when he did, Barren found all his crew staring at him, wide-eyed. He touched his chest, which hurt. He was surprised that there were no bandages around him, and when he looked down, he discovered why. The wound on his chest was gone, but replaced by a black spot. The darkness fed into veins down his chest.

313

He pressed his hand to the wound.

"It's the magic," said Leaf. "It has begun."

So it had. He would repay whatever debt he had begun when he'd destroyed the bloodstone. Had his injury triggered it?

Barren swallowed hard. "It is fitting," he said, and he didn't recognize his voice. "Larkin is a Lyric."

Leaf only nodded.

"Why would she not tell me?"

"Perhaps she was afraid," said the Elf.

Afraid. Yes, because everything she had encountered at sea told her that Lyric was wrong. Even Aethea Moore, who they had just discovered was a Lyric, had used her magic for evil. Perhaps Larkin had felt she must flee to remain good.

Barren sat on the steps leading to the helm. There were splinters in his knuckles. Leaf sat down next to him and began to pull them out. They were silent for a long time.

"Did she look back?" he asked at length. "When she ran away, did she look back?"

Leaf worked for a bit, picking out the splinters. Barren flinched each time the Elf touched the raw skin.

"No."

And Barren asked no more questions. He turned his attention to his crew, who had gathered about, waiting for orders.

"How long since we left Aryndel?"

"Two days," Leaf said. "We're on the border of the Octent and the Orient. I would not make a decision until I knew you were going to live."

"That bad, huh?" Barren said absently.

Leaf was not amused. "We still do not know anything about who sold those weapons to Sabine," said the Elf. "The Corsairs are intercepting ships carrying those weapons. It's likely they've discovered the source. You and I both know this is something that must be stopped at its source."

"No," Barren said immediately. "I will not work with the Corsairs of Avalon. It is against the code!"

"You'd do well to put aside your prejudices and go to them," Leaf argued. "Besides, it's not like you can get in any more trouble with the Elders."

"I don't care about the Elders!" Barren snapped. "The Corsairs have never been our friends!"

"You know who you sound like? Larkin, when she first met us. She hated us, too, and you know why? Because her father said so. You can't hate Corsairs just because the Elders told you they were our enemies. They've never once attacked us personally, and as far as attacking the Orient islands, let me remind you that we are pirates."

Barren was quiet. He knew the Elf was right. Moving forward from here was impossible without knowing how Sabine came by those weapons.

When he had gone to trial, he'd had the same thought he was having now. There were some situations he'd never expected to be in, and this was one. "Sam," he said. "Set sail for Avalon."

***

Cove approached Barren as he stood at the helm. He'd never

315

seen the pirate so quiet or so severe.

"I am sorry, Barren," Cove said quietly. He'd hoped to have better words for the moment, but those were the only ones he could offer. Even he'd been surprised to learn Larkin was a Lyric. But now he understood what she had been hiding.

"It is nothing to be sorry for," Barren said after a moment. "I am only embarrassed that I thought I could love her."

"You do not know her motivations yet," said Cove. "Her choice may be of benefit to you in the future."

"I can't imagine how," he said. "Except that I will not have to answer for my deeds."

Cove grimaced, but he had nothing more to say. He headed from deck to the hatch, feeling lightheaded and lethargic, his breath getting shorter. It was strange to be in this position, especially when it seemed Barren was getting stronger and he weaker.

If he had to sit aside and be useless, he'd rather be dead.

Once he was below deck, he slid to the ground, not wanting to walk any farther.

"You look exhausted," Sara said. He was surprised that he hadn't even heard her approach.

Cove managed to laugh a little. "I am tired," he said.

"Here, eat this," Sara knelt beside him. She handed him a wooden plate with a piece of bread and dried meats. He took the plate, and while he didn't feel like eating, he decided it was best to at least appear as if he had an appetite. He couldn't stand seeing worry in Sara's eyes, especially for him.

"How do you feel?" she asked.

But it was impossible. She would worry. She always had and even if he tried to hide how bad he was feeling, she was going to see it. They knew each other too well.

"Okay," he said.

She look down at her dress and played with the hemline. It was something she did when she was upset. When she was about to cry.

Cove sat up more, ignoring the pain that tore at his side. It was like having an open wound again. He set the plate down, and Sara reached across him. "No, no, eat," she said, trying to put the plate in his hands again.

He placed his hands on her shoulders and gently pushed her upright, looking into her eyes. Before her, he hadn't even thought of favorite colors. But her eyes made the choice simple. Blue. Sapphire blue. Tears ran down her rosy cheeks and over her red-stained lips.

"Don't cry for me," Cove said, begged really.

Her lips quivered. "What will I do without you?"

"You will live as you always have," he said.

"No, no, no," she shook her head, looking away from him. "You don't understand. You never have."

Cove's brows came together. What didn't he understand? She had moved on before, and she had to now. She was engaged.

"When you left before, at least I knew you were here on this earth. But how can I live in a world where I know you don't exist?"

He wasn't sure what to say. So he didn't say anything. He placed his hand on the side of her face and she froze. He kept her gaze as he ran his fingers through her blond hair. It was like silk and curled around his fingers.

And she leaned forward to kiss him.

They had kissed before, but those were innocent kisses. Light kisses. This was desperate. There was anger and fear. It was like they couldn't be close enough, and their kisses were rushed as if time was running out. Cove's lips trailed her jaw, her neck, her shoulders...but he stopped. His grip on her didn't lessen, because he knew that when Sara realized why he'd stopped, she wouldn't want to be in his arms.

"Sara," Cove said, and he moved the collar of her dress back with his thumb. There were colors of yellow, green, and blue. They were bruises, almost healed, but very much present.

She pushed against him, wanting to tear away from him, but Cove kept her firmly beside him. "Who did this?" he kept his voice controlled, calm. If he was to show her how angry he really was, she would be terrified of *him*.

She shook her head and cried harder.

"He did this, didn't he?"

Cove tried to move her face toward his, but she pushed against him harder. It made sense now, why she was so desperate for him to stay. "No!" she cried and stood. She turned her back on him, burying her face in her hands.

Cove stood with some effort, but he kept his distance.

"Are you afraid of me?"

She shook her head. "No," she sobbed, but she still hid her face.

"Sara," Cove said quietly, placing his hand on her shoulder. "Do not be ashamed."

She turned into him and sobbed quietly. He held her, not saying a word. He swore the next time he saw Ben Willow, his rival would die.

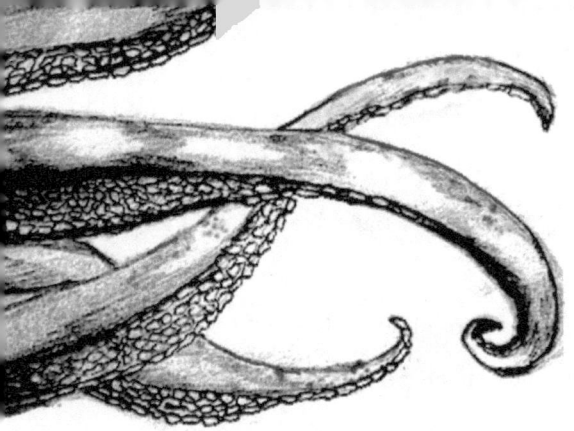

Chapter Twenty-Four
SOIRÉE

Bright sunlight filtered in through the windows. "Up!" Ms. Jennings said. It was the only word she'd spoken to Larkin since her return. "You are requested at the castle."

Larkin opened her bleary eyes. "The castle?"

"The king requests it," she said. "Up!"

Larkin got up slowly, only to be pulled by the hand and pushed toward her bath. The water already rose with steam. "Hurry!"

Larkin glared at the old woman and waited until she left to immerse herself in the hot bath. She scrubbed her skin until it stung and her scalp tingled. Her hair felt heavy as she sat before the mirror while Ms. Jennings arranged the curls, unnecessarily pinning them too tightly. Any other time she might have threatened punishment, but that was not for today. Her eyes were painted, cheeks pinched, waist fitted into a corset. The dress Ms. Jennings helped her into was iridescent pink, which made her skin seem even darker. The sleeves hung off her shoulders, and the skirt was full. She did not remember it.

"Where did this come from?" she asked.

"It was a gift," said Ms. Jennings.

"From who?"

The old woman did not answer. Larkin set her jaw.

When she stood before the mirror, she was not herself.

"You look beautiful," another servant said entering the room with fresh flowers. "It is no wonder Barren Reed was smitten with you." Larkin met her gaze and saw that the woman hesitated for a step, but then gave a small smile. Larkin wondered what she'd seen in her eyes. Hostility? Ms. Jennings huffed.

Larkin turned toward the window. Her habit of looking out at the sea each morning had not changed. After the storm last night, the sun was bright and the sea a marvelous blue. As before, she felt that uneasy pull toward the ocean. She wondered if it ever went away.

"Your father waits for you," said Ms. Jennings. "Go."

Larkin turned, gathering the wide skirt into her hands before she left the room. "Oh, Ms. Jennings," she said. "I would prefer you kept your dissatisfaction with my return to yourself while I am around. I think I might favor you talking behind my back as before."

The old woman raised her head proudly, and the other servant giggled until Ms. Jennings cast her a warning glance.

Larkin made her way downstairs. Her father was waiting for her. He helped her into their waiting carriage without a word and they hurried off toward the castle.

"What is this for?" she asked.

"I warned you to tread carefully," her father said, then sighed, peering out the window. "You said this was not a triumph over Barren Reed, but it most certainly is."

He kept his eyes on the window. Larkin pulled back the curtains and peered out. There were people everywhere. They were marching toward the castle. When her eyes met some of the onlookers, she pulled away from the window and pushed herself to the center of the seat in the carriage.

"Where are they going?"

For a moment, she feared there would be a hanging today.

"Tetherion will present you to the public," he said. "Afterwards he expects you to socialize with the loyalists. They will be brutal."

"Were they not all concerned about my absence?" she asked.

"Concerned, yes," he said. "But that was when you were gone. You're back now. Rumors abound, and one thing remains certain…you are now damaged goods."

Larkin's face felt hot. Damaged goods. As if she were a thing to be traded or bought. She should have expected such.

They arrived at the castle through an alternate route that sloped up a steep hill. Larkin was helped out of the carriage and swept inside. She could hear shouts and commotion nearby and she knew it was the crowd who had gathered to see that she had returned. She wondered what sort of opinions they held about her. Cove had taught her that the most important opinions were those of the common people. There were more of them than there were of the privileged. Their power was great, if only they realized it.

She was led up the grand staircase and to Tetherion's study. She kept her father's arm and cast glances at him now and then to see his expression. It was the same—cold as stone.

When they entered the study, her eyes immediately went to the balcony which was covered with thick velvet curtains Tetherion stood before them, his arms behind his back. Illiana's Relic seemed to glare back at her. She tried to keep her eyes from it, knowing Tetherion would notice her stare. Natherious stood aside to the left of his father, staring outside, while Datherious stood opposite his father.

"Lady Larkin, you look lovely," Tetherion said.

"Thank you, your majesty," she said, and curtsied deep.

"This is a fine day. Shall we?"

They turned to face the velvet curtains. She heard the page announce them, "King Tetherion presents to you, Lady Larkin Lee!"

Fear gripped her heart as Tetherion led her forward. What if this was an execution? And her father had led her into it?

The sun was bright as she stepped onto the balcony. She squinted against the brightness. A roar erupted from below, a mixture of cheers and jeers. She wasn't sure what these people felt of her: relief, excitement, disgust. They would feel many things, believe what they wanted to believe.

Tetherion raised his hand with hers in it and waved. Larkin

did the same, a smile plastered on her face. Tetherion drew her closer to the balcony edge and her heart hammered harder in her chest. He motioned to silence the crowd.

"My people, today we celebrate triumph over Barren Reed, for one of our own has escaped."

The crowd roared and Larkin laughed. One of our own. They had no idea how different she actually was. Even now the magic within her was swirling about. She imagined that it would be beautiful if it wasn't so devastating.

"Remember that while we've had one successful recovery, we have had many failures. Do not let your hatred for this dreaded pirate ebb. We will not rest until he hangs!"

The crowd seemed to explode with excitement. Larkin turned to watch Tetherion, and he nodded at a soldier who raised his flintlock pistol in the air and released a bullet. Then Larkin's eyes focused on movement at the docks where several ships were now setting sail.

"What is happening?" she asked.

Tetherion looked down at her, a smirk on his face. "It's a race," he said. "The first to return with Barren Reed will be heavily rewarded with thousands of pounds, a title, and you."

"Me?" Larkin asked.

"Yes," he said. "It would do you well to wed a wealthy privateer. It is perhaps the only offer you will ever have considering your situation."

"I'm not yours to marry off," Larkin said bitingly.

"Oh, don't worry, if you don't like him, you can just kill him,"

Tetherion said, turning to face the crowd, who had turned to cheer the ships forward.

She felt anger and fear battle inside her, and she knew she had made a mistake. She kept telling herself this was all for one purpose. She had a job to complete; she only hoped she could.

When Tetherion was satisfied with the crowd, he pulled her away from the balcony. "I hope that did not exhaust you, Lady. We've more events to attend."

"Oh, your majesty, I am quite energized," she said. If he was going mock her, she would mock him.

She was allowed to take her father's arm as they descended the grand staircase to the first floor of the castle. She'd forgotten how lacking she'd found the castle of Maris. Though light streamed in from windows high above, the whole castle always seemed dim. The tapestries were all dusty, the dirt covering their history. There was a grandness to everything—the large endless stairs, the blood-red carpet, the massive statues that greeted them as they descended the steps—but it was not awe-worthy. She tried to remember ever finding this place beautiful, and she had to wonder if a different king occupied the throne, if a just king commanded, would it be different?

She and her father were separated from Tetherion and the twins once they reached the bottom of the stairs and were ushered into a room. Through the open windows, Larkin could hear shouts and demands. She knew the crowd had not dispersed. She wondered if they cried for her death.

"They cry for a new king," her father said quietly. "Many have

325

joined the Commonwealth's cause."

The Commonwealth. Her throat felt tight. They were another problem, Ben Willow, especially. What would he do once he found out she was here? Would he attempt to expose her magic since she did not have Barren's compass to offer? Aethea had said that the compass had been confiscated upon her capture, but Tetherion did not wear it as he did Illiana's Relic. Would he not display the other proudly? Perhaps Aethea had been wrong. Perhaps the compass had not fallen into Tetherion's hands, but if the king did not have it, who did?

"Do you agree with the Commonwealth?"

"I think they are false prophets of sorts," he said. "Rumors are that Datherious supports their cause to dethrone Tetherion. He has become their icon. It gives him power he should not have."

Anxiety filled Larkin's stomach. What she wouldn't give to be anywhere else but here.

"Watch your words in there," her father's voice was low, warning. "They will prey on anything you offer."

She swallowed hard and took a deep breath.

Shortly they were retrieved by a servant who led them into the ballroom. The double doors were opened, and she raised her head higher. She paused as she entered the room, hesitating. Men and women were scattered all about. They were loyalists, judging by their dress of fine suits and wide dresses. When they spotted her at the entrance, a strange silence spread about the room, and women leaned in to whisper in each other's ears. She should have guessed this is how it would go, and she realized now that she was here that she wasn't necessarily ready to face their scrutiny. She was reminded of Ben's words. She really had no idea what it meant to be rejected by society, but she had a feeling she was about to find out.

Tetherion and his sons were at the center of the crowd, and when the crowd hushed he turned toward her in his false, animated manner, spreading his hands wide so that the gems on his fingers flashed.

"Lady Larkin!" he strode forward.

The black of his eyes glinted. He was insincere, though she didn't expect much from the King of the Orient. It was strange that she had now become a part of their act.

She curtsied deep, and he chuckled. Her stomach turned as she rose. He reached for her hand and drew her near him. She hated the closeness—darkness radiated from Tetherion like magic radiated from her. "Ah, this is a fine day! Ladies and gentleman, I present to you Lady Larkin! Fresh from the sea."

Some people clapped, but others looked on in disdain. She smiled anyway and nodded in appreciation at those who clapped. As she exchanged a glance with Tetherion, she saw how amused he was. She knew this was deliberate. It was a test, and as terrible a test as it was, she would need to pass it to stay free. This was a place she'd never expected to be.

Tetherion let her hand go, and she managed to take a step away. Then the vultures converged. She stood as a part of a circle, though she felt surrounded like a prisoner held for interrogation.

"So tell us, Lady Larkin, how did you find the company of

Barren Reed?" Lord Covington posed the question. He had a sweet disposition, but his wife's critical stare spoke of her disapproval.

"Deplorable," Larkin said, and the lies she told felt like knives in her blood. "I apologize if you were expecting him to have manners."

"I have heard he is handsome," another woman cut it. She was younger, and Larkin could not recall her name, though her face was familiar. "Would you say the rumors are true?"

The woman beside her was older, perhaps her mother. She had severe features, the lines in her face were deep. "I am sure she was attracted to him. She was the fiancé of William Reed."

"Oh yes," the young woman seemed excited at the thought, but also as if she'd had this conversation before without Larkin. "Ambassador Reed! What a shame. Did you see him die?"

Larkin regarded her in silence for a moment. They were trying to shock her, but she could surely shock them.

"Yes," she answered. The daughter and mother glared at her. "You will excuse me," she said and retreated.

As she turned from that crowd, another one suddenly surrounded her. They were a party of young women.

"Lady Larkin, you must tell us how you escaped the dreaded Barren Reed!" one pleaded.

Larkin hesitated. Why had she not expected this question?

"Well...I...we came to port," she said. "At Aryndel."

"Aryndel?" A man she knew as Sir Williamson stepped forward. "What was the pirate doing there?"

"I-I do not know," she said. "I was hardly told anything."

"The black market is in full swing there," he said. "You know the pirates of Silver Crest once worked heavily with the Underground to move weapons across the Orient."

"I do not know what they wanted in Aryndel," she said. "I escaped through a cannon window before I could discover anything."

"Surely you must have overheard something about their plans," said another man coming forward. "If they are in the Octent, they may be working with the Corsairs of Avalon."

Larkin opened her mouth to protest, but she hesitated. "Barren would never work with the Corsairs of Avalon."

"Oh? And you know this how?" he asked.

Larkin felt the trap closing in on her. She'd backed herself into a corner. "The Corsairs and the pirates are enemies," she said. "It would not happen."

"Do you not think, Lady Larkin, that Barren Reed would make an alliance with those who wished to attack Maris?" It was Datherious who posed that question.

She turned toward him. "That would be an assumption," she said. "Would you risk war with the Octent over an assumption?"

"You are mistaken, Lady, this is war with the pirates, not war with the Octent," he said. "Do you not agree that piracy should be dissolved?"

"Carefully, yes," she said. "Not all of them are guilty of piracy."

"It is a culture," he said. "That must be eradicated."

"That is unjust," she said. "You would deem death appropriate for those who had no control over their circumstances?"

"Everyone has control over their circumstances, Lady."

"Not if they aren't given choices," she argued, and suddenly she realized the weight of the silence in the room. She stepped away from Datherious, who had come to stand too close. "You will forgive me," she said and cut through the crowd. They parted for her as if she were the plague.

At the hall entrance, her father caught her by the arm.

"I know," she said. "I failed."

"Not completely," he said, he nodded to the crowd as if he wanted her to watch what was about to take place. She saw the man who had interrogated her speak with Datherious.

"When you are king you may see to it that pirates *and* Elves are eradicated," the nobleman Sir Williamson said.

"What did you say?" Tetherion's voice rose. Only those closest to him heard the question. Some turned their heads, but most continued to speak. "What did you say?" He demanded, louder this time.

Now the whole room went silent and Tetherion strode forward, his boots clicking against the floor.

The man who had spoken turned to face Tetherion. With a shaky laugh he said, "Your majesty, it was nothing...I...I..."

"What. Did. You. Say?"

No one moved and they scarcely dared to breathe. Larkin watched in horror.

"It is only natural that your son will one day be king. It is

330

tradition."

Tetherion reached forward and wrapped his jeweled hand around Sir Williamson's neck, lifting his feet off the floor.

"I am king!" he seethed. "And I will be king forever. Any who challenge me will die!"

He released the man, who fell to the floor. The people stared in astonishment. Tetherion turned in a circle lashing out at them so that they backed away to the walls. "I am king!" He roared. "I. Am. King!"

There was a demon-like possession in his eyes, but as he looked about at his people, who stared in horror, the light seemed to die, and he became lethargic and his chest heaved. A guttural cry escaped from Tetherion's mouth, and he fled the room.

Larkin looked to her father for an explanation.

"It is magic," he said. His features remained passive, cold.

Larkin swore her heart skipped a beat. "Magic?" she whispered the word, glancing around to see if anyone heard.

"Yes," he whispered back. "The amulet around his neck, it was given to him by Lord Alder. It is called a Relic, one piece of five that make up the King's Gold. It is said to give the bearer the power to use magic, but Alder failed to inform Tetherion that it will poison a mortal man, preying on his greatest fear."

"You know this? And yet you have kept it to yourself?"

"Once the sickness has rooted, there is no reasoning," her father replied.

"Is anyone else aware of this?"

"It is likely it has not escaped Aethea Moore's notice," her father replied.

Larkin gaped at her father. So he'd known Aethea was a Lyric, which meant he'd recognized her from his past. It meant he knew why she'd returned. Lee had not met her gaze since he'd begun speaking about the King's Gold, yet suddenly he did, and she knew whatever secrets he kept, they were dangerous but vital to her success.

***

Larkin's boots thudded against the wooden floor. She knew her father heard her move into the room, but when she entered, he did not look up. He sat behind his desk reading. This had been their life prior to her adventures at sea, her in plain sight and him, oblivious.

What she'd come to tell him wasn't going to be easy, but if she was going to learn any more about the Relics, she was going to have to be honest.

"Father," she said, but he did not look up. "I have magic."

He put his book down slowly. "What?"

"I have magic," she repeated. He was very still. He seemed to be listening. Or perhaps comprehending? She wondered if he would bolt from his chair and cast her out of his home. After a moment, he asked, "How long have you known?"

She shook her head. "Not long."

"You knew this was a possibility, didn't you?" she asked.

"I did," he did not deny it. "Lyrics have only ever been female, and one of Lord Alder's greatest fears was that magic would travel to half-elves and then humans."

"Why did you not tell me?"

"There was no point," he said. "Magic was not in your future until you met Barren Reed."

"You can't blame him for my blood!"

"If you had stayed, you would have never been put into the situation to have your magic unleashed," he said.

She looked away from him. She didn't want to argue.

"I do not understand," he said standing. "You have come back, yet you still defend that worthless pirate, and now you have magic. Why are you here? If Tetherion or the twins find out, they will use you as a weapon."

"They will not find out," she said.

He scoffed. "You can't control your magic. It will try to defend you when you cannot defend yourself. Right now you believe you have returned in triumph, but I can guarantee that after today, the council will move to rule Tetherion unfit to rule. You will be under the control of Datherious then, and he wishes to make your life hell."

"Father, right now, I do not care what Datherious has planned for me. I need to know about mother's Relic."

Lord Lee was silent for a long moment. "So you've come to help your pirate-friends rather than betray them?"

She scowled. "This isn't about enemies, father! Out there, a war is brewing. There are weapons like your hemlock needle rising in abundance. It's only a matter of time before they come to shore. They aren't something that can be stopped by mortals. You know this, so why can't we fight with magic?"

"Because I don't want you involved!" he cried. Standing, he slammed his hand against the desk. "I lost your mother to magic! Do you think I want to lose you, too?"

She didn't know what to say, and Lee turned, taking a deep breath.

"You don't have a choice, father," she said evenly. "I have made sacrifices for this power so I could help."

"Sacrifices?" he scoffed. "You don't know what sacrifices are. Leaving Barren Reed is hardly a sacrifice."

Larkin ignored him and continued.

"You know Aethea Moore is here to find the Relics. She wants the King's Gold. It is only a matter of time before she sets her sights on you. Do you want to lose another piece of mother?"

"You think I won't sacrifice a menial piece of metal and gems to ensure my position and my daughter's safety?"

"Don't you mean imprisonment?" she asked. "I told you, I don't need protecting!"

"You have no idea what you're dealing with."

"Then tell me what I'm dealing with!" she demanded. "If you wish to frighten me away, then tell me the reality you lived!"

"Wasn't your mother's death enough?" he asked, and his voice barely rose above a whisper. Larkin looked away. When faced with her mother's death, and the evil she'd witnessed from Aethea, she knew what she had to do. She heard her father sigh. "I do not have your mother's Relic. When Jess Reed demanded that Alder hand over the King's Gold, I was no longer his friend. Jess has hidden the piece somewhere in Mariana. You'd die before you found it."

"That's no reason to stop looking!"

"Lord Alder and Aethea are both searching for the King's Gold. Do you think you can overpower an Elfin Lord and a Lyric?"

"*I'm* Lyric!"

Lee flinched. "You are an amateur. You can't play Aethea's game, so stop trying."

"You are a coward."

"I never claimed to be a hero," he said.

She stormed away, running to her room. She was stupid to assume her father might help her in this. All he cared about was maintaining his position. It had never been about revenge, and it had never been about her mother, but if he would not rise to the occasion then she would. Aethea Moore would pay for Em's death, and she would never come into possession of the King's Gold.

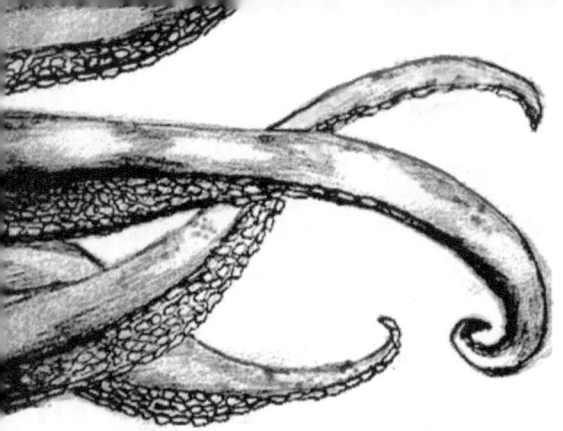

Chapter Twenty-Five
AVALON

Barren stood on deck, staring out at the night. The rest of his crew was here, except Cove who was resting below deck. More and more, Cove was becoming unable to hide his haggard appearance and his heavy breathing. Barren suspected it was from the pain of his injury. But why was Cove growing so weak when he remained so strong? As if unaffected by the weapon that had torn through his chest. Truly, he should be dead. He suspected that's what would happen once this magic ran its course and used him for whatever purpose it intended.

Cool air rushed around them. It was an indication that they were getting close to Avalon which was notorious for its frosty air and icy water. It could prove dangerous, especially in the darkness around them. Barren knew it was a storm. He'd seen the clouds roll in before sunset. Now and then, he felt cold drops of water hit his face, the wind making their impact harsh.

Leaf couldn't quite keep his gaze in one place. It made Barren uneasy because while it could be that these were unfamiliar waters, he might also sense something approaching.

"Do you sense something?" asked Barren. "Other than the storm?"

"I can't tell," the Elf replied honestly. "I feel as though we are being watched."

"But you can see nothing?" Barren's eyes weren't nearly as good as Leaf's, but he began to look around too. The feeling of unease spread.

"No." The Elf walked to the edge of the ship. The water was dark like the night. He placed his hand on the ship's rail. "It's vibrating," he said. "Something's...beneath us."

The ship rippled, as if it had been struck from beneath the surface. Barren struggled to stay on his feet.

There was dead silence.

Suddenly, a shape burst forth from the water beside the ship. As it made its way over the masts, water fell from its body, dropping upon the pirates like rain. A snapping sound broke the night, and a terrible scream filled the air. Whatever had attempted to jump over their ship hadn't cleared the masts. The shadow fell with a loud crash, and the largest mast came with it, tearing part of the ship to pieces.

"Is everyone okay?" Barren called into the night.

"What the hell was that?" Cove demanded. He came up from the hatch.

"Get Sara out of the hatch. Get everyone on deck!" Barren raced to a box near the helm in which he kept supplies. He withdrew a torch and flint. "I don't think it's finished with us."

"Why would you say that? It impaled itself upon our ship!" said Leaf.

And then the ship began to rock again. "I think it believes it's found an enemy."

Barren drew his sword, holding up the torch. He lit it and waited.

"I don't think that's going to help you much against a sea monster!" said Leaf.

"Do you have a better idea?" Barren cried.

"Got any of those powder flasks?"

The water broke again and the monster rose forth from the Orient. In all his years at sea, Barren had never encountered anything like this. Sea monsters were legends. Sure, there were octopi that could reach thirty feet. But this thing. This thing, it was almost human-like. It had a head, crowned with white coral. His skin appeared white, but it also glistened as if covered with scales.

Lightning flashed in the sky, casting the monster's silhouette in light and dark. It had hands but also tentacles that seemed to sprout from all over its body.

"What are you?" Barren whispered.

The thing raised its head, and its tentacles rose up, latching onto the ship, and the monster went after the remaining masts. They groaned under the thing's weight. A terrible scream erupted again. Pieces of wood fell upon the pirates, and then bigger pieces began to fall, hitting the deck hard, splintering and bowing the ship. Barren felt helpless. How was he to fight something so strange? So vicious?

The remaining masts finally broke, and they toppled into the Orient Sea, taking the monster with them.

"What do we do?"

"Kill it with fire! Seamus, Slay! Cannons! Now!" Barren cried.

Barren knew the monster would have nothing else to destroy but their ship when it resurfaced. The storm was worsening, the lightning grew frenzied, and the thunder boomed. Leaf worked to wrap his arrows, Cove and Sara cradled power flasks in their arms, and the others worked to prepare the cannons. As the monster resurfaced, Barren was there to light Leaf's arrows. The Elf fired and it cut through the air, lodging into the monster's chest. A scream filled the darkness and then a burst from cannons mixed with the rage of the thunder.

But the cannons that fired were not from Barren's ship, they were from another. In the chaos around them, Barren made out another vessel. It was smaller in size with a narrow front. There were two large masts at its head, and two smaller at its back. A flag flew high with the image of a red rose. These were Corsair ships.

With the added cannon fire, the monster disappeared beneath the surface. But Barren's troubles weren't over.

"Barren!" Leaf warned, just as grappling hooks dug into the side of the deck's rail. They were being hoisted toward the other ship. Barren raised his blade and his crew followed, hacking at the ropes that pulled their ship toward the enemy, but it seemed the more they cut, the more the enemy threw. It was the shriek of the creature that kept them from fighting. The monster rose again, water beading off it. The Corsairs took up long metal spears and propelled them at the monster. Just as they lodged in the creature, lightning struck from the sky. Electricity pulsed through the thing until it groaned in death, sinking beneath the surface, leaving the lingering scent of charred flesh and smoke.

The waves hardly had time to settle before Barren's ship crashed into the other and Corsairs flooded onboard. There were three times as many of them as there were of Barren's crew, and while he kept his sword raised, he knew it would be in vain. He had two options: surrender and follow their orders or fight and risk losing members of his crew.

So he raised his hands and dropped his sword to the ground. His crew followed, and they were taken to the Corsairs' ship over a boarding plank. The man who held Barren pushed him forward and he stumbled.

"Well now, that seemed too easy," the man who spoke was tall and his accent thick. It reminded him of the accent Aethea had used to cover her identity. He had string-straight hair that fell above his shoulders, and a patch of triangular beard at the bottom of his lip. His skin was brown, and his shoulders were broad. He wore a blue shirt with no sleeves, but a vibrant red cape covered his left arm completely. Barren wondered if he had an arm at all. "I must say, I'm a little disappointed. I was told Barren Reed puts up quite a fight."

"I could be less disappointing," said Barren. "But I don't

usually deal with sea monsters. You can imagine how unsettling that was."

"I suppose they can be quite dreadful when first encountered, but they rise for only one reason."

The man did not elaborate. "Search their ship," he ordered his men and they dispersed to do his bidding. It had been a while since Barren had been in this position. His whole being wanted to fight against it, but he took deep breaths and kept his eyes focused on the captain who had turned to face him again. "You'll be surprised, maybe impressed, to find that even Corsairs of Avalon have laws."

Barren scowled. He was mocking them.

The man looked around at his prisoners, and he seemed to be counting, or perhaps looking for one person. "I believe I had heard Lady Larkin was a member of your crew, yet I do not see her. Disappointing."

Barren tightened his fists.

"Unlike others, I was cheering for you," he said. "But it is so fitting that a noble lass would run to her father when things get hard."

There were things Barren would never be able to hear about Larkin, things that, no matter how angry he might be at her, were never okay. So he snapped. Pulling his knife from his boot, he attempted to launch himself at the captain but found himself on his back staring up at the dark sky. The captain laughed.

"I should kill you for that," he said. "But I'm much more interested in the angry Barren."

He was allowed to stand, but his arms were held tightly behind his back. "Why didn't you let that thing kill us?"

"Do you know what that thing was?" the man said. His accent, combined with his wide brown eyes, made the question feel heavy. Barren just blinked. "Of course you don't. It is a Makar. Do you know why it attacked you?"

"I don't know. Perhaps I was in its territory?"

"No, this is our territory. It attacked you because you have magic," he said. "It is only drawn to magic."

"Captain," a voice called. Barren turned his head and saw one of the Corsair's holding up his hand. "They have them."

Barren turned to the captain. "Have what?"

The pirate walked to the captain and Barren heard the clank of bullets as they were dropped into the man's hand. The captain's eyes met Barren's. Suddenly, he understood. Aryes ship had not been destroyed by Corsairs. It had been destroyed by that creature. The Makar.

"You don't really have to ask, do you?"

Barren turned to face the captain completely, as if he were preparing to pounce. "You don't want to use those."

"I don't?" he questioned, tilting his head to the side. "Don't you?"

"They're not what you think they are," Barren said, and that anger the Corsair captain so much admired from Barren came back. This time, the man's eyes brightened and Barren went still. The thud of the captain's boots sounded as he made his way toward Barren. He drew back the collar of Barren's shirt,

342

exposing the ashy color of his skin.

"You are sick," said the man.

Barren could only glare. The captain seemed pleased as he drew back.

"Take them away," he said and suddenly a cloth hood found its way over Barren's head. He struggled, but not for long as pain spread through the back of his head and all went dark.

Barren wasn't sure how long they sailed, but soon he was being guided to his feet and directed off the ship. The gentle incline of the boarding plank led to a hard surface. Rock, Barren suspected. Which told him he was not on a typical island. This was some sort of hideout. A cave, perhaps.

He was moved forward, a steady hand on his arm. They walked some distance. There were a few twists and turns, and then Barren's feet were kicked out from beneath him. He hit the ground hard and the hood was yanked from his head. It took a moment for his eyes to adjust to what was around him. And what was around him surprised him.

They were in a room. Barren couldn't tell if this was a cave or some sort of stone structure. It was illuminated by a fire which burned at the center of the chamber. And there were several arched openings that allowed for a view of the outside. If it were light enough, Barren imagined the sea would meet him at the window. There were barrels scattered around, probably wine and ale, and sacks of potatoes, cabbages, apples and pears.

After a moment, he heard more footsteps and saw the rest of his crew. He counted. They were all here. His eyes fell on Cove, specifically when his hood was removed. The ambassador was pale, but his eyes were still fierce and determined. Barren was happy to see the fight remained. The men brought Sara last, which made everyone tense. She was guided to the floor to sit, and when her hood came off, her eyes shot to Cove. Barren had to look away.

"Are you impressed?" Barren heard the captain's voice and he turned to see him approach. He had a piece of bread in his right hand. The cape still covered his left.

"Perhaps," said Barren. "If it was light."

The man laughed. "Do you know where we are?"

"At some point, you're going to stop asking me ridiculous questions."

The man just seemed more amused. "These are the marble caves," he said. "Very hard to navigate if you're not familiar."

"Is that a warning?"

The man shrugged. "I suppose that's up to you to determine."

The man walked past Barren and his crew. For a moment, he kept his back to them, and then he removed the red cape. It slithered off his shoulder and to the ground. Then he turned and took a seat. He popped a piece of bread into his mouth, smiling as he chewed. On his right arm, he had tattoos that wrapped around him like a snake. The other arm, which rested on his leg, was covered with an iron cast. Barren couldn't take his eyes off it. It ran from his wrist to the bottom of his elbow. Barren didn't imagine it was comfortable or easy to wear, but it didn't appear to be coming off anytime soon.

"You won't figure out what it is if you don't ask."

Barren met the man's stare, and the playfulness he'd maintained was suddenly gone, replaced by something dangerous. He leaned back in his chair, bringing one leg to rest over the other. "Your father had your curiosity."

"You didn't know my father."

The man cocked a brow. "You sure about that?"

"You're...you look my age. There's no way you knew him!"

The man patted the iron cast. "I suppose this does have its perks. I don't age. Can you guess way?"

"You continue to test me with your questions," Barren said, but the captain was no longer paying attention to him. He clapped his hands and stood. "Oh, I love family reunions!"

Barren wasn't sure what he was talking about until a familiar voice responded, "Shut up, Dom."

He twisted from his place on the floor. "Devon," he said, surprised. "What are you doing here?"

He was not restrained in any way, and he was dressed in clothes similar to those the Corsair captain wore: the sleeveless blue shirt, dark pants, and boots. He looked the same, scars and all, his gray hair in a ponytail.

"Untie them," Devon ordered, and the Corsairs listened. As the bonds came off Barren's wrists and he was allowed to stand, he faced Devon who now stood beside the Corsair.

"You're working with Corsairs?"

"Don't sound so disgusted. I'm right here," said the captain.

"It might make you feel better to know this is a recent

occurrence," said Devon, but when he saw Barren's face, he added. "Maybe not."

"He's just like his father," said the Corsair captain. "He doesn't trust what he doesn't know."

"You didn't know my father!" Barren yelled.

"Devon, help me out here," the captain was enjoying this far too much.

Devon did not look pleased. "Dominique is cursed, and so he does not age and while his behavior might lead you to believe he is younger, he is about my age."

"*Dominique Esquivel*," Barren whispered. "You're the man Em was talking about? The man who survived the *vacair* wound?"

Dominique was also the man who had split from the pirates of Silver Crest after the Barbary Wars and created the Corsairs.

"I wouldn't say survived," he said and he flexed his hand. "This cast keeps me from dying, but not from the pain of death."

Barren looked between the two. "And you know each other how?"

"We both served on your father's crew," replied Devon. "Until he deserted, and my memory was taken."

"By deserted, you mean he left to start the Corsairs of Avalon?"

"He says it as if I didn't have a good reason," Dominique commented to Devon, who wasn't amused by his light-hearted spirit.

"The story goes that you betrayed your captain, my father," Barren said. "Can you have a good reason for that?"

"I do," he said with a smile, and Barren got an uneasy feeling. "Your father is the reason I must endure this curse. He is the one who shot me with the *vacair*."

Barren lifted his head a little, ready to defend his father, but what did he really know about the situation?

Instead of accusing, Barren just said, "Explain."

"Your father and I didn't see eye to eye on this magic thing," Dominique said. "When we intercepted ships, we took the weapons. He wanted to destroy them, and I wanted to use them. I suppose you can guess the rest. We got into a fight, and I took a bullet. It was probably good for me, showed me why your father was so fearful of them. When I split and founded the Corsairs, the curse had not yet begun. It wasn't until I began to feel the pain that I changed."

"And why the cast?"

"Iron keeps the magic from progressing," he said. "I guess you've figured out on your own what it will do. Takes your life force…slowly, it will consume your essence."

"Who gave you the cast?"

"Em gave him the cast," said Devon.

Barren felt the color drain from his face.

"I already know," Devon managed to say. "Who was it? Who killed her?"

"A woman, a Lyric," said Barren. "She calls herself Aethea Moore, but Em referred to her as Halya."

"Halya, you say?"

"Do you know her?"

"Yes," Devon said, looking beyond Barren, and the pirate turned around to see some of the Corsairs depart. Barren wondered what that meant. Where were they going?

"She is a second generation Lyric. Her mother was Ara, and if she is anything like her, she will only ever want power."

"And revenge," said Dominique. "When you destroyed the bloodstone, Lyric came rushing back, along with everything it had created, curse and monster alike. That's how I knew what you'd done. The pain came back. What you have not guessed is that with the destruction of the bloodstone, Lord Alder became vulnerable. As you've learned from Em, I am sure, he is not a popular figure among the Lyrics."

Barren glanced at Leaf. The Elf was very alert, glaring at Dominique, daring him to speak ill of the king. Dominique laughed.

"So it should also be no surprise that some of the Lyrics who escaped D'Avana and survived wish ill upon him."

"Em said the *vacair* are new, that a Lyric has made them recently. Do you think they were made by Aethea?" asked Leaf. "Do you think they are meant for my father?"

Dominique laughed again, as if what he heard was amusing. "You have not yet figured out that your father is the supplier of these weapons?"

"My father cannot use magic," Leaf replied bitterly.

"Of course not, which is why he has enslaved Lyrics at the Ore Mines and drained them of their power."

"I thought the Ore Mines remained unoccupied," said

Barren. It had been thought that Tetherion would use Aethea's attempted assassination to obtain the Ore Mines, but they had heard nothing more on that subject. Further, Aethea had said that Tetherion was not aware of the *vacair*. Had she been wrong? Or was Lord Alder keeping a secret?

"Lord Alder has never been one to follow mortals' rules," said Dominique. "Indeed, his hope is to destroy the human race. I daresay, I never thought I'd see him make the same mistake twice."

"I-I don't understand," said Barren.

"Of course you don't," said Dominique. "Jess Reed was nice enough to protect Alder after he discovered that the Elf King funneled weapons—*vacair*—into the Octent and the Orient during the Ore Wars. Lord Alder's hope was that the Orient and the Octent would go to war and destroy each other. Because if there is one thing Lord Alder hates most in this world, it is mortals. Jess offered Alder an ultimatum. He wouldn't tell a soul about his treason so long as he gave up the King's Gold."

"You are lying!" Leaf accused, and he stood. "My father would never allow something as dangerous as this to happen. He despises magic!"

"Do you know your father?" Dominique asked, his eyes burning with fury. "If you want proof, go to the Ore Mines. See what your father is planning first hand."

Leaf moved to attack, and Barren held him back.

"Leaf," Barren said.

"You don't believe him, do you? You cannot believe my father capable of something like this. He didn't want the bloodstone found. He knew it would bring magic back!"

"He didn't want the bloodstone destroyed because he knew it would give Lyrics the power to destroy him. It would also make him a slave to Tetherion once again," Dominique straightened his shoulders and raised the iron cast so that Leaf was forced to look at it. "I don't blame your father for looking for a way out, but what he's chosen means our world will be destroyed."

"And why should we believe you, a man who turned against his own kind? You're not necessarily known for your good will," said Leaf.

"And neither are you, so we're essentially the same," Dominique started to leave. "Let me not give you the choice. You *will* visit the Ore Mines. You'll see what I'm talking about."

Dominique left them then. Barren turned to face Devon. There was something different in his eyes. Perhaps he was looking at Barren this way because he'd been one of the last ones to see Em alive, perhaps he blamed him. "Devon," Barren said quietly.

"I have to agree with him this time," he said, and he left, too.

Barren met Leaf's gaze. "Whoever my father has become, it is because he has only ever tried to do what is best for his people," said Leaf.

"You may be right," Cove said quietly. "But more than one kind of people occupy this world and all must learn to live side by side."

Leaf moved away from them, and though Barren knew the

Elf could still hear, he looked to Cove.

"He needs time," said the ambassador, his breath was short, his skin ashy. "Everything he knows has fallen apart in the last week."

Barren knew how that felt, but so did Leaf. Was it fair that he had to go through this devastation over and over again?

"If what we've heard is true, Aethea will tell Tetherion of Alder's plans. We have to warn Lord Alder."

"It will be some time before Aethea reaches Maris," said Cove. "Let us hope that is enough time."

While Barren was just as eager to find out what was at the Ore Mines, he wished he could protect Leaf from whatever they would see there because he knew it wasn't going to be good.

Dominique returned after a moment and walked to Cove. He carried a steaming cup in his hand.

"Here, this will ease the pain, help you sleep," said Dominique, handing the cup to the ambassador. Cove drank the tea without hesitation and fell asleep shortly after. Dominique left again, and there was silence for a long moment until Sara rose and came to kneel before Barren. Her wide blue eyes met his.

"You won't let him die, will you?" her eyes brimmed with tears.

Barren's throat was tight. If this had been Larkin, he wouldn't have hesitated in telling her the truth. He would have said he wouldn't promise, he would have explained the reality. But Sara was different. He reached for her hand and squeezed it tightly.

"I'll find a way, Sara," his voice was low, rough. "I promise."

And Barren never made promises lightly.

Chapter Twenty-Six
THE ORE MINES

Barren woke early. He moved outside the strange room and found himself on a stone bridge, which lead to another room. He had no desire to speak, and so he sat outside and watched as the world awoke. He could not see the sun rise, but he followed the light as it burned away the darkness inside the cave. No warmth came from the brightness and the cold ate through his thin clothes, but the beauty before him was distracting enough that he didn't mind.

The water at his feet was turquoise in color, reflecting off several marble structures erupting from the surface of the water. Some appeared to be large, solid walls, and others formed haphazard arcs creating a tunnel-like passageway. Barren wondered where it led, but also believed it to be a trap. At least an opponent with a blade hinted at his next move, but nature was a great deceiver, as it was truly unpredictable.

"You weren't thinking of swimming away, were you?"

Barren turned to see Dominique standing in the door of the

353

opposite room. He wore a long sleeved shirt this time. The red cape covered his injured arm, and in this white and turquoise world, it flickered like a flame. Barren wondered if he hid his arm because he despised it. The pirate turned to stare at the water again.

"I would like to, but I do not trust the water," he said.

He heard Dominique laugh and then the soft tread of his boots as he joined Barren on the bridge. "These marble caves were created by the water. She is a fine sculptor, is she not?" The question was met with no answer, and so Dominique continued. "Of course, she is as fine a killer as she is a sculptor, and as clever with the world as she is with her army."

"Army?" Barren echoed his words.

"We were not called to sea to enjoy its splendor," said Dominique, as if the very thought was a joke. "She is a vengeful spirit, the sea."

There were old legends that spoke of the sea-spirit, just as Dominique was now. Some called her a goddess and others a serpent. The Elves had a name for her, Acionna, and the Elders tended to use her tales as bedtime stories. There were times when Barren echoed those legends and believed he answered to something in these vast waters. He didn't understand it, and wasn't sure he wanted to, so he kept quiet as Dominique spoke, choosing to watch the light dance off the walls of the marble caves instead.

"Come, she will not want us to linger much longer," he said and turned, trusting Barren to follow.

***

Leaving the marble cliffs took longer than Barren expected. This area was meant to be a refuge and was tedious to navigate. They departed in small boats, eyes uncovered this time and Barren much preferred enjoying the splendor of the caves. They sailed beneath magnificent archways of stone, and the ocean was quiet and calm around them, though cold.

At last they came to an area hidden by a large wall of the same marble rock. Behind this, a port had been built, and several ships were docked. His ship was also here, destroyed by the Makar's attack. Barren looked at Dominique.

"We will repair it for you, if you wish," he said.

Barren wasn't sure how he felt about Corsairs repairing his ship, but he nodded anyway and said, "I would be grateful."

They boarded Dominique's ship, and Barren was surprised to see that Devon boarded his own ship. He took in the faces of the crew Devon called his own. They weren't all from the Octent, and he didn't imagine they were all Avalon pirates, which told him Devon merely had many alliances.

The Ore Mines were only a day's sail away from the marble cliffs of Avalon, but Barren found himself more concerned with what awaited them upon arrival and how safe the Elves were in Aurum. He knew Leaf was thinking the same thing.

"Depending on the wind, it could be a seven to eight day sail to Aurum," said Barren.

"A smaller ship would get us there faster," said Leaf.

Leaf was referring to sailing in an Elfin ship, but they would have to find one at the Ore Mines.

"Do you believe we'll encounter Elves at the Ore Mines?" Barren feared finding nothing but bones.

"I'm not sure what we'll find," Leaf replied. "Perhaps I should prepare for the worst so I can contain my shock."

Barren said nothing.

***

When the Ore Mines came into view, it was obvious that the Elves had taken over the island. Several Elfin ships sat along the stone port. Stairs led up a rock hill, and what lay beyond that was not visible from their distance. Barren knew Leaf had seen the island and the ships first, but he hadn't uttered a single word. He couldn't really blame the Elf. Everything he believed about his father was being challenged. Barren would have kept quiet, too.

They came to port, and Barren, Sam, and Slay accompanied Leaf off the ship. If Elves were here, they'd be less likely to kill the pirates if they saw their prince first or so the crew hoped. As soon as their boots scraped against the stone port, Leaf held his hand up for them to stop. They all halted immediately. The pirates seemed to share a common wish to escape the Elves without a fight. Barren remembered observing them in their own halls after he'd been stabbed with the hemlock needle. They were elegant, graceful, and deadly. He'd always been told their best weapons were their hands.

The arctic air from the west blew about them, mixing ash with salt. It was an unsettling smell and it burned their noses. Leaf peered into the quiet and Barren did too, though it wouldn't do him much good. Anything the Elves might attempt would probably be over and done with before he even caught sight of them.

After a moment, Leaf stepped forward, moving up the steps with grace and speed. The crew remained below, waiting.

Then they saw him. A tall Elf with broad shoulders appeared over the wall. He was imposing, and his size seemed above average for most Elves. He was clad as if he were prepared for battle. His armor was a mix of shining silver and black leather— the breastplate of his armor was black, and the outline of Sysara's tree glared back at Barren. This Elf had long black hair that spilled over his shoulders and down his back. His features were severe, his eyes a dark gray. Barren took note of the weapons adorning him. A quiver and bow, a long sword, and two daggers strapped to his thighs.

The Elf's eyes landed on Leaf and he halted, surprised.

"Prince Leaf," he bowed, but his words were tight. Leaf watched as the Elf rose to his feet again. "To what do we owe this great honor?"

The way the Elf spoke, his voice pitched slightly, told Barren he didn't think Leaf's visit was an honor.

"Layce," Leaf nodded. "I need to know what's happening here."

The Elf seemed unable to contain his smile as he said, "A revolution!"

"And what does that mean?"

Layce's features turned to stone, similar to the expression Leaf wore when he got angry. "I suppose I shouldn't expect you to know. You've been gone for so long. I'm surprised we still call you prince."

Surprisingly, Leaf waited. Barren sensed there was something else between these two. There was no civility on Layce's part, and Leaf was patient, as if he understood.

"Come," the Elf tilted his head a bit. "I will show you, then. But I do not trust your friends." His eyes fell on the Corsairs, whose numbers were large. It probably appeared to Layce that Leaf had brought an army with him.

"I trust them. That should be enough," said Leaf.

"You will forgive me, your majesty," said Layce, who gave a sharp whistle. Four other Elves appeared over the wall. They were dressed as he, but lesser in size. Layce commanded them in Elvish. Barren watched Leaf's expression in an effort to guess what had been said, but the prince's face was neutral. Barren turned to glance at Dominique and Devon. They were not happy with this arrangement.

Layce turned and moved up the steps and over the wall. Barren, Leaf, Sam, and Slay followed. What they saw when they crested the wall surprised them all. The Ore Mines were actually one large, desolate pit. The land was terraced like a set of steps. At the base of the pit, strange emerald and blue pools dotted the landscape. There was a disturbing quiet about the place that made Barren feel unsettled, and he knew his crew agreed because they held their weapons tighter. One thing was certain, Barren could feel the power of Lyric all around him. It was strong and made his body ache, and he knew Dominique had not lied.

They made their way down each step of the terrace. While they looked manageable from the wall, they were actually wide steps with a steep drop. Layce and Leaf moved on as if it were nothing, while the rest were left to carefully maneuver down each one. Barren and the others slipped several times, and by the time they reached the bottom, they were covered in dirt and bruised by the rocks they'd hit while stumbling.

At the base of the island, the emerald and blue pools were much larger and their strange water was almost hypnotic. The magic was stronger here, too. They moved forward, and Barren couldn't help but feel drawn to them. He watched them as he passed as if expecting something to rise from them. He knew they were deep, for the water at the center was dark.

He moved around another pool and slipped, falling hard on his back, his legs landing in the water. He gasped at the sharpness of the water and struggled to crawl from its tight grip. Sam helped him to his feet. Layce and Leaf stopped and looked back.

"Careful, mineral wells are cold and deep. If you fall in, no one can save you," Layce's voice was critical and just as cold as the mineral well. Barren decided he didn't like Layce or his voice.

When Barren realized how far they'd walked, he started to feel uncomfortable. They had made it all the way to the other side of the island before Layce moved down a sloping path which led underground, and Barren found himself wondering just how long the Elves had occupied the Ore Mines. This had taken time to build, as the walls were reinforced with wooden slats, and lanterns hung at the center of the tunnel casting green light upon the ground. The tunnel curved, and soon they were moving down several sets of slippery steps. Barren cursed as he went. The green light prevented his eyes from adapting to these conditions, and he imagined Sam and Slay couldn't see at all. The air around them was moist, the walls felt cool, and the sound of water surrounded them.

Finally, they came to a tunnel tinged with green. At first, Barren didn't realize what he'd stepped into. But then he saw them, wraith-like creatures propped up against the wall, their thin arms held in iron chains as if they *had* strength to fight. These were Lyrics, and they were of varying ages, but all were weak, pale. Their skin was pulled tight over their bones, as if they'd been starved and deprived of water. They didn't even react to their approach, not even with a glance, and Barren found that he couldn't move forward.

To add to the insult, guards stood in every corner of the room, and they were armed. With their prey so weak, Barren wondered why they felt the need for them.

"Are they dead?" asked Barren. Part of him was so repulsed he wanted to leave immediately, but another part of him was rooted to the spot. This was real. Then he imagined this happening to Larkin, and he became even angrier.

"No, just weak." There was no remorse in Layce's voice. "Their magic has been drained."

"What do you mean drained?"

Layce looked about. "This is an ore mine...and magic and iron ore do not work well together."

"So where does their magic go?"

He gestured to a small river where sparkling water ran along the floor. "There."

Barren felt his stare harden. This Elf's presence was becoming intolerable.

"So you're saying those wells up there, they're filled with *magic*?"

The Elf didn't say a thing; he just lifted his head higher. Leaf widened his stance and faced Layce. "For what?"

"You're really not that stupid, are you?"

"Do you expect to wield magic?"

"We're building weapons so the human race will grovel at our feet."

"This..." Leaf pointed to the Lyrics. "This is genocide, and no matter what you believe, we are no better than humans."

"You're one to talk!" he spat viciously. "You let mortals kill my sister!"

Barren looked between them. This was Fira's brother. There was hatred here, there was blame. Then his eyes shifted to the Elves who were guarding the entrance to the small cell. They tensed, wrapping their hands around their weapons.

Leaf was careful. It was the slight incline of his head that told Barren he was about to attack, and when he did, Barren and his crew were ready to react, but found that the Elfin guard did not move immediately to assault. Leaf rammed his elbow into Layce's stomach and then slammed his fist into his jaw. Layce's head cracked against the wall behind him, but the blow did not deter him. He pushed against Leaf, and the prince stumbled back.

"I don't know what you think you're going to stop. The weapons have already been dispatched. The humans will destroy each other."

"And what makes you think you won't die in the crossfire?" Leaf yelled. He was so angry, the veins in his neck bulged, and his voice was worn and raw. "You're immortal but not invincible!"

Layce threw back his head and laughed, and Barren knew why he laughed—because now he spied the ashy line running down his neck. "He's drinking the water," said Barren and his blood ran cold.

Leaf stared at him. "Do you know what you've done to yourself?"

"I've become invincible," Layce smiled.

"Until what? Until the magic decides you're finished? Until it suffocates you? "I'm not mortal! I'm not *weak*!"

"Your only weakness is believing you are greater than everyone else," said Leaf.

Then they fought, and Barren couldn't recall a time when Leaf had been so angry or so warrior-like. He used his sword brutally, bringing it down upon Layce with force. There was an intention to kill within those blows, aimed for the neck and head. Layce fought with equal strength, their bitter past fueling their animosity.

And the other Elven guards joined the fight too, engaging the pirates in battle. The space was almost too small to have so many locked in a fight. Barren had not fought Elves before, only Leaf in practice. Even the blade he used was different from those brandished by his opponent now. These Elves used long, slim swords that cut the air violently. The Elf who'd engaged Barren moved forward fast, using every part of the blade; the hilt he rammed into Barren's jaw, then he moved to bring the blade down on his head, but Barren blocked, finding his arms ringing from the blow.

The fight continued like that, unclean and ragged. Barren wasn't sure how to fight. Did he fight to kill, to wound? Did he fight to disarm? He didn't want to be responsible for any Elf's death. Leaf still fought to kill. He ducked as Layce's blade swung over his head and slid his blade along the Elf's legs. Layce's legs buckled, but he still managed to block the blow Leaf had aimed for his head.

"A prince killing his kindred," Layce mocked. "And you say we're responsible for genocide."

That seemed to get Leaf's attention, and he backed away, that evil light in his eyes dimming a little. Layce rose to his full height despite the wound to his legs and attacked, his blows even more vicious. He moved forward and Leaf moved back, blocking the hits, but Barren could tell Leaf was too slow. As the prince jumped back, the end of Layce's blade sliced down his chest. A guttural sound escaped from Leaf's mouth and he reached toward the wall, and taking one of the heavy chains in his hand, he used it like a whip, hitting Layce's body over and over again. Layce folded in on himself and brought his head into his hands to protect it from the blows. Finally, with the Elf against the wall, Leaf pulled the chain tight across his neck, trapping his hands beneath the chain.

"You'll come with me," said Leaf, pulling the chain tight, and breathing heavily. "You'll come with me to Aurum. You will show my father what you've become," he released Layce who slid to the ground. Barren wasn't sure the Elf was even alive anymore.

Leaf turned to command the guards still fighting Barren and his crew. "All of you," he growled angrily, almost demonically. "You will obey me, you will obey me, or you will die for your treason! Leave this place!" Barren wasn't sure they would listen at first, but soon they all lowered their weapons and filed out of the tunnel. The pirates didn't lower their blades until the Elves were no longer in sight.

Barren looked at Leaf, pulling the cloth of his shirt away from his wound. There had been very few times Leaf was injured, and seeing it now wasn't easy for Barren.

"Leaf, we need to get out of here, now," Barren said.

"I know," he said, his voice quiet, but he did not move.

"Leaf," but Barren stopped. He couldn't say he was sorry because that's not what Leaf would want to hear. "We'll make this right. We will, and everyone will be okay. I promise."

The prince smiled slightly. "This isn't for you to make right, Barren."

Leaf moved to Layce. He bent and retrieved a key from his person, then moved to the Lyrics. He began unlocking their shackles. It was sad to see them laying there, eyes opened, but too weak to move. None of them even spoke. Leaf bent and scooped the smallest Lyric in his hands. She was a tiny thing, who couldn't have been more than five. Her hair was dark and tangled. She kept her eyes closed and did not look up at her savior.

Barren kneeled to the floor beside a Lyric who looked older. Perhaps he moved to her because she appeared closer to Larkin's age. Her hair was blond and long. It curled down her thin frame. He brushed it away from her face and her eyes flickered open. She stared at him with soulless eyes, saying nothing. He gathered her into his arms, limbs limp and cold. Sam and Slay followed their lead, and then they began their climb up the steps and into open air.

As they emerged from the tunnel, Barren looked ahead and saw that Sam and Slay stopped as they exited the tunnel. As Barren came upon them, he understood why. Elves had gathered there, several of them. They were a sea of stark faces, frightening, tall, and deadly. Their bodies were lithe and lean, and their strong arms held their weapons aloft with ease. They intended to kill. Barren could see it in their eyes. The hardest part was knowing that Leaf couldn't stop them.

Barren stood beside Leaf, and he watched as the prince carefully kneeled to lay the ailing Lyric child on the floor, then he moved past Barren, facing the arrows and the blades, unafraid.

"You would challenge me?" Leaf stepped forward from the tunnel.

"You are our prince, not our king," said one. "You've no say over what we do here."

"There is no king here to give you orders," Leaf said. "But I am here, and I command you to stop this!"

The Elves laughed, and it made Barren feel uneasy. He kneeled to the floor, laying the Elvish woman on the ground. Her eyes were unseeing, though they were open, and it was her gaze that made him realize that, though these men were Elves, they were not Leaf, and if he must kill them, he would.

"You have never wanted to be our prince or our king, so you have received your wish," one of them replied.

Leaf drew two blades and spread his feet. And then Barren witnessed what it was for an Elf to kill. Leaf used his blade, cutting down his kin as they attacked from all angles. But Leaf also used his body to fight. He would wound an Elf, then use him as a shield, and when he was done with him, he would wrap his long arm around the Elf's neck and snap it. He continued like this alone for what seemed like an eternity. Barren wanted to help, but he found himself rooted to the spot. He knew this was the Leaf who had been sent to Estrellas.

Barren's reality came rushing back to him when he heard cries from a distance—Dominique, Devon, and their crews rushed forward, weapons drawn, prepared to fight the Elves who crowded Leaf. Then Barren joined them, fighting alongside Leaf until few Elves stood, and those who did surrendered.

Leaf stood over his people, as still as stone in the aftermath. His breath wasn't even heavy. He sheathed his blades without cleaning them, and then turned toward the tunnel to retrieve the small Lyric. Leaf knelt to gather the girl gently in his arms and walked through the graveyard he had left behind. It was then Barren realized what this war would become. They would kill what they loved.

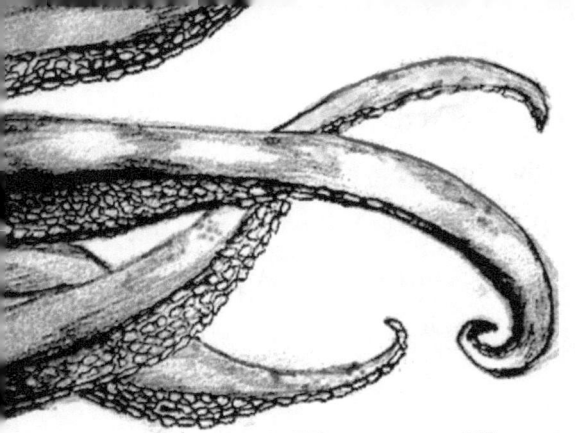

Chapter Twenty-Seven
THE BLACK SPOT

They gathered the bodies of the Elves who had died, piled them up, and burned them. It was the best and fastest way to honor them, even begrudgingly. The smoke that rose from the corpses was bitter, and Barren turned away quickly, avoiding the ruin. The survivors of the Elfin guard were taken captive. Leaf said that they would be taken back to Aurum and if Lord Alder did not punish them, he would.

Dominique approached him. His face was covered with dirt and blood. Barren had never fought alongside Corsairs, but seeing them today had made him glad that he had never encountered them at sea.

"Your Elfin friend, he is like a cannon. One day, he will explode."

"He is stronger than you think," Barren countered.

"So is lead," said Dominique. Then he and his men entered the tunnel, intent on rescuing the other Lyrics. Barren turned toward the Lyric he'd saved from underground. He was surprised to find that she'd raised herself up and was now leaning against the wall. She stared at him blankly, and he found himself wondering if she even had the ability to feel anything anymore.

He knelt beside her. "We're here to save you," he said.

She said nothing. Still too weak to move, he took her in his arms once more. He moved carefully with her, and he found himself thinking of Larkin in this moment. This could be her, as hard as it was to imagine. The blood that ran in this woman's veins was Larkin's blood, too, and there were people who would hurt her. Larkin had been told that, but Barren knew she didn't really believe it because she'd always been protected. Now she wasn't. He didn't want her to know what it was like to be exposed, even if she didn't want him.

As Barren moved toward the ship, Devon fell into step beside him.

"They drained them of their magic. It runs in the water here," Barren spoke between his teeth. "Some of them were drinking it."

Devon said nothing, and Barren glanced askance at him, unable to hide his anger. He knew Devon's memory wasn't completely intact, but he also knew there were things he remembered that he didn't talk about. He could tell by the look on Devon's face now that he was remembering.

"How's your memory looking?"

"I wish it were gone every day," said Devon. "This is our past, but it is coming to haunt *you*."

"It doesn't seem that anyone in your past knew how to clean up, just cover up."

"We did what we could to get by," Devon defended. "You'll understand."

Barren stopped in his tracks and faced Devon. "I might understand at some point, but I will not let this rise up again, even if it kills me."

Devon studied the pirate for a long moment, and the more he did, the angrier Barren felt.

"Don't end up like your father," said Devon. "Your people need a leader, not a martyr."

His people? He spoke to him like he was a prince. "My father was a leader," Barren snapped.

"Your father was always ready to die for a cause," said Devon, taking a step forward. "But what he really needed to do was lead. That's why this mess isn't finished and that's why you're dealing with it now."

Devon stared at Barren for a moment longer before walking off toward the ship. Barren followed him, but at a distance, seething over what the old pirate had said. He was suggesting that Jess should have been the prince he was born to be, but Barren wasn't born to be a prince. He was born to be the captain of a pirate ship. In the end, though, he wondered how different those two things were. Already he found himself intertwined with the future of the Orient and the people in it.

The Lyrics were aboard. There were twelve in total, even more who had not lived to be saved. Those bodies had been burned separately from their captors. The pirates and Corsairs stayed to see that their ashes were spread, and after, they stood in silence, letting the cold gust around them. Now and then, Barren thought he heard whispers on the wind, and he knew the voices of those who had died here in such terror would haunt this place forever.

When it was time to depart, Dominique approached Barren, and he knew what was to come, even before the man spoke.

"We will not accompany you to Aurum," said Dominique.

Barren disliked the disappointment welling inside him. He wasn't sure why he had expected the Corsairs to aid them beyond their boarders.

"I can see you believe me a coward, but consider instead the trouble your alliance with us may cause. You're already in trouble with the Elders, and your involvement with me will only secure your exile. Perhaps we should delay the announcement of our friendship a little longer."

There was truth in that and it wasn't only the Elders who would frown upon him. Lord Alder would not take kindly to Corsairs on his shores, especially those responsible for his exposure. Not to mention the repercussions if word hit Maris. The Octent was already under the threat of war from the arranged assassination of Tetherion. Further, Barren, his crew, and the Corsairs breeched the agreement laid out by the Elfin Treaty, which made things worse for the pirates of Silver Crest.

"I will come with you," said Devon. "And bring a few of my men. If I take a ship, we shall appear greater than we are, which can only be a benefit considering we know not what we will encounter on the Elfin Isle."

It was true. What was ahead was unknown. There were too many players in this game, too many with their own agendas.

Barren and Devon each took an Elfish ship. They were fast and would cut their sail time in half if the weather was good. They would also not draw attention upon approaching Aurum.

Because the ships were smaller, the Elfin guard filled up the brig below deck, which left only the openness of the deck for the Lyrics to rest. Upon setting sail, Leaf went to each one, bandaging their abrasions and lacerations. Sara helped and Barren was surprised to see that she didn't shy away from their wounds. She washed their skin, lifted food and water to their mouths so that they might eat and drink. And then she sang. And her voice was chillingly sweet, and as it carried, it halted everything like a siren's call.

And when the song died, Sara didn't even look up, oblivious to the effect of her voice. It was a reminder of what love and compassion produced, and it was somehow fearless.

Barren's heart felt heavy in so many ways—for Leaf, for Larkin, for Devon. There were few untouched by what had transpired since the destruction of the bloodstone. How could he have known that one simple act would set so many things in motion? He felt conflicted. Had he not done it, Tetherion would have been indestructible, but now that it was done, the world felt like it was falling to pieces.

Barren noticed the Lyric he'd carried to the ship trying to sit up. He moved to help her, and she flinched away from him, so he halted and grimaced.

"What's your name?" he asked, kneeling beside her instead.

The woman looked at him for a long moment, and he began to believe she wouldn't speak. "I don't remember," she said at last. Her voice was a whisper.

"How long were you there?"

"Forever," she replied.

"Do you understand you are safe here?"

Her eyes trailed the wound on his chest. "You have the black spot," she said.

Barren stared. "What is that?"

"It means you are not safe."

Barren drew closer. "You have to tell me what that really means," he said.

She seemed to consider this before she spoke. "It means when faced with battle, dark magic will use you as its weapon."

"What about the others? The others who share this curse with me?"

"No, not the same way. You are Sysara's child. You were born for this," she said. "The curse inside you, it will only amplify your qualities. You have been vengeful and angry most of your life. If you continue so, it will only corrupt that part of you."

Barren swallowed. It was always hard to think of the person he'd been. It was even harder to feel like he hadn't actually come very far.

"You are lucky. The magic still feels you can be of use. That's why it keeps you alive, that's why it keeps you strong." Barren wasn't sure that was luck. After a moment, the Lyric lifted her hand, and her palm began to shimmer. Barren had never seen anything like it before, but the shimmer became solid, and a small vile of ice-blue liquid materialized. She placed it in his hand. The vile was cold to the touch.

"What is it?" he asked.

"Think of it as a wish," she said. "You only get one. Use it wisely."

"Why would you give this to me?"

She shrugged a bone-like shoulder. "You have given us freedom."

Barren tried to give it back to her. "I require nothing in return for such a gift."

She would not take it and smiled. "You would not do me the dishonor of refusing my gift."

And Barren closed his fingers around the vile. "I thought not," she said, and then managed to stand very slowly, and Barren stood with her. She wobbled on her feet, but Barren feared reaching out to steady her. She seemed to understand something Larkin never did. His hands *were* those of a killer.

The Lyric moved along the deck of the ship like a wraith. She kept a thin hand on the rail as she went and Barren found himself wondering how much longer she would cling to this earth, or perhaps she was clinging to the otherworld. Both thoughts made him sad.

He slipped the vile around his neck so it hung where the compass once lay, and then he turned and headed for the helm where Sam stood.

"The wind is changing," said Sam. "We will have a storm."

Barren looked to the horizon, and while he could see no clouds yet, he could feel the change in the wind—it was cool and heavy, damp with the threat of a storm.

"Do you believe these Lyrics have summoned it?"

Before the bloodstone, Barren might have called Sam superstitious.

"If they have, it won't be the first wicked storm we've suffered through and survived," said Barren. "Better call for Slay to come down from the crow's nest—it'll be hard enough for him to hold on."

Sam laughed, and Barren smiled at the sound.

***

The storm was wicked; the rain was harsh and cold. Sara and the Lyrics had taken refuge in the captain's cabin. Cove had been forced to follow, as he was not strong enough to fight the storm. Sam and Barren were at the helm, and the others ensured that the sails were closed and the cargo secured. When lightning flashed on the horizon, Devon's ship was still visible, riding the fierce waves behind them. Barren hoped they weren't separated in the storm.

Water rose up and doused them. The wind was the worst of it all, as it created a chill on their skin that couldn't be broken. At times, Barren thought he felt ice mixed with the rain stinging his face. The weather was so distracting, Barren barely noticed when the Lyric he'd brought to the ship left the cabin. His mind told him to go to her, ensure she returned to the cabin, but his body was frozen in place, watching as she moved like a ghost, barely clinging to this world.

She faced the rain and the cold as if she didn't feel it. The wind whipped around her, lifting her hair and the tattered lengths of her thin clothing. She moved lightly down the deck to the very head of the ship and mounted the rail. She turned with her back to the water and faced Barren, smiling, and then fell into the water. It was over in an instant, and he was suddenly able to move again. A cry tore from his throat and he moved to save her, sliding down the slick deck and hitting the rail with full force. He got to his feet, and began hulking a thick rope over the edge of the ship, but as he prepared to dive, hands were on his shoulders, pulling him back. He stumbled and landed on his back, staring up at Leaf, his body silhouetted by the lightning running rampant through the clouds.

"You must allow her to have peace," he said.

Barren could only gaze at his friend, whose features were just as cold as the rain and the ice coating the ship. He hated that she'd chosen this rather than face any kind of future, but part of him understood. Her pain was too great, and she had not known the world beyond the Ore Mines and her captors. How could she believe any part of it was good?

Chapter Twenty-Eight
DANCING WITH JACK KETCH

Rain tapped on the windows. Datherious walked down the deserted halls of the east wing. In his left pocket he kept Barren Reed's compass, and even now he kept his hand clasped around it, fearing it might disappear. It was his key to power, his key to ruling the whole of Mariana.

Datherious pushed the door of Natherious's small study open and entered. His brother didn't look up at him. He sat behind a desk, reassembling a gun. The pieces were lined up across his desk, organized precisely. Natherious's passion was weapons. He delighted in creating new contraptions and firing them from the courtyard into the ocean below.

Datherious watched his brother for a moment before speaking. "Father fears me," said Datherious.

"Why do you say that?" Natherious asked, still focused on his work.

"Because I will be king," he replied. "Father thinks that the Elf King can offer some sort of way to defy death."

377

"The Elf King is immortal," said Natherious. Datherious felt his anger bubble within him, and his cold eyes fell on his brother, then to his task. He ran his hand across the table, and all the meticulously placed pieces of the weapon fell to the floor. Natherious raised his head but did not look at his brother. He kept his eyes forward, a mark of his anger.

"But he isn't invincible," Datherious hissed, leaning down so that his eyes were level with his brother's. He held his gaze before straightening. "And neither is our father."

"What are you saying?"

"I'm merely stating facts," he said. "I would not be surprised if father attempted to kill his only heirs, you know."

"You think he is that fearful of losing his throne?"

"Have you not witnessed his madness over the last few weeks? He stays locked up in that study, he mumbles to himself, and anytime the council offers opinion, he accuses them of treason. He constantly reminds me that I am not king."

"You are not," said Natherious. He cleared his throat. "When father dies, you will have the throne. That should please you."

"How long until he is dead?" asked Datherious and he watched as his brother narrowed his eyes.

"You've never been so eager for the throne, brother. I suspect Aethea Moore has something to do with your readiness."

Datherious gritted his teeth and grabbed his brother by the throat. "The throne is mine, with or without Aethea Moore."

Datherious released his brother and then placed his hands behind his back, pacing about the room.

"Our father did not teach us how to live with threats, he taught us how to eliminate them," said Datherious, and it was as if he were making a speech. "If anyone stands in my way, *I* will eliminate them."

"With magic?" Natherious questioned.

"And an army."

"You don't have an army, not one that you own," said Natherious.

The only army the crown of the Orient could lay claim to were the privateers, but those crews were privately funded by nobles and any command given to them had to go through the council. Datherious could not sway them to his side.

"Natherious," Datherious chided. "I thought you were smarter than that. I don't intend to have an army of untrained privateers. Indeed, the perfect soldiers have been groomed by our very king. I suppose he will realize their potential when they are unleashed."

"You don't mean to use the prisoners of Estrellas?" Datherious frowned at his twin's obvious disapproval. "They are hardly an army. They...they are murderers!"

Datherious stared. He'd already used the Estrellas army, tested them, really, and they'd met his expectations.

"They aren't disciplined. You won't be able to control them."

"I will control everything," he said. "Once I have the King's Gold."

"You only have two pieces."

"Three pieces," he corrected. "And with Aethea's help, I will have the last one," he said. "It is discouraging, your lack of faith in me, brother. I have to wonder what has happened to you."

Natherious said nothing and looked away. Datherious threw back his head to laugh. "My poor brother, do not be afraid. *I* will protect you," he placed his hand on his brother's shoulder and squeezed. Then he turned to leave the room, but paused at the door. "You can let go of your blade," he said.

Natherious looked down at his hand. He let go quickly, as if he hadn't realized he had been holding it. Datherious offered a smile and then moved down the hall.

***

There was a loud, rapid knock on her door and then it flew open.

"Up!" Ms. Jennings ordered.

Larkin sat up. "Ms. Jennings," her voice was shrill and high. She'd had enough of the woman's disrespect and thought to discipline her, but once she was up, she found Ms. Jennings and two soldiers entering her room. She gathered her covers around her.

"This is highly inappropriate!" she cried, but the soldiers moved forward.

"His majesty Prince Datherious has ordered you to the castle."

"His majesty would prefer I was decent."

"His majesty has ordered that you come in whatever state you are detained in," replied the soldier, seizing her hand. Larkin used her feet and slammed them into the soldier's stomach. She reached for her knife, which sat on her bedside table, and as the other soldiers came forward, drew the knife along his neck. She fled from the room, ignoring Ms. Jenning's shocked expression. She hurried toward the staircase but found too late that the downstairs was occupied by two other soldiers. When they spotted her, they raced upstairs. She hurried down the hall and into another bedroom. She looked out the window. She was two stories high, and below her was a carriage guarded by two more soldiers. She heard footsteps outside the room and opened the window. If she could make it to the roof, she would at least have more of a chance.

Behind her the door opened, and she was surprised to hear her father's voice.

"Larkin," he said. "Do not do this. Let them take you."

She turned and glared at him. "I will be imprisoned and hanged. Is that what you want?"

"If you run, you will not make it to the sea," he said.

She narrowed her eyes. Had he helped them organize this trap? She looked outside the window again. The soldiers there had already taken note of her. They waited to pounce. She felt tears in her eyes and stood straight, lifting her head to her father. "You would let them do this?"

"It will be safer for you if you don't fight," he said.

And the soldiers filed in and seized her. The servants watched as she was led outside in her bedclothes. The soldiers helped her into the carriage. Her father had followed them out, but he did not move to accompany her. Even if he had, she wouldn't have noticed. She did not look back.

She sat across from the man who had received her blade. He

glowered at her. The solider had indicated that Datherious had summoned her. Had Tetherion been ruled an unfit king as her father had predicted? Was Datherious calling the shots? If so, what plans did he have for her? Would he imprison her? Would he kill her?

Arriving at the castle was much different this time. Everyone still stared but in a smug way that made Larkin both angry and embarrassed. She was led to the throne room. To her surprise, the doors were open and Tetherion appeared to have visitors. The guards halted her at the entrance, though she wasn't sure if she could have taken another step. In fact, everything in her being wanted to hide. On the other side of the door, she found familiar faces—those of the Elders, Eva and Tobias. Why where they here?

It was then she realized that Tetherion wasn't even in the throne room. It was Datherious's voice that rose, clear and resounding. Her heart fell into her stomach.

"Why would you tell me this?" Datherious's voice rose.

"Ambassador Rowell has gained too much power. He thinks he can hold the Network over us, defy our rule. Well, we are one step ahead of him. We're giving you the Network locations, and we declare to you that Barren Reed is an exile to the pirates of Silver Crest. With his association void, you can have no reason to wish ill upon us. We'll sign new agreements, run stock through the Underground, anything you need."

This was something she should not be surprised to hear, and yet she couldn't quite believe it was happening. The Elders were here, betraying Cove and the whole of the pirates of Silver Crest, directly defying the code they swore to uphold. If Eva and Tobias were so fearful for their people, for those who lived on Silver Crest, they would not be here right now.

Datherious's eyes turned toward the entrance where she stood with the guards. Eva and Tobias's eyes followed. Eva appeared shrewd, and there was no hint of remorse in her eyes for her betrayal. Tobias seemed resigned, though he had to be. There was no way to take back what they had just done.

"Lady Larkin," Datherious's voice was like sharp glass. "It is good that you have arrived, and just in time."

The soldiers dragged her forward. Their arms pressed into hers painfully. She did not move her own feet.

"I have already heard you are acquainted with Elders Tobias and Eva," Datherious gestured to them, and Larkin met their gazes. They were both unfriendly, but Eva in particular.

"Yes, I have met them," she agreed.

"They were just proposing an alliance," he said. "What do you think of that?"

She didn't answer.

"Your silence is telling," he said. "But more telling is the bit of information I was given from Miss Aethea Moore." Datherious stepped down from his elevated place near the thrones.

"Eva, Tobias, have you ever heard of Relics?"

The two exchanged glances. It was clear they hadn't.

"Let me enlighten you," he said. "Relics are devices the Lyrics sometimes used to contain their power. Together, they act as a channel through which even a mortal can wield magic."

Datherious reached and drew a gold chain from under his shirt. Barren's compass settled in his hands. "This is Sysara's Relic. But I should not tell you all this," he paused to laugh. "But now that I have, there is but one question left to answer: why would I require your services?"

Eva and Tobias began to protest, but Datherious was finished. "Take them all to the dungeons," he said. "We will have a hanging in the morning."

The guards dragged her away. Did Datherious mean to hang her too? Did her father know?

Those who stood guard at the entrance laughed at her approach. She stared straight ahead. They threw her in the cell, and she stumbled forward, falling to her knees. She sat there for a moment before turning and sitting on the dirty ground. She was not there long before Eva and Tobias were led into the cell adjacent to hers.

"Your plan didn't work," her voice was harsh, but they deserved scorn. She would accept no excuse for their treason. "Surprised?"

Eva glared at her. "You've no idea what we've been through. You wouldn't understand why we did it."

"To hide a little longer?" she said. "The magic you're dealing with, it cannot go unopposed any longer."

"Silly girl!" Eva spat. "Magic cannot be opposed! It is best you align with those who can give you protection."

"So they can hang you?" she responded vehemently. Eva

glared. Tobias had moved to sit on the bench in the corner and hung his head in his hands. Larkin turned from them, and moved to sit on the ground on the pile of hay meant to be her bed. While she was angry with them, she hoped someone came to rescue Eva and Tobias. She did not want to see them die.

She lay down on her side and dreamed that Barren and Cove had seized the castle and rescued them.

***

"Get up!" the voice commanded her. She was wrenched from sleep and pushed from her cell. She staggered, almost falling into Eva and Tobias's cell. She met their gazes. They were weary and darkness pulled under their eyes. She guessed neither had slept that night.

"What's happening?"

"You've got to get ready. There's gonna be a'hangin'," the guard said.

Larkin felt the color drain from her face. She was led upstairs where servants waited beside a hot bath. She was made to bathe and dress. Bile rose in her throat when the servant girls beamed as they said, "His Majesty the prince picked this out for you."

It was a bright red dress, as vibrant as a flame. And when she put it on, it ignited against her skin. It was meant to make her a beacon, a target. She slipped the dress on, and then they arranged her hair, pulling and pinning strands until it cascaded over her shoulder. There was jewelry too, diamonds. They felt heavy against her skin.

When the servants were finished fixing, poking and prodding, they stepped back and admired her. They had no concept of what was happening. She was sure they didn't even realize she'd spent the night in the dungeon. Their only thought was how lucky she was to have a dress chosen by the prince.

She was escorted downstairs where Datherious, Natherious, and Aethea waited.

Aethea appeared very pleased. She was dressed in a shimmery, emerald green dress, which made her dark features stand out. She and Datherious made a good pair, though unfortunately, the prince only had eyes for Larkin at the moment. She told herself it wasn't for any other reason than to make her uncomfortable.

"Lady Larkin," Datherious's voice rose to her, and he beheld her with satisfaction, his eyes trailing the length of her. Her stomach rolled. "You look lovely." He extended his hand, and she took it, still confused about what was happening. He guided her forward, out of the castle and to the courtyard where the hanging stage was erected and ready for its victims. They entered the tower and moved up several flights of stairs. Their seats would be on the balcony, which overlooked the gallows from above. So she would not hang today. But that meant Eva and Tobias would.

Why couldn't her dream come true?

She was made to sit beside Datherious. From this height, she could see the ocean on the horizon. She kept her eyes there, searching for any sign of pirate ships. If not Barren and Cove, perhaps other Elders? Or pirates from Silver Crest? Would they rescue traitors?

In the pavilion below, the crowd gathered. Before she had

sailed with pirates, she had hated hangings. She never understood the wish to watch others die, murderers or not. She'd never watched people she knew hang before. Perhaps she could look away when the lever dropped.

The jeers started when Eva and Tobias entered the courtyard. Larkin watched in horror as the two were hit with rocks and rotten vegetables. They were taunted and thrashed. Wasn't it bad enough that they now walked to their death? They moved up the stairs and filed in under the two nooses. The hangman placed the nooses around their necks like fine jewels. The color drained from Larkin's face when Eva and Tobias's gazes met hers.

Datherious leaned close to her, whispering in her ear. His hot breath slithered down her neck. She wanted to lean away, but his words kept her still.

"If you turn away, I will send you to the noose next. It has already been arranged."

So she kept her eyes glued on Eva and Tobias. Their charges were read by a solider dressed in a fine red suit and golden sash. His voice was diplomatic. No remorse touched his words.

"You have been charged with the crimes of piracy and murder. You have been sentenced to hang by the neck until dead, dead, dead."

There was no drum. Nothing to count the minutes until their deaths, or soften the blow. In the stark silence, the lever was pulled, and the harsh snap of their necks shot like an arrow through her heart. She gasped, and she squeezed the arms of her chair tight. The bodies twirled on their ropes, and people cheered. Larkin wanted to run, but she didn't. She stayed as still as stone until Datherious rose to his feet and led her from the balcony.

***

Larkin been returned to her cell promptly after the hangings. She'd immediately began tearing away at the red dress, shrieking as if she were covered in Eva and Tobias's blood. When she no longer hand the strength to tear the dress, she sat in a pile of tattered fabric and sobbed. She wasn't sure how long she cried or when she'd fallen asleep, but she awoke when a door slammed in the distance.

The soft rustle of skirts and click of heels became louder. Aethea approached her cell, and Larkin felt her face grow hot with anger. Aethea pursed her lips, as if she were holding in a laugh. Aethea looked like she was prepared to leave. Her skirt was short in the front, and longer in the back. She wore a long jacket, and beneath that was a ruffled shirt. A hat sat cocked to one side upon her head. Her hair had been pinned beneath it, but some curls escaped free.

"Does Datherious know you are a Lyric?" Larkin asked. Perhaps it was still dangerous to be so bold, but the only people in this dungeon who knew what Lyric meant had been Tobias and Eva, and now they were dead.

"No," she said, and her voice held warning. "Let's keep our secret."

"Why not tell him? Are you afraid he will use you?"

"I do not trust mortals," she said.

"Are you afraid you are not strong enough to fend him off?"

Aethea gave a cold laugh. "I'm strong enough. He is still mortal."

"But Datherious's mother was half-Lyric. Surely he can withstand our magic a little better."

Aethea lifted her head. "I pity you. You've lived among mortals so long, you hardly have any understanding of us."

"I understand that you aren't as powerful as you lead us to believe," said Larkin. "If so, you would not have to fight on the level you are. You wouldn't be in search of the King's Gold."

"Well," her voice was even. "I was not wrong when I said you were smart. But you don't understand the power of the King's Gold."

"I understand you can draw upon all Lyric."

"Yes, but you haven't even considered: Why would I, a Lyric who can already draw upon magic, wish to possess the King's Gold?"

Em had said Aethea merely wanted more power.

"The King's Gold, when brought together, can be used to resurrect Sysara's spirit. She will have no body of her own to inhabit, of course, once she is awakened, so she will have to possess the most powerful being nearest her. I intend to be that person."

Larkin had no words. Now that she remembered, Em had said something like this, but it was brief. *Relics are powerful magic...she could raise your mother from the dead.* That's exactly what Aethea had intended to do. "You could stand alongside me," she continued, and Aethea's eyes seemed to ignite at the thought. Larkin thought that strange. She'd always considered Aethea as someone who would prefer to be alone. "We might rule together."

"You seem to misunderstand the point of being Lyric."

"What? Being a guardian?" she mocked. "Those are the old ways. The world out there is too hostile. We cannot be guardians or we will become slaves again."

"I will not be a slave," said Larkin. "But I will not stand beside you."

Aethea's face hardened and she stepped away from the bars. "Have it your way," she said. "But I only offer once."

Aethea left, and Larkin listened until the heels of the Lyric's boots faded into silence. She knew little about magic, and even less about resurrection, but she knew nothing good could come of it. Worse, Sysara was the most powerful Lyric to exist. Was anyone alive who could resist her power? Destroy her? And what would Barren do if Sysara's spirit were to be resurrected? He'd watched one parent die, and lived without the other for so long. Could he do it again?

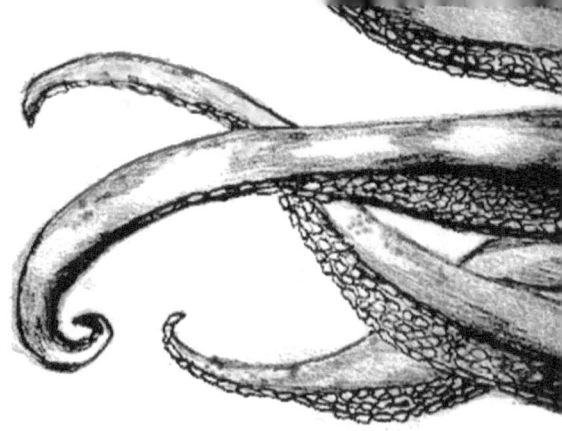

Chapter Twenty-Nine
PANIC

The carriage door opened for her and she stepped outside under an umbrella held open by one of the footman. She smiled as not long ago, she would not have had the opportunity to enjoy such amenities, but things were changing for her. Beyond the cover of the umbrella, rain poured down, and she took a moment to watch the rivers of water run down the hill and pool at the bottom. She turned to face the two-story house before her. She remembered her initial impressions of the home: she had felt it was nice. Now, after enjoying the splendor of the castle of Maris, it was somehow lackluster and as she moved up the steps to knock on the door, she found herself impatient to leave.

She knocked on the door and waited. The rain continued to pour, and the skirts of her dress were beginning to soak through.

Finally a small, frail girl answered. She was pale, her hair blond. She took note of how similar she appeared to Sara Rosamund, the girl she'd seen on Barren Reed's ship when she'd sailed with them to Aryndel. The servant led her to the left and through a set of dark doors which opened into the familiar study. There Ben Willow sat, his chair facing the window. His legs were spread apart, his hand resting against his chin. He wore a tan suit, and he did not acknowledge her as she entered.

"Tea ma'am?" The servant's voice cracked when she spoke, and Aethea snapped her head around to look at her.

"Yes, please," she said and watched the servant go. Aethea turned to survey Ben again. He was as still as a statue. Aethea set her lips.

"Your servant girl is a frightened little thing," she said. Pulling off her gloves, she moved toward the fire. She noted the soot that stained the brick, the coal and ash scattered across the hearth, and stepped carefully. She moved so that he was within her sight.

"You could at least acknowledge me," she said. "I would not have come here had I known you would be silent."

In response, he began muttering a song. She only caught part of the words, but she straightened as he spoke them, anger welling inside her.

The sea she will deceive me

Lock me up and keep me!

Give no bread to feed me

No drop of drink to ease me

Then he stood quickly and turned toward her, the words he sung louder, harsher, and his gray eyes seemed possessed. She drew away toward the wall, heart beating in her chest as he strode forward.

The sea she will deceive me

Lure me in and keep me!

Give no love to please me

No sight of sun to guide me

The sea she will deceive me

Draw blood and destroy me!

When he finished the song, he breathed hard, his hands pinning her against the wall, one on either side of her face, and she held a knife to his throat, ready to kill.

"I gave you everything!" he yelled. "And yet I have seen nothing in return! That was *not* the agreement! I brought you from obscurity! I made you what you are!"

She smiled, false pity colored her features.

"*You* gave *me* everything?" she asked, and pushing the knife against his face, he took a step back. "Half-breed."

Ben's eyes widened and he turned to look into the mirror. She watched in pleasure as he touched his face in a fury. "What have you done?" he cried, clawing at his face. Blood pooled down his cheeks, and he took the mirror and threw it at her. She dodged it, and it crashed against the wall, shattering to the floor. "Fix me, Gypsy-Witch! Fix me!"

His voice was raw, and he hardly let his face show, covering as much of it as he could with his hands.

"Did mother hide your face because she was ashamed, Isaac?"

Ben looked up at her, glaring, and she pulsed energy toward him, restoring the illusion that hid his true appearance. He writhed on the floor, seeking to forget the truth of his blood.

"Never forget what I have given you, brother," said Aethea. "And what I can take away."

Ben stood slowly then, the fissures he had gouged into his face still ran with blood.

"You have given *him* everything you promised me," he said, taking in a breath. "That compass was *mine!*"

"Don't look so pitiful," she chided. "I did give Datherious the compass, but you need not worry. He does not know I intend to resurrect Sysara's spirit with the Relics, and when her spirit is resurrected, she will possess only the strongest of us. That is me. I will fulfill your wish, half-breed. Until then, we have Datherious's trust and the songbird caged."

"How long until her spirit is resurrected?" he asked, retaining some shadow of the man he presented himself as to the world.

"We have only to find two more pieces of the King's Gold," she said. "Be patient, dear."

"And how do I know you will make me human at the end of this?"

"Oh, brother," she said. Stepping forward, she placed her hand on his cheek, letting the blood that pooled there press against her palm. She drew back, taking her blade and slicing her palm. Ben watched her, and his blood and her blood mixed together and bubbled. Where there had been an injury, there now was none. "There now. A blood oath exists between us. If I fail, you fail. If I succeed, you succeed."

Their gazes met, and there seemed to be peace between them. Aethea moved to leave, but paused at the door.

"Oh," she said, and approached him again. She pulled back the collar of his shirt where a horrific scar lay above his chest.

"It is a pity you swore by the mark."

"I did not swear," he spat, glaring at her. "I was born to a pirate father who branded me...but that part of my life is over."

"Is it?" she asked. "You had a lot to recover from, having once joined sails with Barren Reed as Isaac Noble and betraying him. If he discovers you, he will kill you."

He jerked away from her. "My father abandoned me to sail the seas," said Ben. "Pirates are cowards and I intend to eradicate them, including Barren Reed. With your help, of course."

She gave him a half smile and placed a black velvet pouch in his hand. The contents of the purse clinked together as it landed in his hand. "You will have time to gain the upper hand here, half-breed. I would not want Datherious to consider you useless."

He opened the pouch in front of her, and the wicked smile they shared cracked across his face.

"Sister, you shouldn't have."

***

Hollow stared down at the bold letters. They glared at him from the page and he glared back.

ROSAMUND'S DAUGHTER GOES MISSING: AMBASSADOR ROWELL AT SEA

When he saw it, he wanted to drag his fingers along the grain of this fine wood desk. This article was speculation, of course, but it would breed rumors, and they would spread like wildfire. It would succeed in damaging Sara Rosamund's reputation and might garner sympathy for Ben Willow. Cove had certainly gained naysayers since his departure, people who had watched Ben Willow drag Dr. Newell into the courtyard. People who had doubts before suddenly found themselves on a side. If Cove were here, he would quash those rumors with some pretty words and a party, but he wasn't, and Hollow would only hurt this situation if he tried to step in. So he had to let the rumors swirl and build.

"Hollow!" There was urgency to the voice that made his heart rise in his throat. "Hollow!"

Maddox burst through the doors, out of breath. "The church is on fire!"

Hollow was on his feet instantly. The adrenaline that rushed through him was the same as the night Cove had been shot, and what had transpired from there had been one long and tiring string of events.

He hurried with Maddox out into the night. The air smelled of ash and smoke, and he could see orange over the trees in the distance. It looked like a sunrise in the middle of the night. He and Maddox broke out into a run, not sharing words about the subject, just hoping to get there in time to save some people.

The closer they got, the more people joined them in the run toward the church. As they rounded the corner, they could see a large crowd, and the tall pinnacles of the church were completely consumed. The fire was great and rabid. It crackled and raged, catching the trees on fire as it went. Some attempted to carry buckets toward the blaze, but they had to move back once the structure of the church collapsed.

Hollow and Maddox came to a dead stop. "No one could survive that," said Maddox.

No, they couldn't.

Suddenly, a word was thrown into the air that Hollow did not expect.

"Murderer! He's a murderer!"

The crowd agreed in a rushed yell. "I say we hang 'em!"

The crowd agreed again, and Hollow was reminded of the night John Newell was almost hanged. He moved forward, pushing through the crowd with Maddox behind him. When he burst through, the heat of the fire was on his face, and the bodies of the brothers of the church lay on the ground, including Alaster. Ben stood before them.

"By Cove's word we let him roam our streets, and this is how he repays us!" Ben roared. "I say we deal justice tonight! For the brothers of unity!"

The crowd agreed.

"Find John Newell!" Ben ordered and the crowd obeyed like a wave, darting off to retrieve the doctor from his home.

Hollow pulled Maddox toward him. "Go, see if you can evacuate him before they get to him."

Maddox nodded and hurried off into the woods. Hopefully the other privateers had the forethought to get John out of here.

Hollow approached the bodies that lay in a row before the blaze. Some of them were burned, but each had clearly been killed in another way. A wound above their hearts had taken their life.

Then Hollow turned to Ben, and he knew this had been orchestrated by him.

"Senator Dallon," he cried when he noticed Hollow. "What have you to say for your friend's behavior?"

"John Newell could not have killed these men, nor the men Cove brought to Arcarum. He was nowhere near them and was only consulted to find the cause."

"And were you a witness to these murders or these fires, Mr. Dallon?"

The crowd jumped to back the question.

"No," Hollow said evenly.

"Then we have little reason to believe you, Senator."

"You will kill an innocent man if you do this!"

"And we risk more deaths in this manner if we do not! To the courtyard!"

The crowd surged forward and Hollow was pushed back and forth as they rushed past him. The fervor of the crowd to kill made Hollow sick. He had only one hope now, that the governor would intervene.

He took off on foot, hurrying to Matthew. He found the governor holed up in his study. Hollow was wary as he approached him, for he was pushed into a corner of the spacious room, head bent, his thumb and forefinger rested on his nose.

"Governor, Ben Willow is going to hang Dr. Newell!"

"Yes, I have been informed," he said in a restless voice and looked up at the senator. Hollow had a feeling it took a lot for him to meet his gaze at this moment.

"You will do nothing?"

Matthew's eyes were pleading.

"If he has threatened you, I can protect you. Just stop this," said Hollow.

"You cannot stop this," Matthew said. "And you cannot protect me."

Hollow glared. "Tell me when Ben gained so much power."

"When Cove Rowell became a liar."

"Cove protects, he does not lie. If you think him a liar, you are not his friend."

"If he protects, where is he?" Matthew said between his teeth.

Hollow turned to leave, and Matthew stopped him. "You'd do well to tell Cove to stay where he is."

"It's too late for that. This is war."

Hollow left the governor's house and hurried toward the courtyard. His lungs burned.

"Any in opposition to this crime?" Hollow heard the question, and no one rose to protest.

Hollow came upon the scene just as the hangman released the lever. John fell from the hanging stage, his neck snapping and while Hollow's heart fell out of his chest, the crowd cheered in approval for the death of an innocent man.

Beside him he felt the presence of the other pirates.

"What will we do?" asked Jonas.

"We prepare for our end here in Arcarum."

"You do not really believe Cove will lose?"

"All good things come to an end," said Hollow.

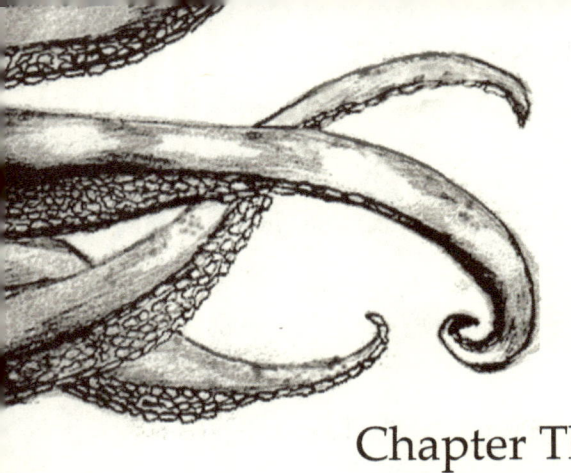

Chapter Thirty
AT ROPE'S END

The edge of the horizon was dotted with the tree line of Aurum. Barren didn't remember the last time he'd arrived here. He had been slowly succumbing to the poison racing through his blood. Later, after Lord Alder had healed him to the best of his ability, he'd learned he'd been stabbed with a hemlock needle laced with magic. Christopher Lee had been the possessor of that hemlock needle. Barren was just now learning it was only one of many weapons created by the Lyrics.

It was easy to try to place blame on Lord Alder, but Barren knew that the Elfin Lord wasn't completely at fault for his actions. Mortals had played a role in this, too. It had started when Lord Alder had given Eadred the bloodstone. The bloodstone ensured Alder his kingdom, but it also made him a slave to the mortals and all their lustful wishes. This did not justify Lord Alder's actions, but it did make them understandable.

"I don't believe that Elves and men can exist together in a

world with magic," said Barren.

"They haven't been given the chance to live with magic," said Leaf. "Think about what you knew of magic before the bloodstone. Nothing. It's this secret only shared between those who sit at the top of our world. It's a power play. Elves and men, they could live with magic, but it must have boundaries."

Barren scoffed. "How do you put boundaries on something so unruly?"

Leaf glanced at him, and his gaze was not kind. "You know nothing of magic but that it has been used against you. In truth, it has not been good. Magic in Mariana has not been given the chance to be good. It has been twisted and used for evil." The Elf turned to face him fully. "You must think of your mother when you begin to believe magic is evil, and you must think of Larkin when you begin to wish you could destroy it altogether."

Barren pressed his lips together and looked away. He heard Leaf laugh quietly. "Trust me when I say, it is easier to live with the knowledge that she still exists, even if you are apart."

The words fell heavily onto his heart, and it hurt.

***

There was no place like Aurum in the whole of Mariana. No place as ancient, no place where the earth and trees seemed wise and alive. No place with such fearful things, the living forest, the Elves themselves.

The island was serene and as they approached, everything was still. There was no breeze in the trees, no ships or port crowding the white shores. No signs of life. This was not uncommon.

Barren knew the ports were built into the bank of the river which ran straight to the palace at the center of Aurum. Despite this, Barren couldn't shake the feeling that something was wrong, and it was amplified by Leaf's unwavering stare.

"Something's not right," Leaf said. His eyes searched the tree line.

"What do you see?"

"It's what I don't see," he said. "There are always archers in the trees. Guardians of the forest. They are not present."

Leaf turned to Layce. "Where are they? Where are the guards?"

"Do you think Lord Alder would call away his guards? At a time like this?" Layce asked. "I know as much as you."

"What do we do?" asked Barren.

"You and I will sail up the river with Layce and the other captives," said Leaf.

"It will be safer than walking through the woods."

"Captives?" Layce's voice echoed Leaf's. "It is as if you are not one of us."

"I am not," said Leaf. "As far as I'm concerned, you are my prisoner until my father releases you."

"Then I will not be a prisoner much longer. You seem to think your presence will change your father's mind about what he has done."

"I don't expect to change my father's mind about anything," said Leaf. "But I do intend to make it known that I disagree with him and that I will fight to change what he has done."

"You're ridiculous," Layce said. "You think you can win a war against magic?"

"Perhaps I can't, but then you won't withstand the magic coursing through your veins and you will die, too."

Then Leaf turned to Barren. "Cove and Devon can keep watch for approaching ships. I hope we are not too late."

Cove was at his weakest yet. If he entered into battle, Barren was not sure he could hold his own.

Leaf understood the concern. "I do not intend to fight a battle on these shores," said Leaf. "If I can evacuate my people, I will."

"Evacuate? To where?"

"The place my father used as his prison," Leaf said simply. "D'Avana."

It was safe, providing they could sail past the storm guarding it again. Barren wasn't sure that privilege was given twice. It had barely been granted the first time, but Barren didn't argue. They had few options. With Dominique and the other Corsairs retreating to their hole in the Octent, they were left outnumbered against any force Tetherion might dispatch their way. All they could do was run.

The orders were given that Cove and Devon would stay behind and scout the waters. Barren and Leaf prepared two dinghies and, after settling Layce and the other Ore Mine guards inside the shallow boats, they departed, paddling the small boats toward the river.

The mouth of the river was wider, and planks of wood and tree roots seemed to work together to create a port where elegant

Elfin ships were tethered. Beyond this, the river narrowed, and the branches overhead seemed to reach over the river and entwine creating a canopy of gold. It was fall here in the forest. Barren watched as one of the leaves broke free from its stem and floated slowly to the water below.

"The leaves do not usually fall in Aurum," said Leaf. "They turn gold and red in the fall and linger, and then return to green in the spring."

Barren looked at the Elf, and then their heads snapped to the forest. There were noises in the distance, footfalls and the sounds of metal, and even Layce seemed concerned. Through the thicket of trees, men dressed in black ran toward them. There was the stretch of bowstrings, and Barren yelled, "Take cover!"

As he did, arrows rained down upon the boat. Some splintered the wood, others plopped into the water, and some of the Elfin guards were hit. Leaf hurried to cut the ropes from Layce's wrists.

"Free the rest," he said.

There were no comments from Layce. Instead he turned and hastily did as he had been commanded.

Leaf withdrew an arrow from his quiver, strung his bow, and shot into the forest. As soon as Leaf loosed his first arrow, others followed. At first Barren thought they were being attacked from both sides, but the stream of arrows had come from the trees, and they took down a row of men running just inside the forest. He looked up. There were Elves in the trees, the Elves Leaf hadn't seen guarding the forest near the shore.

As their attackers drew closer to the river, Barren realized who they were: not just privateers, but men from Estrellas, recognizable for their deformities. They had been under Aethea's command in Aryndel. Did that mean she was here now? And what did that mean for Lord Alder?

Another round of arrows fell on the dinghy and Barren jumped from the small boat into the river below. He swam to shore and drew two blades—his sword and cutlass. Leaf followed suit, as did the Elfin guards who still lived, and though they had no weapons, they stormed forward with Barren.

It was then Barren witnessed, in the chaos of it all, the true terror of the Elves. He was sure part of it was in their nature, the other was in the magic they'd consumed. Layce and the others fought with their bare hands. They were graceful but murderous, snapping necks and sending bodies flying. When they had the chance to take up a weapon, they did, and then there was bloodshed.

Leaf ran ahead, using his blade to cut down anyone in his path. He was a different person in this battle, the raw anger explicit on his face. Barren's blade met with the blades of the Estrellas men with sickening familiarity. He fought hard, cutting down anyone who dared step forward to fight him. Overhead, the Elves moved among the trees, their arrows raining down in a methodical release, wiping out a row of men in seconds. Some Elves fell from the trees, arrows through their bodies, eyes still open. There was a time when it would have startled the pirate, but it didn't anymore. It just made him angrier.

Suddenly, Barren began to feel dizzy and light headed. The colors around him melded together. He kept fighting. It was the only way to stay alive. He stumbled but managed to stay on his feet, his sword rising weakly to block another blow.

"Barren!" he heard Leaf call his name and he turned to find a man running toward him, blade lifted high above his head. Barren charged, ducking as the man swung over his head. Barren swiped his blade along the man's stomach, felling him, and Barren turned to bring the final blow to his head. The pirate breathed heavily as he turned to fight more men. His blade clashed with others and blood spattered, the sound rising over the roar of fighting and the singing of the arrows in the air.

The sting in Barren's arm was unexpected and he cried out, jerking toward the pain. A gash lay across his arm, deep and oozing blood. It slid down his arm fast, coloring his vision in red. He gripped his sword as hard as he could, ignoring the blood that stuck around his fingers, and engaged the man responsible. He was a man from Estrellas. He was large, his skin badly burned from torture. It made his eyes look dead, but it didn't lessen the fervor with which he fought.

The man hit Barren's blade hard and sent it to the ground. Barren lifted it again but another blow sent the blade flying out of his hands. His arm ached and he cradled it to his stomach. Then pain spread from his head down his back and he fell to his knees. He looked around blindly seeing men running past him, continuing their battle.

Where was Leaf? He couldn't see him.

Another blow and there was nothing.

***

Cove and Devon sat before Aurum on their ships. They kept their eyes on the horizon, on the water, and on the island, which Cove trusted least of all.

"There is unrest here," one of the Lyrics from the Ore Mines stared at the island. He wasn't sure if she'd ever known this place, so it was strange to hear her say such.

"We are connected to this land," said another, as if guessing Cove's thoughts. "The magic in our veins is the same magic that makes Aurum dangerous."

Cove nodded once, and then set his eyes on the island again.

When the trees began to move, Cove reached for Sam's spyglass. As he looked through it, several men in dark clothing emerged from the forest, weapons drawn.

"There are Estrellas fugitives here," he said.

"Cove," Sam's voice drew his attention. "That's a distraction. Look." Cove followed the helmsman's gaze and found that two Elfin ships raced for them. They were fast and glided upon the water. They had come from the river and were lining up to attack the two ships. They had no time to run for their guns.

"Down!" The command was ordered and everyone on deck flattened. Shots were fired and cannon balls tore through the ship at all levels, destroying the sails and splitting the mast, which tumbled to the deck below. Wood split and exploded, becoming just as lethal as lead. Gunfire sounded and men fell, lead through their bellies. Then the ship crashed into theirs, groaning with

407

impact. Shrill cries rang out and the men on the enemy ship boarded. Those who boarded were privateers as well as former prisoners from Estrellas, and they were having fun. They sliced and shot, filling the air with terrible cries and thick clouds of smoke.

"Get to your posts!" Cove roared. They would have to fight to get there, but it was the only thing they could do to survive. Cove took up his blade, though he was weak, and he fought. His arms had little strength, and these men wanted heads, so he found he had power in blocking, and when they got too close, he sent a dagger through their hearts. There was gunfire all around, and the shouts and screams from Devon's ship echoed their own.

"Cove!" Sara's voice rose shrilly, and Cove turned in time to find an arrow through the man who was about to kill him. He turned and saw Sara had taken up the bow Leaf had given her. She persisted, stringing arrow after arrow and killing any man who approached him. It was then he felt a pain shoot straight through him. It spread through his chest, and he couldn't move. Sara screamed. Somehow, he managed to stay upright, though he knew he'd been shot through the chest. He didn't have long.

The ambassador turned and saw Sam kill the man with the gun.

"Cove! We are surrounded!" Sam's voice rose above the clamor.

Cove looked around. There was no way this ship or Devon's ship could survive another set of cannon fire.

"Abandon ship!" he yelled, and he turned to Sara. Wrapping

his arms around her, they dove overboard. The cannons sounded again. And with him and the crew, bits of the ship and artillery followed them into the sea.

Cove opened his eyes momentarily to see the ocean colored with his blood. He wondered if this would be his end. Death had always been a possibility, as he'd been reminded over and over again by Sara. Another day was never guaranteed, but there was no way he could have gotten this far believing that.

Suddenly he felt himself being pulled, and he broke through the surface, spitting out salt water and taking deep breaths, though they were labored and painful.

He looked up, and the sun was in his eyes. Through the bright rays, he could make out Sara above him. She was laboring as she dragged him to shore. With the sun on her head, she seemed to be an angel. Finally she dropped him in shallow water. Soon after, Sam pulled him farther to shore.

"Look!" Sara pointed to the horizon and Cove managed to sit up. Several ships now dotted the landscape. At first Cove's heart fell. If they were the enemy, he and those with him would be doomed. Sam took out his spyglass.

"It's Dominique," he said. "They are Corsairs."

And almost immediately, the Elfin ships were surrounded and the battle there appeared fierce, leaving Cove and the others to deal with the men on the shores. Cove tried to stand, and when Sam attempted to stop him, he snapped.

"I demand you stop," he said. "I *will* fight. If I do not, I *will* die."

Sam hesitated, and then shut his mouth. He nodded and helped Cove to his feet. Sam gave him one of his blades. He surveyed the men and women who had made it to shore. There were few of them, but enough.

Then there was Sara. He turned to her. "I love you, I have always loved you, and I will continue to love you."

She swallowed hard. He reached forward and kissed her. When he drew away, Sara's eyes were hard. As she spoke, her mouth quivered. "Let me fight with you."

His brows came together, and he brushed her cheek. "No," he said, shaking his head.

"I will fight with you!" she said between her teeth, and he felt her fingers tighten around the hilt of the blade at his waist.

He gazed at her for a moment longer, and then nodded. He unsheathed the blade and gave it to her. Then he turned with Sam and the others, raised his own blade, and charged.

Their enemies did too, and as they came upon each other, the pirates watched as arrows flew down from the trees to take the invaders down. Cove couldn't see them, but he knew they were Elves. Those who escaped Elfin arrows engaged. Cove fought, and his adrenaline rushed so high, he didn't even feel the pain anymore.

He fought hard, using his blade and his dagger. He fought to harm, to incapacitate, to spill blood. If this was to be his last battle, they would win.

Behind them, the last Elfin ship fell and the Corsairs made their way to land. Dominique led them, his blade held high, his red cape splayed behind him. Their cries rose up for battle, and when they joined the pirates of Silver Crest, a fury was unleashed unlike any other. It was almost supernatural to watch the Corsairs fight, the way they used their bodies like a weapon, finishing the deed with blades, axes, or bows.

The Lyrics fought too, but not with magic, with real steel. They fought to save themselves, to protect the freedom they'd recently gained. They slew many, and the way they fought only hinted at their anger and their pain. They were vicious and unflinching.

The Elves in the trees began to pinpoint the bodies of the privateers and prisoners. One by one the invaders fell. Those who attempted to flee fell, surrounded on all sides by pirates and Elves.

When the battle neared its end, Cove moved toward the water and sat. His head felt light and his chest hurt. He refused to look, refused to accept. Suddenly he found himself falling back into the sand, and everything moved slower—the sky, the screams. He could see Sara's face, but her voice was far away, and though he knew she wanted him to speak, he couldn't form words.

"Can't you help him?" Dominique demanded of the Lyrics.

"Our magic is not strong enough," one said. "Not to restore a life."

"Someone...someone go get Leaf!" Sam demanded.

"If we cannot save him, the Elfin prince cannot," another Lyric said.

"I don't care what you say!" Sam sneered, and then took off

toward the forest.

Cove took in deep breaths. When he closed his eyes, he could feel someone touch his face, and he knew Sara was begging him to open his eyes, but they were so heavy. And when he could no longer open his eyes...he knew that he was dead.

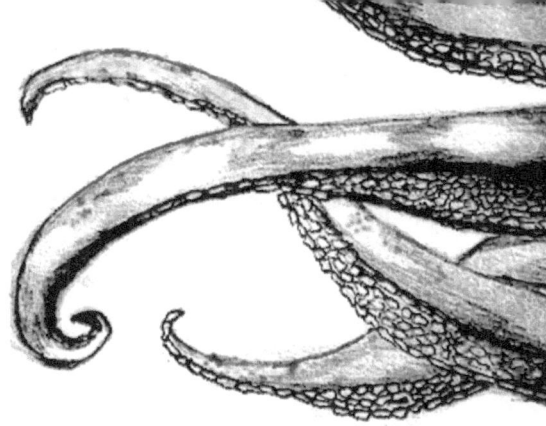

Chapter Thirty-One
BLOW THE MAN DOWN

Barren woke with a start when cold water hit him. He was then jerked upright by his hair before he could even fully understand what was happening. It took only a moment to adjust because what he saw before him made his heart speed up and beat out of his chest. He wasn't sure what to do, but his mind raced instantly. His hands were tied behind his back, there were guards all around. He had no weapons. But Datherious did. The prince stood with a long knife pressed to Lord Alder's throat. The Elfin king was on his knees, his back to the prince, head raised in dignity. He was always so proud, even now, silver hair spilling over his shoulders, icy eyes that only hinted at anger, not fear.

They were in Lord Alder's throne room and everything was white. Lord Alder himself was clad in fine white robes.

"No!" Leaf's voice was both desperate and harsh.

"Oh, look. Your son is awake," said Datherious. He was too amused. "He's just in time to witness his father's execution for

413

treason."

Barren's eyes snapped to Leaf who was struggling to break free, but the guards who held him stepped hard on his bent legs and he gave out a cry. "Don't you dare!" Leaf spat. "Don't you dare touch him!"

His voice was filled with raw fear, raw anger. Barren knew there was also a part of Leaf that wanted to beg...maybe even take his father's place.

"I do not serve you," Lord Alder said calmly, but his voice carried throughout the hall. "Therefore, I cannot commit treason."

Datherious laughed. Then grabbing a handful of Alder's long hair, he yanked his blade through it, and the strands fell to the floor. Alder did not move.

"You signed a contract with your king, agreeing to serve him with magic!" Datherious cried.

Leaf stared and so did Barren. This was the confirmation they had been waiting for, but not like this, never like this.

"Why don't you explain this agreement to your son," Datherious's voice was mocking. "He doesn't seem to understand."

Though his head was still held high in defiance of the prince, his throat now worked. "It was the only way to protect you, Leaf. It was the only way to protect the kingdom."

Datherious kicked the lord hard in the back so that he fell forward on his face. He let out a grunt as he crashed to the marble floor, and when Datherious dragged him up, blood stained his face, his white robes, and the white marble.

"Tell him what else you did!" Datherious screamed, and his face seemed to morph into something dark and inhuman.

"I sold weapons to your king, and I sold weapons to the Underground....in hopes that humans would destroy themselves," Lord Alder spat blood on the ground. "If you kill me, you will lose magic forever!"

Datherious laughed. "It is intriguing to see you beg for your life in this manner. It might please you to know that I've found another way to your magic."

"A direct way," said Aethea, who now walked down the hall, her boots clicking against the marble. She was in her human form, but Alder seemed to recognize her.

She smirked. "You remember me."

Alder said nothing.

"You see, Alder, I don't need a middleman anymore," said Datherious. "Aethea has agreed to offer her services and give me access to the tools you once possessed. Tools you kept quiet about," and he reached down and pulled a gold chain from around the Elfin King's neck. At the end of the chain was a blue crystal. As it rose, it shimmered like the sun on the sea. Barren recognized the power radiating from the stone; this was another piece of the King's Gold, and if he had to guess, it was likely to have belonged to Ara, Aethea's mother, the keeper of the heart of the ocean. Barren's eyes followed it as Datherious pulled it over his head. "What? Were you hoping to use them against me?"

Then Datherious grabbed a handful of the Elf's hair and

pulled his head back so his neck was taut. Barren's heart beat faster in his chest, and Leaf began to struggle.

"There is only one punishment for treason," he whispered near Alder's ear. "But it must be a relief to you after fighting for power so long to know that you can rest."

That was when Barren began to struggle, too, but the flick of the knife was fast across Lord Alder's neck and Datherious cast him away to the floor as blood poured fast from his wound. The sound Leaf uttered was one Barren had never heard but understood—it was one of unspeakable pain. Shattering pain. Barren felt it deep in his core, to the depths of his soul.

And Barren watched as Leaf struggled forward, hands bound behind his back. He crawled through the blood and nudged his father onto his back, and he wept over the body, begging him to live again.

There's so much blood, Barren thought as it coated the Elven king's pale hair like a vile headdress, and he knew without a doubt that no matter the sins Lord Alder had committed, he had done it with the wish to protect his people and his son.

How could there be evil in that?

And Barren began to rage. Something within him broke free, and he found the strength to break the ropes that bound his arms together. The guards moved slowly, taken by surprise, and the smirk on Datherious's face faded quickly.

"Go! Let's go!"

Barren twisted and brought his head against the guard's, cracking his skull. The man fell back, holding his nose. Barren reached for his blade and unsheathed the sword, skewering him. The man fell, and Barren turned to meet more blades. He knew this show of strength was unnatural, it was powerful, and it was dark. He was possessed with bloodlust. The guards raced forward, and Barren cleaved them in two. And when others tried to escape, he used his sword as a spear and impaled them.

Not long after, he stood surrounded by a ring of bodies, and the anger that had possessed him was overtaken by the sobs of his best friend. He ran to the Elf and untied his wrists from behind his back. Then he stood aside as Leaf shakily took his father into his arms. He cradled his father against him and rocked back and forth, sobbing.

Barren took up a bow and quiver of arrows from one of the guards and left Leaf to grieve. He went in search of Datherious and Aethea. He would kill them and it would be brutal. As he hurried down the hall, he caught a glimpse of them entering the forest.

"Come back here and fight me, you bastard!" Barren yelled.

He hurried into the woods behind them and sent up a silent prayer that the woods would work against them. Each time he caught a glimpse of them, their images disappeared into the brush. Barren ran forward as fast as his legs would carry him, and when they moved out of sight again, he decided to chance it.

He strung an arrow. The bow was not his strongest weapon, but by Saoirse he would hurt them. The arrow cut the air and he heard a satisfying scream. He wasn't sure where he'd hit, but he knew Aethea had taken the blow. Now for Datherious.

But another cry caught his attention. It was Sara, and he knew without a doubt that Cove had fallen.

No. The rage he felt was unrecognizable.

Barren rushed through the forest, as fast as he could. Ahead of him, he saw Sam hurrying to meet him.

"I know!" he called, and together they ran toward shore. When they broke through the tree line, his feet slid in the sand. In front of him he could see Cove on the ground, Sara bent over him.

"Cove!"

Sara screamed Cove's name as if her heart had been ripped from her chest. There was fear, there was pain, there was anger. It made his blood run cold.

Barren hurried forward and fell to his knees. "Albatross," Barren picked up Cove's head, but he was not responsive, and then Barren saw the new wound in Cove's chest.

"Albatross," he said through his teeth. "Albatross, don't you leave me!"

He looked up at Sara, and her wise blue eyes met his. "You said you wouldn't let him die," she sobbed. "You promised."

What could he do? He'd meant he wouldn't let dark magic take him, but this was different. There was no way he could breathe life back into Cove. He didn't heal wounds, and he wasn't a necromancer. And at that thought, he paused and reached into his pocket. He withdrew the small vial the Lyric had given him before she was lost at sea. The liquid inside was crystal blue and it seemed to glow, even in the brightness of the day.

"His pulse is faint," said Sam. "He's still alive, but not for much longer."

Sara's eyes were on the bottle. "Give him the magic. It can save him!"

"Yes, but at what cost?" Sam asked. "Cove's life? Maybe Barren's."

"There is no cost to me," said Barren after a moment. "This curse upon me, it wants me alive for now."

Barren uncorked the vial and forced half of the liquid in it down Cove's throat. They waited but there was nothing. Barren didn't know what he was supposed to do.

"Poor it on the wound," Sara ordered.

Barren was surprised by her command, but he did as she said and poured the remainder of the contents on Cove's wound. It immediately began to sizzle and smoke, and the skin bubbled and closed up. What happened inside, Barren wasn't sure, but he saw the ambassador's chest rise and fall. There were cheers, but Barren only smiled for a moment. As he rose to his feet, the cheers died down.

"Lord Alder is dead," Barren said and paused. "Leaf is king."

Barren never thought he would utter those words.

***

Barren wasn't sure where all the blood had gone, but when he returned to the throne room, the floors were spotless and white. When he went in search of Leaf, he was escorted to a room along with the other pirates and Corsairs. Cove was taken to a healing suite and tended by Elfin healers. That night, dinner was brought to all of them, and Barren inquired after Leaf.

"His majesty sits with his mother at their king's side until he is buried tomorrow."

The Elf said nothing more and left. Devon came to his chambers soon after. He had changed and was free of grime from battle.

"Cove is recovering well, I have been told," he said. "The Lyrics said Morrigan gave you the remainder of her life-force. That is why you were able to save Cove. It was not dark magic with which you healed him."

"Morrigan?"

"That was her name," he said. "The other Lyrics have all been given quarters here. I am not sure of their future. The old ways have been gone for so long."

"Do you really believe the Lyrics were sent to be their guardians?" asked Barren.

Devon did not answer, and so Barren prompted him again.

"What do you believe?"

"That they are a test," he said.

Devon didn't expand on the subject, and Barren didn't ask. Since the moment Barren knew anything of Elves, he'd known they believed mortals to be power-hungry and careless, yet he had seen the same characteristics in Elves. The Lyrics, with their ties to magic, could mean the end of Mariana, the end of any world as they knew it.

"What of Layce and the others?"

"They were all found dead. There were no wounds to their

bodies, so we are left to assume the magic they consumed at the Ore Mines killed them."

That did not surprise him. The magic had only created temporary war machines. Bodies that were not made for magic couldn't handle the power, but there were always people who felt they could defy the odds. Barren wasn't so sure he could. He'd turned into a war machine as soon as Lord Alder was killed. He shuddered, remembering the rush of power that ran through him, the ease with which he'd broken the ropes around his hand, as if they were paper. He was still alive, but for how long?

"How will we stop this?" Barren said quietly.

"Any way we can," Devon replied.

***

The next day, at dusk, they were called to the courtyard. The entire palace emptied and Barren watched as Elves made their way out of the forest dressed in white and gold robes, some carrying white lilies and others lanterns. They created a walkway, forming a line from the doors of the palace to a path in the forest. Barren and his crew felt out of place. They did not have nice clothes, and they had not been brought white robes. At first Barren had thought they had forgotten, but when he saw Leaf exit the palace doors, he was dressed as they were. In his arms he carried his father. The Elfin Lord was clad in white and gold robes. A heavy crown of gold and diamonds rested on his head. Though everything was crisp and bright, Barren could only see blood.

Behind them, Leaf's mother walked. She carried her

husband's sword in her hands. She, too, was dressed in white, and as she moved, her dress glittered with gold. A white veil covered her face, and a circlet of gold held it in place.

They moved like spirits down the lane and into the forest. The Elves then turned and followed. Barren and the others marched with them. As they moved under the canopy of the trees, the elves began to sing. Now and then their voices rose together, and the haunting melody made Barren's skin ripple.

They continued to sing until they came upon a grove of willow trees that overlooked the sea. At the center of a grove, a marble pyre sat. Upon it was a bed of dry wood. Leaf was the only one who moved forward. He placed his father on the pyre, situated his hands and his hair gently, and kissed his brow. Then he stepped back and his mother moved forward, placing the king's sword upon him, folding his hands over the hilt, and she kissed him.

She moved to stand beside her son, and for a moment, there was a pause, and Barren knew Leaf was preparing himself for this moment, the moment when his father would no longer be on this earth. The moment he would never see his physical form again.

Then he reached for one of the Elf's lanterns, and with all his strength, he cast it at the pyre and it erupted into flames.

The fire burned fierce at first, cracking and popping. It made Barren flinch, but Leaf stood perfectly still, watching it consume his father. After a moment in silence, he began to sing. No one joined him, but his voice carried throughout the woods, and Barren knew that everyone, near and far, felt his sorrow.

***

After the funeral, there was a great dinner. Music played, and there was laughter, but Leaf and his mother were nowhere in sight. Just as Barren had thought to go in search of him, he entered the great hall. He had not changed, his clothes were those of the profession he swore to. The Elves grew quiet at his approach and they bowed. Leaf watched them for a moment before he spoke.

"Rise," he said, and his eyes were still searching for something or someone. He saw Barren, and then he spoke. "War is upon us. War is upon our world. I do not speak simply of Aurum, but of Mariana, for if it falls, you fall, too," he stepped toward them. "My father did many things right, and he was motivated to protect, but he was not always right. I know some among you believe that making war upon mortals is a solution. You hoped that by giving them weapons laced with dark magic, that they might destroy each other. Did you not consider that they might destroy you, too?" He let that question sit in the air as he walked among the Elves. They parted, and he made eye contact with those who would look at him. "And if mortals are so terrible, what are you? What traits did you believe separated you from humans? All I have witnessed is a people willing to kill for a chance to regain the past."

He paused and then placed his hand over the 'X' on his chest. The Elves would know nothing of it, but Barren did. He was making a promise. "To those who still believe my father's solution was best, if there are any of you left within this territory by morning, trust that I will find you all."

He did not promise life and he did not promise execution.

Leaf left then, and Barren followed like a shadow. The Elf had come to a balcony which overlooked Aurum. He stood straight with one hand upon the rail. Barren took a deep breath and joined him. They did not speak for some time. They didn't even look at each other.

"Do you blame me?" Barren asked at last.

"No," he said.

"I'm sorry I did not save him."

"It was not your place to save him," said Leaf, and he met Barren's eyes. "At least I can rejoice that Cove is alive."

There was silence again. "Do you not intend to be a king to your people?"

"We have a lot to do beyond these boarders before I can be king of anything," said Leaf. "We will come to war against magic. It has already begun. Datherious killed my father, and he has another piece of the King's Gold. We cannot let him wield magic."

Datherious was turning out just as his father and grandfather had, power hungry but somehow more capable.

"If he cannot find all the pieces, he cannot wield magic," said Barren. "Em said there are five pieces to the King's Gold. We can only account for four. That means the other one is still hidden."

"So the question is, where would your father hide it?" asked Leaf.

"No," said Barren. "The question is, how did your father find two of them?"

They stood together in silence, neither knowing that answer.

"What shall we do?" asked Leaf.

Barren looked at the Elf, stunned by his question. "You are a king asking for my advice."

"I am a quartermaster asking for my captain's guidance."

Barren took in a breath. "I would wish to return to Silver Crest where my allies have gathered. Where friends of my father still live. Our only hope is to find the rest of the Relics before Datherious, before we must face the *vacair* in battle."

There was silence between them, and after a moment Barren spoke. "I fear that I will not always be your ally," he said. "I fear that this curse, it will use me for evil. I would wish that you, at least, were armed against me."

"I could not kill you," said Leaf. "Even at your worst, and you will not ask me to do it."

"Is that a command, King?"

"It is a promise.

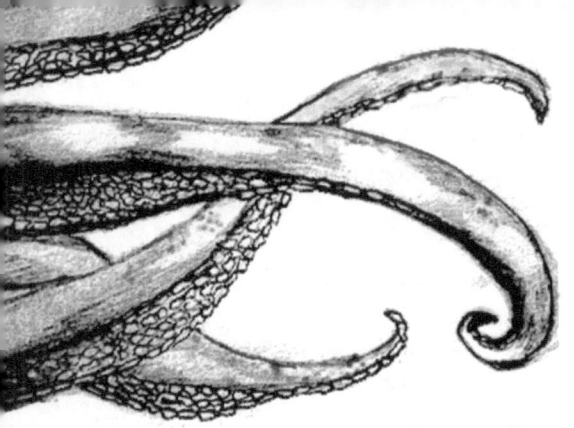

Chapter Thirty-Two
GIVE NO QUARTER

There was an explosion and Larkin woke with a start. Her heart beat erratically in her chest, and she rushed to her feet. There were no windows in her cell, but as the gunshots and screams sounded, she knew they were under attack. Another explosion shook them, and Larkin went to the door of her cell. Guards hurried past shouting orders. "We're under attack! Call to arms!"

Then they were left alone unguarded as the commotion above continued. The other prisoners in the cells started to shout and clank things against their cell in hopes of escaping during the chaos. Larkin couldn't deny that she had that hope, too.

In the cell opposite hers, there was a window, and a large man waited there, staring idly outside. After a moment, he began to whistle a tune. It was harsh and jagged; it made Larkin's blood run cold. Then he laughed and turned, his eyes finding hers immediately.

"Someone's a'coming for you," he said.

426

Her first thoughts went to Barren, but she quickly pushed them aside. Barren would not come for her. She'd known that the moment she left. No, this attack was something different.

"They've broken the gate!" she heard someone cry, which meant they were in the castle now.

"Who's coming?" she called to the man. "Who is it?"

But he only looked at her with a scornful smile.

Larkin scowled and turned from the bars. She hurried to the corner of her cell and began to pry a small section of the brick away where she'd managed to hide the makeshift shiv she'd been forming since she had been placed here by Natherious. The edges of the rock weren't yet sharp enough, but it was still a weapon.

The door to the dungeon opened and voices rose in the hall.

"She's in 'ere, least that's what he said!"

She recognized that speech, and suddenly she knew that the man in the cell across from her hadn't been lying. They were looking for her. These were the men of Estrellas. She'd left an impression on more than one guard at the fugitive island, killing their leader, Cas, and wounding another. To make matters worse, she was the daughter of Lord Christopher Lee, the man who was partly responsible for their torture.

Larkin turned so her back was to the corner, holding tight to the makeshift weapon. She watched as two of the Estrellas guards walked into view. They were dressed in black, their faces masked. They had those strange long swords with the bent ends. She shivered. The two were almost past her cell when one stopped and swiveled toward her.

She tried not to breathe when she saw his face. He wasn't wearing a mask like she'd thought, just a black leather helmet. The torture he'd experienced was clearly mapped on his face. Burns covered the right side, and knife marks the left. One of his eyes was missing, and when he smiled, deep scars made it seem endless.

"Well, well, well, so it is true. Christopher Lee's daughter has found herself in a cell," said one.

"Betcha don't remember me," the other sneered, but she would remember those yellow eyes anywhere. It was the Estrellas guard she'd stabbed through the hand just before Cas had found her. She'd known he'd wished her dead the moment he'd discovered who she was, and now he was here to see to it.

The man with no eye raised his hand. A set of keys clinked against each other as he twisted them around his finger. "Look what I got. Your freedom," he said, and that strange smile deepened hideously.

He inserted the key into the lock, and the man with yellow eyes moved forward. He was the only one who advanced; she supposed the other felt this was his opportunity for revenge. He raised his blade. "I'm gonna stick you good, then hang you so your father will know my pain."

He was upon her, blade raised to meet her neck. She watched it, unable to take her eyes off it. She could feel the magic rise within her. It was in her stomach and moved from there, through her veins. It was strangely a part of her just as much as her blood and skin.

"If you close your eyes," he said. "It won't hurt a bit."

But she watched the blade, and when he went to move it forward, he found that the blade would not budge. He looked between her and the blade, and when he loosened his grip enough, she took over. Jamming her feet against his legs and shoving the rock into his face, she dragged her makeshift blade down. He screamed and wrenched away from her. His own blade clattered to the ground. She went for it and heard the words she'd dreaded to be called.

"Witch! Sea-witch!"

She ran the blade through the yellow-eyed prisoner and then pulled it from him harshly. He fell slack to the floor. The other Estrellas prisoner rushed forward, sword drawn. She blocked his initial blows, but he used his body to fight. He hit her face, and she fell back, blocking his next blow at the last second. She needed to get closer to the open door of her cell. It was the only way she might escape him.

The prisoner brought his blade down harder, and he hit her again. This time she fell to the floor. She rolled to miss a blow to her head and hurried to her feet in time to nick his arm. It was only enough to make him angry. He charged at her again, and each blow rattled her to the core. She knew he'd hit her when her arm started to burn, but she refused to look at it. She wouldn't survive if she did.

The magic inside of her had a reaction to the pain, however, and as she went to strike a blow against the prisoner, a swirl of energy exploded from her hand and hit the man square in the chest. He was blown backward. He hit the floor and fell in a heap on the ground.

She was stunned for a moment, completely out of breath. She lowered her blade and looked at her hand. She marveled at how normal it appeared. It was her hand, calloused, but hers all the same.

"Sea-witch!" she heard someone say, and she whirled around. It was the man in the opposite cell.

"Sea-witch!" he called again, and the others in the prison began to join him. They chanted it over and over again. Their voices rose in a terrible rhythm. Just then, the one-eyed man stirred and awakened. He growled and started getting to his feet. She turned and hurried out of the cell. The prisoners' haunting voices followed her as she made her way down the passage to the door.

She heard the one-eyed man bellow as he came after her, the girth of his body seeming to shake the dungeon.

"Little wench! I'll teach you a lesson!"

As she ran, the passage curved and more cells were on either side of her. The people inside joined in the chant and reached for her. She lashed at them with her blade and some fell away, but the chanting continued.

She came to the door. It was ajar. She hurried through and then turned to pull the heavy door shut behind her, but she wasn't fast enough. The guard wrenched the door open and she stumbled back, raising her blade prepared to fight.

The man fought hard and fast. He lashed out at her with his

blade. There was nothing graceful about it. He wanted blood. She fought against him, her arms shaking from exhaustion and ringing from blocking heavy blows. Then there came a point where she couldn't hold onto the hilt of her blade anymore and with one heavy blow, it slipped from her hands. The guard hit her again, and she fell to the floor. Larkin spun, reaching for her blade, the only defense she had against this man.

His heavy footfalls sounded, and his boot met viciously with her hand. She screamed, and he stepped harder. There was only pain. Pain and magic. Why did the magic only come with pain?

He brought his blade over his head, and she reached out, her other hand spread wide. She could feel the energy gathering there, but it was weak. As his weapon came down, a blade exploded through the man's chest, sending blood splattering across her face. She covered her head as the one-eyed guard dropped his sword. It clattered to the ground and he fell to his knees. She scurried out of the way, and he hit the stone with a hard thud.

Behind the fallen man, Natherious stood. For a moment she lay stunned, wondering if this was him just defending his castle, if he would take her prisoner as he had before. When he reached forward, it was all the confirmation she needed. She wrenched away from him.

"I'm not going to hurt you," he said. "And if you delay, you're not getting out of here. Come on!"

He took her arm and pulled her up the stairs to the first level of the castle. He paused at the door, peering down the halls

431

before moving forward again, keeping to the shadow. Now and then they would stop when footfalls drew near. The sound of gunfire and clashing blades continued in the background. Screams and howls accompanied the symphony of the battle.

She held her left hand to her chest, the pain reverberating through her entire body, and even her teeth ached. She had no idea how this would heal. And if it did, her hand would never be the same again.

"Who are they?" she asked as she followed Natherious.

"These men who have attacked are from Estrellas," he said.

"Did they escape?"

"I do not believe they escaped on their own," he said.

"What do you believe?"

He paused and looked at her. "Only the strongest survive in Estrellas. Those men were made to be weapons."

He turned and continued.

Cove had said Estrellas was made in the hopes that the men would destroy each other, but instead they'd united around a single purpose, the hope of destroying those who had put them there. So who had they found as their savior? She could only think of one man—Datherious.

They were in the west wing at the moment and from here the ocean could be viewed from any window. Once, not too long ago, the Cliffs could also be seen from here, but they had all been destroyed. She peered out now as they passed each open window, streaming with moonlight. There were ships upon the horizon, dark ships with sails that seemed to sprout out of the ocean like blades. How could she hope for escape when their shore looked like that?

Finally, Natherious ushered her into a room. It was dark, but moonlight poured in from the window, and she could see that it was a sitting room. He moved her to the back of the room toward a large bookcase. "You'll take this passage here," he said. At first she saw nothing but a wall, but Natherious managed to pry open a seamless door which revealed a dark and narrow passage. "It leads upstairs to the second floor, right into my father's study. He will be there. He's locked himself up with his madness. I know you've heard that my father has a piece of the King's Gold. Lord Alder gave it to him, but my father is mortal, and the gold bears the curse of madness. I don't care how you'll do it, but get that piece from around his neck and run. Get on a ship and don't look back."

Larkin stared at him pointedly. "How long?"

It was more of an accusation, but she was also angry. Natherious was one of two brothers who had caused Barren and his crew much toil and strife, and suddenly he was acting more friend than foe.

"How long have you been on our side?"

"Always," he breathed. "Now go!"

He pushed her toward the passage and into the darkness she stumbled. "Wait," she whirled around. "What will you do?"

"I still have a part to play until I am called elsewhere."

He pushed a sword into her hand and she took it, then he closed the door on her. She turned and faced the darkness. She felt around for a moment, found the first step and then another. Her confidence rising, she moved up the steps fairly quickly until suddenly she lost her footing. She gave out a cry as she caught herself with her injured hand. Her sword clattered down the stairs, and she followed.

She sat in pain for a long moment before standing and grasping her sword once more. Exhausted, she moved up the steps again, slower this time.

Finally, she came to the second floor and found the door before her. She held her breath as she pushed on it, careful to open it slowly. The passage opened beside a fireplace whose coals were now glowing embers. She could feel the warmth as she slipped into the room. Everything was dark. The curtains were closed, the doors shut tight. Outside she could still hear the howls and screams of those who were encountering the men of Estrellas, and she wondered if the massacre would ever end.

She looked about her. The room was not large, and there were few places to hide, so where could Tetherion be? In the back of her mind, she wondered if Natherious was just as deceiving as Datherious. She moved forward into the room and a scream caught in her throat as a hand touched her shoulder. She whirled, pushing the person away, holding up her sword.

There she found Tetherion, but something was wrong. He was bent over, holding his waist. His breath was shallow and haggard. He wasn't on his feet long before he fell. She lowered her sword and moved toward him.

"H-help me," his voice was that of a ghost's.

Her eyes moved toward his stomach were the hilt of a blade protruded. He had been stabbed. She reached for it and withdrew the blade, blood following fast.

"Who did this to you?" she asked.

But when her eyes met Tetherion's again, he was dead.

Then the doors to the study opened. A servant stood before them, eyes wide and terrified. She screamed. Larkin knew what this meant for her. She was bent before the body of the king, the bloody blade in her hand.

"King killer!" the servant cried, and her voice rose, horrible in its accusation. She was reminded of the men in the dungeons chanting sea-witch.

She threw the dagger aside and reached for Tetherion's neck. The fur of his cloak and the collar of his shirt were fastened tight, and it took some time to find the fine gold chain that held Illiana's Relic, a beautiful sapphire-colored stone with thousands of star-like flecks. When she did, she pulled it from him, the chain snapping with the effort. She stood, placing the Relic in her pocket, and grabbing her sword, she fled. The woman was still screaming, drawing attention. Others had joined her and stood as witnesses.

"Larkin!" the voice was familiar and strangely gave her hope. Her father was running toward her, his blade drawn. "Come! Run!"

And he ran with her. Together, they cut down any who came upon them, Estrellas prisoner or Maris guard.

As they came to the grand staircase, the exit in view, a line of

Estrellas men caused them to stop in their tracks. Their weapons were drawn, their faces flecked with the blood of their victims. Behind them, more enemies were gaining on them. They were surrounded, and there was only one way out.

Larkin continued forward, despite her father's protests. She could hear him move down a few steps, reaching for her, but she continued. She took in deep breaths and concentrated. She would need all her energy for this. She dropped her blade, drew her hands together and screamed. All the pain, all the anger, all the loss rushed from her body and into the men who blocked her way.

By Saoirse she swore she would never be prisoner to them. To anyone.

And they all fell instantly. Smoke rose from the bodies as if they'd been burned.

Silence followed after, and she felt drained. She collapsed to her knees. Her father's feet pounded on the marble floor. He drew her to her feet and hurried out of the castle. Behind them were the witnesses to her magic and to a murder. They were the servants of the king, the nobles in his court. Life would never be the same for her. It hadn't been since she'd met Barren Reed, but this time it was different. This time she knew she was meant for something greater, and if she was going to defeat the evil rising in Mariana, she would have to embrace the magic she'd been taught to hate.

Once they were in the cold night, they ran. Larkin's chest burned, her eyes stung with tears, the wind ran its cold fingers through her hair. There was pain, there was exhaustion, and there was darkness. But she kept running, following her father to the coast where they would make their escape.

***

Barren sat in the stone courtyard outside his room. The forest of Aurum had encroached upon this space since his last visit. Vines stretched across the stone and seemed to reach for his mother's statue which stood erect in the center of the space. He liked to imagine Sysara was here with him, and that her embrace was the cool wind surrounding him. Truly, this was the coldest he'd felt in a long time. He wished Larkin were here to fill the space beside him, to offer her warmth. He wondered how it was so easy to miss her and be so angry with her at the same time.

Larkin's absence was just one way things had changed. When they departed Aurum this time, Leaf would be a king. Barren's alliances would lie with the Corsairs of Avalon. Some of his greatest enemies would belong to the only family he'd ever known, and Mariana would be one step closer to spiraling out of control. How ironic that he sat at the center of such a fragile thing.

He was brought from his thoughts by a frantic call.

"Barren!" It was Devon's voice. Barren turned to step into his room. He left, hurrying down the palace hallway. He found Devon and Leaf racing toward him. "I've got news, and it isn't good."

Barren felt his features harden. He was preparing himself for the worst.

"Maris was attacked by the Estrellas prisoners and the king is dead. They are saying…they're saying Larkin is the king slayer."

"Surely that is not true," said Leaf. It couldn't be true. And if Estrellas men attacked Maris, it was because Datherious and Aethea had ordered it. The people of Maris would not know that.

"Where is she?" Barren asked immediately. If they found her, Datherious would hang her immediately.

Devon shook his head. "They cannot find her or her father."

She'd fled with her father? And where would they go? No one would welcome them. Should he go in search of her? What would he even do if he found her?

"There is one more thing," Devon said carefully. Barren's eyes grew wide. How could there possibly be more?

"Eva and Tobias were also hanged. They compromised the Network locations."

So the Elders had thought to quash Cove's threat first by exposing the Network, but what did that mean for their brethren? For the women and children who also occupied those locations?

"Were they warned to flee?" Barren asked.

"Cove's Network is vast," Devon shook his head, his eyes were sad. "Not everyone was reached in time."

"Wake everyone," he said. "We set sail tonight."

"We are too late, Barren. We might as well wait until morning," said Devon.

"No," he said. "If we start now, we're four hours closer to

where we are needed, Silver Crest."

"Very well," Devon nodded and retreated to wake the others. Leaf still lingered, watching Barren closely.

"Just say the word, Barren. I will find her. I will bring her back to you."

Barren sort of laughed. "Why are you so desperate for me to have her?"

"Because you aren't the same Barren Reed without her."

"If she wants me, she will find me," he said.

ACKNOWLEDGEMENTS

I love this book, and I think it's a fantastic sequel to CUTLASS. It's also the middle book, which means I only have one more left. This makes me incredibly sad. However, I'm very thankful I have gotten the chance to spend time with Barren and Larkin, and most importantly share their story with you.

I want to thank my Daddy and my Momma because they're awesome, of course, and believe 'I am the brightest star.' I love you guys!

I want to thank Michelle Albanese Parson for being the best fan and friend ever, for sharing CUTLASS with everyone she could, and for offering support every step of the way. I am so indebted to you.

All the bloggers who shared Cutlass and helped me spread the word—THANK YOU SO MUCH. You guys are amazing.

I also need to thank Capri East, Jason Hampton, Holly Holland, and Molly McCool for all their love and support.

My BFF Emily because you're a badass and you remind me everyday that I'm awesome. I'm so lucky to have a BFF like you!

Shryl, Shelby, and Allan for all your support and extra love!

Mrs. Applegate because you never cease to believe in me.

Armand because without you this book wouldn't look so fantastic! For telling me every morning that I'm awesome. For believing in me, and for generally being awesome.

Lastly, but most importantly, thank you to all my readers, old and new. Those of you who have discovered my Cutlass Series, and those of you who will—I do this for you.

©Jessica Pearl Photography

ABOUT THE AUTHOR

Ashley was born and raised in Oklahoma, where the wind really does sweep down the plains, and horses and carriages aren't used as much as she'd like. She has a Bachelor's degree in English Writing and a Master's degree in Library Science and Information Technology. When she's not writing, she's reading, working out, or pretending she's Sherlock Holmes. Her obsession with writing began after reading the Lord of the Rings in the eighth grade. Since then, she's loved everything Fantasy-- resulting in an unhealthy obsession with the 'geek' tab on Pinterest, where all things awesome go.

www.ashley-nixon.com

COMING SOON!

Nacoma Knight

Anora Silby wants her mother alive again. She'd do anything to feel her touch, hear her voice, and understand the strange circumstances surrounding her death. So when the new kid, Thane Treadway, offers outlandish answers, Anora listens.

Thane believes Anora's mother had her soul stolen by the Cercatore di Anime, a race of soul eaters. It isn't until Thane starts forgetting things and having random outbursts of anger that Anora begins to wonder if Thane has personal experience with the Cercatore.

Anora's search for answers leads her into the center of a mid-world battle between good and evil—the soul and the soulless. Not only that, she is the Eurydice, the only one of her kind who can enter and exit spirit. Her gift makes her a target, and soon Anora finds herself faced with the loss of her mother or the love of her life.

Can Anora see past her grief long enough to make a decision or will she lose everything?

www.ingramcontent.com/pod-product-compliance
Lightning Source LLC
Chambersburg PA
CBHW051536250626
47157CB00001B/72